PENGUIN BOOKS

HEARTS THAT CUT

T0333132

HEARTS THAT CUT

KIKA HATZOPOULOU

PENGUIN BOOKS

PENGUIN BOOKS

UK | USA | Canada | Ireland | Australia
India | New Zealand | South Africa

Penguin Books is part of the Penguin Random House group of companies
whose addresses can be found at global.penguinrandomhouse.com.

www.penguin.co.uk
www.puffin.co.uk
www.ladybird.co.uk

First published in the USA by Razorbill,
an imprint of Penguin Random House LLC,
and in Great Britain by Penguin Books 2024

001

Text set in Centaur MT Pro
Design by Alex Campbell
Cover design by Kristie Radwilowicz

Printed and bound in Great Britain by Clays Ltd, Elcograf S.p.A.

The authorized representative in the EEA is Penguin Random House Ireland,
Morrison Chambers, 32 Nassau Street, Dublin D02 YH68

A CIP catalogue record for this book is available from the British Library

ISBN: 978–0–241–61466–2

All correspondence to:
Penguin Books
Penguin Random House Children's
One Embassy Gardens, 8 Viaduct Gardens, London SW11 7BW

TO MAMÁ,
THE HOPE-GIVER

PART I

THE CUTTER

BURNT ORANGE

THE WORLD WOBBLED around the girl's feet. The wooden window frames mewed like a cat before breakfast, the desk chairs tilted to the left, and all across the classroom, pencils rolled over wood and hit the floor in chimes of *ting, ting, ting.* The sky had deepened to a graying mauve, the lights had come on, and the mud-tide was rising beneath the floating foundation of the school, setting it adrift.

At the front of the class, the teacher let out a long exhale and announced they were free to go. At once, every seventh grader in the room burst into action, notebooks stuffed into bags, chairs screeched back, textbooks abandoned in a tower on the teacher's desk. Within moments, the only person left in the classroom was the girl.

She was still bent over her notebook, fingers rubbing circles against her temples. She didn't jolt when the bell rang; she stood and let the throng carry her past the school gates.

The swaying was even worse here. The streets of the slums surrounding the Golden City of Nanzy were fashioned out of mismatched chunks of wood atop makeshift floats, the oscillating exacerbated by the feet of passersby. Every step was like deadly hopscotch—one wrong move and you might slip right into the murky tidewater peeking between the gaps.

The girl kept her eyes to the ground. She could hear her teeth grinding, the disgusting sound drilling all the way through her skull. Gods, this headache. Would it never end?

Someone bumped into her from behind. Her schoolbag slipped

from her shoulder, tipping her body forward. The sudden jerk felt like someone had stabbed her between the brows. She wiped tears with the back of her hands, gathered her schoolbag in her arms, and stood—

She could only see dark orange, the color of maple leaves in the fall. It was on some people's skin, shimmering blazons of color in the muted cacophony of the rest of the crowd. The marks were on their legs, on their arms and necks, on their faces, in swirls and whorls, like otherworldly tattoos of burnt orange. A few were inked from top to bottom, others only in small patches on their cheeks.

She knew instinctively what the marks meant: *Crimes*. Crimes in need of punishment, and her own hand to deliver justice.

A figure appeared before her. "There you are," the man said jovially, as if he recognized her. "I've been looking for you all day. Such furious eyes you've got."

His hand circled her wrist; he pulled her into the crowd, practically dragging her behind him in an unknown direction. She couldn't make out his features, only the orange twisting around his flesh, from wrist to elbow. She blinked and blinked, rubbed her lids, and kneaded her eyeballs, but the blasted color just wouldn't come off.

"Who are you?" she asked. Did he know her? Had her mothers sent him? "Where are we going?"

"Just here." The man pulled her around a corner.

The alley swallowed the streetlight. The bustle of the busy streets quieted. The girl heard the man shuffle closer and squat down to her height. Her heart hammered in her ears.

"You have been given a purpose." He rubbed her back, as though comforting her. As though he wasn't the one causing her terror. "It's time for you to fulfill it."

2

The girl didn't want a purpose. She could guess at its essence—already it was pumping through her veins with every frantic beat of her heart: *punish, punish, punish*. But punishment meant pain. She didn't want to cause pain.

His fingers splayed over her chest, and something sinister tugged at her insides. It was painful—a sting on her skin, but also deeper, through the very essence of her being. A cry tore from her lips. She pulled away, her senses wild and disoriented.

"Hush now," he crooned. His hand fisted in the back of her shirt, rooting her in place. The girl could just make out the outline of his face: his brow knit in concentration, his eyes twinkling a bright silver.

"It's over now," he said—then came an aching, world-shattering *SNAP!*

SILVER AND GOLD

THE THREAD SHIMMERED like liquid flames on Io's palm, a razor of silver-and-gold twine. It was woven twice around each finger of her left hand, forming a misshapen mesh of fear and purpose. At night, before she dropped into whatever sad excuse for a bed she and Bianca had procured, Io would bind her left fist with cloth, then secure it in a sling across her chest.

It was a god's thread, her only clue to the heart of the blasted conspiracy she had unearthed in Alante—she would rather cut off circulation to her hand than risk it slipping free.

She flexed her tired fingers, watching the raindrops scuttle over her knuckles. The thunderstorm had tailed them from Alante like a stray dog: five weeks of a relentless cycle of dust-stained rain, thundering blizzards, and infuriating drizzle. Bianca had pinched two leopard-print waterproof boater hats from canal drivers back in Poleon, but despite that, they were constantly drenched to the bone, so much so that Io's leather jacket currently smelled like a dead rat dipped in moldy cheese. Five weeks of sloshing through rain and mud from one Wastelands town to another, of haggling for food and shelter, of bickering with the mob queen, of jerking awake, drenched in cold sweat, fumbling to check the knotted thread on her left hand.

Five whole weeks, and the thread had led them to this: the shack across the street and the figure inside it.

"It's been six hours," Bianca Rossi said. The mob queen was crouching on the slanted tin roof next to Io, eyes hooded beneath her wide-brimmed leopard-print hat and locked on the block of shanty houses. "I think we've waited long enough, cutter."

Io was still *cutter* to Bianca: sharp, lethal, a threat. It didn't matter that Io had broken her out of police headquarters, plotted the betrayal and punishment of Io's sister with her, forsaken everything she knew so they could track down whoever had masterminded the mob queen's fall. It didn't matter that they had prowled through the Wastelands together, huddled close for warmth, fought back to back, cooked and ate over the same fire. In Bianca's eyes, Io was and would always be a moira-born, the youngest of three sisters descended from the goddesses of Fate, able to see and cut the threads of life and love. Io would always be the girl who handed her over to the wolves who severed her life-thread and transformed her into an unwilling fury-born.

A lifeless wraith and a heartless cutter, what a pair they made.

"Six hours," Bianca repeated, "and your stakeout has yielded nothing. Let's just smash through the door and punch them until they spill all their secrets."

While that did sound alluring, it would also be disastrous. For five weeks, the god had been giving them the slip, always two steps ahead. If they rushed into action now, they might not get another chance like this.

"The point of a stakeout," Io replied sharply, pushing her long-distance spectacles up her nose, "is to *watch*. We can't act until we know who or what they really are."

"They're asleep, that's what they are." Bianca flicked a wrist at the shack across the rooftops, where the figure had indeed been stationed for the entirety of these six hours.

Through the shack's windows, outlines were cast in bronze firelight. Several bodies were nestled on bedrolls and in hammocks hanging from the ceiling, all of them refugees seeking shelter from the Great Tide that had slowly been scaling up the coast of the Southern Peninsula. Most were asleep, but one of them paced the tiny space from the stove to the window. He was an older, bald man who had arrived from the Southern Peninsula earlier that afternoon, in the same refugee group as the owner of the gold thread. His face had been tearstained and solemn; Io suspected that he might have been separated from family or friends on the journey here. Now he stuck his crooked nose against the rain-spattered glass of the window—for a moment, Io and Bianca tensed.

But the man couldn't see them. To him, Io and Bianca were just two of the hundred shadows clinging to the roofs. Such was the perk of a water town like Hagia that balanced on thousands of thin stilts, tin shanties stacked on top of each other like a child's toys, tidewater claiming the ground below at night; its access to electricity was very limited. No streetlights speckled the horizon—the dark was broken only by a few carefully tended fires, willowy smoke rising to meet the leaden thunderclouds above. Bianca, born and raised under the barrage of neon lights that was Lilac Row, hated the lack of electricity, but Io found it oddly charming. Firelight tinted everything in a rosy orange, like lips freshly kissed.

The man dropped the curtain back into place and lay on his bed-roll. Minutes passed. He didn't stir again.

Bianca cocked her head in that feline way of hers. "Is he asleep?"

Io called forth the Quilt, a tapestry of the silver threads woven between people and the things they loved. It was invisible to all but the descendants of the Moirae, the goddesses of Fate. The moira-born always manifested in three siblings: one to weave the threads of fate, one to elongate and measure them, and one to cut them. Io was the third, a cutter. In the Quilt, she could see past wood and concrete, right to the bundle of silver threads that burst out of a person's chest. The old man's threads were completely motionless, and so were the threads of every refugee in the tiny shack.

"Yes," Io said. "They all look asleep."

"Finally," Bianca drawled. *"Now* can we kick down the door and demand answers?"

"Yes to the second part, no to the first," Io said. "We need to move slow and steady if we want to stay undetected. If the god feels even the slightest vibration in the thread I'm holding, it might alert them to our presence."

Which was why Io had stayed almost completely motionless, up here on this rooftop, ever since the hooded figure with the god's thread had arrived in Hagia with the southern refugee caravan six hours ago. Even now, she was unfolding from her crouch as slowly as humanly possible, which produced an exaggerated eye roll from Bianca.

Io ignored it, turning instead to survey the pile of tin boxes that made up Hagia, the haphazard metal bridges and winding steps, the spiked nets between streets keeping the larger chimerini from crawling out of the waters. Currently, the town was packed with refugees fleeing the tsunami waves of the Great Tide. Hundreds were stuffed in shanty houses, and nearly two dozen curled into every nook and cranny on the rooftops and streets.

"I'll take the lead and you stay in the shadows, all right?" Io said. "Just like we planned."

"Yes, yes, the plan," Bianca said with a dismissive flick of the wrist. "Let's just go already, cutter."

The rain hissed against their coats as they jerked into motion. Bianca's body sliced the air, her strides spasmodic, unaccustomed to her new speed and agility. Io followed her at her own, snail-like pace, careful not to disturb the thread in her left hand. They dropped onto the adjoining bridge, landing low on their knees for minimum noise. In stilt towns like Hagia, the trick wasn't choosing the most direct or safest path—it was all about sound. Everything was made of tin and iron, and every step pulsed across the neighborhood. Even with the constant pattering of rain, the residents were so accustomed to the familiar groans and squeaks of their town that anything out of the ordinary put them on immediate alert, as Io and Bianca had quickly realized back in the first stilt town they stopped at.

They hurried across the streets, every screech and slosh of their boots magnified tenfold by their alertness. Several tiny, many-legged bodies skittered across Io's path, making the hair on her arms rise in dread. Over the summer, Hagia had become infested with these blasted chimerini bugs—hybrids of every kind of pest—so much so that the locals had started to include them in their daily diet: fried toad-fleas, winged-centipede chips, snail-trout soup.

"Yeech!" A few feet ahead, Bianca jumped from foot to foot. "Get it off!"

Candlelight flowered from the window above their heads, warm yellow reflecting kaleidoscopically on the rain-sleek tin roofs. Io brought a hand over Bianca's mouth and flattened them both against the wall. She heard the creaking noise of the window opening over-head, felt Bianca's hot breath between her fingers, sensed something scuttling up her calf. Her throat vibrated with a silenced scream. Damn these tiny demons!

After a pause, the person retreated into their house. Io and Bianca immediately started patting every inch of themselves down in a silent stampede, looking for the blasted chimerini bugs.

"They're gone," Io breathed. "Let's keep moving—oh gods."

The only way to the shack was a set of cantilevered stairs hammered into the side of a particularly tall block of shanty houses. "Gull-stairs," the locals called them, for the seagulls that often perched on them. The stairs were mere planks of metal, rusted red at the edges, glistening with rainwater, escalating to a ridiculous height. No handrails, no balusters, no risers or any kind of support between the planks.

Worse even, thought Io, *than cat bridges.*

Bianca was already climbing, though, and Io wasn't about to let a homicidal wraith out of her sight. She took the floating steps of the gull-stairs slowly, both arms out for balance, every accidental glimpse of the abyss between each plank a kick to the stomach. Her heart was drumming senselessly against her ribs by the time she reached Bianca at the top of the steps. Her breaths came out shallow and panicked, her vision blurring at the edges.

Settle, Thais whispered in her memories. *Name your feeling. Find the thought behind it, the reason. Breathe in through your nose, out through your—*

No. Io exorcised Thais from her mind. Her oldest sister's advice was a house pest, uninvited and unwelcome yet always there, parasitizing Io's thoughts and feelings. She didn't want Thais's comfort; she didn't want her tricks and manipulations. Sure, they would make her feel better, perhaps even calm her terror, but they were a scheme. An imitation of reassurance thieving Io of honest support, of real love.

How it pained her to remember: for two years, she had been racked with guilt for sending Thais away from Alante. When her sister returned and seemed forgiving, happy even, Io had rejoiced. She had hoped for reconciliation, for absolution, for a second chance. All these weeks on the road, Io kept reliving the few moments they had had together, back in Alante: Thais's arms enfolding her after killing the second wraith, Raina. Thais comforting her among the slaughtered bodies of the Nine Muses. But it was Thais herself who

9

arranged Raina's attack, who masterminded the Nine's assassinations. It was all Thais: Thais hurting her, then Thais dressing the wounds *she* had inflicted.

Gods, Io felt like a fool.

She wouldn't be made a fool ever again. Her lungs transitioned from panic to anger, nostrils flared, exhales stabbing vapor against the chilly rainfall. She glanced down to find her hands fisted and her boots planted in a fighting stance, as though she was about to launch herself at someone.

With a quiet, deliberate gait, she crossed the narrow gangway that led to the row of tin shacks their target was holed up in. Bianca stood ramrod straight at the foot of the gangway; there was something eerie in her rigidity, something dangerous.

Immediately, Io blocked the mob queen's path and clasped her elbows. Bianca's glassy gaze was nailed to the shack—it blazed the orange of fury-born.

"Hey," Io whispered. *"Bianca."*

"I can see the stains of crime on some of them. They're not good people, cutter." The words slithered between Bianca's unmoving lips, an unnerving effect that made Io's heart jump to her throat. "Will we punish them? Will we sow vengeance? My hands itch so."

Io glanced down to find Bianca's fingers clenched into claws. It was no longer visible, not even to Io in the Quilt, but there was a severed life-thread in her fist. It had been cut and wrung into a fury-born's whip, all in the gods' attempt to bring back the extinct line of the Furies' descendants.

This was Thais's crime, too: she had turned Bianca into this wraith, prone to violence and doomed to an early death.

Io allayed her body into stillness. The promise of violence was thick in the air, filling her nose, pressing on her chest, clawing at her ribs. In the five weeks they had traveled together, Bianca had only gone into this trance twice, and both times Io had had to physically restrain her until she recovered her senses. But now there could be no wrestling Bianca to submission—it would wake up the entire town.

"There will be no punishment," Io told Bianca. "No vengeance. You'll stay hidden while I approach them. We won't get another chance like this. You need to *focus*, Bianca."

"Focus," Bianca repeated. Her gaze shifted to Io. They stood there, eyes of orange meeting eyes of silver, Io's palms folded over Bianca's fists.

Thunder rattled through the town, ominously loud. Bianca's face flashed white with lightning: her pale skin, her ashen blond hair, her clever, clever gaze. Her eyes had reverted to their normal brown, no longer the orange of flames.

The world returned to shadows. Io's chest was tight with tension, her shoulders aching from withheld terror. Bianca slipped out of Io's hold and took another staircase up to whatever dark corner she was going to keep watch from. Io was left alone with the pattering rain, the gangway, and the door.

Her wet fingertips stretched over the metal. Beyond this door could be the answer to her myriad questions. Io had uncovered the facts of the gods' plan: Obeying their orders, Thais had arrived in Alante, seeking people who had weak fury-born blood and severing their life-threads to activate their powers. Then she had set these wraiths free in the city to assassinate all those involved in the genocide of the original fury-born twelve years ago. But Io still hadn't figured out *why*. Why were the gods hell-bent on avenging the genocide and reviving the line of the Furies? What was their end goal?

And what was Io's place in this mess? The patron artists of the Muses had been painting and writing a prophecy regarding Io: *The cutter, the unseen blade, the reaper of fates. She cuts the thread and the world ends.* What was the part Io was supposed to play in this mayhem, and could she avoid it?

Io clenched her jaw. She would be patient no longer. She would be caught a fool no more. Cunning was her weapon now, and she would wield it with precision.

She tucked her spectacles into her pocket and slipped out her lockpicking tools, making quick work of the lock. Propping up its bottom with the tip of her boot in order to avoid creaking, Io slid the door open. The shack was a tiny square space, made even smaller by the refugees' wet coats drying on lines across the ceiling. A wood stove stood to her left, a pot and a ladle laid on top of it; a small desk packed with knitting supplies was to her right; and tattered roll-up mattresses lined the opposite wall. Seven bodies were sleeping atop them. The scent of sweat mixed with days-old salt water was stifling.

Agonizingly slowly, Io closed the door but didn't turn the lock. She brought forth the Quilt, blinking furiously at the overwhelming sight: there were too many people in the room, and too close to one another—it looked like an explosion of silver, so bright her eyes stung. But even so, the gold thread stood out, there in the cot farthest from the stove.

She was a woman, as far as Io could discern through the hanging laundry. Her face was obscured, but long, blood-red hair trailed over the bundled sweater she was using as a pillow. Her threads sprouted from her chest in iridescent silver; Io took a step along the line of sleepers, ducking under dripping coats and trousers, bending at the waist for a better view.

She couldn't quite comprehend what she was seeing. The silver-and-gold thread that she had been tracking for the past five weeks led to the sleeping woman—but not to the woman's chest. The thread was looped around the woman's ankle, one end leading to Io's hand, the other to somewhere outside this shack, in a north-western direction. It didn't belong to the woman. She wasn't a god. It belonged to someone else and had been tied around this woman's leg to misdirect them.

Io deflated, her arms falling to her sides.

The woman was a decoy—and Io and Bianca had spent *five weeks* chasing after her.

When they left Alante more than a month ago, the god's thread had pointed northwest. Io and Bianca had followed, crossing the Wastelands at a breakneck pace through blizzards and dust storms, spending almost every coin they had—only for the thread to suddenly change direction and point southeast. They took off again, from outpost to village to town, but the moment they got close, the thread deviated once more: straight west.

That was when Io began to suspect they were being misled. That someone was sending them on a wild goose chase around the Waste-lands that was quickly depleting their funds, energy, and will. A week ago, they had been deep into the Peninsula, tailing the thread south, when news broke out that the dreaded Great Tide was now headed for the southern coast. Io knew this was their chance: she had pored over every single dot on her map—then stabbed her finger at Hagia.

The stilt town was the largest border town between the Peninsula and the Wastelands; its town council was unusually generous and its borders always open to refugees. Anyone fleeing north from the tsunami waves of the Great Tide would have to at least pass through Hagia. If Io and Bianca hurried north to Hagia, the god would be walking right into their waiting arms.

A soft rustling sounded somewhere in the shack. Io dropped the

Quilt and studied her surroundings: the figures seemed asleep, but much of the room was concealed by the hanging coats. *I can see the stains of crime on some of them*, Bianca had said. *They are not good people, cutter.*

Heart pulsing in her ears, nerves alight with adrenaline, Io drew a hanging poncho aside. There, curled at his father's side, was a child, barely five years old; the boy was writhing in place, brow scrunched as though in a nightmare. Io glanced at the father—still asleep, thank the gods—then at the red-haired woman carrying the god's thread—

Her eyes were open wide and staring straight at Io.

It happened fast: The red-haired woman's thin mouth became a hard line. Her eyes snapped to something—*someone*—behind Io. Io spun fast, bracing herself. She caught the image of an arm flying through the air. Of a ladle flashing scarlet with firelight.

A bludgeoning thud drilled through the side of Io's head.

CHAPTER II

NORN OF THE WORLD OAK

PAIN FOLLOWED, ALONG with a distant trill. "Thief! Thief!"

Then the metal grate of the floor, digging into Io's cheek, wet, cold, and achingly soothing. The floor vibrated with footfalls. Io's eyesight was swimming, but she managed to roll onto her back, giving her a better view of the room.

The old man was standing over her, ladle still raised as a threat, chest heaving with frantic breaths. The dripping coats flapped overhead, like the haggard sails of a storm-torn ship.

"Thought we were easy targets, huh?" the old man snapped.

But Io couldn't care less about him, or the other people rising from their cots—her eyes went to the redhead. She was standing in a long burgundy coat; she had slept in her clothes, the clever fox. By her feet was a backpack, into which she was hastily stuffing her belongings. Candlelight caught on her profile to reveal a button nose and wisps of hair so crimson the color could only be artificial—Io had a sudden pang of familiarity.

She had no time to dwell on it, though—more bodies crowded her vision: the father holding his boy; another child, older; and two women gripping each other's hands.

Io rolled to her knees and splayed her palms. "I'm not a thief," she said quickly. "I'm not here for you—"

The redhead dashed for the door, slipping past the old man with the ladle. Oh, hell—Io had no more time to waste. In one swift motion, she rose to her feet and knocked the ladle straight out of the old man's hand. A startled croak tore through his throat, momentum twisting his body to the side, which cleared a path to the door. Io raced out, one hand reaching for the knob behind her. The moment the door was closed, she raised her knee to her chest and kicked, breaking the knob and locking them inside—she didn't need any more ladles to the head, thank you very much.

Outside, the rain pelted every tin surface in Hagia, its relentless drumming the only sound in the gangway. The woman was rushing ahead, almost at the gull-stairs already. To hell with caution, to hell with silence; the Quilt pulsing silver around her, Io reached for one of the woman's threads that was throbbing in midair a few feet away. She grabbed it and *yanked*—up ahead, the woman screeched as she flew back onto the gangway, landing on her bottom.

Io was already running. She was there in seconds, with the aim to neutralize her, but the woman was just as fast. She rolled back into a crouch, her coat flapping around her legs, and smacked a fist into Io's belly. Io folded over herself, crashing into the wall of the nearest shack.

One of its residents howled, "Quiet!" followed by bangs on the tin walls.

Io felt the impression of a body moving through air—in a flash, the woman was on her, not with a punch or kick, but grabbing instead for Io's arms, trying to pin them to her sides. Io brought her elbow down on the woman's grip and slipped away, placing her body between her opponent and the gull-stairs. Her mind was muddled with panic; it urged her to flee, but then what would happen to the plan, to the answers she needed, to—

Too late, she realized the woman was moving again: she took off in a run, stepped on the rail of the gangway, and launched herself into the air. Io tried to escape her trajectory, but there was nowhere to go in the narrow gangway. The redhead landed on Io with both arms outstretched. It was all Io could do to bend her knees to break her fall—still, her spine reverberated against the metal, the whole gangway shaking with them.

Io tried to catch her breath, tried to force her body to obey, but the woman had positioned herself right on top of Io's chest, trapping Io's arms beneath her weight. This close, the details of her face became clear: a pale-skinned woman in her late thirties, her carefully painted kohl smudged by rainfall, her hair a vibrant, unnatural red as though spun from fire itself.

It was a face Io knew. It only took her a moment to place the light skin, the expensive coat, the artificial red hair cascading over strong shoulders—

Hanne.

The woman had been part of the entourage of Luc Saint-Yves, the former Police Commissioner and current Mayor of Alante, and Thais's ex-fiancé. Io had met her at that tension-filled dinner at Thais and Saint-Yves's house in the luxurious District-on-the-Hill, where Hanne had introduced herself as Saint-Yves's campaign manager. It was evident now that Hanne was much more than that.

"How," Hanne said in a sweet, feminine voice, "did you manage to find me?"

Io's ribs groaned with pressure as the woman leaned back to take a better look. Io's stomach fell—Hanne's blue eyes had turned silver. *A moira-born.* It made sense now, how Hanne had managed to evade them all this time, to alter her direction the moment they got close. She had the same powers Io did and could sense every shift and vibration in the Quilt.

"You're moira-born?" Io hissed between gasping breaths. That single time she had met Hanne back in Alante, there had been no reflection of silver in her eyes, no hint that she had powers.

"The Moirae are your gods, Alantian. Mine are the Norn of the World Oak."

The Norn were three sister goddesses, originating in Jhorr. Their descendants, the norn-born, dealt in fate and threads, but their powers were rumored to extend beyond the moira-born's. Io had heard that the norn-born could see images in the workings of a thread, snippets of the past or future.

"Back in Alante," Io said, "you helped Thais to create the wraiths."

Io had always wondered about this hole in Thais's confession. Her sister had admitted to reshaping the wraiths' severed life-threads into fury-whips, but who had cut these life-threads to begin with? Only a cutter could do that, and Thais's power was weaving. Hanne could be the missing piece.

It was merely a guess, but the woman didn't even try to deny it. "It had to be done. Justice demands sacrifice."

Io wanted to gag. She had heard these self-important doctrines before at that horrible dinner: *We are conduits of the divine. We will be harshly judged, and we, more than anyone else, do not want to be found lacking,* Thais had said. *Justice is the virtue of great souls,* Hanne had replied. Io should have known then that the two were working together.

"But how did I not see you coming? How did I not spot you when I arrived in Hagia?" Hanne said, staring at the bundle of threads above Io's chest. "Ah, I see. You used to be a beacon of silver, Io Ora. What happened to you? Where have all your threads gone?"

Hanne's fingers danced over Io's threads—twenty in total, a fairly average amount. Before escaping to the Wastelands, before starting this hopeless search, Io had had thirty-five.

"And where is your precious fate-thread?" the norn-born continued, her thin lips stretching into a smile, all teeth and gums. "Isn't it supposed to shine brighter than all your threads put together? Is it this one?" She pinched Io's fate-thread between thumb and fore-finger. "Honey, this one is a goner—I might as well cut it for you now and save you some time."

Every rational thought flew out of Io's head. She broke into kicks and punches, hitting nothing but air, hissing incomprehensible sounds. She was frantic, she was quake and storm and hail.

A plea broke through her lips. "Get off me! Get off me!"

Hanne raised her hands, palms up placatingly. "Calm down. I was merely curious—your beloved fate-thread is not what I'm looking for."

Io gritted her teeth and jerked her hips, trying to dislodge Hanne. She wiggled her torso and kneed Hanne's back—but there was no escape, not with the weight of the norn-born's entire body on her.

"Ah," said Hanne, eyes falling on Io's left hand. "*This* is what I'm here for."

No—no! Io felt as though she were far away, removed from her mind and body, as Hanne pinned her left wrist between her hands and started unwinding the precious god's thread from her fingers.

"I've been running for a long time. First to wrap up loose ends in Alante. Then to intercept this thread before you could follow it to its end. Then to lead you up and down the Wastelands like a dog on a leash. But I am tired, little Ora." Hanne's voice quieted, almost as if she was talking to herself. "The Great Tide—it took me by sur-prise. Surviving it depleted all my strength. I don't want to run any longer. I want to go home. You finally found me—congratulations. But you won't find me again."

Io felt helpless and trapped. Defeated. *I don't want to run any longer,* Hanne had said. *I want to go home.* Io wanted the same thing, a return to all the things that meant home. She made herself stop fighting. She looked away at the tin walls sleek with rain, the warm firelight through a nearby window, the ravenous gray of the sky. The god's thread was her only clue to the mystery at the heart of this conspiracy, the thing she had fought and lost so much for—

Io watched it beam its golden light against Hanne's hand. She watched as Hanne brought out one of her own threads and sliced.

The god's thread was severed. It dropped to the floor in loose tendrils like chopped hair, where its iridescent light began to fade. In moments, it had disappeared altogether.

Io pressed her lids shut. Moisture escaped down the side of her cheeks, dripping into her hair. All this time she had spent guarding it, nursing it, tracking it—*gods*.

"I will let you go just this once," Hanne said. "Because Thais loved you. Because she made me promise, that day we turned Bianca Rossi into a wraith, that I wouldn't hurt you or Ava. But this will be your one and only warning. You are going to abandon this quest. You're going to return to Alante and live the rest of your days happy and healthy and free. Aren't you, love?"

There was a motherly quality in Hanne's voice, a didactic tenderness that reminded Io of Thais. What a sick ploy to pretend either Hanne herself or Thais cared in the slightest whether Io got hurt or not.

Io looked straight into the norn-born's silver eyes. "It's far too late to stop now, *love*."

There was no going back. No returning to Alante to live out the rest of her days happy and free. She had unknowingly assisted in the murder of the Nine. She had been manipulated by one of her sisters and betrayed by the other. She had abandoned Edei as he lay bleeding, fighting for his life. The past was a disappointment, a disaster, a rotting corpse best left behind, and Io had no intention of ever returning to it.

She moved fast: clenched her core, raised her torso, and head-butted Hanne right in the face. The woman's head arced back, hands flying to her nose. Her breaths came out short and labored around the blood flowing from her nostrils. She was cursing under her breath, in what Io recognized as Jhorr insults.

Then, in Alantian, "You little brat!"

Hanne stood in one fluid movement, her long coat flowing like a queen's cape around her, and kicked Io hard in the ribs.

Io's sight went all white. The pain was immediate, so all-consuming that she couldn't even scream. She cradled her side and curled, breathless and silent, into a fetal position.

"Listen to me carefully now, little Ora."

Io had the impression that Hanne was squatting right over her, but she couldn't bear to open her eyes. Drawing a breath felt like inhaling scissors; her insides writhed, hot and swollen with agony.

"The gods are not your villains," Hanne stressed, her long hair tickling Io's forehead. "They are saviors. They have sacrificed their lives to save us, to save this entire world time and time again. Stop looking for them, or it will be the last thing you ever do on this earth."

Io's chest was racked with small, stabbing breaths. She heard Hanne's footfalls recede, then the echoing vibrations of the grated gangway. She opened her eyes and craned her neck in the norn-born's direction.

There she was, walking down the gangway in the pouring rain, burgundy coat silky with droplets. She passed by two hunched fig-ures huddled at the foot of the gull-stairs. One of them reached a hand to her, as though asking for change, and Hanne flattened her-self to the wall, startled. She ignored the man's pleas, climbing the rest of the steps two by two. Within seconds, she had disappeared.

Io rolled to her back on the gangway, staring straight up at the dark sky. The raindrops looked funny from this point of view, round and fat and gray. A hand on her aching ribs, she timed her breaths, trying to get her heartbeat under control. Inhale: one, two, three. Exhale: one, two, three. Inhale: one, two, three, four. Exhale—

A lithe body appeared above her, a smirk peeking beneath a wide-brimmed hat.

"That sounded like such pure *fun*," the mob queen said. "Kind of like a whale whipping an elephant around by its tail."

Io would have chuckled if her whole body wasn't in such pain. "Why didn't you help?"

"You told me not to, remember?" Bianca countered. "Told me to stick to the plan."

"Well, did you?"

Bianca craned her neck in the direction of the gangway.

"Ey, you two!" she shouted. "Did you get her?"

The beggars beneath the staircase had unfolded to their full height and were now making their way over. In the smothering dark of Hagia, the two men's eyes shone like beacons. Bronze, the color of dioscuri-born, descendants of the gods of paths traveled.

The two brothers joined Bianca to peer down at Io.

"Aye, boss," said the shorter one. "We got her."

CHAPTER III

GROOVED PATHS

BIANCA THREW OUT an impatient hand.

Io reluctantly took it and let the mob queen pull her up. Her side was still pulsing with pain, but after a few moments of gingerly poking her ribs, she was relieved to find none seemed to be broken. Surprisingly, neither were her spectacles, tucked into the front pocket of her jacket. She stepped beneath an awning by the staircase, where Bianca and the two dioscuri-born had found shelter from the heavy rainfall—on the other end of the gangway, she could hear the refugees trying to knock the door down. Soon they'd release themselves; Io needed to have made herself scarce by then.

The dioscuri-born, named Leo and Vito Ferrante, were identical in everything but height: in their late thirties, rough looking and wide shouldered, scars peeking from beneath their patchy beards. Leo was taller by at least ten inches, while Vito's neck was short, thick, and hunched. They stood side by side, hands limp in the pockets of their gray coats as they stoically studied the tin planks of the gangway at their feet. There was nothing there that Io could see, but the twins' eyes blazed with the bronze of their power: as descendants of the twin gods Castor and Pollux, the Dioscuri or Gemini, they had the ability to see the paths a person had taken in the past and would take in the future, in the form of thick grooves the color of rusted metal.

"Well?" Bianca said. A lit cigarette was hanging from her lips, its tip blazing red in the darkness of the stilt town.

Vito answered, lilting every word like a question in the accent common in these parts of the Wastelands. "What do you want first, past or future?"

Well, that was a loaded question. If she was really being honest with herself, Io wanted neither. The past was laden with rejections and betrayals, and the future didn't look too bright, either, not with the Nine's damned prophecy hanging like a scythe over her neck. But this wasn't about her and the running joke that was her life, so she squared her jaw and said, "Past."

Vito twirled a hand at his brother, prompting him to talk. Leo must be the oldest twin, then, gifted with the ability to interpret the paths a person had traveled in the past. The dioscuri-born had been handed a hard skill: they could trace trails of bronze on the ground, but deciphering where exactly each led was notoriously difficult. Needle in a haystack, in other words.

Face scrunched up in thought, Leo sat on his haunches and traced the metal grate of the gangway with his fingers, looking beyond the mud and grime Io could see there.

"Your runaway friend has been busy," he said.

Their runaway friend—that was how Io had phrased it when she approached the twins for this job. She was desperate to find a friend who owed her money, Io had told them, and who was sure to give them the slip at the first opportunity. She needed their help to track her friend's next stop on the road, so she and her partner, Bianca, could get their money back. Leo and Vito were going to get a cut of that money in advance, roughly thirty notes, if they were ready to help the moment Io called on them.

"Your friend was just in Blue-Temple, and before that she stopped briefly in Poppy Town and that fishing town southwest—what's the name, Vito? Berry Hill?" His brother grunted agreement in reply.

"And before that, I think she was in Alante. There are cobbled streets in her path, their slick surface reflecting neon lights."

Bianca was the fastest to realize. "Lilac Row?"

"Yeah," said the man. "Looks like it."

The mob queen's eyes sliced to Io. "What business does our *friend* have in the Fortuna's turf?"

Io gave her a pointed, bulging-eyed look, in the vein of *I'll tell you later.* But her mind was cataloging clues: Hanne had admitted she had been "tying up loose ends" in Alante, and Io herself had met her in the opulent District-on-the-Hill, but Lilac Row was unexpected. Smack in the heart of the Silts, the slums of Alante, Lilac Row was a street lined with clubs, gambling dens, and dream palaces. Its crown jewel was the Fortuna Club, home to none other than Bianca Rossi and her gang. It was no place for a fancy Jhorr woman who was running the Police Commissioner's mayoral campaign, much less a disciple of the gods, so what had Hanne been doing there?

"How long ago was this?" Io asked.

"Lilac Row?" Leo replied. "A little more than a month. She was there a few times, from what I can tell."

The gods' strongarm had visited Lilac Row *a few times.* That was alarming, to say the least. Io said, "And before that?"

"Lots of places, all over the continent. Jhorr, for the first few years of her life. But she seems to always return to the same cement sidewalks, patterned like cobblestone and interrupted by drains . . . That's a telltale of the streets of the inner city of Nanzy. I'd wager that's your friend's home. Brother," Leo said, "can you confirm?"

Vito needed only to glance down once at the bronze paths his twin was studying before giving them a curt nod. "That's her home, all right. She visits it often in the future."

By last count, the Golden City of Nanzy was the largest city-nation in the world and the seat of both the Mayoral Council and the Agora, the governing body of the other-born population. It made sense for Hanne to live there—it was where Thais had been stationed during the two years she had disappeared from Io and Ava's lives, and so, by extension, the most likely place she might have been enlisted by the gods.

"Is she going there now?" Io asked, watching Vito closely. There was something about the shorter twin's casual indifference that felt too composed, artificial almost. "Back to Nanzy?"

Vito nodded with a smile verging on greedy.

"You need to be more specific." She had been hunching against the wall, a palm cradling her tender rib cage, but now she straightened. "Nanzy is a city of millions. Where exactly will she be? Where can we intercept her?"

The smirk launched fully on Vito's face, as though this was precisely the question he had been hoping for. "Your friend knows how to hide from our powers. Her steps are intended to confuse a dioscuri-born or any other kind of other-born with the ability to track her. She walks on mud when she can, overlaps her steps, circles back to a different path. But she can't trick me."

It was a trap of some sort, but Io couldn't help but willingly walk into it. Through her teeth, she asked, "Where is she going?"

"Uh-uh," Vito said nasally. "I will need better compensation to reveal that to you."

Io knew instantly what would follow. Her head dropped back against the tin wall with a soft thud.

"Brother," Leo intervened, "don't—"

Vito spoke over his twin, stepping in front of Io. "I hear you're a cutter, girl."

Io let her eyes flutter shut. Gods, she was exhausted.

The money she had snatched from her savings before escaping Alante had quickly run out, spent on travel fares and town entry fees, on food, housing, and the necessary medicine to keep Bianca alive. They tried doing odd jobs here and there: porting goods, washing dishes, doing laundry, hunting chimerini—but these sorts of jobs paid little, even less if their employers noticed the silver in Io's eyes. Until one of them—the owner of a dodgy inn—approached Io with a job: cut his thread to his former lover, for a hefty twenty notes.

For two days, Io battled with herself: she didn't want to start cutting threads for money again. It had taken her years to admit she didn't like doing it for Thais. Longer still to stop hating herself for it. But money. Damn necessary money. Eventually, Io had had to take the innkeeper's job, and a dozen others after that.

You used to be a beacon of silver, Io Ora. What happened to you? Where have all your threads gone? Hanne had asked. Io had thirty-five threads when she left Alante, much more than average. Her sisters used to call her a hoarder, because Io collected loves like shiny marbles: the delicious éclair she ate, the nice librarian at school, that very green frog she had found when she was six. Threads to the things she cherished appeared out of nowhere, her love given essence in gleaming silver.

Not so anymore. It was impossible to find new things to love, new connections to form, when your heart had been broken so thoroughly. Now Io was down to twenty threads. One thread could only be cut by another, both sacrificed to the severing. In total, this side business had cost her fifteen threads; no wonder she no longer looked like a beacon in the Quilt.

Breaker of hearts, cutter of threads—her destiny was inescapable.

Io heard someone hiss, "You filthy, greedy vermin."

Too late, she recognized Bianca's voice. There was aggressive shuffling as bodies slammed together, and a thunderous vibration on the tin wall at her back—Io snapped her eyes open to find the mob queen had nailed Vito Ferrante to it, an arm pressing down on his windpipe.

"We had an agreement, for which you were paid handsomely," Bianca seethed, her face inches from the man's. "You'll uphold your end of the deal, or you will find yourself without a tongue to speak ever again."

The shorter twin's eyes were round and bulging, his hands struggling to unlock Bianca's hold on him.

"Hey, hey," Leo said soothingly, palms up as he tried to wiggle between them. "My brother meant no offense . . ." He trailed off the moment he registered Bianca's face. "Gods," he whispered. *"What are you?"*

Uh-oh. That wasn't good.

Io unstuck herself from the wall. Bianca's eyes were reflecting the orange of flames, the telltale sign of a fury-born, whom the man—and the rest of the world—believed to have died out twelve years ago. Leo was right to fear her: a throw of Bianca's fury-whip would snap his neck in an instant.

"Bianca." Io's voice was hard, an order.

Twice now, she had seen Bianca lose control of her newfound fury-born powers. The first was forty miles outside Alante, when they had stopped at one of the roadside elevated stalls for some clean water. The vendor tried to haggle half of their notes for two glasses, and Bianca had lost it. Her eyes had ripened to burnt orange; next thing Io knew the mob queen was jumping over the counter and tackling the man to the floor. Io tore her off the vendor just before she smashed his head in.

The second time was three weeks ago in the last stilt town they visited, Poppy Town. They had been scarfing down stew at a packed taverna, while an ever-present storm raged outside. One of the patrons had caught Bianca's eye. *Stained,* Io had heard her mumble before she rushed at the woman. This time, Io couldn't drag her away—it took three of the other customers and two of the waiters to restrain the mob queen. Needless to say, they were kicked out, their bowls of stew still steaming at their table. The woman, according to the information Io had scrounged the next day, was a grace-born who used her thrall-inducing powers to run a business based on child labor. Io had located her in the town's infirmary; her life-thread was fraying, her spine broken in two places.

Io had gone straight from the infirmary to the innkeeper and accepted his offer. She cut the thread to the innkeeper's ex-lover right there in his office, while the last dregs of the storm siphoned out of the fishing town. Then she went to the oneiroi-born operating through a side room in his tiny apartment and bought Bianca five bottles of sleeping tonic.

Now Io's voice dropped to a soothing whisper. "Where's your calming tonic? Shall I get it for you, boss?"

"Boss" was what gang members used to address someone they respected. Io had learned the term while working with Edei back in Alante and used it often on the road; Bianca seemed to like it. She reached out uncertainly—when Bianca didn't react, Io fumbled through the pockets of the mob queen's oversized coat until her fingers closed around a little vial. The liquid was a vibrant blue, the kind of color you only see in neon signs and dream-palace cocktails. Io popped the cork with her teeth, then stuck the vial under Bianca's nose.

Manufactured and used by oneiroi-born, the descendants of the gods of sleep, to help their customers fall asleep, the calming tonic was hard to procure in the Wastelands, where there was scarcely any drinkable water, let alone dream-palace cocktails. But it was the only thing that worked effectively to quench Bianca's bloodthirst. It dulled the mind, making her slow and groggy, but also offered a reprieve from a fury-born's lust for vengeance.

"Drink up," Io urged, prodding Bianca's lips with the vial for good measure.

The mob queen moved fast, as she was wont to do, so swiftly it was a blur: she stepped away from the dioscuri-born, snatched the vial from Io's hand, and gulped down a good sip.

Vito collapsed sideways into his twin's arms; his face was sculpted into wrath. Standing so close to them now, Io suddenly became aware of how much bigger they both were. How easily this could escalate into a fight she and Bianca would lose.

"Forgive her," she said, plastering a smile on her face. "She can't control herself sometimes—you know how the keres-born are."

Descendants of the Keres, goddesses of violent deaths, the keres-born had a nasty reputation for being aggressive and sadistic. Fittingly, Bianca actually was a keres-born—or had been, before becoming the dying wraith she now was. Keres-born's eyes shone red when they were using their powers, a shade so close to the orange of fury-born that Io hoped it would convince the dioscuri-born twins of her lie. Vito was still watching Bianca with the look of a caught fish released back into the sea. His breaths were labored, his cheeks red and trembling.

Io stepped in front of Bianca, trying to draw the twins' attention back to her. "What is the thread you'd like cut, Vito?"

After a long moment, Vito's head seemed to clear. "We used to have a winery, Leo and I. But this bug-infestation . . . We get waves of insects every summer, but this time, it has been worse than ever before. None of our usual repellents work. All the vineyards around Hagia are suffering. We have an offer to buy the winery, but I—I can't sell it, even though I know it's best to try our chances elsewhere, at a more hospitable place. I love it too much."

Io nodded. She knew that helpless devotion all too well.

Winery, she thought, and blinked on the Quilt. Her hand charted over the threads bursting out of the man's chest. He had dozens of them, which was always a good sign; hearts that loved a lot tended to be kinder. Io got faint impressions of their essence as her fingertips skimmed each thread. Here was one of the deepest love and bursting laughter—a child, perhaps, or a lover. Here was one of smoked paprika and cool yogurt—one of Hagia's traditional dishes. Here was the smooth skin of sun-warmed grapes, the sharp smell of wood barrels. Vito and Leo's winery.

"Are you sure?" she asked.

"Brother," Leo said softly, an arm still supporting his brother's weight. "You don't have to."

"I know." Vito's face had sobered. "I want to."

Io felt like an interloper. This was a moment between brothers who held each other up, who mourned with each other and sacrificed what they loved for each other. She had lived these moments herself, in Ava's arms, in Thais's, and to be looking at them now, from the outside in, was gut-wrenching.

She grabbed one of her own threads from her chest and brought it down on Vito's.

Both threads snapped, disappearing. Such was the price a cutter had to pay: each slice cost them as much as it did their victims. Io knew the loss of this thread, of the fifteen before it, would register soon, accompanied by a great melancholy, but these were thoughts for later, when she was alone and sorrowed.

Vito placed a palm over his chest, eyes drooping, and began speaking in a low, fast tone, giving her exactly what she had paid so dearly for. "Before returning to Nanzy, your friend will stop at Tulip, two days' travel north from here. She knows you might be following her—she's using a bog pirogue right now and is planning to walk on nondescript dirt, but she's in bad luck. I recognize the sandstone beneath her feet; it's used to hold rainwater in terraced farming towns like Tulip."

"Thank you—" Io began to say.

But the mob queen spoke over her, a dark looming presence in her large coat and wide-brimmed hat. "If she knows how to hide from you, then how can you be sure she will return to Nanzy?"

"It is her home," Vito answered. "She will go back to it, soon. We humans like to return to grooved paths."

Grooved paths: that sounded about right. The truth of it was in the mud-tide beneath their feet, claiming the land each night, releasing it each morning. It was in the second moon, Nemea, peeking between the storm clouds at the edge of the horizon, like it did every day. It was in Bianca Rossi's tense posture, arms crossed over her chest, always in battle with herself, the mob queen and the wraith. It was in Io herself—hadn't she started cutting threads for money again? Back into the grooved path she'd gone.

> *The cutter*
> *the unseen blade*
> *the reaper of fates*
> *she watches silver like a sign*
> *she weeps silver like a mourning song*
> *she holds silver like a blade*
> *she cuts the thread*
> *and the world ends*

The prophecy sprang unwelcomed into her mind. Chills ran down her spine as she remembered the Nine, the all-knowing muse-born, flinging copies of this poem in the air. Scattering portraits on the floor of Io with a thread in her hands and the world burning behind her. Destiny, again, coming to haunt Io. Was it really as inescapable as Vito claimed? Was Io bound to return to it, her grooved path, simply because the Nine's artists had said so?

"Come, brother," Leo said, ushering his twin away.

Io stood there in the rain, watching them go. Leo's arm was around his brother's shoulders, their strides in tandem. After a moment, they burst into laughter, and Vito reached up to ruffle his twin's hair.

Brother—it was so close to what the Ora sisters called each other: *sister mine.* Io imagined Ava's fingers combing her hair after a long shower, Thais's arms closing around her in a tight hug—*no.* Now wasn't the time for bittersweet memories.

"I knew her," Io said to Bianca. "The person the gods sent. Hanne. She is a norn-born from Jhorr. She was introduced to me as Saint-Yves's campaign manager, but I think she was working with Thais on—"

On you, she almost said. *On making wraiths like you.*

She glanced at the mob queen. Her lips were stained blue from the tonic and pursed in a tight line. "Taking a detour to Tulip is foolish," Bianca said. "We should head straight to Nanzy. It's roughly two weeks away by foot, ten days if we can afford to ride on a caravan. We can move incognito; no one will be expecting us. We can wait for this Hanne at the gates and shadow her when she arrives."

"Sure," Io said.

It was a good plan, safe, sensible, and forethoughtful, just the kind of thing Io usually went for. It gave them an edge, an advantage, placing them a step ahead when they had been two steps behind for weeks.

But Tulip. With its sandstone dirt and terraced fields and the caution Hanne was taking to hide her destination. What could the gods' norn-born be doing in Tulip? What if she was going there to find yet another helpless person with distant fury-born heritage? To trace their life-thread up to the sky, then snap it off, exactly as she had done to Bianca?

What if, this time, Io was there to stop her?

Bianca's groan broke the smooth pattering of the rain. "*Cutterrr*," she whined. "Nanzy is the smarter choice."

Io knew it was. Still, she was going to make the foolish one.

CHAPTER IV

THE RIGHT WORD

THE TIDE HAD been arriving slowly from the south, creeping over the barren hills and valleys of the Wastelands until Io and Bianca had to wrestle with the mud for their every step. Dusk had fallen upon them unheralded; in fifteen minutes, half hour at most, the land around them would be submerged in water.

Io hated the Wastelands. Hated the mud and the chimerini, hated how fast the tide came, seemingly out of nowhere, hated the constant need to scan the horizon for a roadside outpost or mound high enough to save them from the coming tide. Dread was an insistent, unwelcome companion on the road, to the point where Io's thoughts became hazy with terror and her limbs jittery with fright.

"Just a while farther," Bianca Rossi called over her shoulder. "Then we'll be nice and safe on the transmission tower."

Io eagerly slipped her long-distance spectacles on. A few hundred feet ahead of them, a beacon cyclically emitted red light across the plains. Bianca had spotted it twenty minutes ago and set them on a track toward it, sloshing through the rising mud-tide at a brutal pace. Now Io could make out the spindly metal legs and wiry arms of the tower itself. It looked like a scarecrow in a wheat field, or maybe a too-tall birdfeeder, draped as it was with squatters perching on its steel latticework.

"Will we make it in time?" Io shouted ahead to Bianca.

Instead of replying, Bianca turned around, marched through the squelching mud, and tore the backpack off Io. She shouldered it on along with her own, and croaked, "Now we will. You better keep up, cutter, because I'm not coming back for you if a buffalo-bear sets its eye on you again."

Io nearly dislocated her skull snapping her head around in search of the telltale horns of a buffalo-bear peeking through the mud. She would very much rather *not* happen upon one again, ever in her life. It had been a terrifying experience: the chimerini had burst through the mud like a fiend and started galloping toward Io, head bent, horns at the ready. The only reason Io was still alive was Bianca—the mob queen had pretty much tossed Io onto an elevated tide-guard outpost, then hauled herself up behind her. The buffalo-bear had rammed the outpost legs for hours before admitting defeat. It had been a hard, sleepless night.

Io's jaw tightened as she sprinted to catch up to Bianca. It was easier to wade through the mud without the added weight of the backpack, but still, when they finally reached the transmission tower, Io's legs trembled with exhaustion.

Bianca was unfazed. She handed the backpack to Io and warned, "Not a word about heights, cutter. Just climb."

The first time Io had needed to climb up an elevated roadside shelter, she had frozen, jaw clenched, fingers clamped around the ladder. The mob queen had looked down at her, rolled her eyes, and said, *Get over it. There's no room for phobias in the Wastelands.* Io had decidedly *not* gotten over it, but she did teach herself to just soldier through it, fear and all. Typically, the alternative was death, so terror it'd have to be. The backpack straps dug into her shoulders as she dragged her tired limbs from beam to crossbar to beam again.

"Just in time, kardesi," a voice said from above.

A middle-aged Kurkz man with curly eyebrows reached to help Bianca onto a large grille doubling as a platform. He gestured at the ground beneath them—Io risked a look. Indeed, tidewater was now lapping around the legs of the tower; the entire valley glistened with the sickly green of an algae-ridden lake.

The man clasped Io's hand and hauled her up. "Tesekur ederim," Io thanked him in Kurkz.

"Ah, no worries," he said, giving Io a hearty thump on the back. "No one left behind."

It was a popular saying among Wastelanders. Io had first heard it on the busy roads outside Alante when she and Bianca had run out of water. Another traveler had offered them a drink from her canteen, these same words muttered instead of a greeting. No one left behind—because it was only through communality that one could survive the Wastelands.

"Gods," Io gasped, resting her hands on her knees. "It feels like the mud-tide arrived much faster than normal tonight."

"It did," the Kurkz man said. "It's the Great Tide—it's changed direction overnight. It's heading north now, toward us, and it's bloating the mud-tide on its way up."

"North? But the Agora warned it'd be heading west."

"Aye, it seems they were wrong."

Oh, this Great Tide was a cheeky one. The tsunami waves usually formed somewhere in the Timid Sea and often dissipated before they ever hit land. Those that had crashed into the coast in the past had devoured entire chunks of the continent. Io's family on her father's side had had to migrate to Alante when a Great Tide flooded their fishing town.

But Io had never known the Agora's predictions to be so wide of the mark before. Comprised entirely of descendants of the Horae, goddesses of time, the Agora were the leaders of the other-born population. They used their knowledge of past, present, and future to warn about coming disasters, advise on investments, and mediate in times of conflict. Compared to the domineering Mayors, they had little power—seeing as how all other-born were considered dangerous criminals and whatnot—but any warning they issued was instantly taken to heart. In a world as unstable as their own, a heads-up could save the lives of thousands.

"But don't worry, kardesi. We'll be safe come morning." The man pointed with his chin. "I'm afraid we've taken up this platform, but there's space for you farther up."

Indeed, the grille platform was filled to the brim with travelers and their belongings. They all shared the dark coloring of the Kurkz; probably his family, relocating from one city-nation to another. Above, squatters nestled in every nook and cranny of the transmission tower. Some had even started a fire.

"Drifters," the Kurkz man explained, following Io's gaze. Drifters were nomadic travelers who traversed from town to town, hunting seasonal work. They knew a lot about the Wastelands, about surviving them as well as enjoying them. Whenever they crossed paths with a Drifter caravan, Bianca insisted on following them until their paths diverged. "They've offered to roast everyone's meat after they're done with theirs."

Io gave the man a kind smile. "Alas, we don't have any meat."

They hadn't had meat for a good while, a fact that Bianca often lamented. The mob queen was skin and bones; her appetite had diminished since her life-thread was cut. The only thing she ate with pleasure was freshly grilled steak. Anything else was mechanical, as though chewing was torture.

"Neither do we," the Kurkz said, "but at least—"

"Girl!" Bianca snapped from somewhere above, which was what she called Io when she couldn't say "cutter" in public. "Hurry up."

Io didn't. She saluted the Kurkz man with a nod, then took her time climbing, mindful over every hand- and foothold. When she reached Bianca, the mob queen had already slung their hammocks between the beams and was nestled inside the bigger one, scowling at the rowdy Drifter group a few feet below them. Their setup was impressive: they'd stretched a canvas between the four tower legs and arranged a whole dining room on top of it, complete with a portable gas stove and wooden cutlery. They were roasting sausages—the smell was divine. The children were playing a card game by the fire, while the adults were huddled beside a portable radio, listening intently.

Io hooked a leg around the beam and twisted her ear in the direction of the sound. Across from her, Bianca was leaning half-out of her hammock to catch the transmission of the latest news.

"—conflicting reports from the riots in Rossk. Officials claim the unrest has settled down, but our correspondent on the ground sends frequent updates on the reignition of violence in the popular Merchant Square. Meanwhile, Obinova, the Mayor of Rossk, is currently in Nanzy for the Mayoral Assembly, which is expected to begin discussions tomorrow. Mayors of every city-nation on the continent have congregated in the Golden City to deliberate on new measures to satiate the insurgencies after the assassinations of major other-born leaders across the world five weeks ago. The Assembly meets at nine tomorrow morning in the historical bui—"

The signal cut out abruptly. One of the Drifters rose to fix the wire antennae. The whole thing was an impressive feat of ingenuity that Io had seen at pretty much every outpost on the road: all caravans carried small radios, which they illegally connected to these transmission towers for electricity and signal. Travelers tuned in around midnight, when the latest weather report was broadcast. With the Great Tide hitting the Southern Peninsula and a sudden resurgence of hurricanes on the western coast, one could never be too careful these days.

"Hey," Bianca called to the person in the hammock directly beneath theirs. An oil lamp hung over their head, a book propped open on their belly. "Any news of Alante?"

"None today," they replied in a husky voice. Io couldn't see their lips moving through their bushy beard; its ends were braided and clipped with marbled beads. "The riots came to an end there three weeks ago, but there's been no arrests for the murders of the Nine."

Io tensed, but Bianca brushed the comment off, revealing nothing on her face. "Yeah, we've heard that. Have there been arrests in other cities?"

"I know the Jhorrs recently held a public funeral for their fallen æsir-born," they said, "and that the Police Commissioner there had to resign after failing to catch the culprits before they escaped the city. Last week, I heard someone was arrested in Kurkz for the murders of the sabazios-born, but rumor is the assassin died before the police could get any information out of them."

The æsir-born were one of the oldest bodies of other-born units in the world, similar in power and notoriety to the Nine, and the sabazios-born were the relatively new leaders of a consortium of other-born in Kurkz. Their assassinations had happened in the same week as the massacre at the House of Nine.

The mob queen was silent for a moment, then: "What did the assassin die of, do you know?"

The person made a noncommittal sound and turned to watch the Drifters fumbling to get a signal back.

While their attention was elsewhere, Io whispered at Bianca, "Will you stop?" The mob queen made a point to keep track of news of Alante at every stop on the road, regardless of how many times Io asked her not to. "What was the point of the fake papers we paid a fortune for, if you're going to shout left and right we're from Alante?"

"Cutter," Bianca hissed back. "Nobody cares about us. Don't you see they've all got their own problems to worry about? A tsunami is clawing its way inland, for gods' sake."

"But if they realize who we are—"

"If our names and faces had been given to the press or the police, we'd already be rotting in a cell back at City Plaza. For *some* reason, which we can all guess is saving his own ass, your sister's boyfriend hasn't publicized what happened at the House of Nine."

The mob queen was right. There had been no mention in the news of their involvement in the slaughter of the Nine, nor of Thais's part in it, despite the fact that there had been several witnesses and photo evidence taken by Rosa. Saint-Yves must have buried the news to *save his own ass*, as Bianca so eloquently put it. But their relief had been brief—within a week of them leaving the Sunken City, news had broken of other-born assassinations in every major city-nation: Jhorr, Rossk, Kurkz, Iyen. Most culprits had evaded arrest, but a few had been discovered dead, or they'd passed away soon after they were brought in. Wraiths, Io suspected, created by the gods' lackeys just like Bianca was. Whatever the gods' plan, it was bigger than avenging the genocide of the fury-born, bigger than restoring balance to the world—Io just had no idea how it was all connected yet.

The radio cranked up again: "*—three new disappearances have been reported this week from bogland villages. Two women and a man. Local constables remain perplexed by this strange occurrence, while Wastelanders demand the city-nations' help.*"

An angry murmur went through the crowd. This string of disappearances—or abductions, depending on which outlet was reporting—had started a month ago, after Io and Bianca had already been on the road for a week. It wasn't uncommon for people to go missing in the Wastelands, but this was something bigger. At every village and shantytown, solemn faces in black-and-white police sketches or the rare photograph gazed back at them from noticeboards, people of varying ages, races, and genders. There was no common thread to connect the missing people, which had baffled constabularies across the Wastelands. They seemed to disappear into thin air. An Iyen man had approached Io in Blue-Temple to hire her to track down his missing nephew, but Io had to turn him down. She could see no thread connecting them, nothing that she could follow to find his nephew. Either the man didn't care for his nephew as much as he claimed or—the boy was dead.

"Assassinations, riots, disappearances . . ." A Drifter's voice rose over the murmuring. "Now a Great Tide chasing our tails north. What's next?"

Sounds of agreement from the crowd, followed by quiet conversations in smaller groups.

Io slipped inside her hammock, backpack and all, and stayed there for a moment, staring up at the dark clouds.

No moons tonight, no stars, either, just the clockwork scarlet light of the rotating tower beacon. Space had lost all meaning after five weeks on the road. Time, too. Io longed for the familiar walls of the apartment she shared with her sister Ava, for the creaky floorboards in the kitchen, and the worn, fuzzy throw on their sofa. She longed for a normal day: to wake up early and grab a slice of spinach pie before heading out, then return late in the evening to slouch on the sofa with a warm drink, her body tired from the day's work, her mind content, and her belly full. Most of all, though, she longed for those precious moments in between, a stroll and a chat with Ava, a night out dancing with Rosa, a book analysis over coffee with Amos.

Gods, what she wouldn't give to be back at home, with her people, the past few months erased from history.

A boot stabbed Io in the thigh. She jostled, her hammock swinging back and forth, which sent a nauseating wave of terror up her throat. *"Bianca!"*

"Get your backpack off," the mob queen ordered. "It's bad enough that we have to smell that . . . *feast*; you don't have to squash our bread, too."

Io gingerly maneuvered the backpack off her shoulders, slipped it open, and ceremoniously slathered two pieces of bread with fig jam. A feast of kings, one could say. When she offered one between the hammocks, Bianca snatched it with unnecessary force. The brim of her hat concealed her eyes, but Io could tell the mob queen was stabbing daggers at her.

"What?" Io said, suddenly uncertain. "Is this about Tulip?"

"No, cutter. I'm just sick and tired of fig jam." Bianca flapped her slice of bread as though it were goat droppings topped with moldy cheese. "Your insecurities grate on my nerves, you know that? You made a choice. It is done. We'll be in Tulip in the morning. What is the point of doubting yourself now—and dragging me down with you in this needless conversation?"

The trouble with Bianca was that she couldn't fathom that there didn't *have* to be a point. It was just how Io's mind worked now. The two people Io had cared about most in the world had betrayed her. She had loved them, she had trusted them and forgiven them, and she had been *wrong.* How was she supposed to ever feel certain of herself and her choices after that?

"I've told you before and I'll say it again," Bianca said. "If you want to go to Jhorr, I'll go to Jhorr. We can find your sisters. We can get your justice. Then we can go right to Nanzy and finish what we started. If I'm still hanging on to this pitiful imitation of life, that is."

Jhorr: a city-nation built out of ships and ice islands, far in the north. Jhorr: where Thais's and Ava's threads had been pointing ever since they left Alante in a hurry. On the very first night on the road, Bianca had given Io this same choice, to track down her sisters instead of the gods. Demand answers, seek justice, then deal with the gods afterward. But Io couldn't.

She was a talented detective, a skilled cutter. She worked with clues and suspects and motives. The god's thread had been her clue, the gods her suspects—motive was what she was looking for now. If she found the gods, if she outed them as the masterminds of all these assassinations, she would put a stop to whatever dark plan they had brewing. She would get Bianca the revenge she had promised her. Then and only then would Io face her sisters. When she had proven she was right. When she had proven they had made the wrong choice.

"It's not justice I want," she said quietly. "It's an end to all this death."

"You sure about that?" the mob queen asked. "They left you, cutter, blood-soaked and brokenhearted."

"I told you, Thais has always been like this—"

"Yes, Thais, your oh-so-wicked sister. But I'm not just talking about her. I'm talking about Ava. Ava chose to leave you. She chose to leave me, too, beat-up and threadless. She assigned me to your care, as if I'm a pet to be walked while she's on vacation. Why aren't you angry?"

"Because this is not about anger, or insecurities, or guilt!" Io snapped.

She *wished* she was angry. Every day on the road, alone with her thoughts, Io wished for the all-encompassing heat of wrath, to scorch and incinerate every ounce of doubt and grief and longing in her heart. But she had too level a head for that. Nothing useful ever came out of anger—no, what Io needed was to be smarter this time. Stronger. Less naive.

"What's it about, then?" the mob queen snapped back.

Io's mouth opened—but she couldn't think of an answer. Sadness? Sorrow for the family she'd thought she had, the love she had lost? Ah, there was the right word—

"Loss," Io whispered, all her irritation deflating.

Bianca's gaze wandered off, meditative, as though the statement required time to process. Io began feeling self-conscious. This conversation had taken an odd turn. Screaming matches they did on the daily, bickering pretty much every hour on the hour, but heart-to-hearts, even in the form of snappy back-and-forth? No, she and Bianca didn't share their *feelings*.

After some empty, soundless moments, the mob queen said, "You haven't lost them, you know. They're alive. You can have them back if that's what you want."

"No," Io said quickly. "I can't. What they were to me, what we used to be to each other—that's gone forever. People change."

"You say that like it's a bad thing."

Because it was. Io was certain.

Silence stretched, too long, growing uninterruptible. Io slipped farther into the hammock, disappearing from view. She gazed at the sprawling gray sky again, at the beacon washing its red light over every beam and line.

People change. The thought pounded in her head, like the drum of a funeral lament. It wasn't just her sisters who had changed. It wasn't just her sisters who Io was grieving.

As if bespelled, her fingers probed the space above her chest. The silver latticework of the Quilt spilled over her surroundings.

Io reached for the fate-thread.

CHAPTER V

ROT AND DEATH

ONCE, THAIS HAD taken Io to her old Rossk moira-born mentor. Sonya was her name; she had a gray mane and little curly hairs that peppered her jawline like a man's stubble. Mama had found Sonya for Thais when Io's sister was still a thumb-sucking, silver-eyed toddler. Sonya had taught Thais everything she knew about the moira-born—for a price, of course.

Sonya lived on Thyme Street, close to the Docks. Every now and then chimerini reptiles scuttled across their path, claws and fangs and pinchers shining ominously in the light of the three moons. Io had just turned ten, but she held Thais's hand tight as they traversed the darkly lit neighborhood. It had been years since Thais had seen the moira-born tutor, as their parents could no longer afford the lessons. The burden of teaching Ava and Io had fallen on Thais herself, and just last week, Thais had discovered Io's fate-thread—and didn't know what to do with it.

Thais had stood Io before Sonya and asked, "Is this what I think it is?"

Sonya had been sitting in a chair on the building hallway, fanning herself with one hand and holding a small radio to her ear with the other. *Reign of Hearts* was on, the long-running tragic love story of a poor other-born boy and a nonpowered rich girl, hiding their relationship from their rival families. Sonya had shushed them with a spotted hand; Thais and Io stood there for a long time, waiting for the episode to end.

At last, Sonya stuffed the tiny radio in the folds of her skirt and reached for Io's chest. The jolt stole Io's breath. She would have fallen right on her bottom had she not been gripping Thais's hand. In the Quilt, Io's fate-thread pulsed a luminous silver in Sonya's stubby fingers.

"It's so bright it can be nothing else," the old moira-born said, releasing the thread with a flick of her wrist.

Thais's mouth had scrunched up, in that way it did when she was upset. "How can it go away?"

Even Sonya's eyebrows were graying. They scowled now as she examined Thais. "Why, malishka? Did you try to cut it and found you could not?"

Io's heart had begun beating very fast in her chest. She schooled her face to indifference, lest her sister realize how scared she was, how precious this thread was to her already.

Thais said, "Of course not," and it was so truthful, so absolute that Io suddenly felt guilty. How could she have believed even for a second that her sister wanted to cut her fate-thread? It would be a terrible thing to do. Her sister wasn't terrible.

The old moira-born's eyes landed softly on Io. "It's an extraordinary thing, a fate-thread. All threads exist outside the concept of place. No one can see or touch them but our kind. But a fate-thread also exists outside of time. It is a thread of the future, bound to you in the present." Her fingers snaked around Io's wrist. "Such a precious light should never be snuffed out. Do you understand, moy luchik?"

Sunray, the word meant, Io had later learned. She had nodded her head profusely. Even at ten, the fate-thread was already the most precious thing she had. It promised a brighter future filled with love, a future that made all the hardships of the present—the lack of food, the hand-me-down clothes the neighborhood kids mocked her for, her parents' dark moods, and Thais's constant worrying—far easier to bear. Io would ensure it was never snuffed out.

Now, on the transmission tower above the flooded valley, Io opened her eyes and looked at the fate-thread in her palm.

Its light was dim, its essence fraying. Gone was the lustrous shine, gone was the precious glow. Not snuffed out entirely, but on the way there.

Io gripped it tight. The familiar dread cocooned her in a shroud of sorrow. As he had bled in her arms, Edei had said, *I do care.* He had said, *I promise, the moment I'm better, I'll come find you.* He had taken her palm and placed it on his chest, over the fate-thread. *I will follow this. I'll always find you.*

But it had been five weeks, and he wasn't here. Surely, with Samiya's help, he had healed by now. Surely, he had sorted things out in the Fortuna gang. Surely, he knew Io was treading dangerous waters and would welcome his help. Surely. But Edei hadn't even *moved*—the fate-thread always disappeared to the southeast, back in the direction of Alante. It never shifted, never vibrated; he had taken not a single step toward her.

And now the fate-thread was fraying. Its light was fading.

It had happened so slowly, so quietly, that Io hadn't even noticed at first. She had crawled onto the mattress she shared with Bianca in that dreadful inn back in Poppy Town, after a particularly nasty day of cleaning up after rude, loud drunks, and she had sought the comfort of the fate-thread. Of knowing someone was out there, fated to be her destiny. Soon they would be reunited, soon all would be all right again.

The fate-thread had shone with a broken, dimmed light that she had never seen before. Upon closer inspection, she realized a few tendrils were sticking out as though it was an overused sail rope finally succumbing to the elements. Io knew what she felt, she knew what Edei was to her—which could only mean the fate-thread was fraying because *his* feelings were no longer the same. He had said, *I'll always find you*, but perhaps he had changed his mind.

People did that, after all, didn't they? Even the people you thought you knew best. They changed and it was catastrophic, it was an ending, no matter what Bianca might believe.

Io closed her eyes and hoped for the thoughtless oblivion of sleep.

She jolted awake at the sound of a shriek.

For a few incoherent moments, she couldn't remember where she was. Her attempt to rise sent the hammock swinging—her stomach plummeted, hands flying out to steady her. Lucidity came slowly, the last dregs of sleep holding fast to her mind.

The scarlet light of the beacon washed over the tower. Bianca was sitting up in her hammock, narrowed eyes scanning the dark horizon. Below them, the bearded person had climbed onto the beams, a knife in their hand. Most squatters were still asleep, but at least three of the Drifters had risen on their elbows in their blankets, gazes intent on the overcast sky.

Bianca spoke under her breath. "Something's out there."

Io grabbed for the closest beam, hooking her feet into the framework of the tower. They were sixty feet off the ground in the middle of a flooded valley—what could there possibly be all the way up here?

Then she heard it: the flapping of wings.

A cry slit the night, from a big-shouldered Drifter woman, "*Night-beast!*"

Io froze. She could feel it now. A disturbance in the air, a *something*

49

where there ought to be only dark sky. Instinct took over: she ducked to a corner of the tower legs, where the scaffolding was thick with beams. A moment later came the sound of wings beating, so loud that their owner must be enormous. Talons scratched the beams where she had been only seconds ago. As Io whipped her head to take a look, she thanked the gods she had drifted off to sleep with her spectacles on.

It was an avian chimerini, a hybrid unlike anything she'd ever seen before. Its body was that of a raptor, albeit three times its normal size, its belly glimmering with fish scales, its talons long and curved like an eagle's, and its head the lustrous mane and square snout of a lion. Its jaws closed around the leg of one of the squatters sleeping in the uppermost beams of the tower.

The scene was horrible—its fangs around the man's flesh, the raptor-lion beat its large wings backward, dragging the young man away from the tower. It took two flaps of its wings, three, then abruptly, the young man slipped through the beams and hung in midair. His weight was too much for the raptor-lion; he slipped from its jaws and plummeted, arms flapping. A wretched scream followed him all the way down.

Io waited for the splash of the body hitting the tidewater below, but her heart was roaring in her ears, drowning out all other sounds. She had to press her forehead against the cool iron of the tower, waiting for the immobilizing terror to subside. Suddenly, Bianca was there, filling Io's vision.

"You hurt?" the mob queen asked, only it sounded like they were both underwater, sound distorted, time decelerated. When Io took too long to answer, Bianca reached through the beams and shook her. "Girl! Are you okay? The blasted thing is coming back."

She was moving before Io could reply, scrambling down the tower. A glance below told Io why she hadn't heard the man splash into the water: he had managed to grab hold of a thick plank on the bottom level of the tower and was now trying to bring his legs over it, while his right ankle bled profusely. Io heard wings beating again on the other side of the tower. An instant later, the raptor-lion burst into view. It swooped around the tower in a wide arc, then dove for its prey with bared fangs.

Bianca was close, a few feet above where the man hung. As Io watched, mouth agape, breathing hard, the raptor-lion closed in on the young man, and Bianca *did the most harebrained thing*. She jumped from the center of the tower, grabbed on to a bar with her hands, then, with built-up momentum, rammed her boots into the chime-rini's snout. It snarled—a lion's snarl, terrifyingly unnatural coming from a flying beast—and soared away again.

It wasn't done with them, Io knew. It would come back; its prey was already hurt and primed for eating. Io studied the space around her. It would take her a few minutes to join Bianca where she was trying to haul the young man back into the cover of the belly of the tower, and what good would that do? There were two dozen people perched on the transmission tower, and those farther below, like the Kurkz family, didn't have the latticework beams to protect them from the raptor-lion's fangs. Even if every squatter managed to hide inside the safest parts of the scaffolding, the chimerini would just land on the tower itself and try to snip off their flesh through the beams. They needed to get rid of the beast, once and for all.

Io glanced at the Drifters directly below her who were moving in a fury. In the chaos of the attack, their portable stove had overturned, and their bedding had caught on fire. Most were trying to douse the flames, but the hulking woman who had first sounded the alarm was watching the sky for any sign of the raptor-lion, a metal net with spiked ends in her hands. She was at a disadvantage, though. Squatters were flooding the Drifters' makeshift canvas platform, as it was the largest and most protected area in the tower. The woman could hardly take a step through the crowd.

Io began climbing, a half-formed plan in her mind. She didn't dare scale the exterior of the tower, exposing herself to the night beast, but the inner beams should be safe enough. It took her a long time to navigate through the abandoned hammocks, but finally, she reached the Drifters' platform and waved furiously at the woman.

"Hey!" she called over the panic of the gathering travelers. "Give me that!"

The Drifter searched for the source of her voice, located her, and tossed the metal net without hesitation. Io caught it and nearly toppled over—the thing must have weighed a hundred pounds. Heaving it over one shoulder, she glanced at the sky and squeezed between the framework of the tower. Scaling on the outside was the only way to get past the busy platform.

The lacing metal of the net clattered too close to her ears, and her breaths were too loud; she couldn't hear any hint of the bird. Beneath her, Bianca was still struggling to haul the young man up. There seemed to be something wrong with his left shoulder—it hung limp from its socket as though he had dislocated it when he broke his fall. He was holding on with his good hand and his knees, struggling to keep his weight off his injured ankle. His whole body was on the exterior of the tower, exposed to the raptor-lion's attacks, while Bianca was half-in, half-out of the tower, trying to help him.

Io slipped back inside the body of the tower and came to a stop. She needed clarity; she needed silence. She hooked her knees around the beams and tightened her core to keep herself upright. Hands freed, she loosened the net over her lap. How did one use such a thing? It was so heavy Io doubted she could fling it far. The beast needed to be close for this to work—close and distracted.

A roar sounded from up above, throaty and vengeful. The raptor-lion was coming around again. Io's head shot up, but she could see nothing but dark clouds and metal glistening with the red of the beacon. Air whooshed at her cheeks, carrying the earthy smell of woods and blood—then the beast was upon them, swooping past Io to get to its prey. Its wings were larger than Io was tall, twigs and leaves tanged in its mane.

The young man let out a cry of desperation. Bianca glanced up: her eyes went to the raptor-lion first, then past it, to Io. The mob queen became utterly motionless. It was an unnatural stillness, incompatible with the panic around her. Predatory, lethal.

Io knew this stillness. She had seen the mob queen employ it half a dozen times before: when she ordered the fury-born slain during the Moonset Riots, when she attacked the Nine five weeks ago, when she jumped at that grace-born in Poppy Town. It was the quiet before the storm, the silence before a gunshot, the boxer gearing up for a knockout punch.

Bianca was going to *do* something. Something absurd, granted, but also something sudden and ferocious and brave.

Io had to help her.

The seconds ticked by like a leaky faucet. *Drip* and the raptor-lion dove toward them. *Drip* and Bianca slipped wholly out of the beams. *Drip* and it snatched at the man's bleeding leg. *Drip* and Bianca lunged for it.

The mob queen wrapped an arm over its neck in an ill-advised headlock and began pummeling punches into the soft part of its belly, scales and all. She was wearing her brass knuckles; they echoed hollowly against its scales. Its mouth snapped open, its head reared to latch on to whatever part of Bianca was closest—

But Io was already there.

With one swoop of her arm, the net was over the raptor-lion's head, her boot on its snout, pushing, kicking, stomping with all her might. Abandoning her furious punching, Bianca focused on the headlock, grabbing her other wrist and tightening her grip. The raptor-lion began thrashing uncontrollably. Io wasn't sure how she was holding on to the tower; she could feel metal digging into her arm and waist, and her kneecap was threatening to pop right out of her flesh, but she held on and Bianca held on, and they kicked and punched while the raptor-lion beat its wings around them, for minutes and minutes it seemed, until finally, it slumped in their hands, limp and heavy.

The raptor-lion's body had been rescued from the tidewater. The portable stove had been relit. The squatters had all rearranged their hammocks around the Drifters' platform. The Kurkz man and his eldest daughter had volunteered to take first watch, high up beneath the beacon. The young man's arm had been popped back into place, and a Drifter healer was treating his ankle by the fire. The air was hot with the smell of grilled meat and freshly baked pitas. In return for the raptor-lion's hide and feathers, the Drifters had offered to cook its meat to feed everyone tonight. They'd even spared some of their own valuable flour and cheese to make perek.

No one left behind on the road, not even the carcass of a beast of prey.

Raptor-lions hunted this area in the wintertime, the large Drifter woman—Ozalia—had told Io. Travelers knew to take measures against them, namely to carry spiked shields to sleep beneath at night. But in the summertime, the avian chimerini flew south to lay their eggs.

"The presence of this one here now's very troubling," Ozalia said to Io grimly as she handed her a bowl piled high with slices of perek and juicy raptor meat.

Io didn't know how to respond; she thanked her quietly and began the slow, one-armed climb to where Bianca was sitting, far up above the festivities. The mob queen had gathered her legs against her chest and was looking at her knuckles, slowly picking the raptor-lion's scales off her skin.

It looked painful, but Bianca didn't even flinch. She had refused professional help; the Drifter healer was a horus-born, descended from the Sumazi gods of mummification. If he turned his emerald-green gaze on her to heal her wounds, he would see nothing. Because Bianca *had* nothing: no threads in the Quilt, no bronze path for the dioscuri-born to follow, no emerald-green veins for the horus-born to heal.

The mob queen was dying.

Her body knew it, every other-born's powers knew it, but her spirit held on. How, Io had no idea—but lately, it felt like even this borrowed time was running out. Io studied Bianca's hollow cheeks, her sunken eye sockets, the deathly paleness of her skin. The nicks on her knuckles that should have been oozing blood but were instead leaking a translucent pus, as though she was already a half-dead thing.

Io pushed the plate into Bianca's hands. "Meat," she said, "and cheese perek."

They were quiet for a while, inhaling the warm food. Io kept slipping glances at the mob queen; her eyes were downturned and unfocused, her movements slow and mechanical.

After a while, the urge to ask became unbearable. "What's wrong?"

Bianca spoke without turning. "Look at them. They didn't hesitate a second. They rallied around each other, offering healing and food, volunteering for watches. The Kurkz have offered to carry the injured boy all the way to the nearest town."

"*No one left behind*," Io said, repeating the Wastelanders' mantra. "But that's good, isn't it?" Why did the mob queen sound almost bitter about it?

"Of course it's good," Bianca hissed in that tone that always confused Io, hinging between anger and passion. "I just wish people had rallied around me when—"

She cut herself short. She always did when the conversation steered to the past. In all these weeks together, Io had collected only bits and pieces. Bianca had grown up in the barren mountains north of Alante. She was one of a set of triplets—as all keres-born were. Both her sisters had died in a mining accident. Bianca had had to fend for herself from an early age. Io could guess the hardships; this world was not a hospitable place for a young girl who could see violent deaths.

Bianca could no longer see the red dust of violent deaths. For a while there, when she had first turned into a wraith, she could wield both other-born powers—that was how she had saved Edei's life when he was shot. But over the weeks that followed, her keres-born powers had dwindled. She was keres-born no more. She wasn't even a queen.

Not bitter, Io realized. Melancholic.

Her chest tingled with a soft warmth. Io glanced down to find a thread weaving itself into being. It was no brighter than a dying ember, no wider than a hair, but it was bridging the space between her body and Bianca's. Io counted: one second, two, three—the thread began unraveling. It wasted away as swiftly as it had arrived.

This wasn't the first time a thread of friendship had attempted to form between her and Bianca. It had happened before on that night Bianca had taught Io cards when they were stranded indoors by an acid rainstorm, on that waitressing shift they had spent rolling their eyes at a client's irrational demands, on that gloomy morning after Io had discovered the fate-thread was fraying. Bianca was unpredictable, crass, and supremely annoying, but these moments of kinship kept cropping up, pretty weeds breaking through cement.

But kinship wasn't strong enough to compete with this half-thing Bianca had become. No thread could connect you to someone who had no essence herself.

Oblivious to the intricacies of the Quilt, the mob queen asked, "How did you know? That I was going to attack the chimerini?"

"You had that face," Io said.

"What face?"

"That face you always get when you're about to—"

"Kick ass?"

Io huffed a laugh. "Decide violence on the spot."

Bianca passed the near-empty bowl to Io and studied her ruined knuckles. "Violence is best like that, cutter. Staying still is rot and death," she said. "The more you stand still, the more the world finds obstacles to place in your way. Grit your teeth and just go for it."

At the edge of the horizon, the sun was announcing its arrival, spilling fuchsia in the patches of sky visible between the clouds. Io swallowed her last bite and glanced at her backpack, packed and ready, hanging from one of the beams. Gods, what she wouldn't give for an hour or two of sleep. But dawn was here; the tide was ebbing; they had to set out again.

Io gritted her teeth and stood.

CHAPTER VI

DEEP QUILT MODE

"HOW ARE WE ever going to find Hanne in this place?"

Bianca wore a scowl of epic proportions, brow furrowed, lips a downward curve. They were standing in the mud, along with dozens of other travelers, in the long toll line to enter the town of Tulip. The mob queen looked as tired as Io felt, hair frizzy and legs caked with brown up to the shin. The only bright spot on her was the caramel raptor-lion feather decorating her wide-brimmed hat; one of the Drifter kids had gifted it to her this morning, before their paths split.

Io followed Bianca's gaze up, and up again. Tulip was huge, far bigger than the Wastelands stilt towns they had been visiting so far. It rose from the dirt in neat, man-made tiers, wide and concentric, so tall that it rivaled the luxurious District-on-the-Hill back in Alante. It even had a cable lift system, so that rich folk wouldn't have to climb steps between tiers like plebeians. The bottom tiers were farmsteads; Io could make out pens and fences and the rancid smell of pigsties. They had spotted the livestock grazing in the valley on their way here, and Io could see large wooden drawbridges all along the wall surrounding the town. The next tier was human housing, made from stone and wood, which was quite fancy in comparison to the tin shanties of Hagia. And above it was all farming terraces: the long golden stems of wheat, the gnarly branches of olive trees, the emerald leaves of vineyards.

Io couldn't wait to enter; she had a rising suspicion that the mud they were on wasn't *just* mud. There was a reason earthworks were always built like that: livestock on the bottom, humans a level up, agriculture all the way to the top—sewage spilled downward from one tier to the next until, Io's parents had explained once, it ended up at ground level. In other words, exactly where she and Bianca were standing now.

"I'll find her," Io answered. Sure, Tulip looked like it housed at least thirty thousand people, but Io was a moira-born detective. Finding people was her job, and she was darn good at it. Now that she knew where Hanne would be, what she looked like, she was confident she could locate her.

The line moved, and Io silently passed their papers to the border patrol officer.

He glanced at them over his glasses. Mia and Laeticia Marrow, the papers presented them as, sisters born in Clyde and traveling the Wastelands as seasonal workers. Of course, their papers were very obviously fake—the stamp was entirely the wrong color—and Io and Bianca looked nothing alike. But they had more than enough notes to pay for a day's entrance fee, which Io had made plain to the officer by slipping a few extra in the folds of their papers.

"Clyde, huh?" the officer said, pocketing the extra money with a subtle twist of his palm. "People disappearing on you there, too?"

"We wouldn't know," Io replied smoothly. "We haven't been back in years."

She reached for the papers, but the man gripped them tighter. "I visited Clyde on my honeymoon. Picturesque place, for a Wastelands town, especially that view of the Flying Orchards."

Face half-covered beneath her hat, Bianca said crisply, "I don't know which Clyde you visited, but you certainly can't see the Orchards from *our* Clyde."

It must have been a test, because the officer gave them an appeased nod and allowed Io to take the papers back. Io steered them toward the throng gathered in front of the noticeboards. Dozens of jobs were scribbled on a blackboard, along with their location, wage, and benefits—that last one was usually a meal or a place to rest for the night. All around the board, thin, yellowing papers were pinned, the posters of the missing that had become a fixture of every town in the Wastelands. Io skimmed them: a dark-haired girl that could have been her cousin, a thin-faced young man with spots on his cheeks, a slim woman with a head of ginger curls. No names that she recognized, although the towns were familiar, a few that Io and Bianca had visited in the past five weeks. All these people disappearing out of thin air, no clue left behind—it left a bitter taste in Io's mouth. If she had more time, if she wasn't entangled in this blasted conspiracy, she could have stopped. She could have helped.

But the gods took priority, and by extension, whatever Hanne was doing in this town. Io focused back on the board, scanning it for a very specific kind of job—there. *Chimerini watchmen, Tier Six, five notes per day, free meal.* She shouldered through the crowd and tore out two of the bronze pins pressed next to the job description.

"Watchmen?" Bianca groaned. "Do we need more run-ins with chimerini after last night?"

"Shush," Io said. "I have a plan."

"Oh, I didn't doubt that for a second," the mob queen said dryly.

But she wasn't really objecting. Bianca liked to complain about Io's plans, but in the end, she always went along with them, and carried them out with relative success. Even now, she had fallen right into step, joining Io in yet another long line outside the employment office.

When it was their turn, the clerk instructed them to grab a pair of binoculars, a whistle, and a long, rusty trident each. "And something a little extra, for my services," the clerk said, shrugging a cashmere-clad shoulder. Her cardigan was the kind only rich folk could afford—with the new refugee wave flocking to the town from the south, the clerk must be swimming in bribes.

"So hospitable," Bianca muttered as Io placed yet another two notes in front of the woman. "The moment we step off the road, it's back to the usual cheating and corruption."

Io ignored her. Now was not the time to philosophize over the intricacies of their society. As they began climbing the endless steps between tiers, her eyes roamed: the livestock terrace was enormous but nearly empty of people at this hour. She doubted that was where Hanne was hiding, anyway, not with that fancy leather coat of hers and her soft, uncalloused hands. The housing terrace, on the other hand, was packed full of passersby, apartments stacked over busy shops, laundry hanging between balconies. It was all very bright and colorful, even the streets; they must have street sweepers cleaning the mud from the cobblestone all day long. Io meandered on the steps of the housing terrace, her eyes tracing every face riding the cable lifts and winding down the narrow main street that circled the entire town. No sign of Hanne, which Io had expected, but she did spot a couple of inns and tavernas that they could try first—the norn-born had to sleep somewhere, right?

The worker behind her grumbled in annoyance. Io began climbing again, shepherded upward first through sloped plains of wheat and orange trees, then vineyards sagging with red and green grapes. Tier Six, their post, was the second above the housing tier, all rich, turned earth; the midsummer wheat crop must have just been harvested. There were haystacks in a line by the steps, waiting to be plaited into baskets and hats or fed to the livestock. Farmers were plowing the earth, preparing the seedbed for the winter crop. The smell was distantly familiar. Io could remember her parents coming home after summers in the Neraida Plains north of Alante, their noses spotted with freckles, their clothes aromatized with seed and earth and wheat stalk.

Their whole group stood, flushed and panting, while the overseer handed out shifts. Much to Bianca's chagrin, Io volunteered them to be the walking patrol, which admittedly involved a hell of a lot of pacing, but also offered the perfect cover for what Io was planning. They were sent out, instructed to keep the binoculars glued to their eyes, and were sweating pools into their shirts almost immediately. The sky had cleared while they were on the road, and the midsummer sun blazed hot and pleasant on their skin.

"Can I have the sunglasses?" Io asked.

She was being generous with the word "sunglasses"—they were merely two pieces of dark glass strewn together by copper wire that Bianca had nicked back in Clyde—but they'd do the job.

Bianca handed them over. "So, what exactly is the plan?"

"Do you know how the Quilt works?" Io asked.

Bianca gave her a scathing *of course I do* look.

"When we were younger, me and my sisters had this game. We would choose a stranger, say the baker or our geography teacher, and try to find them in the Quilt from miles away. It took hours and had some side effects—"

Io paused. She'd told this story before.

She and Edei had been standing outside a stranger's apartment, piecing together the latest clue of their investigation. She had mentioned this game to Edei, and how it had once made her bleed out of her nose and ears and eyes. *So you almost stargazed to death?* He had teased her, that wonderful, delightful boy, and Io had reached up and kissed him. His tongue had slid her lips open, his arm had snaked around her waist to pull her close, her fingers had grazed his neck and ear and the short hairs at his nape.

The memory was tinged with longing, with affection. Io glanced down at her chest, looking for the sparkly shine of the fate-thread. But all she saw were her twenty or so threads, undistinguishable from each other. It was foolish, wasn't it, to keep stabbing herself in the same, never-healing wound?

She cleared her throat and tucked the sunglasses over the long-distance spectacles already on her nose. "Ava called it deep Quilt mode," she told Bianca. "It might take me a long time, but I'll find her."

Bianca didn't look convinced, yet she only asked, "What do I have to do?"

Io looked at the sprawling town around her, tiered like one of those glazed white wedding cakes she and Rosa used to see when paging through fashion magazines. It would take hours to walk around the tier to locate Hanne, and her poor legs were already shaking from the climb. Never mind. She would manage, as she always did. She would see this through.

"Keep me from stepping off the tier, I guess," she answered Bianca.

The mob queen sighed through her nostrils. "What a wonderful, exciting day."

Io found Hanne late into the afternoon when the sun battered their backs with the force of a thousand fires. She spotted the norn-born's burgundy coat first, in the main street that ran concentrically through the entirety of Tulip. Then Io's gaze fell to the woman's left hand and the silver thread gripped in her fist.

"Gods," Io whispered. "We need to get down there."

Bianca snapped her head in the direction Io was looking. "You found her?"

"There." Io pointed out Hanne, two tiers below them. "Next to the fruit vendor."

"What's she doing?"

"She has a thread in her hand." Io narrowed her eyes. The norn-born was a good sixty feet below her, but Io could tell from the way the thread changed directions that it belonged to a deliveryman weaving through the hundreds of passersby. "I think she's following that person pushing the cart."

"He's just a boy," Bianca commented. "What does Hanne want with a child?"

Io risked dropping the Quilt for a moment to get a clear look at Hanne's target. Indeed, he was barely fifteen, his cheeks hairless and acne-spotted, utterly oblivious to the norn-born cutter stalking him.

"There's someone else with her," Bianca said. "Look."

As they watched, the boy paused before a busy tea shop to unload packages by the front door. Hanne pulled to a stop a few feet behind him, and soon another person joined her, a man in his twenties. He wore construction overalls spotted with paint, and his long hair was tied back in a low ponytail. Heads bent together, he and Hanne spoke in whispers, eyeing the boy all the while. When the boy hoisted his cart again, Hanne and Ponytail Man broke off. The cart was nearly empty, teetering up and down the cobblestone. Whatever Hanne and her accomplice were planning, now would be the time to act, when they could finally corner him alone. A tall building rose on the main street, blocking Io's and Bianca's view.

"Shit," Bianca muttered, but Io was already pulling on the Quilt. Luminescent silver drilled into her eyes, pulsing a stabbing pain deep inside her skull. She had been at it for hours, seven, or maybe even eight. Her nose had bled twice, but she had swept it away with the back of her hand and kept watching.

"We need to go now," Io said. "Before they reach him."

Bianca gave a grunt of agreement and turned toward the stairs, then paused in midstride. "Let me just get our wages first." Io made to argue, but the mob queen gripped her elbow. "We're in no position to waste money, girl. I'll be back in a minute—don't lose them."

Three minutes the mob queen was gone, during which Io tracked Hanne's and the boy's threads. He was making the last of his deliveries to a tiny jewelry shop crammed between two fancy boutiques. Io dared not move. She had been in the Quilt for far too long; the real world had become blurry at the edges, her sense of space and distance distorted.

When Bianca returned, she grabbed Io's hand and guided her through the wheat stalks. They fell into an easy, thoughtless rhythm. Down the steep staircase they went, past the olive orchards and into the housing tier, Bianca laboriously warning Io of every step and gutter. When they were finally on solid ground, Io took the lead, whispering instructions—left, straight on, left again—until Bianca's strides slowed.

"I see her," the mob queen whispered.

The Quilt had become painfully uncomfortable in the presence of so many people and threads. Io let the shimmering latticework drop with a sigh, tucked her spectacles into her pocket, and rubbed her eyes until they were wet with tears. Gods, she would have a *splitting* headache in a few hours.

"Is that the boy?" Bianca asked.

Io turned her tired gaze to the crowd. There was Hanne, the collar of her burgundy coat pulled up, her russet curls shoved into a black cap. A few paces in front of her, the boy was wrestling his empty cart against the cobblestone. Ponytail Man was nowhere to be seen, but Hanne was following the boy, sticking to the shadows. Io and Bianca began following *her*, sticking to even deeper shadows.

The boy cut into a side street, then slipped into a nondescript alley. The pulsing bustle of the crowded streets disappeared here, the silence broken only by cawing gulls flying overhead. He deposited his cart by a squat basement door and rifled through his pockets for his keys.

Hanne moved fast, with the focused efficiency of a practiced attacker. One second, she was at the mouth of the alley, just a few steps ahead of Io and Bianca—the next she was on him, her palm over his mouth, her lips next to his ear.

"Stand still," she ordered, "and this won't hurt a bit."

Io and Bianca were already moving, springing from the shadows to barge down the alley—but it was too late. In a single swoop, Hanne swept a hand over his chest. Io dragged on the Quilt and came to a stop, mouth hanging ajar, shoulders clenched with terror.

Hanne had his threads in her fist. *All* his threads besides the one tying him to life itself, which shot up to the sky like a lonely branch of a winter-torn tree. As Io watched, in the space of a second, Hanne twisted the boy's threads to form one thick bundle of them, then *sliced*. The threads were cut in a single blow, costing Hanne only one of her own threads. Io didn't know whether to be impressed or horrified. That kind of precision, that kind of ruthlessness—it was savage. It was *wrong*.

The boy's eyes rolled back in his head. Hanne had to slip her hands beneath his armpits to keep him upright. She whistled sharply, and Ponytail Man appeared at the other end of the alley, hooking the boy's arm over his shoulders.

"*What*," Bianca barked, "*did you do, demon?*"

Hanne's face slackened with surprise, eyes jumping to Bianca and Io. She shoved the boy toward her partner and placed her body in front of them. "Little Ora. What did I tell you," she hissed, "about sticking your nose where it doesn't belong?"

Io knew a threat when she heard it. She began backtracking, skidding on the cobblestone, but she wasn't fast enough. In the Quilt, Io saw the woman grab on to one of Io's threads, the closest she could reach, then slice—pain jabbed through Io's chest, stealing her breath. The earth slipped beneath her feet, landing her hard on her bottom.

Lightning flashed overhead, and rain cascaded down, a proper torrential outpour, as if the very gates of hell had opened right above their heads. Thunder followed a few moments later, raking the silent streets. Io gathered herself up and glanced at the alley.

Hanne, her accomplice, and the boy were gone—and so was Bianca. Their footsteps splintered the street up ahead. Io set off in a sprint, leaning to pick up a metal bar sticking out of the drain at the corner of the building. She came out to a main street in chaos: vendors hurrying to pack up their stalls, shop owners dragging down awnings, people running for cover, arms held over their heads.

Bianca was closest to Io, her leopard-print hat easy to spot in the thrashing crowd. Hanne and Ponytail Man had quite a lead on her, a good twenty feet, the boy hauled, almost unconscious, between the two of them.

Io began waving the metal bar and yawling, "Out! Out! Out of the way!" in such a frenzied voice that the crowd simply parted for her. Within seconds, she had caught up to Bianca. They shared a glance, Bianca's eyes all orange fury, and split up: Io took the left side of the street, Bianca the right, in order to close in on the trio from both sides. They were fast, gaining ground with every footfall, but Hanne—

Hanne and Ponytail Man were pushing the boy up the steps to the cable station, elbowing past the rest of the line. They shoved him inside, and Hanne dragged the door closed, then rammed down the lever, to the astonishment of both the driver and the other passengers.

No. *No.*

It was barely five seconds, barely two breaths, before Io reached them. Up the steps she flew, past the waiting line. She jammed the metal bar against the handle, trying to pry it open, but nothing happened. *Gods damn it*—she slapped her palm against the windows, two, three, four times. A few passengers jumped back, startled and fearful.

Lips quivering, shoulders hunched, the boy locked eyes with her. It was not acne on his skin after all, but Ersa's kisses, the same skin discoloration that Bianca had, his cheeks dusted with soft pale marks. Above, the cables groaned to life. The cable car started slopping over the town, agonizingly slow, as though it was designed that way specifically to taunt Io.

"Cutter."

Io watched it go, panting puffs of steam into the suddenly frigid air. It was headed past the farming tier and toward the vast expanse of the Wastelands, which made no sense. Where was Hanne taking this boy, so close to the arrival of the night tide? She was looking at Io still, through the glass, her hand in a death grip on the boy's nape.

"Cutter!" Bianca grabbed Io by the elbows, shoving her down the elevated station and backpedaling her all the way to the closest wall. "We need to get inside."

"We can catch up to them on the next cable car—"

"No, we can't." There was an undercurrent of vicious wrath in the mob queen's voice. She raised Io's arms to eye level.

Already, Io's skin was blistering a dangerous kind of red.

It didn't register, not the swelling, not the redness, not the pain, until Bianca said it out loud. "The rain is acid."

CHAPTER VII

ERSA'S KISSES

IO'S SKIN FELT like it was on fire when they finally dove into the cover of a nearby pub. The place was packed with dozens of townies and visitors seeking refuge from the sulfurous rain, everyone undressed to their undershirts, draping their coats and hats to dry on every available surface. The whole place smelled like burnt hair soaked in stale ale.

Bianca shouldered her way to the bar, leaned over the counter, and grabbed a wet cloth, then proceeded to furiously dab at Io's bare arms. It stung like hell, but Io endured it; the acid would do double the damage if left unattended. She'd need a proper healing salve and perhaps some anti-inflammatory medicine—but she hadn't the mind to go looking for them right now.

Hanne got away. Io let her head droop into her palms, kneading her temples with her knuckles. This damned headache was growing worse by the minute. Gods, she had been a fool. She should have been more careful, more focused, more cunning. Now Hanne and her accomplice had run off with a scared, helpless kid whose threads of love were severed. Now the gods would know Io hadn't abandoned her quest; worse, they would know she was coming.

"Evening, travelers," came a voice on the other side of the bar. "I'm Po, your bartender tonight. What can I get you?"

Io looked up to see a dazzling smile, all bright, white teeth and lips glistening with dark plum gloss, piercings peeking on the person's upper lip, septum, and left eyebrow. Po had on a worn black leather vest and striped white-and-gray pants, and their hair cascaded over their shoulder in pitch-black waves, razed to the scalp on the sides.

"Two glasses of your finest and cheapest drink," Bianca said, plopping her chin on her hand.

The barperson laughed, which seemed to please Bianca, and deposited two glasses of ale in front of them. "I've never seen you before. Came here from the Peninsula?"

"Nah," Bianca drawled. "We're seasonal workers."

Po was already nodding. "Tulip is a great place for that kind of job. All these fields and animals—we need all the help we can get. Too bad our acid storm decided to make an appearance so out of order."

"*Your* acid storm?" Bianca asked.

With a twirly hand, Po indicated the acid storm raging outside the windows. The glass was stained with fat, milky-white droplets that would slowly erode the windowpane if left unattended. "Yeah, you know, Tulip gets these storms every year. But they're usually well behaved; they arrive at the height of spring, when the cherries are beginning to bloom, giving us fair warning to cover our crops, and only last a week or so. We've never had acid rain so late in the summer—that's why we were wholly unprepared today."

Bianca breathed a disinterested grunt, but Io's curiosity was piqued. Po's description made it seem as though the storm was as much a staple of their lives as morning coffee or cake on your birthday, and that its appearance today was odd.

"Why do you think it has arrived late this year?" Io asked.

"Same reason the bird chimerini have flown back from the south so early and the Great Tide keeps changing directions." Po leaned forward conspiratorially, letting the silence drag on for extra creepiness. "To make sure none of us get a single day of rest."

"Sounds about right," Bianca mumbled around the glass she'd brought to her lips.

"Just when you think you've got this world all figured out, *bam!*" Po slapped their hand on the counter, startling Io. "It's suddenly in shambles again. Oh—excuse me for a moment."

Somebody had called for a drink; Po went to serve them, leaving Io to stare forlornly at her ale. The glass was sweating; Io pressed a finger against the wet ring at its base, feeling every nick and splinter in the wooden counter. *The world in shambles again, not a single day of rest* was a pretty accurate description of Io's life.

A long exhale streamed through her nostrils.

"Whatever self-pitying hole you're about to fall into," the mob queen drawled, "don't. All is not lost. Let's skip the drama and move straight to planning, shall we?"

Rude, Io thought, but truthful nonetheless. They had no time to wallow, no time to doubt; when the acid storm was over, they needed to have a battle plan ready.

"What I don't get," Bianca said to her glass, "is why Hanne would travel all the way to Tulip after barely escaping a Great Tide just to abduct a random delivery boy."

"He's not random," Io said.

Because he couldn't be. That wasn't how the gods worked: they were meticulous planners themselves. They had sent Thais and Hanne to Alante to find and try to reawaken the powers of people with latent fury-born blood. According to the news, they had done the same in every major city-nation in the world. They had instructed Hanne to intercept the thread Io had gotten hold of and lead her in a goose hunt all across the Wastelands. Then they had directed Hanne here to help Ponytail Man with the delivery boy's—

Abduction.

Io was up from her barstool in a second. She squeezed through the crowd, her mind racing ahead of her, and came to a stop before the noticeboard by the pub door. Her eyes roamed over sales leaflets and drunken love notes, landing at the missing people posters. Solemn faces stared back at her in black-and-white photos and police sketches. Disappearances, or perhaps, *abductions.*

In the street just a few minutes ago, Io had gotten the impression she had seen the boy before. Those blond curls, that weak chin, those cheeks dotted with pale spots. She began snapping posters off their pins to unveil those hidden beneath. It took her a minute and a dozen papers, but she found him. There, on the bottom left corner, was another face with the same blond hair and weak chin, the same pale blemishes across his cheeks: Ersa's kisses.

The name beneath the poster was Eliott Lowe. He wasn't the delivery boy, not exactly—he looked older by at least a couple of years, the hint of stubble on his jaw—but he had to be related to the boy Hanne and Ponytail Man had kidnapped.

"Clever, clever detective," Bianca commented, coming up behind Io, the ale in her hand. "And look there, another one."

Io's eyes fell on the poster Bianca was slipping out of the stack in Io's hands. The mob queen flattened the new poster next to Eliott's. It was another missing person, named Lena Lotz, older than both boys but with the same spots of discoloration across her nose, the same curly hair, the same triangular face.

"Siblings?" Io mused. The different surname didn't matter— people picked up dozens of different names when traveling the Wastelands, in order to avoid getting flagged at town entry gates.

She stepped back for a better look at the posters, her gaze renewed with this revelation. "These two," she said, eager and breathless, tapping a poster in her hand of a long-haired man in his forties and another on the noticeboard of a round-faced person a few years younger. They had the exact same eyebrows, thick and black, and the same prominent bottom lip. Their names were both Kurkz.

"Make it three," Bianca noted, pointing to another poster on the top right corner of the board: the woman depicted had identical lips and pitch-black hair.

Within minutes, they had found yet another trio of siblings, all women with the same striking eyes—even in the black-and-white photos, Io could tell they were an unusually light shade, probably pale blue. None of them had the precise same surname, but their resemblance was evident.

"Look at the places where they disappeared." Io prodded Bianca with an elbow and read aloud, "Blue-Temple, Poppy Town, Hagia. We've traveled through all of them, on Hanne's tail. And didn't Leo say Hanne was in Berry Hill?"

"She's been helping her accomplices kidnap siblings?" Bianca guessed.

"I think . . ." Io's chest felt too tight to hold her breaths. "I think she's helping them kidnap *other-born*."

For what other reason was there, to target trios of siblings all across the Wastelands? Her mind instantly made a list of all the other-born that appeared in three: moira-born, grace-born, fury-born, zorya-born, norn-born, morrigan-born, sanxing-born, and a dozen others.

"But if they are all other-born," Bianca said, "wouldn't it be all over the news by now?"

Yes, it would be. The media would never pass on the opportunity to connect a story to other-born; it made for much juicier news. "They could be hiding their identity, like we are. They've adopted different surnames. And look"—Io raised two of the posters in her hands—"it's even listed that they had no known relatives."

"Maybe they don't," Bianca said quietly. "Maybe we're grasping at straws."

No. Io's instincts had flared like an alarm. She was on the right path, she knew it. "She severed his threads of love."

"What does that mean? Will he become a"—the mob queen inhaled—"wraith?"

"No. His life-thread is intact. He won't die, but he will be disoriented, aimless, without the threads connecting him to the people and things he loved. That man who approached me in Blue-Temple, do you remember him? His nephew had disappeared, but I could find no thread to follow. I thought he was lying. That he didn't care for his nephew as much as he said or that the young man wasn't his nephew to begin with. But what if—" What if she had been wrong yet again? *Stop it*, she ordered herself. *No time for wallowing.* "What if Hanne cut his threads so that no one could find him?"

Bianca emptied her ale in rapid, loud gulps. "She severed his threads so that he'd be easier to manipulate, cutter."

The *just as they did to me* was implied. Io flashed back to finding Bianca in that cell at City Plaza, cold, beaten-up, and threadless, curled into a ball in her silken pajamas. It was yet another of the gods' elaborate plans, this one orchestrated by Thais: they had bet on the fact that Io would want to save Bianca by bringing her to the Nine. They had counted on Bianca succumbing to her fury-born bloodthirst and slaughtering the Nine for them.

"The gods wanted to restore the other-born policing body, to create a new Order of the Furies," Io said. "But according to the news, the wraiths they created keep dying."

Bianca nodded. "So now they're recruiting again."

"*Gods*," Io breathed.

"That word sounds ironic now," Bianca commented dryly, "all things considered."

Io turned on her heel and marched back to the bar. She slipped onto her barstool and waited for a few minutes, until Po sidled close. Bianca sat next to her a moment later, looking befuddled.

"Hey, so . . . You don't happen to know a guy who works in construction here, right?" Io pretended to anxiously twirl a curl around her finger. "Long hair in a ponytail, very cute green eyes?"

The barperson watched Io fumble for words with a kind smile, then said, "Sure, I know Wilhem."

"*Wilhem*," Io repeated dreamily, trying to ignore the bemused look on Bianca's face, lips pursed as though to hold in her guffaws. Io wished suddenly for Nico, who'd gone along with her lies with the skill of a seasoned actor. "I met him the other day, and I, um, wanted to ask him out, but I chickened out at the last moment. Do you know where he lives, so I can leave a note or something?"

"He came to Tulip last month for work; he's been staying at one of Signor Marco's rooms. But he's a little old for you, no?" Po asked with a side glance to Bianca.

"Right? I keep telling her that," the mob queen lied smoothly, finally picking up on Io's plan. "But you know how delusional first crushes can be. Don't worry, I'll go with her. If this Wilhem guy tries anything funny, he'll have these to deal with." Bianca brandished her scabbed-over knuckles, rather dramatically in Io's opinion.

But it seemed to do the trick. With a sympathetic sigh, Po reached out behind the counter for a pen and paper. They wrote an address and slid it over to Io.

"Since you seem to know everything about everyone," Bianca went on, "what's the news on the missing people from Tulip? There's a girl, Ilaria Radinsky, who's been missing for three weeks—we know her. Friend of our cousin's."

"Is that so?" Po said. "I've never talked to her, but her boss, the local baker, was always praising her strudels. The constable suspected the doctor for a while—he was the last person to see Ilaria before she disappeared, but he had a strong alibi."

"What was she at the doctor for?" Io asked.

"Headaches and nausea, supposedly. Doc suspected some issue with her eyes."

Io found Bianca's gaze, trying to communicate *other-born* with the bulge of her eyeballs. "Did any of the other missing people have any health issues?"

"Not that the doctor knows of. Funny," Po said. Their attention was on the counter; they had located a dried-out bit of gunk on the wood and were trying to scrape it off with a black-lacquered fingernail. "We got another visitor just a couple of weeks ago, asking questions about the missing people from Tulip. A Sumazi guy— friend of yours?"

Io thought her skull might have suddenly shrunk to half its size. It couldn't hold all the feelings, all the thoughts, racing in her head. A Sumazi guy. Here in Tulip. Asking questions about the missing people. Io couldn't remember how to breathe properly anymore.

"Cutter," Bianca muttered under her breath, "calm yourself. Not every Sumazi guy is your lover boy—"

"He was with another guy," Po went on, oblivious to the chaos they had just caused in Io's head. "Ginger. Cute but short. Gods, he wouldn't stop talking."

Nico.

There was no doubt anymore.

Edei and Nico had been here, only two weeks ago.

Io didn't know what to do with herself. Frantic energy pumped down her spine with every heartbeat, making her limbs jittery. She couldn't sit on the barstool any longer. She slid off and rushed for the door—when she was outside, it took her a couple of seconds to remember the acid rainstorm and flatten herself against the wall beneath an awning in the side alley. Lightning traced through the clouds above, hueing the dark sky with white; thunder cracked a few seconds later, and a gust of wind sent the rain pattering against Io's legs. She didn't move. She couldn't remember how to.

Edei had been here. Nico, too. Asking questions about the very same people who had become central to Io's own investigation. But how could Edei have passed through Tulip, a couple of weeks ago no less, when every night, the fate-thread firmly pointed back southeast in the direction of Alante?

Io brought forth the Quilt. Threads of silver sprouted like vines from her torso, reaching in all directions to the horizon—looking at them sent stabs of pain behind Io's eyes. The headache pulsed in her skull, worse with every heartbeat. Just a little bit longer, she promised herself. Then she'd go looking for painkillers.

With trembling fingers, she leafed through her threads. One less now, after Hanne had severed one in that alley—the thread to the Cellar, her and Rosa's favorite dance club, Io realized with a pang of grief. She had loved that place, but no matter. She had a job to do. Her fingertips went on, locking around the fate-thread. She couldn't tell it by its shine alone anymore, but its feel was inimitable: the smell of Edei's neck, the whisper of his voice, the shape of his shy smile when he teased her.

The fate-thread still pointed southeast, toward Alante.

Io's reaction was visceral; fury and disappointment all bubbled down to their essence: *Why?* Po could have lied to her but had no reason to. It must be the fault of the Quilt, then, the fault of her powers, and Io had never encountered such a betrayal before, from her own self. She gripped the fate-thread and pulled, not with her usual gentleness but with all the berserk longing in her heart. She wanted Edei; she wanted him close; she wanted him as he had been, a brilliant pulse of light in her future, a destined love, a—

There was something snagging at the fate-thread.

She couldn't quite wrap her mind around it—she had never felt anything like this in the Quilt. There was a block on the thread, resisting her pull. She twined the fingers of both hands in the fate-thread and heaved again, putting all her strength behind it. The fate-thread vibrated with the force; the obstacle snapped; Io could feel it giving way under her fingertips, like the wind tearing the roots of a tree from the earth. In an instant, the fate-thread snapped back into place, taut and pointing . . .

Not toward Alante any longer. The fate-thread was pointing west.

Edei was somewhere west.

Io sat there against the pub's wall, breathing through clenched teeth. The fate-thread throbbed between her fingers. It was still dim, still fraying, but something felt changed, truer in some way. What had just happened? *Thais would know,* Io thought. Thais would know what was happening to her, what was happening to the fate-thread, but Io didn't have Thais any longer. She had neither of her sisters, just Bianca and her own wits.

They would have to suffice.

Wilhem clearly hadn't intended to stay in Tulip long. The small loft he was renting from Signor Marco was almost completely bare: no personal belongings, only a couple of pieces of clothes, takeout boxes collecting dust by the door. He must have known he would be leaving town today. His towels were tossed in the middle of the floor, his water canteen nearly empty, a few folded notes left for Signor Marco beneath the bedside lamp.

Io went straight for the bed, lifting the mattress against the wall, then moved to the wardrobe, tracing her fingers over and under each drawer, looking for hidden objects. She found a few pairs of socks and a worn deck of cards, but nothing of use.

"Cutter," Bianca said from the bathroom.

Io stopped at the doorframe. The bathroom was far too small to fit two. Bianca was squatting beneath the sink. One of the pipes was misaligned from the wall; when Bianca shook it, it plopped right off. A piece of paper fell from inside. They moved back into the main room, to the bed, where Bianca unrolled the paper.

It was a map of the continent. There were no words, but dots specked the paper roughly where the main towns were. The land was separated from the Timid Sea by a wavy border. Known caravan roads and village paths were inked in dotted lines. But there were other shapes, too, that Io couldn't quite decipher. Small, wavery strokes traveled up from Suma into the Southern Peninsula then northwest toward Nanzy. Pointy arrows crossed east to west in the Wastelands, and north to south up in Rossk. A cluster of tiny stars clouded the towns where Io and Bianca had just been: Hagia, the valley, Tulip. In the north, east of Jhorr, a massive amorphous shape was outlined in a faint jaggy line.

"What the hell is this," Bianca mumbled.

What the hell indeed. "A warning system perhaps? So the gods' lackeys can track each other's progress?"

The mob queen shook her head. "No one with half a brain would carry all of his colleagues' secret missions on a piece of paper, much less leave it behind."

"Look," Io said. She took the paper from Bianca's hand and lifted it to the glare of the streetlight beneath the narrow window. There was a faint oily indentation on the paper, as though Wilhem had often traced it with his finger. "He was marking out the route to Nanzy."

Bianca scoffed, crossing her arms over her chest. Her leopard-print hat was spotted with white where the acid rain had dried. "I don't like it."

"What do you mean?" Io asked.

"Hanne. This Wilhem guy. The missing boy. The emergency Mayoral Assembly with representatives of every city-nation. Now Edei and Nico. Even the damned Great Tide is heading to Nanzy."

Yes, Io thought. Everything was coalescing. It could be nothing but planned, nothing but bad news. Even so. "Shall we join them, then, partner?"

Bianca's face soured. "Don't call me that," she said, and held the door open for Io.

CHAPTER VIII

WATCHING, WATCHING HER

THE FIRST THING Io noticed was the leviathan.

"They call it Le Cauchemar," Bianca explained, her hips rolling smoothly with every shift of the camel-horse below her. "*Nightmare.* Local lore says the original Nanzese slayed the beast after a year-long battle, but scientists believe the leviathan crawled this far inland to die some two hundred years ago and that the city was repopulated long after it was dead."

"Regardless," Io said, "it's breathtaking."

The leviathan was colossal. The city was still a speck atop a hill across the valley Io and Bianca were currently traversing, but the leviathan was so enormous in size that Io could make it out even from this distance. Its body curled around a towering wall built on the spikes of its spine, and farther up, whole districts were laid on the bones of its wings and fins. Its head, now a fleshless skull, sat at the very top of the city, above a glimmering dome that mirrored the brilliant blue of the sky. Le Cauchemar must have once been the color of molten gold, because the ivory of its bones was etched with golden swirls. Io used to joke like every other kid: why was Alante the *Sunken* City and Nanzy the *Golden* City? Unfair, wasn't it? But here, faced with all this pristine ivory and white marble, all this gold and reflecting light, the nicknames seemed very fair indeed.

Bianca clicked her tongue. "I'd hold off on any declarations of awe until you see the city in its entirety."

Io was about to ask what the mob queen meant, but at that moment the camel-horse beneath her gave a mountainous jerk—Io had to hold on with hands, elbows, knees, *and feet* to keep upright. When Bianca had said she'd book them a caravan, Io hadn't expected *this*: gigantic camel-horse hybrids strapped with saddles. True, they had crossed the Wastelands in six days' time—half as long as it would take on foot. The camel-horse's legs were so long that they could travel *while* the tide was rising—but gods, at what cost? Io's bottom and thighs felt like the meat Mama used to pound to granules when making giouvarlakia soup.

She righted herself on the saddle and gave her camel-horse, Ajax, a pat on the neck. As far as chimerini went, to be fair, these were the nicest, sweetest ones Io had met. Ajax turned its head back to her and licked her arm through its muzzle. Cute, but always misbehaving.

Almost an hour later, a chorus of excitement tittered from the caravan riders ahead of her. They had come to the crest of the hillside, and the city of Nanzy had become visible in its entirety: the enormous valley it was built in, the surrounding hills and lakes, the sprawling urban architecture.

It was huge, just as Io had expected of a city of three million. But it was also rottenly ugly.

The City Proper was a shimmering jewel, marbled and engoldened, but it was a king seated on a throne made of waste. Factories surrounded it on every hill, squat cement structures with no windows, puffing smoldering gray plumes into the sky. Miles and miles of slums stretched from the factories to the walled city, floating shanties strewn together like makeshift puzzle pieces. Bridges and floating streets connected the tiny houses, while a dark mud sea churned below, its surface glistening a sickly shade of green. It was all so huge, so crowded, so dirty that Io was momentarily speechless.

"Why is the valley flooded?" was the first question that popped into her mind. Granted, the mud-tide wasn't even knee high around Ajax's legs, but it should have been nonexistent. "It's nowhere close to tide time."

"Ah, but see," said the mob queen, "the people who first repopulated the city have their pretty little apartments inside the walls and their handy factories manufacturing everything they need and their sprawling fields down south importing them their favorite foods. Who cares if the rest of the population has to live in a bog, right?"

"A *bog*?" Io's voice came out shrill and childlike. "You can't be serious."

Bogs were death. Dangerous, unexpected death—that's what Io's parents always said. After the Collapse, when the triple moons swelled the tides to unfathomable proportions, some parts of the land became unreliable. One moment you might be stepping on solid ground; the next you might be slipping into a sinkhole, never to be seen again—that was how Baba's best friend had died, long before Io was born. These places were called bogs, for lack of a better word, and they were death traps: festooned with water at all times of the day, sheltering chimerini in their mud. Building on a bog was the highest level of brainlessness Io had ever encountered.

"The mud-tide comes straight out of the earth itself. In the morning, it's like this," Bianca explained, gesturing at the earth beneath the camel-horses' feet, wet and sludgy, "and at night, it rises fifteen feet. It turns the whole valley into a lake—see there? You can spot the mark it leaves on the Spined Wall."

Indeed, the bottom one-fourth of the so-called Spined Wall was entirely brown, like a rotten tooth. Io squinted at the shanties coming into view as the caravan began their descent toward the city; their roofs were polished tin, glistening like mirrors in the sunlight, but their bases were wood patched with clay, connected by hanging catwalks. Some were even perched on enormous floats the color of weak tea.

"They're made of waterproof canvas," Bianca explained. "And there are lots of houseboats, too. As the mud-tide level rises, so do the Shards. Clever, isn't it?"

"The Shards?"

"That's what the slums are called. The mirrored roofs mimic the glittering gold of the City Proper. As though the slums are shards of inner Nanzy."

It was an apt description: although derelict, every shanty Io could see had a spotless, shining roof, the poor man's imitation of the wealthy walled city standing guard above. Io couldn't decide if copying the rich was pitiful or a clever way of mocking them.

"Listen up!" Paula, the caravan leader, had dismounted from her camel-horse and was now addressing their group. "This is as far as I go. The rest you have to walk. Stick to the floating streets and get your papers ready. We're at the Fen District. Entry fee is seven notes per person—"

"But this is the slums!" one of the travelers called out. "I knew Nanzy was expensive, but I'm not paying a single note to enter this filth!"

Paula leveled him with a tight-lipped scowl. "The Shards are the turf of the Sarris-Nakano brothers. If you want in, you've got to pay their entrance fee. Otherwise, you're welcome to travel back to Tulip with me—for another twenty notes."

Bianca leaned sideways on her saddle. "The Sarris-Nakano brothers are the mob kings of the Shards—well, four of them are. The fifth district is ruled by the eldest brother's widow. They're erotes-born, rumored to be extremely powerful. We're lucky to be entering at the Fen District, which is Ryou's turf. He's an Anteros; his deals are always fair and well kept."

Io had never met an erotes-born before but knew they were descendants of the gods of love. Like most other-born, each sibling had inherited a specific god's power: Eros was the god of desire, Anteros the god of mutual love, Himeros the god of unrequited love, Hedylogos the god of flattery, Pothos the god of yearning and longing. Their eyes shone a soft rose-pink, but Io wasn't quite sure how their talents manifested.

"You seem to know a lot," Io told Bianca.

The mob queen didn't take her gaze off the slums as the caravan started moving again, Paula leading them on foot through the mud to the border patrol station before them. "I did a brief stint here, when I was setting up my smuggling network," Bianca said. "I've never met the mob kings themselves, but I've dealt with their accountants."

"Accountants?" Io huffed—this had to be a joke, right?

A smile quirked Bianca's pale lips. "The Shards are not like the Silts, cutter—gangs squabbling for turf rights and haggling with small shop owners. The Sarris-Nakano brothers are entrepreneurs: they have set up proper, legitimate businesses; they own fancy restaurants and five-star hotels; they even have shares in some of the biggest factories."

A silent *wow* formed on Io's lips. When they reached the platform before the border patrol, Io dismounted, patted Ajax on the cheek, and handed his reins to Paula with a nod of thanks. Bianca had already joined the waiting line, their money pouch in her palms, counting out notes—they should have just enough for entry, perhaps for a meal or two as well, but definitely not enough to rent a room. The streets it would have to be tonight.

Io took a couple of cautious steps on the floating platform, feeling like a boat out on the monstrous waves of the Timid Sea. Every step was instability, her legs wobbly on the rocking surface of the floating slums, her thighs burning with the effort of keeping her upright. Thank the gods they hadn't had the money to afford anything but bread and fig jam—otherwise, her breakfast would be a gross yellow puddle at her feet. Travelers wobbled on cautious, uneasy feet, arms out for balance, faces scrunched in concentration. Of course, there were no railings to hold on to—*what does this world have against railings?* Io lamented—but the locals didn't seem to mind. The border patrol squad dashed across the floating street with impossible speed and marvelous agility, like those tiny geckos that frequented the walls on the balcony of Io's family's old apartment.

Bianca was faring much better than Io. She had her apathetic face on, trudging along the waiting line with her nose stuck in the air. "Lots of guards around, huh?" she whispered, her eyes latching on to the patrol guards pacing up and down the line. They weren't wearing uniforms, but identical guns rested on their belts, their handles rimmed with golden patterns. "Twelve that I can see."

"That's unusual?" Io asked.

"Twelve guards for one entry point? Yes, it is. Or it used to be, back when I moonlighted as a smuggler here. I wonder . . ."

The pause took too long. Io prodded, "What?"

"There've been attacks on every other-born leader in the city-nations. The sabazios-born in Kurkz, the zorya-born in Rossk, the clan kings of Iyen, the Muses—all have suffered losses. The æsir-born in Jhorr were completely wiped out. But we've heard no news of assassinations in Nanzy. Strange, isn't it?"

"If the Sarris-Nakano brothers are as powerful as you say, perhaps the wraiths didn't manage to get to them," Io said. The wraiths hadn't managed to get to the Muses, either, not until Thais manipulated Io into bringing Bianca into their home.

"Perhaps. But all this added security is suspicious. The wraiths should be dead by now. What could the Sarris-Nakano brothers be so afraid of?" Bianca shook her head. "Which way did you say your fate-thread is pointing, cutter?"

It was still weird to hear the mob queen discuss the fate-thread. After Bianca had found her gulping down furious breaths in the acid rain outside the taverna, Io had come clean. About the fate-thread she shared with Edei, about how it was fraying, about the way it had been blocked by something and was now pointing in the right direction: west, to Nanzy, where they now stood.

A fate-thread, Bianca had repeated dryly, then gave Io a long look that quickly became uncomfortable. *Any other secrets you'd like to share, cutter?*

Io had shaken her head. The existence of the fate-thread felt enough of a confession for now. She didn't have the courage to go into the other secret she had been keeping from Bianca: the Nine's prophecy. Either the mob queen would laugh in her face in disbelief or she would get violent—Io had seen how Bianca Rossi treated those she considered a threat, and what bigger threat was there than a girl who would end the world? Neither reaction was something Io had the stamina to deal with right now.

Io summoned the Quilt. She could see it before she touched it; the fate-thread was vibrating with Edei's proximity. He was close, finally *so close*, that Io felt packed to the brim with anticipation.

"Straight ahead," she replied.

The mob queen must have shared some of Io's eagerness, because she nodded emphatically. "All right, then. Let's get to it—"

"You there," said one of the patrol guards. He had been watching the line trudge along, a hand on the golden-rimmed gun at his hip.

Bianca shifted, placing her body between Io and the guard, with a whispered "Drop the Quilt."

Io obliged, plastering surprise on her face for good measure. "Me, sir?"

The patrol guard wasn't convinced. His hand clasped Io's upper arm, dragging her out of the line. "Come with me."

"Hey, hey, boss," Bianca said, following close behind. "What's this about? We've got the funds to pay the entrance fee, and our papers are squeaky clean—"

"Let me see those." The man snatched the papers and notes from Bianca's hand. He gestured to the clerk at one of the checkpoint stations, then shoved Io and Bianca in front of the booth.

An older couple who was next in line started complaining, but the guy flashed them a scowl, and they instantly quieted. Io didn't dare glance at Bianca; they both knew to play it cool in front of border patrol. The checkpoint clerk, a woman barely older than Io, went through their papers at a leisurely pace, checking every page, then slid them across the booth to Bianca.

"What's this about, Alek?" the clerk asked.

"I saw this one's eyes flash silver," the guard said. He was still gripping Io's arm. "We've got orders to flag moira-born upon entry, for interrogation."

Moira-born flagged at entry? For interrogation? For gods' sake. This wasn't going to end well, Io could already tell. They were going to bring her in for questioning at best, arrest her at worst. There was no way she was getting out of this with polite smiles and fake papers this time.

She acted on instinct alone, with a crisp "*Bianca.*"

The mob queen needed no further instruction—they bolted.

Bianca stomped her boot on the man's knee; he went down with a groan. Io slipped past the checkpoint booth, blindly throwing out a hand at the desk. Papers flurried in the air as they dashed into the tightly woven shanties of the Shards. The streets were a blur of color and sound as Io and Bianca dashed through the crowd. The backpack banged against Io's spine as she ran, straps digging into her shoulders, slowing her down. Bianca wasn't ten feet ahead as per usual, but had slowed her sprint to match Io's, stealing furtive glances over her shoulder at the guards. Io could hear them, clumping down the alley, blowing their shrill whistles to call for backup. She looked straight ahead at the floating streets, dodging obstacles and trying to think of a way out of this. It was unlikely they'd lose the guards in the streets—they knew this part of the Fen District far better than Io and Bianca did. Taking on a mob king's guards also seemed unwise—they'd get in far more trouble for assaulting them, and besides, it looked like backup had *already* arrived.

A man and a woman holding golden-handled guns appeared out of a side alley ahead. They paused and frowned, uncertain what was happening, which was all the opening Bianca needed. As they sped past, the mob queen swung her backpack, hitting the woman in the chest and the man straight in the jaw. The poor guards landed on their bottoms in the gap between two rafts and slipped straight into the mud-tide beneath.

Io was suddenly dragged to a stop by Bianca's fingers looped in her backpack strap. Panic lined the mob queen's bugged-out eyes. Io turned: at the other end of the busy street, three more guards were pushing through the crowd. Time slowed as their eyes skimmed the crowd in the street, falling finally on them.

Well. Assaulting a guard it would have to be.

Io lowered her chin to her chest, then looked up through her lashes. In the Quilt, they were barely more than outlines, but Io knew what *they* saw: her eyes blazing the menacing silver of fate, the silver of life, the silver of death. She gave her wrist a theatrical twist, looping the thread she had been holding around her fist. The heel of her boot dragged against the wooden raft as she rotated to a stance of attack. They wanted dangerous moira-born? They'd *get* a dangerous moira-born. She threw her free hand out in the direction of the three officers before her—

"Psst!" Bianca hissed.

Io hadn't noticed the mob queen leave her side, but now she spotted her among the threads of the Quilt, a few feet away, her back flat against a wooden fence between buildings. Her hands were interlaced, low on her torso, creating a perfect—

A perfect step.

Io launched into a run to build up momentum, placed her boot right on the step of Bianca's laced fingers, and *jumped*. The mob queen thrust her up, then the top of the fence was digging into Io's hipbones and gravity took over—in seconds, Io was on the other side of the fence, landing headfirst in a pile of sacks. Dust sprang up all around her. Io began sneezing and sneezing *and sneezing* and didn't stop until Bianca climbed down the fence and clapped a palm over her mouth.

The mob queen backpedaled Io to the fence and pressed down on her shoulders until Io was a small, hunched bundle among the sacks. Bianca raised a finger to her lips, then threw an empty sack over Io's head. Io didn't move, not when she heard Bianca's footsteps fade, not when the fence at her back quivered with the guards' weight, not when they landed on the sacks to her left, snapping orders at each other in that lilting Nanzese accent. She just squeezed her nostrils shut and waited. Bianca was risking herself to lead them away from Io, and Io wasn't about to let it all go to waste because her damn nose was feeling sensitive today.

In barely a minute, the alley was silent. Io peeked out from under the sack—no one there—and set her nostrils free. Sneeze after sneeze after sneeze came, rattling her entire head. Of all the times to be acting out, why did her damned allergies have to choose now?

She unfolded from her hiding spot, edged toward the mouth of the alley, and began to dust herself off, holding her breath. Her boots crunched against spilled grains: oats, as tasteless as they were allergenic. And they were all over her hair. Bending at the waist, head upside down, she began shaking the oats out of her curls—

She felt a tug at her chest. The fate-thread was vibrating with movement. She straightened. Her pulse was a hammer at her throat. She traced the thread with her eyes as it rotated like the hand of a clock nearing the hour. She heard footsteps come to an abrupt stop. She dropped the Quilt.

Both of his hands were flat against his chest, right over the fate-thread. His face had gone slack, mouth slightly agape. His hair was longer, curling over his brow and beneath his ears. He wore a white shirt, the sleeves rolled to his biceps. The brass knuckles gleamed from their hook on his belt. His gaze found hers and did that thing she loved, skipping fast from one of her eyes to the other, watching, watching her.

Edei's lips curved up, then bloomed into a smile.

PART II
THE UNSEEN BLADE

CHAPTER IX

QUIET TERROR

IO'S HEART WAS suddenly thudding in her chest. She felt like a child again, called to the front of a class, or like when she'd stood before the committee for her detective license examination. She had an acute awareness of her body, her curls shaken up and sticking in every direction, her nose red and running from sneezing, the kitschy leopard-print hat hanging from her neck. She must look very silly, standing there gawking at him—she *felt* silly, light-headed, and thoughtless with excitement.

"Io," he said.

His smile was a brilliant thing; she wanted to stay in this moment forever, looking at him looking at her, beaming at each other.

But then a whistle sounded to his right. His face spasmed with worry. He held out his hand to her, and Io went to him, her fingers slipping into his. The world narrowed down to that point of contact between them. Io's mind filled with all the times he had held her back in Alante, all the casual touches and softness, all the little ways he had cared. They walked like this, fingers threaded, into a larger street lined with yellow lights hanging from awnings, a flea market of some sort.

People jostled by, guards holding gold-rimmed guns pushing through, but Edei kept a brusque pace, winding through floating alleys and hanging bridges. Within a few silent minutes, they had crossed into a new district, marked only by a simple toll booth. Edei barely glanced at the guards posted there as he handed them a few notes, then slipped into another street, this one narrower but busier. Street vendors advertised their fare in the local Nanzese dialect. Io got whiffs of the food as they passed by: steaming buns, fried chicken wings, some sort of broth, fresh coffee accented with cinnamon.

The traffic slowed in front of a busy square where a group of teenagers was performing a dance routine. Edei huffed in annoyance and switched directions, taking them along a passageway built on the shiny, mirrored roofs. From up there, Io had a better view of the Shards: she was closer to the Spined Wall now, shanty houses stretching endlessly behind her. But the sensation of being on board a ship was all but gone, and now Io could see why. This part of the Shards was built on stilt platforms, their legs visible above the mud-tide, the entire district elevated some fifteen feet over the rest of the slums.

Edei tugged her through a labyrinthine maze of narrow alleys, then up again on a winding staircase that creaked with every footfall. At the top, there was a narrow gangway with five doors; Edei knocked on the one on the far left. Two beats slow, pause, three beats fast, pause, two beats slow—the knuckle raps that the Fortuna gang used as a secret code.

The door opened to a tiny room with two bunk beds facing each other, a sink and a tiny icebox between them. Nico stood there, as rosy-cheeked and redheaded as ever, in a gray tank top, black shorts, and socks pulled up to his calves. When he saw Io, his face broke into a wide, toothy grin. "Boss!"

He drew Io into a hug, while Edei quickly shut the door behind them. She hadn't known Nico long enough to memorize his smell or the feel of his arms around her, but she found his arms comforting nonetheless, even his boyish stubble stabbing her cheek. Over her head, Nico whooped to Edei, "You found her!"

Edei gave a nod. He was moving with purpose around the tiny

room, kicking his boots off, gulping down a glass of water, sitting gingerly at the very edge of a bed, then standing again. Io took note of the rest of the room: their luggage shoved under the beds, Nico's brass knuckles hanging by a hook on the door, a money pouch sitting on the chest of drawers—and a Muse, sitting cross-legged on the floor, a bite of noodles halfway to her mouth.

"Hello," Urania, Muse of astronomy, said.

Her glossy black hair was wrapped in a colorful scarf, highlighting her smiley, upturned eyes and heart-shaped face. She wore a simple gray sweater and matching cotton pants, rolled above the ankles. The last time Io had seen her, she was cowering behind a sofa as Bianca Rossi attacked her sisters in a bloodthirsty frenzy.

Io didn't know what to say besides a stunned "Hi?"

"Urania has been traveling with us," Edei explained. He had returned to Io's side and was now lifting the backpack from her shoulders. Io let him take it and shrugged off her hat and leather jacket—it was hot enough to bake a cake in here. "She refused to join her sisters in a safehouse. She wanted to help us."

Io kept nodding, as if this was making any sense at all.

"Are you hungry? We just got food." Edei gestured silently at Nico, who proceeded to step over Urania's legs and fish out a carton box from a takeout bag. "Come, sit," Edei said, squeezing his tall body into one of the bottom bunks, "eat."

Io sat next to him on the creaky mattress. She took the steaming noodles from Nico and mindlessly brought a bite to her mouth, then another. On the third, she paused, lowered it, and said, rather unintelligently, "How are you all here?"

Edei's lips parted, but Nico was—naturally—faster. "We've been looking for *you*, obviously—and Bianca. We thought she was traveling with you?"

"Gods, Bianca!" Io blurted. She really was a fool: she was munching on spicy noodles while Bianca was trying to throw five guards off her back. Edei's presence had accosted her with such shock that she hadn't spared a thought for the mob queen ever since. "I've got to find her—"

"Don't worry," Edei said. "I stumbled upon her first, pummeling a guard into the ground. Another two, she had already tossed in the mud-tide below. She pointed me in your direction, and I tossed her my hotel room key. She'll find us."

"You said you've been looking for me?" Io asked.

"Since the day you left Alante," Nico said. "It all went to shit after that night: the police raided the Fortuna Club, riots broke out in the Silts, Edei had to take charge of the gang—"

Quietly, Edei added, "Rosa has been fighting tooth and nail to publicize the events of that night in the House of Nine, but Saint-Yves buried the story on the grounds of this being an ongoing investigation. We have a system in place, for Bianca to reach us if she's out of town. But she never contacted us. And I couldn't—" He cut himself short, then breathed, "We started to worry."

Io sucked her bottom lip into her mouth. Edei was looking at his hands, rubbing off invisible dirt. He couldn't find her. Because the fate-thread had begun to weaken and fray.

Nico puffed out his chest, his face lighting up with a smug, self-congratulatory smile. "So, I convinced Edei to ask for the Muses' help. Clio and Polyhymnia refused to put themselves in any more danger, but Urania came to find me after our visit. She offered to use her powers to find out where you and Bianca were. She's been a great help."

On the floor between the beds, Urania kept chewing her noodles, as though this conversation didn't involve her at all. As though Nico wasn't mooning over her with heart-shaped eyes.

"And you agreed?" Io asked.

Edei and Nico's friend Chimdi had been swindled by the Muses before. She had been forced to create sculptures for them, even when her hands were bleeding. Edei still carried the guilt of being unable to help his friend all those years ago. For him and Nico to trust the muse-born now, to travel and eat with her—Urania must have gained their trust in some astonishing way.

"It had been weeks since you left," Nico said. "Edei—*we* were getting quite frantic. So, I agreed to let her powers inspire me, and oh, it was unlike anything I've ever experienced before, Io! We set up a telescope and a star chart, right there on the roof of the Fortuna, and suddenly, I felt inspiration taking over me. It was like those moments when you first wake up after a vivid dream, convinced it was real. I could see the planets and galaxies clearly, I could read the meaning behind their alignment in the skies, I could tell exactly what the position of each star meant, and, well, I found you. The stars were clear: a shabby pub in Tulip, and a tiny hotel room in Nanzy."

He spread his arms wide to indicate the room. "We set off the same day. We waited for you in Tulip for a week, but when you didn't show, we decided to come to Nanzy instead, because that part of my stargazing had been clearer. Was I right? Did you go to Tulip before coming here? The stars only showed me where, not when, so I realized I might have the timing wrong. I convinced them to come to Nanzy, because I thought if we waited in one place long enough, you'd appear, and I can't believe I was actually right! I'm never right!"

This last part Nico said in a breathless torrent, so fast that it took several seconds for it to sink into Io's mind. Under the influence of the Muse of astronomy, Nico had interpreted the constellations in the sky to figure out where Io was.

"How long have you been waiting?" she asked.

"Eleven days," Edei said in a soft voice.

All this time, all those lonely, grief-stricken nights Io had spent gazing at their fraying fate-thread, Edei had been *waiting* for her. *Looking* for her.

"And then, today," Nico went on, "when we had just gotten our takeout, Edei suddenly hopped up and said, *Io is here*, and simply dashed out the door. We've been sitting on hot coals for half an hour, but all's well that ends well, because here you are."

He patted Io's knee affectionately, like Rosa used to do when they sat together at school. Edei was still perusing the skin of his knuckles with a hint of a blush on his cheeks. Io was awash in relief, in warmth, in roaring giddiness. She didn't know what she'd done to possibly deserve friends like this.

"Stop it," she said, but mildly; she was only teasing.

Nico flashed a quick grin, then said somberly, "Io, where have you been? What have you been doing?"

The noodles were going cold. Io folded the flaps of the carton box and set it on the floor by her feet. "How much do they know?" she asked Edei.

"Everything," Edei replied without pause. "I knew that when you left Alante, you were holding a thread and that Bianca disappeared that same night. The only thing uniting you two is your desire to find the masterminds behind the wraiths, so I gathered that must be your plan. When Urania offered to help us, she held nothing back. She told us that her surviving sisters suspect someone very powerful orchestrated the massacre at the House of Nine and the other-born assassinations that followed."

"I did not say *someone*," Urania interjected with a scowl. "I said *the gods*."

Nico gave her a flustered look, halfway between appeasement and panic. "Yeah, but it has to be someone else, some kind of other-born we've never heard of. There can't be actual gods out there. They died millennia ago. We would have heard of them if they didn't! Right, Io?"

They all turned to look at her. "I'm afraid Urania might be right, Nico," Io replied. "At the greenhouse of the House of Nine, when my sister was confessing, I got ahold of the thread that linked her to whoever was guiding her. The thread was golden. Unlike anything I've seen before, unlike any *human's* thread I've seen before. And just a week ago, the suspect I have been following through the Wastelands warned me to stop looking. She told me, *The gods are not your villains.*"

"But—" Nico started. A dozen emotions passed over his face, setting on bewilderment. "It can't be gods. How are we supposed to face off against gods?"

Io could understand his dread. She felt it, too, in the rare moments she allowed herself to think past the task at hand, past the thread she had been tracking, past the mystery of the abductions. But the fact remained: the thread was golden. Thais had hinted at the existence of gods. The Nine had, too. Last week, Hanne had outright admitted it.

"What else did your sisters tell you?" she asked Urania.

"You have to understand." Urania's voice was high and her cheeks round, the girlishness at odds with the composed way she spoke. "Polyhymnia and I were twenty years younger than all of our sisters. We were told very little and were never part of the decision-making. Our eldest sisters, Calliope, Euterpe, Clio—their eyes had turned indigo when they were still toddlers. They were raised with the knowledge they were one of the rarest and most powerful kind of other-born in the world. There had been assassination attempts against them since they were teenagers. We have always been careful, always prioritized safety. But something changed after the Riots."

The Moonset Riots, an eight-day gang war in the slums of Alante twelve years ago that had cost hundreds of lives, including the complete eradication of the fury-born. Until recently, their deaths were blamed on a rogue gang, whose identities were kept a secret through the vow of Roosters' Silence. Except Io had discovered that wasn't the whole truth: it was the fury-born themselves who had originated the violence, launching senseless attacks on other-born leaders across the world. The Nine had employed Bianca's help to put an end to the rampage and wipe out the entire fury-born bloodline.

Io had drilled Bianca on her involvement in the Riots extensively when they first left Alante. But the mob queen had only been a young smuggler back then—she wasn't privy to the Nine's machinations. The Muses had asked for her help, and Bianca had obliged, to save her gang and the Silts. The only information Bianca could offer was that the Nine believed the Order of the Furies was being *influenced* by someone to target and assassinate the other-born leaders, much like the wraiths were doing now.

Urania was silent for a while. When she spoke, it wasn't to elaborate but to ask a question, "Do you remember what it was like when the fury-born were alive?"

Io shook her head. "I was only six when the Riots happened." Urania nodded; she must have been the same age, perhaps a year or two younger. "But the way my sisters describe it, the Order of the Furies supervised the other-born population of the entire continent. They stepped in when other-born were arrested and conducted their own investigations and trials. Their population was small, so they weren't present in every city, but their proceedings were fair. Much better than those of the police."

"That's the extent of what I know, too. After the attack on our House, I tried to get Clio to explain why someone would target us, but she refused to reply to any of my questions, not one. I lashed out and told her that Bianca Rossi's eyes were burning orange like the fury-born's and if it's the fury-born who came for us, then we must have done something *rotten*—" Urania pursed her lips, averting her gaze. "I didn't mean it. I didn't really believe that. But Clio was furious. She started speaking for the first time in weeks, screaming, to be precise, and—she told me about the Order of the Furies.

"They were based in a compound just outside Jhorr, which they shared with the valkyrie-born and other justice-focused other-born. A few months before the Riots, a neo-monsoon destroyed their compound. The fury-born sought refuge here, in Nanzy. That's when they started changing. They began targeting other-born leaders with little cause or reason. Clio said that the fury-born are incredibly powerful; once their fury-whip is around your throat, there is little you can do to fend them off. So, Clio and the rest of my sisters decided to end the fury-born's rampage. They hired Bianca and the city's strongest other-born to do it, which led to the Moonset Riots.

"After the Riots," Urania continued, "my sisters started acting as if everything was a threat. They turned our House into a fortress. We weren't allowed to step foot outside the city. When anyone visited, especially officials, we'd have twenty security men on site. One time, Polyhymnia and I found a sniper keeping guard in the attic. Other-born were completely forbidden from entry. You're probably the first to cross the gates in a decade, and even then, they had us rehearse your visit for days. Where we'd be, what we'd say, escape routes if things turned ugly."

The memory of the day she met the Nine was vivid in Io's mind. The luxurious living room, dressed in vibrant indigo, the Muses' eerie performance, the tricks they had tried to play. The portraits of Io's face flurrying through the air. A canary yellow scarf pulled back her hair, while her fingers clawed around a thread and the world writhed in flames behind her.

Rehearsing for days, hiring a sniper, keeping two teenagers cooped up for years—this wasn't normal behavior, not even for someone with as many enemies as the Nine.

"What were they so afraid of?" Io asked.

"I think," Urania whispered, "that my sisters were planning something twelve years ago. Something big. Something that angered the gods enough to send an army of fury-born to stop them. And not just my sisters. I think every other-born leader who was targeted then, and every leader who has been targeted now, was in on the plan."

Io watched the girl's reactions closely. There was no lie or pretense in her quiet terror, no odd lilt to her voice or extended eye contact. Urania wasn't trying to manipulate them, which meant she truly believed that the gods were punishing other-born leaders for something they'd planned twelve years ago. Io already knew the gods were meticulous; she had no trouble accepting their revenge might be twelve years in the making. What she couldn't understand was what kind of plan could have brought about this response? What had the Nine been planning that was so terrible the gods would cause violence and upheaval across the entire world?

Knuckles rapped at the door, startling all four of them. Two beats slow, pause, three beats fast, pause, two beats slow again.

Bianca.

Nico shot up and threw the door open. The mob queen stood at the threshold like a bull about to charge, chest heaving, forehead dotted with sweat, a bruise forming on her jaw. Her gaze went past Nico to Edei, to Io, and then finally—to the Muse.

"*You*," the mob queen hissed. Her eyes blinked burnt orange.

Io sighed. *Not again.* She sprang from the bed and tackled Bianca to the floor just before the mob queen's hands could close around Urania's neck.

CHAPTER X

TAKE A WALK

BIANCA DIDN'T FIGHT Io. They dropped like stones on the wooden floor, rattling the whole room. Shifting her body beneath Bianca's, Io snaked her arms under the mob queen's armpits and locked them above her head, completely immobilizing her.

"In the left pocket of her trousers," Io shot at Nico, who was closest, "there's a blue vial. Tip it into her mouth."

Obediently, Nico made to move, but Bianca hissed at him like a feral cat. "Muse," she barked at Urania. "Who else knows about the prophecy?"

Urania's chin was trembling. "What proph—"

"Don't lie to me, you venomous viper!"

"Hey." Nico circled around their bodies to stand before Urania. "There's no need for—"

"There's every need!" Bianca screeched. "Who did you tell about Io's prophecy, oh Muse of nothing?"

"N-no one," Urania stammered as Nico pulled her up to her feet. Her eyes were two perfect orbs of fear. "Edei already knew. He's the one who told Nico and Chimdi. But no one else knows. My sisters haven't ventured out of the safehouse for a single minute. And all the portraits, all the poems burned with the House."

"Yeah," the mob queen snapped, "I made sure of that."

A startled "*Huh?*" escaped Io's lips.

It was news to her that Bianca knew about her prophecy to begin with, but to have burned down all evidence of its existence? They really needed to calm the mob queen down and get some answers out of her. Io released one of Bianca's wrists and shot her hand into the mob queen's pocket. But the vial came out empty. It had run out, Io remembered, back in Hagia.

"Could it have reached people's ears anyway?" Bianca went on. "Perhaps one of your precious patrons leaked it to someone, or an artist re-created their painting."

"No, no," Urania said quickly. "My eldest sisters were terrified when the art began trickling in. They made us all stop sending inspiration to our patrons and went to great lengths to retrieve every piece of art created about the prophecy. We didn't want news of the end of the world reaching the media. No one else knows, I swear."

"Then why," Bianca spat, "are the entire Shards looking for a moira-born cutter wanted for crimes against humanity?"

Dear gods. Arms and legs still clenched around Bianca's body, Io let her head drop back to the floor. She stared up at the ceiling, the fan whirring shadows against the walls. The words sprang to her mind: *The cutter, the unseen blade, the reaper of fates. She watches silver like a sign, she weeps silver like a mourning song, she holds silver like a blade. She cuts the thread and the world ends.*

She was so tired. Her body was a patchwork of bruises and pulled muscles, her mind frantic with worries and panic. A series of kidnappings, a secret network of gods, a twelve-years-long revenge plan, a fraying fate-thread—and now this? The mob kings' lackeys looking for her on the grounds of *crimes against humanity?*

There was some shuffling in the room. Edei appeared above her and lifted Bianca off as if she was a rag doll. Holding her by the lapel of her raincoat, he backtracked her against the door and placed a hand on her chest. Urania had crawled to the very corner of the bottom bunk bed, while Nico crouched at the foot of the mattress, his eyes on Bianca like a hawk. The mob queen's chest rose and fell against Edei's bunched fist. But her eyes were no longer orange. Leisurely, almost as if teasing them, Bianca reached into her pocket and took out a cigarette.

"Please, don't," Io muttered from the floor. "The air's already thick enough to lick in here."

Locking her gaze to Io's, Bianca lit the cigarette and puffed a billowing gray cloud at her. Io sighed. How was it possible that the mob queen of the Silts was in fact a child in a trench coat?

Io pulled herself into a sitting position, leaning her head against the post of the bunk bed. "When did they put out the arrest warrant?" she asked.

"Yesterday," Bianca answered around a plume of smoke.

Yesterday. When Hanne was due to arrive. The norn-born had let her superiors know that Io had tracked her down in Tulip. That Io had defied their warning to stop looking. That she was coming for them. And now Io was a wanted person.

Time for Io's next question. "How long have you known about the Nine's prophecy?"

"I started suspecting something was amiss when the Nine allowed you into their House," Bianca explained. "The night of the elections, after the gang arrived and Edei was taken care of, I sneaked into their mansion. I found the portraits and the poems. Then I doused them all with the Muses' cherry brandy and set it ablaze."

A pause followed, where Bianca opened the tiny window and stuck her hand with the cigarette outside. It had gotten so smoky in here that it was hard for them to see each other. "I kept waiting for you to mention it, but you didn't," she went on, voice empty of emotion. "I don't blame you. Only a fool would go around talking of being prophesized to bring about the end of the world, and you, cutter, are no fool."

Io said nothing. The silence stretched, long and heavy with apprehension.

"It doesn't mean anything," Edei said. Io realized he had been watching her under furrowed brows. "The Nine used it to try to manipulate you—"

"It means *everything*," Urania spoke up. Gone was her childish scowl, gone was her coddled uncertainty. "My sisters and I have never been wrong before. This is the future."

"How can one girl, one severed thread, bring about the end of the world, girl?" Bianca snapped at the Muse. Sweat had matted her hair. Her jaw was bruising a sickly black color. Her chest labored with every inhale, her lungs wheezing with every exhale. Even so, Io knew she would smoke her cigarette to the butt.

Urania said, very gravely, "We don't know. That's why we planned to get Io to ask us that day. We could use her question to inspire a true answer."

"Well then, cutter, ask the question!" snapped Bianca.

The prospect of finding out how she was supposed to end the world sounded absolutely horrific, but Io turned to Urania nonetheless. If she had to pay for the truth with her sanity, then so be it. The end of the world was a much steeper price.

Edei was drawing a breath, as though to object, but he needn't have. Urania was already shaking her head. "I can't."

"You inspired Nico," Io said.

"I did. My power requires only one thing: an artist with a personal connection to the subject to be created. I could inspire Nico because he knows you and he wanted to find you. I granted him the creativity to decipher astronomy to locate you, the stars did the rest. But it doesn't work the same way when an artist attempts to create something beyond their sphere of knowledge. That required our collective power, all of us working together. That power is gone now."

Gone, because Io had been fooled. Because Thais had orchestrated the murder of Urania's sisters. In a night, one of the most important other-born skills in the world became obsolete. Clever and vicious, these gods; whatever their plan, they had managed to eliminate their enemies in one stroke, not just in Alante but in the entire world.

"I could, however," Urania said, "inspire *you*."

She raised her eyes across the room—to Bianca.

Io was closest to Edei: she felt him tense, saw his fingers clench into fists and his feet prepare to place himself between the Muse and the mob queen.

But Bianca simply leaned out the window and flicked the butt of her cigarette into the air, with no care where it landed. "What would be the point of that?"

"You were there." Urania's brows were knitted together in a vicious scowl. "Twelve years ago. You were part of my sisters' plans."

"Girl, if I had any more information to share on the matter, I would have gladly shared it." She paused, cocking her head. "Maybe not with you, but certainly with the cutter. I was twenty-one when the fury-born started their rampage. All I knew was my friends were getting picked off by fury-born left and right. Much more powerful gang bosses than I was at the time. I was scared, for my life as well as the lives of everyone working for me. It's the only reason I agreed to your sisters' plan. They used me to put an end to the bloodshed. We didn't have a heart-to-heart over tea."

"I could try," Urania insisted. "You were privy to their plan, you were there when it all went down. Perhaps there's something you missed that I could bring to the surface—"

"It wouldn't work," Io cut her off. "Bianca can't be affected by other-born powers anymore. Go ahead, take a look."

Urania's brow scrunched in confusion. An indigo hue draped over her brown eyes; after a few moments, it disappeared. The girl deflated into a limp tangle of arms and legs on the cot. "There's nothing there. Nothing to inspire."

Io expected a smart quip from the mob queen, but none came. Bianca was studying the floorboards, her arms crossed over her chest. *A pitiful imitation of life*, the mob queen had called her existence. No creativity to inspire, no thread of love to weave, nothing but this mission and this vengeance. Io wondered how long justice could sustain a dying body.

The mob queen spoke quietly. "Could you inspire Hanne if we found her? Force her to reveal the gods' location and their schemes?" Oh. That was a good idea. A great plan.

"Inspire someone against their will?" Urania said. "I could try—"

"Who's Hanne?" Nico interrupted.

Right. She had yet to fill in Edei, Nico, and Urania on what she and Bianca had been doing all these weeks. She went over it swiftly and decisively, skipping over any unnecessary details. She told them about the wild goose chase up and down the Wastelands. About the Great Tide and the trap they had set in Hagia. About Hanne and Wilhem and the poor boy they had kidnapped in Tulip. She showed them the map they had found at Wilhem's place and told them about the sets of three siblings that had started disappearing all over the Wastelands.

"Not just the Wastelands," Edei said. "People went missing in Alante, too. Rosa and Xeno had just started investigating the disappearances when we left. Rosa even traveled with us as far as Clyde to interview one of the missing people's family."

Hearing Rosa's name was like a spoonful of thyme honey, laced with a heady sweetness, warming Io to her core. What she wouldn't give to be lying on a couch with her best friend, their feet propped on the table, giggling at their favorite comedy show on the radio.

"I've seen missing people posters all over the Shards, too," Edei added. "We could start there. We could figure out why the gods are choosing these particular people to abduct or even locate one of the abductors. The Shards are jam packed—someone's bound to have seen something."

"And Urania and I can find out more about this Hanne," Nico offered. "The border guards must have seen her pass through the gates."

"The border guards?" Urania said, a little dryly. "What makes you think they'll tell you a single thing?"

"Because I am a *charmer*," Nico replied. "Tell her, Io."

"He's a charmer," Io supplied with a smile, which seemed to irritate Urania even more.

"All right," Edei said. He was standing in the middle of the small room, arms crossed over his chest, a general commanding his troops to action. "We split up. Io and I will investigate the missing people. Nico and Urania will look into Hanne and see if they can track her arrival in the Shards." He turned to Bianca. "And you—"

"Oh, you're giving the orders now, are you?" Bianca drawled. "I heard a rumor a while back that a young Sumazi man is the new mob king of the Silts—that true?"

Where had Bianca heard that? She'd never mentioned it to Io.

Edei didn't bow from her hard gaze. "I took care of them. The gang, the Silts, all the mess you left behind."

"And?" Bianca's tone was playful, but the glint in her eyes was anything but. "Was it exactly what you had imagined? Did you fix everything, just as you begged me to all those years?"

Edei didn't answer.

"Ah, you finally realized why ruling requires brass knuckles, huh?" Her tone had turned outright mocking. "Don't look so sour, Edei. It's a necessary lesson in this life."

Io studied him; there was something impossibly sad in the way he was holding every emotion back from his face. He had been forced to take over the Fortuna gang, put an end to the rioting, and reclaim the gang's turf—no doubt through less-than-savory means. He had been welded into the very thing he hated: vicious, perhaps even cruel. Once, he had told her that tolerating violence was a violence in itself—what had it cost him, Io wondered, to do everything he had to do to protect the people he cared about?

Io cleared her throat. "Let's all calm down. You need to lie low, Bianca, and perhaps get yourself some more sleeping tonic."

"Is that right, cutter?" Bianca said, leaning away from the window. "For six weeks, I'm at your beck and call for every foolhardy plan you conjure, and the moment you're with your friends again, I'm supposed to just what? Go shopping?"

"You *need* the tonic—"

"What I need is my life back!" Bianca shot out. "And I'm never going to get that, so I'm going to aim for the next best thing: revenge. You promised me revenge, cutter, and I'm not letting you off our deal until you deliver! Even if it's the last thing you do, thread in your hand, the world burning behind you and all that nonsense—"

"Take a walk."

Edei didn't raise his voice or alter his tone. He might as well have said *hello*.

But Bianca was instantly silent. Her face was furrowed with wrath, her eyes blazing with hatred, but she didn't speak a word.

Edei reached an arm out and grabbed the money pouch from the drawer. He threw it at Bianca. It hit her in the chest, and she caught it before it slipped to the floor.

"Get yourself the tonic or don't," Edei said. "I don't care. But I won't tolerate one of your tantrums right now. We're finally together, all of us. We've got enemies around every corner. We're going to stick together, and if that's too hard for you, if it's too much for your delicate ego, then there's the damn door."

He was breathing hard when he finished. His face was marred with intensity, muscles flexing silently at his jaw.

The room was frozen in anticipation of Bianca's reaction. Bianca's violence.

Her lips split in a smile that could cut diamonds. She bowed at the waist and hissed "Yes, boss" through her teeth. Then she disappeared out the door.

CHAPTER XI

OLD DEATH

IO STARED AT herself in the mirror, nipping at the inside of her cheek.

She turned her face this way and that; the quick shower she had just taken in the hotel's shared bathroom had left her cheeks rosy and her hair sticking in all directions, but she was clean at least, after five days of travel. She was wearing crisp, fresh clothes: a pair of cargo shorts she had been carrying since Alante—too petite to be of use in the mudscape of the Wastelands—a dark gray shirt borrowed from Nico, rolled high over her biceps, and Ava's booties, finally polished free of mud.

But she had an ugly deep mauve bruise on her side where Hanne had kicked her back in Hagia and a series of scratches along her thigh from the fight with the raptor-lion. Her face was sunburned and starved for moisturizer, and her eyebrows, gods, they needed some *serious* plucking.

It was airheaded to spend this much time in front of a mirror right now, when there were missing people to track down and clues to follow and blasted *gods* to find, but here Io was, nitpicking every aspect of her reflection. Because outside the hotel's communal bathroom and down the gangway, *Edei* was waiting for her.

Io ran her hands through her wet curls, squared her shoulders, and threw the door open. Edei's head perked up from where he was leaning against the balustrade, hands in his pockets. His gaze traveled from her bare legs to her arms to her hair to—no, he didn't look at her face. Instead, it seemed that the grille of the gangway was suddenly of keen interest to him.

"Where should we start?" he asked.

"Um," Io replied, the very picture of articulation. "Announcement boards? We can visit the missing people's homes and see if anyone's willing to talk to us."

Edei nodded and started down the spiraling staircase, plunging them into the traffic of commuters. It was early afternoon, the sun blistering on every mirror rooftop of the Shards, the air hot and humid. Edei smelled good, though—he always smelled good, clean and soapy. Io wished he would look back at her, wished he would smile again and pull her into his arms and tell her they were all right. That they were just how they used to be, all smooth camaraderie and shared experiences and bad jokes and, eventually, fleeting kisses. It had always been easy, with her and Edei.

It wasn't easy now.

Don't wallow, Thais said in Io's mind, as she had so many times before. Thais would have followed it with *go find what you don't like and change it,* but that felt naive now. Life could never go back to how it used to be; that was a fact, a truth far beyond Io's control, so what was the point of even trying? Best to just cherish what she still had, even if it was merely awkward stiffness and zero eye contact.

"So," she said, "how is Rosa? And Amos and Chimdi and everyone else in the gang?"

The streets were crammed with people and laden with noise. Edei had to shift his head toward her and raise his voice. "Rosa is good. She stopped by the Fortuna nearly every day while I was there, often with Xeno. He was far more . . . personable than the first time I met him. Amos is also good, but his café suffered some damage in the riots after the death of the Muses. The gang has been helping him restore it, as they're doing with all businesses in the Silts that suffered damages."

"Who's leading the gang now that you're here?"

"We had a vote. Chimdi was the unanimous winner." In a softer tone, he added, "I felt so shitty, bringing the surviving Muses under the protection of the Fortuna gang after the assassinations. But Chimdi was great about it. She hates Clio with a passion, as expected, but she doesn't mind Urania and Polyhymnia."

Edei had mentioned how much Chimdi's torment at the hands of the Nine still affected her. It must be hard for her to be in charge of protecting her very tormentors. Even harder to run the gang in a time of such turmoil.

"What do you make of Urania?" Io asked.

Edei pulled them at a stop in front of a public noticeboard. Posters had been crammed in every spot, lapping over each other like waves of a churning sea. About two dozen people crowded before the board, scanning the notices for gods-knew-what. The crossroads was extremely busy, a gambling den on one corner, a fancy restaurant in the other—Io had to squeeze right into Edei's side, to wait for space to clear up in front of the noticeboard.

"She's nice enough, but she, um." He hesitated. "She grew up in a bubble, I guess."

Io couldn't help it; she *had* to tease him. "You know, she's not listening, you can just say she's spoiled."

A brief laugh puffed through Edei's lips. "Yes, she's spoiled. Which can get pretty irritating when you're traveling through the Wastelands during the worst summer weather of the decade."

"Hasn't it been horrible? There have been so many acid storms back-to-back. And the damned Great Tide."

"Yes, it's been very bad. We got caught in the hailstorm at Peony."

Io didn't know what to say besides "Gods."

"At least the Great Tide won't reach us here. Nanzy is too far inland."

"Mm-hm," Io said. "While we were traveling to Nanzy on the caravan, we heard rumors of a neo-blizzard in Jhorr. I didn't know there could be neo-blizzards in summertime."

"Me either," Edei agreed. "The weather's been acting strange."

Silence followed. Great, even the weather was an awkward topic of discussion for them.

Suddenly, Edei piped up. "Urania and Nico are kind of a thing, you know. Or, rather, Nico very much wants them to be a thing."

"*Oooh!*" Io said, all grumpiness instantly forgotten.

Edei glanced back at her. "I've never seen him so smitten before."

Io remembered that line Nico's sisters used to tease him with: *All his mouth'll ever do is talk, talk, talk—never kiss.* Her eyebrows scrunched together. "I suddenly feel like a million years old, because all I want to do is ask her what her intentions are toward Nico."

"I know, right?" Edei snorted under his breath. "Nico's been trying to tell her how he feels for weeks—but he always chickens out at the last moment."

"*Nico* chickening out of talking?"

"You've got to see him, Io. He gets so flustered, it's adorable."

They grinned at each other, toothy and giddy. Hope coursed through Io, warm and electrifying. He was looking at her and grinning and sharing a joke—perhaps not all was lost.

The crowd parted before them, creating an opening. Io and Edei slipped through and cast their gaze upon the posters. Edei produced a tiny notebook and pen from his pocket; they put their heads together and began untangling their newest web of clues.

They visited six homes, all of them utter duds.

The first two led nowhere; the missing people were travelers passing through the city. The innkeepers knew little about them, and their belongings had been handed over to the mob kings' officers. The next three were locals, a man and two younger women, but their families were not in the mood to answer questions from two strangers, especially when those questions had to do with whether their loved ones were unregistered other-born. Io discreetly peeped in the Quilt, but found no threads connecting them to the missing people. The sixth was a complete disaster: the missing person's young wife began raging over all the debt collectors her husband had left her to deal with. No, he had no other-born powers, but yes, he had two sisters, and if Io and Edei ever found them, they'd better tell them their brother was a wart-nosed loser.

The seventh, however, looked promising.

Io and Edei were seated in a cozy living room, every surface draped with doilies: the back and armrest of the couch, the tables and drawers, the big transistor radio. There was even one on the domed pendant light hanging low from the ceiling. Tea and honey cakes were served on a heavy mahogany coffee table. Io and Edei had had to take off their shoes at the door; even in her socks, Io felt like she was fouling the pristine, homely place simply by being here.

"My baby Torr," the woman on the armchair across from them was saying. Her name was Brigitte Vidal, and she was a pastry chef. Her daughter, Torr, had disappeared without a trace three weeks ago.

"This is her. She's frowning in every photo," Brigitte said fondly, sliding a black-and-white photo across the table to them, "because her brothers were fussy and the photoshoot ran so long that she had to miss her mathematics test in school."

Io glanced at the photograph—it depicted two women, Brigitte and her wife, and three children: a baby in Brigitte's arms, a toddler in her wife's lap, and Torr, the eldest, standing beside them, her shoulders ramrod straight and her smile not quite reaching her smart, upturned eyes—then quickly returned her gaze to the mother.

Io was wary of her, but she couldn't quite pinpoint why.

When they had knocked on Brigitte's door, claiming they had been hired privately to investigate the disappearances, the woman had welcomed them eagerly into her house. She had closed the door to the nursery, where the baby was sleeping, and brought out tea and snacks and every photograph and piece of evidence she could find. They were all laid on the coffee table now, among the porcelain teacups and doilies.

"The police said she ran away, but Torr wouldn't do that." Brigitte produced a police report from the pile of documents on the table. "She was having a bit of a hard time, but she wasn't unhappy. She was *excited*; we were finally so close to gathering the money to pay our permanent residence fee for the City Proper. She was going to go to L'Académie des Sciences, starting this fall—"

The woman stopped, blinking hard at the ceiling as though pushing down tears.

Edei reached out to lay a hand on her arm. "We'll do everything we can," he said softly. "Could you go over the day of her disappearance?"

Brigitte gave a tight-lipped nod. "It was a day like any other. She ate breakfast and helped me feed Andre—that's my youngest, the baby—then she got her and Mario's—that's my second oldest—bags ready. My wife, Ola, walked them to school, left Torr at the gates, saw her go in. The school's right around the corner, so Torr usually walks home on her own and picks Mario up from his school on the way. But on that day, half an hour passed, and they hadn't shown up. I grabbed Andre and went by Mario's school first, where I found him waiting. When we reached Torr's school, the teacher told me she had seen her leave just fine after the final bell rang."

Io frowned. If someone had intercepted the girl between her school and her brother's, it meant they might know her route from school to home. "How far away are the two schools?"

"Five minutes' walk, through Charity Square."

Io glanced at Edei for clarification. "It's a safe area," he explained. "Mostly schools and universities, a heavy guard presence."

"Were the teachers questioned?" Io asked Brigitte.

"Yes. The officers interviewed them. They are all accounted for, in the building with other students."

"Was anyone spotted around the school?"

"A couple of people. They were all interrogated and released."

"You said your daughter was having a hard time lately?" Io asked.

"Life with a newborn is always hard," Brigitte said, "for the entire family. At first, Torr was a dream, helping with the cleaning and the cooking, watching over Mario, keeping me company while I nursed. Then, about a month ago, she started having headaches and couldn't sleep at night. She kept saying there was something wrong with her eyes, but the doctor found nothing." Brigitte's fingers glided another paper at Io, a medical report. "The doctor said it's stress, probably because of the new baby, and prescribed a very light sleeping tonic."

Io's gaze found Edei's. She had told him that in Tulip, the doctor had been a suspect because all the missing people had come in for headaches and eye issues. Torr fit the profile: one of three siblings, with similar medical issues, disappearing without a trace. Io had done a quick sweep of the mother's threads while she was in the kitchen; she had no thread to her daughter, even though it was obvious she loved her.

"Did Torr take the tonic?" Io asked, skimming the medical report.

"Just once," the woman said quietly. "She went missing the next day."

"Miss Vidal," Io said, "may I ask a sensitive question? You don't have to answer if you're not comfortable sharing, of course."

"Go ahead."

"Did you and your wife use the same donor for all three of your children? Is there any chance there is other-born blood in Torr's lineage?"

The woman frowned deeply. "Yes, we used the same donor. We requested a nonpowered donor, but you can never be entirely sure with that sort of thing. Me and Ola have no other-born in our families." A pause, then: "Why do you ask?"

"We believe," Edei replied, "that it's a possible connection between all the missing people. That they may have latent other-born powers."

Brigitte's eyes went glassy as she glanced between Edei and Io. "The headaches, the eye problems . . . you think those were related to latent powers?"

Io nodded. "Did Torr's eyes ever change color?"

"No, but—" The woman's eyes grew wide. "You need to get in touch with Seto Sarris-Nakano. His people were investigating the disappearances. He hired a geb-born and nut-born pair to study the earth and sky around the school grounds. They found no malicious intent, but with this new revelation, he'll no doubt ask them to look again."

Io frowned; she had heard the names before but wasn't certain what these gods' descendants could do.

Quietly, Edei provided, "Geb is the Sumazi god of earth and his sister, Nut, the goddess of the sky. Their descendants can interpret clues in the earth and sky. In my neighborhood in Suma, there was a geb-born who could predict earthquakes by watching the patterns of moving sand." He turned to Brigitte. "My apologies, Miss Vidal, but I think geb- and nut-born powers work best when the clues on the earth and sky are fresh. But we'd love to collaborate with Mr. Sarris-Nakano on this. The more hands we have on deck, the better."

"You can find him in the Oleander Club, on the other side of the district—"

Wailing burst out from the nursery.

Brigitte stood, rattling the tea set on the table. "Excuse me for a moment."

"Miss Vidal," Io asked before the woman disappeared into the room, "could we see Torr's room?"

"Of course. It's the one over there."

Io shot out of her chair, heading for the half-open door to Torr's room. "If there was no malicious intent in the geb-born's and nut-born's readings," she whispered to Edei, "that means that either her abductor wasn't malevolent or that Torr ran away."

"Her mothers say she wouldn't," Edei said, following her in.

"What do mothers know?" Io muttered, a little snappily, surprising even herself.

She paused and let herself feel: she had been getting increasingly irritated as Brigitte talked, but why? The way she had been describing Torr's day, the expectation that she would chip in with taking care of her brothers, all the little things she did during the day to parent them, the extra stress and headaches . . . it had sounded like *Thais's* life.

Io had few memories of her mother, like the sun-warm smell of her skin, her dark mop of curls, her fried tilapia dish, her arms full of flowers when she came back from work. She had no apparent reason to distrust mothers. But she also had a slew of images of Thais stark in her mind: Thais age twelve, being told to weave a thread to Sonya, her tutor, so that the old moira-born would teach Ava and Io without pay, and when she refused, having to teach them herself instead; Thais yawning over her own homework late at night after she had helped Io and Ava with theirs; Thais at seventeen, fresh out of school, having to hide her grief beneath a mask of composure as she faced the solicitors handling her parents' will. Thais tired, always tired, hissing at Io and Ava to be quiet while their parents slept.

But Brigitte wasn't Io's mother. Brigitte had taken Torr to the doctor to help with her headaches, Brigitte had been saving money to provide a better future for her children, Brigitte was stricken with worry and exhaustion and yet welcomed two strangers into her home in the hopes that they might find her daughter.

"Io?" Edei asked. He was watching her.

"I'm sorry," Io said aloud, even though only Edei was there to witness her baseless projection. "I was being unfair. The girl's disappearance is striking a nerve."

He nodded, as though it all made sense, and gestured to the room. "What am I looking for?"

Returning to the task at hand was a welcome relief. Io had been hired for a missing kid case back in Alante, one of her first jobs. A boy, barely a year younger than her, had disappeared—Io quickly realized he had run away, because his rain boots and coat were gone, even though it had been summer. "Look for any missing essentials: backpack, shoes, underwear, knickknacks you wouldn't part with."

The room was as neat and inviting as the rest of the house. Shelves loaded with books were stacked above the desk; soft, sweet-smelling pillows were plopped on the bed; a slew of toys towered in bins on one side of the room next to a crib, which must belong to the second-born, Mario. Io went to the wardrobe; Edei went to the desk.

"Anything?" he asked after a minute.

Io grunted *nuh-uh* through her nose. "What about you?"

"This looks odd," Edei said, pointing to the bookcase.

Io came to stand next to him. She caught a better sense of his smell now: lavender soap and the essential oils of his aftershave, bergamot and tangerine and something else. His finger rested between two books, where there was a gap in the series of worn and dog-eared mystery novels that Torr evidently loved. *The Mysteries of Thistle Manor* skipped from volume six to eight. And even more bizarrely, there was a visible absence of dust where volume seven should have been.

"Interesting," Io whispered. She took a step back and surveyed the room again.

There was a thin layer of dust everywhere: the bookshelves, the desk, the bedside table, the windowsill. There didn't seem to be anything else missing from the bookshelves, but when she crouched down by the bedside table, Io could make out the outline of a wristwatch that must have been removed recently. In the windowsill, dust lingered at the corners, but not in the center.

The window had no latch—it opened noiselessly when Io pushed it. She was instantly met by the heated, humid air of the Shards. The family's apartment was on the second floor of a stilt building. There was no way to reach this window from the ground, but one could certainly lower themself to the sill from the rooftop. Io could pinpoint a potential route: footholds on the planks sticking out, hands scaling along the drainpipe for balance, then right onto this windowsill.

"Look at that corner," Edei said from inside the room.

A glistening liquid had been scraped at the rim of the sill, the color of tar flecked with neon-cobalt specks. Io reached out and touched it—not exactly wet but not completely cakey, either. Someone had climbed on here, recently. She retreated back into the room and showed Edei the black-and-cobalt tip of her finger.

His response, bizarrely, was to sniff it. Almost immediately, his tongue stuck out in a comical gag. *"Aman,* that stinks."

Io sighed. Now she needed to take a whiff, too, and *gods,* it was just as horrific as Edei's reaction suggested.

"What the hell is that?" she hissed. "It smells like death."

"It smells like *old* death," said Edei, which made her raise an eyebrow at him.

He gestured with his chin out the window. The Shards stretched before her, a sea of mirrored rooftops, cliffed by the mud-stained wall of the City Proper—and the scaled carcass of Le Cauchemar. From this district, Io could see a part of the leviathan that she hadn't noticed before: a thick cluster of run-down scaffolding holding up a bulging growth where blackened flesh and neon-cobalt sinew still held on to the skeleton.

"It smells," Edei said, "like the Guts."

UNMOORED

THE SMELL WAS absolutely foul.

Io's fingers cupped her shirt over her nose as she scaled the steps carved on the leviathan's skeleton. The Guts loomed before her like an aggressive tumor growing out of the smooth stone of the Spined Wall. Le Cauchemar, Edei explained, was named after a local Nanzese myth: a nightmare spirit that sits on its victim's chest while they sleep, suffocating them. The leviathan had attacked at night; for hours, the residents of what would become Nanzy fought it in the pitch dark, until the cleverest among them devised a snare: they fed a large herd of oxen with poison and released it in the leviathan's lair. Within hours, the beast slumped dead, its warped body coiled around the settlement. The Spined Wall had been built on its remains.

Over the years, the locals had found a dozen different uses for its carcass: its tusks became jewels, its scales armor and weapons, its golden-veined skeleton support for their structures, its skin and entrails balloons for the floating slums around the city. Now, hundreds of years later, all that remained were its bones, sucked of marrow, and a bulb of blackened mass halfway up the Wall, where its belly used to be, charmingly called the Guts.

There was no electricity in the Guts, but Edei had bought a lantern and a very expensive scent-repellent mask from a vendor at the base of the skeleton stairs. It comprised two long, coarse pieces of canvas cloth, stitched together around a massive bundle of mint, sage, and rosemary, which worked to neutralize the rancid smell of the Guts.

"I don't understand how people live here," Io said as they reached the entrance, a mouth of rotting flesh propped open by slimy wooden pillars. Beyond it, the dark narrow tunnel consumed all light. The place would have been disgusting even without the reek: the walls were being held up by steel skeletons and wooden braces, and were very visibly made of rotting flesh, sagging beneath their touch, coated in a neon-cobalt layer of slime that looked downright toxic. A black liquid ran down the steps and platforms, making Io's shoes sticky and squelching with every step. Sound distorted, as though sucked by the membrane of the walls.

"People don't really live in the Guts," Edei explained. The tunnel was so low and narrow that he had to duck his head and keep his elbows close to his sides so as not to touch anything. "It's mostly scavengers and black market dealers who come here. There's something unnatural about this place. All year round, scavengers chip away at the flesh and grime, to use in medicine and beauty products, and yet the raw material never ends. It should all be marrowless bone by now, but miraculously, the Guts seem to be able to regenerate."

How damn creepy. A shudder scuttled up Io's nape. "It keeps getting better and better. What's next? Wait, I know. The slime on the walls is actually flesh-eating chimerini bacteria."

"Well . . ."

"No."

"The locals call them the Devouring Bile."

Io sucked in a hissy breath, pulling her arms to her chest—of all the times to wear a top and shorts! "Really?" she squealed. "And they eat flesh?"

Edei huffed a quiet laugh and glanced at her over his shoulder. The smirk on his lips was absolutely devious.

Understanding sank in, filling Io with instant relief. She smacked him lightly on the back. "That's not something to joke about, you demon!"

A proper laugh broke out of Edei's lips. "But your shocked face is adorable."

Io's cheeks went hot with embarrassment. Her heartbeat roared in her ears and throbbed in her neck—for a few seconds, she couldn't think properly. Edei had used the word "adorable" about *her*. Io felt as gooey and fluorescent as the slime around her.

Edei cleared his throat, a minuscule sound, then turned his back to her. Had she been staring too intently? Had she been quiet too long? He began moving again, down the tunnel, but Io remained still. The Quilt rose around her, spilling iridescent silver on the sleek black walls. The fate-thread was the first thing she saw, stretched taut from her chest to his back. This close, she could see its every detail: some of its shine had returned, thank the gods, but it was still tattering. Strands were sticking out of the thread, like split hairs.

Io's fingers closed around it, featherlight.

In front of her, Edei pulled to a stop. His shoulders moved in a shallow breath, then he turned toward her. "I haven't felt that in a long time."

"The pull of the fate-thread?" Io asked.

The lantern shadowed his eyes and brows, making his expression inscrutable, but his voice—it was whisper-soft. "Yes. Ever since that fortune-teller told me the fate-thread existed, I had a vague impression of it, of you. I could tell when you were near, and when we began working together, the sensation became even stronger. But when I woke up in the Fortuna Club after you left Alante . . . I could feel nothing, Io. I tried to follow it instinctively, as I had so many times before, but there was nothing there to guide me. I feared something had happened to you, I thought—"

He quieted and raised the lantern. Light slunk into the grooves of his face; he was looking at her clasped hand, suspended in midair between them, and the invisible thread in her fingers. "I thought," he said, "that you had cut it."

"I didn't," Io hurried to say. "I wouldn't."

His eyes found hers at last, his mouth forming an almost soundless "Oh?"

He was waiting for an explanation, but the right words couldn't come to Io. She knew Edei wasn't cruel. He wouldn't be standing before her, wide-eyed and soft-spoken, if he had decided the fatethread was not what he wanted. Perhaps he hadn't recognized this in himself yet, or he was trying to turn her down gently. Io had decided long ago that she would never lie to him. He was the one person who knew all her truths, even the darkest ones, and he would know this one, too. But she wanted to offer him a way out if that was what he craved.

"It has been different for me, too," Io said. "The fate-thread pointed east, toward Alante, when you have been here, in the west. Threads are not supposed to be unreliable. It can only mean that . . ." Gods, would the earth just open up and swallow her already? "That things have changed."

Edei's face remained smooth, carefully empty of emotion. "I see."

He did? Because Io herself didn't see, she didn't understand, and it was heartrending. "You do?"

"These are hard times. It's understandable if things have changed. If our feelings are different."

Our feelings. She had offered him a way out, and here Edei was, taking it. She should tell him her feelings hadn't changed, not in the slightest, not since she felt the fate-thread tug at her chest when he arrived in Alante three years ago, not since she met him and knew him and fell for him two months ago. But she could say nothing of the sort, because he wasn't talking about her, was he? He was talking about himself and trying to be polite about it, because he was the kindest person Io knew, even when he was breaking someone's heart.

"It's all good," he said, and now there was a distant smile on his lips, as composed and tactful as his voice.

All of a sudden, anger seized her. She wanted to shake him by the shoulders until he was senseless. What did he mean, *it's all good*? What an inane thing to say—

"We still make a good pair, you and I," he went on, oblivious to the turmoil in her head. "We're going to see this through to the very end."

Gods, was *that* what he was worried about? Working together and seeing this investigation to the end? A reaffirmation of his loyalty was very much not what Io needed right now. In fact, she had never heard anything more annoying in her life. She didn't want to be someone's *responsibility*; she had been Thais's all her life, and look where that got her. She wanted to be swept off her feet and kissed passionately under falling rain. She wanted the epic, fated love the threads had promised her.

No, she wasn't going to settle for lukewarm feelings any longer, begging for people's affection, fighting tooth and nail to be worthy of their love. Edei could take his *it's all good* and his *we still make a good pair* and shove it.

"Come on, then, *partner*," she said, with a profuse amount of sarcasm, and stepped around him, delving deeper into the belly of the rotting beast.

It took them a while to navigate through the maze of tunnels that made up the Guts, but at last, they arrived at a large cavern, propped up by beams and a domed structure of interlaced steelwork. People came and went through several side tunnels, stopping by makeshift scavenger stalls to browse their wares.

She and Edei had taken turns wearing the herb mask—right now, it was luckily Io's. Even so, she was envious of the scavengers' rain boots and protective gear, and their full-face masks connected to air tanks on their backs. Asking around, they were quickly directed to a man at the very back of the cavern, a scavenger named Alexei.

The man sat on a folding chair beneath a naked bulb hanging from a beam. Various jars and trinkets were laid on a thick canvas at his feet, and the arms of his chair were draped with masks similar to theirs. He was tinkering with an intricate apparatus of magnifying glass balanced on his round belly, but when Io and Edei approached, he paused and peered at them through the bronze-rimmed goggles of his face mask.

Edei extended the photograph. "We're looking for this girl."

The man peered at the photograph, then back up at Edei. His voice came out deep and hushed through his face mask. "You her family?"

"No, but we work for them," Io said. Not technically true, but honest in all the ways that mattered.

"I've seen her." Alexei paused and tapped one of his wares with his boot—a large cylinder filled with what looked like chunks of flesh floating in a neon yellow liquid. "I think you'll really like this one: pickled liver. It's good for stomach issues. Boil it in milk and drink it first thing in the morning."

Io ruffled in her pockets for five notes, the last dregs of her and Bianca's travel money, and placed the money on the lid of the pickled liver jar. She could recognize a request for a bribe when she saw one.

Alexei's eyes wrinkled, as though he was smiling beneath his mask. He pocketed the notes, leaned back into his chair, and said, "Ask away, my friends."

"Was she alone?"

"There was a woman with her. Dark haired, tattooed, very pretty. Neither talks to us."

"When did you first see them?"

"The woman has been coming and going for almost a month now. I first saw the girl about three weeks ago. They always appear through the north-bound tunnel over there."

"When did you see them last?"

"I saw the girl coming down this morning."

"Where are they going?"

Alexei shrugged. "To the slums, I gather."

"What's up there?" Edei gestured at the tunnel entrance Alexei had pointed to.

"Hell if I know. Tunnels up there are too tight for a man my size. But rumor is the northern branch leads to an opening through the Spined Wall, into the City Proper."

"How long is the girl usually here for?" Edei asked.

Leisurely, the scavenger tapped another jar with his other boot, this one packed with some kind of dried meat that had an other-worldly lime-green hue. "Amygdala preserves," he said. "Chew on them when you're hungover and you'll be in shape in minutes."

This time, it was Edei who pulled out five notes. He didn't bother to pretend to be buying; he placed into the man's waiting hand.

"Never long after nightfall," Alexei said meaningfully—it would be nightfall in less than half an hour. "There's a tiny cavern before the tunnel becomes too narrow to cross. You can wait for her there. But if she sees you, she's going to bolt, and boy, is she fast."

"How do *you* know?" Edei growled.

The scavenger shrugged.

Edei moved fast, grabbing a fistful of Alexei's lapel. With his other hand, he snatched a face mask from the arm of Alexei's chair.

"Hey!" the man crowed.

"I'd say we've paid enough for this," Edei said. "If I find out you've laid a hand on her, I'll come back for the rest."

Io hurried to follow him as he turned to the narrow entrance to the northern tunnel. She glanced over her shoulder; Alexei watched them, wearing a trouble-stirring scowl.

"Golden City, my ass," Edei murmured as he grabbed the cloth from Io and handed her the face mask. "Is there a single city-nation in the world where things are . . . good?"

"I very much doubt that," Io replied. She guided them to the entrance of the tunnel and took the lead, climbing at a sharp pace, mindless of the slime splashing the backs of her calves with every stomp of her boots.

For a long while, they scaled the tunnel in the oppressive silence of covert fury. Edei's was no doubt directed at the scavenger, and Io's . . .

It was strange, being angry at someone completely oblivious to it. They'd been in the Guts for close to fifteen minutes now, and she bet Edei had no clue that *it's all good* was playing like a broken record in Io's mind. She bet he would never even notice; Io wasn't very good with anger. She only knew how to withhold it, either until she burst out and said something mean, on very rare occasions and only to Ava, or until it simply fizzled out, unspoken and unacted on, in pretty much every other situation.

She could already feel it fizzling out. Anger was a clingy pet, in constant need of feeding and nuzzling. An all-around exhausting experience, a waste of time.

"I think this is it," she said when they came upon an opening in the tunnel. It could hardly be called an alcove, more like a bloated piece of bowel. But the two beams holding it up offered some cover from anyone coming up the tunnel. Io took one side, Edei the other.

She turned her gaze to the fluorescent cobalt slime slithering down the fleshy walls of the Guts. She was squatting, elbows on her knees, chin tucked in her palm; soon, her whole body would be cramping. She hoped Torr made an appearance soon. She hoped the girl was unharmed and that she could be returned to her mothers by nightfall.

A quiet sort of sadness squashed her chest. Io was used to patience, to steadiness, to deliberation. But in the span of one day, she had argued with Bianca, made an unfair comment about Brigitte, and was suddenly annoyed with Edei. Her emotions rattled in her chest like loose stones, a cacophony of disorder.

"What's wrong?" Edei whispered.

He was a human-shaped shadow against the black-and-blue tunnel, the lantern blown out and tucked by his legs. But the cadence of his voice was clear, his intentions as straightforward as ever: gentle, caring, a little shy.

Astonishment stilled Io into quietness. He had seen. He had noticed she was upset. She thought, *I have missed him.* She had missed the way he knew her but never judged her, the way he gave but never demanded anything in return. She had missed the way he cared, quiet and all-giving and always *there*.

"I just feel so disoriented, so in doubt of myself," she answered. "These last few weeks, my thoughts storm around my mind, all jumbled and pointless."

"I know what you mean. I've been feeling the same way. Like everything's changing, very fast—"

"Changing, yes, exactly."

"—and I don't have time to get used to one thing before the new one comes along. It's like I'm . . . what's that word, for when a boat is drifting in the sea?"

"Unmoored?"

"Unmoored," he confirmed.

"It's a good word."

Unmoored was what she felt, too. Wrestling waves on all sides, her only purpose to stay afloat instead of simply voyage. Anchorless in a sea of twists and revelations. Io's breaths slowed. She settled back into herself, freed of anger and melancholy. She was not alone in this; the relief was elating. Words formed on her lips—*how do you stop feeling unmoored?*—but they didn't feel right. She and Edei had shared how they felt. They had found some kinship in each other. They were not alone in this, and that was enough of a balm for now. Perhaps solutions could wait. Perhaps she should stay in this part— the sharing part, the feeling part—for a little longer. Io so rarely allowed herself the time to just . . . *be.*

Perhaps Edei was right: *it's all good.* As long as he was her partner, as long as he was her friend, it would all be good.

The sound of footsteps traveled up from the bottom of the tunnel.

Io widened her eyes at Edei. Soundlessly, they burrowed deeper into the shadows of the slime-filled alcove. The footsteps neared, squelching determinedly down the tunnel. Io could see a figure hued in the pink light of a lantern: black hair in a sharp bob framing upturned eyes that peeked over a half-face mask. Torr wore black dungarees, their legs rolled multiple times to reveal tall boots caked with the black tar of the Guts. She was carrying a packed messenger bag that clinked and clanged.

Io slipped into the Quilt, but thank the gods, Torr's life-thread sprang up to the sky, unharmed. There were other threads, as well, two of them. Thin, which could mean they were freshly woven. Back in Tulip, Hanne had cut all the boy's threads. And every other family Io visited today had no threads to the missing people. What had changed with Torr?

She had no time to ponder—the moment Torr stepped into the alcove, Edei gave Io a signal with his hand. They stepped out simultaneously, blocking both of the girl's escape routes.

Torr came to a stop, her eyes sweeping from Io to Edei.

"We're not here to hurt you," Io said quickly, putting her palms up. "Your mothers sent us. They're very worried, Torr. Whatever is going on, we can help you. Let us help you."

The girl's hazel eyes narrowed on Io's face. "I *have* help. I don't need you."

"Whose help?" Io asked. "Who's that woman that you've been seen with? Is she the one who kidnapped you? What is she making you do?"

The girl scoffed. "You don't know anything."

Of course Io didn't. That was the very reason she was here. "Then tell me—"

"It's not my job to tell you things," Torr hissed. Whatever was in her messenger bag rattled—it sounded like glass. "I don't know you; I don't trust you. I don't trust anyone. I should be at school. I should be having pizza with my friends. I should be playing with my brothers. But I couldn't stay, not with that creepy man stalking my house—"

"What man?" Edei asked, his voice lethally low.

"How should I know? He made a grab at me in the streets; he did something to me—it felt like he was cutting through my soul. I managed to escape and tried to get to my moms, but he was there when I reached home. He was waiting for me. So I turned around, and I've managed to evade him ever since. Like I said, I don't need your help." It all rushed out of her in a ferocious torrent. When it was done, the girl was panting, her chest rising and falling against the straps of her overalls. "Move out of my way."

"We can't," Io said. "Your mothers—"

"Tell my mothers—" The girl's face spasmed, her chin jutting out as if she was struggling to hold back tears. "Tell them I'll come back when it's safe."

Then she sprang, rushing at Io with her arm swung back. Io planted her feet on the ground and hoped her defense wouldn't hurt the kid. But instead of tackling Io, Torr simply swept her arm forward, her fist clenched as though gripping something invisible.

Too late, Io thought, *Other-born.*

Heat seared her skin; pain dug into the soft flesh of her throat. Torr brought her arm down—Io went tumbling. The fall reverberated through her palms as she clumsily caught herself before smacking face-first into the blackened ground.

But Torr had gotten what she wanted—an opening. She darted over Io's fallen body, the contents of her bag click-clacking. Io kicked her legs out, trying to trip the girl, but Torr easily jumped over them.

Her pink lantern swayed, spilling a kaleidoscope of light down the dark tunnel. She glanced back at them over her shoulder, her forehead glistening with sweat, her lips parted in a gasp, her eyes—

They blazed the orange of flames.

Torr was a true fury-born.

CHAPTER XIII

PEOPLE LIKE HER

IO LEAPT AFTER her.

The tunnel tapered threateningly around Io; she felt pressed on all sides, the incline so steep she had to drop on all fours to fit her body through. Her knees were covered in black-and-cobalt slime, and her breath came out hot and raspy, fogging her mask. But she was gaining ground on Torr—she could see the soles of the girl's boots now.

For a few minutes, they went on like that, crawling through the dark, moist tunnel of the Guts like a cat and mouse on a chase, then the walls opened up around them. Torr must have taken this route before, because suddenly she was dragging herself upright, setting the lantern aside, and grabbing for a rope with thick climbing knots for footholds. Up above, a cavity exposed the twinkling lights of the cityscape.

Io dashed for the swinging rope, but the moment she tested her weight on it, the rope slipped down a few inches. Torr, already a few feet above Io, gave out a shriek and hugged it tight.

A voice rang out, laced with panic. "Torr? What's going on?"

The young girl shouted, "Someone followed me! Pull me up!"

The person standing at the top of the opening lost no time. The rope began retracting, vibrating from the person's effort. Io let her fingers go slack around the rope, afraid that holding on would send Torr plummeting to the tar below. She stood there, in her fuming rage and bouncing adrenaline, and simply watched. In the Quilt,

Torr's threads were nowhere near Io. She was going to get away, and Io was going to let her, because anything else would put the girl's life at risk. Torr reached the narrow cavity, braced her legs along the walls, and hauled herself up.

Swift words were exchanged, then a face appeared.

Long dark curls swung in front of a face Io knew well: *Ava*. Her sister's features were bathed in the soft pink glow of the lantern now discarded near Io's feet. Shadows cloaked her skin, but Io could make out her eyes, so wide the whites were showing all around her irises.

Ava breathed—"Io?"

A small hand closed around Ava's bicep, and Torr's young voice came out shrill from somewhere out of sight. "Come on! We've got to go!"

Io didn't know what to think. Couldn't find something to say. Ava was right here, in Nanzy, with one of the very people Io had been looking for. Astonished and half-wild, she only gaped as Ava's face shifted from astonishment to determination. As her body lingered above the opening, just for a moment longer, then disappeared.

The rope tumbled down by Io's feet, like a viper coiled up.

On the slimy tar, something glimmered, left behind. A glass vial, filled with a neon blue liquid.

"Slow down," Edei rasped, practically jogging to keep up with her.

Nightfall hadn't changed the Shards much—the streets were still wobbly; the passersby still hurried, the mud-tide still reaching for their ankles between the planks—but now the whole slums were elevated, a good twenty feet closer to the top of the wall. The golden shimmer of the City Proper was even brighter at night, spotlights roaming the sky, garlands decorating the spine of the leviathan.

Beneath it, the Shards were an imitation, swathed in neon signs and bobbing lanterns of all colors. Io and Edei were marching through the Glade District, mob king Haru Sarris-Nakano's turf. It had the features of the beating heart of any city or slum: bars, clubs, gambling dens, and dream palaces were strung up in stilt buildings stacked on top of each other. The scent of cheap beer and piss was strong enough to almost drown out the stink of the Guts clinging to Io's and Edei's clothes.

"Io, *slow down*," Edei said for what felt like the tenth time. "First of all, you're drawing attention to us. And secondly, we need to talk about this."

"Talk about what."

"Well, the girl, for starters. Her eyes were *orange*. And she didn't look like a wraith. Could she really be a true fury-born? I thought their line died in the Moonset Riots."

"Apparently not." Gods, she was being snappy again. She stuck out an arm to draw Edei aside as a group of rowdy drunks ran past, laughter trailing after them. In a calmer tone, she said, "At the House of Nine, Thais said that the gods tasked her with creating the wraiths to avenge the fury-born and restore order. She said the gods promised her that's how the fury-born line could begin anew."

"But that's not how other-born powers work, is it? They don't just come into being because order needs to be restored or whatnot. It's about *family*—your ancestors and your siblings?"

Io gave a sharp nod, then launched down the street again. "I know it doesn't make sense, Edei. But we both saw Torr's eyes. I felt her whip around my throat. She is a real fury-born. I suspect they might *all* be fury-born."

"The missing people?" Edei asked, then: "Gods, you're right. The headaches, the sight problems, the trio of siblings—it all lines up. But why are the gods abducting fury-born?"

Io's jaw clenched. "I think—I think they want their army back."

Twelve years ago, the gods had directed the fury-born to attack other-born leaders across the world for some reason Io had yet to uncover. The carnage had led to the Nine conspiring with Bianca Rossi to eliminate the fury-born, under the guise of the Moonset Riots. But now the Nine were no more. Bianca Rossi was slowly dying. The wraiths had attacked the other-born leaders of every city-nation. The line of the fury-born had been resurrected. It only made sense that the gods were picking up right where they left off twelve years ago.

Io cut a sharp turn left, hopped across a floating bridge, and hurried down the main street. She could see the neon sign now, pulsing hot pink atop a run-down wooden house. SALAMANDER'S, the sign said, framed by cocktail glasses with little umbrellas.

"Io," Edei breathed. "Io, will you stop for a moment?"

His fingers hooked into her elbow. Io let him turn her around, clasp her shoulders. His eyes were wide with panic, and Io got that panic, she even *shared* it, but there really was no time for them to break down right now.

"If the gods are building an army now," Edei said, "if they're attacking every powerful other-born in the world, it's because they are preparing for *war*. A war that started twelve years ago. We can't keep following one clue to another—it is pointless if we don't understand what their motive is. We need to think this through. Nico and Urania will be back in the hotel room, probably Bianca, too—we need to regroup and discuss our next steps. We can't just go marching into—"

Rage coursed hot and fiery through Io's body. To hell with slowing down, to hell with keeping a low profile, to hell with regrouping and discussing. It was better to strike when the iron was hot, and oh, was the iron blistering right now.

With all the composure she could muster, Io said, "Edei. It was *Ava.*"

Concern burdened his brow. His fingers on her shoulders loosened, trailing down to her wrists. "I know, but—"

"No, you don't know," Io said. "Ava is here, in Nanzy, but her thread is pointing north, toward Jhorr. It has pointed north since we left Alante. That means Ava drew our thread out. She purposefully elongated it and laid it out to point in a different direction, because *she didn't want me to find her,* Edei. And just half an hour ago, I *did* find her, albeit accidentally. What do you think Ava's going to do now?"

Edei didn't even hesitate. "She's going to flee."

"Or at the very least," Io said, "cover her tracks and go into hiding. So, there's no time to slow down. It's got to be now, and it's got to be fast."

"Okay." His fingers slipped into Io's palms; he squeezed. "Okay, let's do this. But, Io, do you really think Ava is involved in the abductions? She's a good person; she wouldn't steal a twelve-year-old girl from her family."

Io glanced down at their clasped hands, at Edei's thumbs running circles on the back of her palms. She broke the touch and pulled out the vial from her pocket. Neon blue swirled inside the glass. Io had recognized it instantly: it was the blue of a sleeping tonic, just like the one Bianca used to dull her fury-born's bloodthirst.

"If Ava's not involved with the abducted fury-born," Io breathed, "why was Torr carrying a bag of this for her, Edei?"

"But would a true fury-born need the tonic?" he countered. "Torr said she escaped her abductor and chose to stay away from her

143

family of her own free will. She said someone was helping her—and then Ava appeared."

"We can't be sure," Io said. "Not until we know why she was carrying *this*."

Edei threw a glance at Salamander's and heaved a breath through his nose. "All right, then. Let's do this."

The steps groaned in protest as he climbed up and threw the doors of Salamander's open. The dream palace was a downgrade from what Io was used to. Unlike the spacious, velvet-draped luxury of the palaces on Lilac Row back in Alante, this one was all mismatched furniture, peeling floral wallpaper, and chandeliers with busted bulbs. That was the cost of building an entire city on a bog: you had to forgo beauty.

Some things, however, were irreplaceable—like the animal masks that all palace workers wore. The one in question was a young man with a stubby goatee, sporting a swan mask and a vest and suit shorts in a lovely shade of olive, a walking stick in his right hand.

"I'm Nautilus," the oneiroi-born said, "and I'll be your guide on this ethereal journey."

Io plastered a smile on her lips. "Hi, Nautilus. Can I ask, is this one of yours? My friend gifted it to me, and it's by far the best tonic I've taken. I slept like a baby!"

"That good, huh? You'll have to hand it over, darling." He extended a palm, and Io dropped the vial in it. Nautilus traced its bottom with his fingertips. "Oh, yes, it's one of ours. Notice that *SAL* engraved at the bottom?"

Io had, indeed, noticed the *SAL*, and asked around for a dream palace of that name the moment she had stepped out of the Guts. "Oh, that's wonderful! Could I get some more of it?"

"Of course. We have an excellent collection to choose from. You sure you don't want a sleeping session in our premises? You and your"—the man gestured in Edei's direction— "*friend* can have the regulars' discount. Two for one."

"That sounds great," Io quipped, "but alas, we barely have enough notes for the tonic."

Nautilus gave them a respectful bow of his head and led them down a narrow hallway. Io realized he was blind, or perhaps partially sighted, as he used his walking stick to navigate through the space. Several kinds of other-born powers relied on sight, like the moira-born, but low vision didn't limit them. It was likely that Nautilus applied his other senses to use his skills as an oneiroi-born, gifted with control over dreams.

"Forgive me for saying so," Nautilus commented, "but you two smell . . . *funny*."

Io and Edei exchanged an alarmed glance.

"It's our first time in the Shards," Io replied quickly, "and we're not quite used to the floating streets just yet. I'm afraid Edei here slipped and got properly dunked in mud-water."

Edei rightly gave her a flat look.

"Ah, you poor thing!" Nautilus said. "Where are you two from? Your accent is so lovely."

"Clyde," Io replied, sticking to her old, familiar lie. "Are you from the Shards?"

"Born and raised, darling! Ain't no place as glamorous, don't you think?"

Io definitely didn't but spat out a generous "Oh, yes" for the sake of small talk.

This part of Salamander's was even more derelict. The paint on the wall had chipped in myriad little places, and the floorboards beneath their feet were a squishy kind of wet. There must have been a leak somewhere in the building, quietly depositing mud-tide water right through the floor.

"Do you have a lot of regulars here?" she asked, careful to keep her voice neutral.

"Oh, yes, hundreds. Sleepers come to Salamander's for *quality*."

Quality? In this dump? Gods. "So my friend . . ." Io went on, dripping her voice with worry. "She brought me the tonic as a gift because she knows I suffer from night terrors, but I'm concerned she's a little young to be hanging out at dream palaces. She's about twelve, kind of a big mouth?"

"Oh, I know her!" Nautilus said. "Don't you worry about Torr. She just picks up her sister's weekly order and leaves without even entering the building. We would never sell to a child! Salamander's is a respectable business."

Io forced a bubbly yelp of excitement through her throat. "Gods, her sister! I haven't seen her in ages. How is she? I remember she had the loveliest voice."

"Amazing voice," Nautilus agreed, "and she's well, I think. She hasn't stopped by in a while."

At the end of the corridor, the oneiroi-born threw open a door and crossed a sketchy-looking set of floating steps and entered into the building across the canal. Io exchanged a glance with Edei—where exactly was the man taking them?—but Nautilus was already holding the door open for them on the other side. Io could see rows of shelves in the room, packed to the brim with tonics in all shades of blue and green. With a sigh, she stepped onto the floating bridge, felt it quiver beneath her foot, then leapt the rest of the way as fast as she could.

In the storeroom, the oneiroi-born had his back turned, skimming vial labels with a finger. "Take a seat. It might take me a moment to find the one you liked so much."

Io obliged, plopping down on the ramshackle sofa by the door. The room must have belonged to a club of some kind; fast-beat music was coming through the walls, and the ceiling was vibrating with the stomping of feet. The light fixture swung slightly, like a grandfather clock with the chills.

Seated next to her, Edei leaned his elbows on his knees and raised his eyebrows. "I'm impressed," he whispered. "You're very good at this."

"Lying?" Io whispered back. "Another glowing compliment from Edei Rhuna."

He instantly went pink, which made her smile furiously. "I didn't mean—oh. You're teasing," he said around a laugh.

"Sorry?" Nautilus asked, twisting his head toward them.

"We were just saying," Io ventured, smothering her smile, "what might be wrong with her, our friend's sister. A weekly order of sleeping tonic is far too much for one person . . ." She trailed off, hoping the oneiroi-born would take the bait.

He did, in less than two seconds. "You know, I've been wondering that, too. But it's not an oneiroi-born's job to question the dreams of his sleepers."

That was some top-tier mumbo jumbo, but Io could still turn this around. "But is it safe," she asked, "you know, for people like her?"

She was fishing. "People like her" could mean anything. The words were open to interpretation; Io was hoping Nautilus would just fill in the blank with the information he believed Io also knew.

Indeed, the oneiroi-born wagged a finger. "You know what, I've thought about that, too. It's fine for office clerks to be addicted to our tonics, no harm done, but a fancy tram driver in the City Proper? That could prove deadly, quite fast—but as I said, I'm not one to snoop."

Gotcha.

"Listen, darlings," Nautilus went on, "it looks like I'm out of stock on your particular tonic. Will you give me a minute to check if we've got any upstairs?"

"Sure thing," Io chirped. She was basically vibrating with excitement.

She tracked the oneiroi-born's movements as he crossed the room and disappeared through a door to the club beyond.

The moment he was gone, she turned to Edei. "How about now? Even more impressed?"

He breathed a chuckle. "As impressed as a man can be. So, your sister's working as a tram driver in the City Proper?"

Io shook her head. "Unlikely; she doesn't even have a driver's license. But Nautilus must have a reason to think that. She could have told him she's a driver, or maybe she had a driver's papers? Regardless, we have somewhere to start now."

I'll find her, Io thought. She would find Ava and demand answers. The fury she felt was almost shameful. She didn't want to feel that way about her sister. Once, Ava had been Io's favorite person in the world, but change had ruined that, too. Because Bianca was right: Ava *had* abandoned Io back in Alante. She had drawn out their thread to keep Io away. Io had every right to be angry.

The door creaked open again; Io's and Edei's heads swung in that direction, words already forming on Io's lips. "That was fast—"

But it wasn't the oneiroi-born standing in the door.

Five guards spilled in the room, carrying guns rimmed with gold.

CHAPTER XIV

ROOSTER'S WATTLE

THE MOB KINGS of the Shards had dealt with moira-born before.

Io's fingers were forced into fists and clasped in iron gloves that had been designed specifically to nullify her powers. Knuckles were etched into the metal, the inside inlaid with stubby spikes. There was no wiggle room, no way to touch the threads of the Quilt. The cold, heavy cuffs pulled on her arms, making her slouch as she stood rigidly in the middle of the office.

That's them, isn't it, boss? I smelled the Guts on them, Nautilus had told the mob kings' lackeys as they dragged Io and Edei farther into the Oleander Club, the building the oneiroi-born had tricked them into. The office overlooked the dance floor; all walls were sound-proof windows tinted black, the only evidence of the party raging below the vibrations of the glass. A dark green moquette covered the entirety of the floor. The furniture was modern and stylish: a huge glass desk, a short, white sofa, and matching armchairs, four narrow floor lamps in each corner of the room.

When Io and Edei were brought in, their friends were already seated. Urania perched on the white sofa. Nico was next to her, stooping uncomfortably with his hands cuffed behind his back. Two guards held Bianca's shoulders, keeping her down in one of the armchairs. Her hands were in other-born manacles identical to Io's; her mouth was gagged.

This ambush was well-planned and finely executed—it made Io all the more nervous. Her eyes traced the room: only one exit, the door she had come in. She doubted the windows were breakable, but even if it were, it was a good twenty-foot drop to the dance floor below. There were nine guards in total in the room, all clad in long black robes and carrying the golden-handled guns of the Sarris-Nakano mob.

Only one other person was seated, in an armchair by the big desk. His dark blue suit jacket was folded nearly over his lap. His tie ran a smooth, straight line from his neck to his abdomen. Metal frames supporting his legs peeked beneath the fabric of his suit pants; two walking crutches leaned against the desk at his left. He was tall and square shouldered, his graying hair neatly combed, his skin luminous and clean shaven—Io would mistake him for a simple businessman were it not for the scraggly scar running from his hairline to his lip.

"Do you know my name?" the man asked.

Io didn't, but she could take a guess: his face carried some of his Iyen heritage in his features, and there was only one family of mob royalty in the Shards. She said, "You're a Sarris-Nakano brother."

"Seto Sarris-Nakano," Edei supplied. "Second oldest of your erotes-born brothers. Mob king of the Moor District. What is this, exactly, sir?" Edei's hands, too, had been bound behind his back, but there was an unmistakable shade of authority in his voice.

Seto Sarris-Nakano studied him with calm, inquisitive eyes. "And you are Edei Rhuna, current mob king of the Silts." His gaze transferred to the sofa. "Your associate, Nico Petrelli. Urania of the Nine, Muse of astronomy. And of course, Bianca Rossi, former mob queen of the Silts. But you," he said finally, to Io, "are somewhat of a mystery."

Io very much doubted that. It was apparent he knew *what* she was—the gloves around her fists were proof enough. Seto's calm voice, his neutral face, his curious eyes: they were hypocritical. He had brought them all here in *chains*.

Io inhaled and exhaled slowly, counting the seconds. She had to get everyone out of here—she felt it urgently, in the pit of her stomach and the stiffness of her spine. They were her responsibility, because she was a cutter, powerful and deadly, and because she was the one whose choices had led them all to this, cuffed and guarded before the most powerful mob king in the world. If she couldn't use her powers, wits it would have to be.

She threw her shoulders back and said, in a nasal drawl, "My name is Io Ora. I'm a private detective in Alante, and a moira-born, but I believe you know that. You did, after all, tell your people to flag all moira-born at entry. We are all busy people here, so let's cut straight to the chase, shall we? What do you want from us?"

Seto wasn't riled in the slightest. He regarded her with his dignified gaze and said, "I would like to know, Io Ora, why you're harboring the woman who slaughtered the Nine, and why exactly I found her asking around about *my* family."

That took Io aback. She had been expecting this to be about *her*—it was her kind the border patrol was flagging on entry, which she had assumed had to do with Hanne alerting the gods that Io was still on their tail. But the mob king seemed more interested in Bianca. The fact alone that he knew the truth behind the murders of the Nine meant he had gone looking for them in particular, since Bianca's involvement hadn't been broadcast anywhere public. He even brought them all here, to his office, to interrogate them himself. Mob kings didn't stoop to interrogations when there were a hundred gang members to do it for them. It meant that Seto was invested in this *personally*, somehow.

Io's mind jumped back to this morning, standing in line at border control. *We've heard no news of assassinations in Nanzy,* the mob queen had said. *Strange, isn't it?* Had Bianca spent her day investigating these suspicions? What sort of answers was she seeking that Seto didn't want unearthed?

"Mr. Sarris-Nakano," Io asked, "were you ever attacked by a threadless assassin?"

She watched closely for Seto's reaction. There was no shift in his tranquil features, but the strongarm behind his shoulder, the oldest out of all the black-robed guards, shifted on his feet, casting a sideways glance at his boss.

Now they were getting somewhere. Io went on. "Or your family, perhaps?"

The strongarm's hand moved through a slit in his robes to the holster of his gun—Seto's brothers, then, Io deduced. A wraith had likely killed one of Seto's brothers.

"Sir," she said, softening her tone, "the assassin who hurt your family is probably dead. Without a life-thread, they couldn't have lasted more than a week. If you'd like, I can help you look for them, but you must understand we had nothing to do with—"

"A week, you say," Seto interrupted. "And yet, here is Bianca Rossi, who by all accounts became a wraith six weeks ago, still alive. Here you are, the private investigator who helped put her behind bars, pleading for her life. Here is Urania of the Nine, whose sisters died at Miss Rossi's hand, traveling with her. I think it's best you stop asking the questions, Miss Ora, and start answering them."

Oh, he would be a hard one to crack. "What would you like to ask me?"

Seto didn't miss a beat. "How are you keeping her alive?"

"I'm not—"

"I would prefer it if you didn't lie, Miss Ora," Seto said. "My guards are kurbantes-born."

The Kurbantes were Kurkz gods: nine brothers who wielded ferocious powers through dancing. Their descendants could create illusions or enhance their physical skills by stamping their feet and twirling to a unique drumming beat. Io had never encountered kurbantes-born before, but Ava had in one of her music seminars; she had said their dancing was the most magical performance she had ever seen. Io's eyes trailed from one guard to the next. They had the same tan skin, short foreheads, and silky black hair, all roughly in their late thirties, in black robes of various fabrics and designs.

"I can extract the truth from you with their help," Seto continued, "but I would prefer not to. It would be a waste of time, and as you said, we are all very busy people."

A straightforward threat, shaped into pretty words. On Io's right side, Edei was brimming with tension; his body was stiff, his breaths coming out in short stabs. But not even all four of Io's friends together could take on the kurbantes-born. The truth it would have to be.

"We're not entirely sure why Bianca has survived so long," Io answered the mob king. "It might be that she was already a keres-born when she was turned into a wraith. For a while, she could access both powers. It might be that she's been self-medicating with sleeping tonics."

Seto nodded to the kurbantes-born standing behind him, who reached into his robes and produced a vial. Neon blue sleeping tonic swirled inside it; it was the same vial Nautilus had taken from Io just minutes ago.

The mob king held it between thumb and forefinger. "A scavenger was kind enough to alert me that two Alantians had been snooping in the northern tunnel of the Guts today, in search of a girl. He said that when they returned, they were whispering furiously over *this*."

Io schooled her features into indifference. They had really been digging their own graves with this investigation, first by trusting that scumbag Alexei, then by following Nautilus into this trap. And she feared that these weren't the only clues Seto had stacked up against them; any good investigator would have staked out their suspects a little longer, hoping to catch them red-handed. There must be something more, something he wasn't saying. Io decided to let the silence lengthen.

After a long minute, Seto spoke again. "The northern tunnel, Miss Ora, was where the wraiths who attacked my family were last seen, six weeks ago."

Io saw the story taking shape. The gods had sent the wraiths to the Shards to kill Seto and his brothers. They'd succeeded—to what extent, Io didn't know yet. Then the gods had sent Ava to retrieve the wraiths through the northern tunnel and bring them back into the City Proper. The gods must have reached the same conclusion Bianca had, that the sleeping tonic could dull the wraiths' blood-thirst. Ava was using Torr, an inconspicuous young girl, to bring in fresh supplies from the Shards. But there was a missing link here. What reason did Torr have to obey Ava? What did any of this have to do with the man who had tried to kidnap the girl, with Hanne and her network collecting true fury-born all around the Waste-lands? Did Seto even know about the fury-born, about the gods?

"Your records must show that we have just arrived in Nanzy this morning," Io told the mob king, "so what exactly are you accusing us of?"

A hustle broke out to Io's left. The two kurbantes-born hold-ing Bianca in the armchair were suddenly thrown against the wall behind them as the mob queen jerked their hands off her shoulders and stood. Using her wrist, she slipped the gag from her mouth and snarled—"He thinks that I've come to finish the job. Because he's the only Sarris-Nakano left, aren't you?"

Her head cocked in that dangerous way of hers. The guards clasped her arms, forcing her back into the armchair, but Bianca wasn't done.

"I've been asking around," she said. "No one has seen your brothers in weeks. Rumors have been circulating that they have abandoned Nanzy to lie low in your safehouses in the Wastelands. But I don't think the mob kings of the Shards would just abandon their turf. I think you're trying to keep their deaths under wraps, to avoid the fearmongering and rioting that all the other city-nations have fallen prey to."

Seto ran a hand over his jacket. "You of all people, Miss Rossi, must understand the necessity of order, whatever the cost might be."

"Oh, believe me, I do," Bianca said. "What I don't understand is why you're looking for the wraiths, when we both know they are mere weapons. It's the hand that wields them that you should be after."

The mob king leveled a calculating look at Bianca. "I feel like you're leading up to a proposition for me, Miss Rossi."

"Yes." Bianca pushed against the kurbantes-born's hold, the stringy strands of her blond hair swooping in front of her face. "Tell us why the Order of the Furies attacked every other-born leader twelve years ago. And then we will help you find those who sent the fury-born—and kill them."

It was a gamble on Bianca's part. It would only work if the Sarris-Nakano brothers were a part of the mayhem twelve years ago, if they knew someone had been puppeteering the Order of the Furies, if they were as afraid of them as the Nine had been. It hadn't escaped Io's notice that Bianca hadn't explicitly mentioned the gods. She was fishing, just like she had watched Io do dozens of times on the road.

"The fury-born?" Seto repeated. His eyes became sharp arrows, piercing them each in turn. Io couldn't decipher the intensity of his gaze—surprised? Suspicious? "You think you know what the fury-born did twelve years ago, Miss Rossi?"

"Why don't you enlighten me?" Bianca replied without missing a beat.

"You know I can't do that."

"Ah, yes," Bianca drawled. "The Roosters' Silence. I've always wondered who invented the Silence. The threat of a rooster's wattle was a nice touch. Was it you, boss?"

The Roosters' Silence was the vow that everyone involved in the end of the line of the fury-born had taken. They vowed to never mention what really happened during the Moonset Riots, how the Nine and Bianca conspired to slaughter the entire Order of the Furies that had been terrorizing the world with unjust and targeted executions. The rooster's wattle was what happened to you if you ratted them out: your throat was sliced, your larynx ripped out to hang from your flesh like a bright red wattle.

Seto said nothing. He went on looking at the mob queen, his fingers twined over his crossed legs. Bianca's riling up wouldn't work; he was far too collected, too methodical to let a secret as big as this one just slip out. No, they needed to pull the truth out, with violence and brute force, like a rotten tooth from a fighting patient's mouth.

"But you were there," Io said. "You could tell us, if you wanted."

Seto's silence was answer enough.

Io turned to Urania, sitting at the edge of the sofa. The tendons of her neck were prominent, bulging with barely constrained panic.

She was the only one of them still unbound, perhaps out of reverence to what she and her sisters had been, perhaps because her powers were nonthreatening. It was the mob king's only mistake.

Her skills could tip this interrogation to their advantage. Io's mind went back to their conversation earlier today, when Urania had admitted she could only inspire an artist with a personal connection to the subject to be created. Well, here the artist was: the kurbantes-born dancers. And here was the personal connection: if Seto had been there, then it was likely his guards had, too, judging from their age.

"Urania," Io said. All eyes in the room swung to the young Muse. *"Inspire them."*

For a few moments, there was only confusion on the Muse's lifted eyebrows and half-open mouth. A tall kurbantes-born behind Urania stepped forward, her hand reaching for the Muse; Seto made to leap out of his chair; then Urania's gaze locked on Io's with sudden clarity.

Her eyes flared indigo blue.

The hulking kurbantes-born sister trying to grab Urania moved first. Her foot began tapping a rhythm against the floor, soft and muffled against the moquette. Within seconds, the guards on either side of her picked up the beat, clapping or slapping their palms against their chests. All nine of them shifted through the furniture, coalescing in the middle of the room. Io and Edei stepped back as the kurbantes-born formed a tight circle. They began dancing, their loose black robes flapping like the wings of a raven. Their legs and arms swung in tandem, nine bodies coming together into a single form.

An illusion was being spun into place. It started from their stomping feet and traveled up their legs. Another layer of reality draped over their bodies, like acrylic paint coating a charcoal sketch. Io felt entranced, transcendental; she wasn't looking at the nine dark-haired siblings any longer, but a mass of people of all races and genders, packed into a large auditorium.

There was no sound, but their gestures were full of tension and argument. Figures dressed in pure white stood up, taking over the conversation and coming out victorious. The illusion cast them in warm light, as if the sun itself was blazing through them.

The scene wavered and resettled: a dark windowless room, with two factions placed in opposition, the white-clad figures on one side and the Sarris-Nakano brothers on the other. One looked like Seto; he was younger, but the same scar ran over his face. The kurbantes-born's dance became frenetic, heightening the illusion around it. More and more people joined the brothers' side, a great crowd pressing closer to the figures clad in white—when suddenly, the mob kings and their allies were thrown back, as though a gust of wind had blown them off their feet.

The illusion displayed a tidal wave, a raging storm, shaking earth. The Sarris-Nakano faction was flattened against the floor. They got up and tried again, but their bodies met resistance until the oldest among Seto's brothers was able to place one foot in front of the other. Slowly, meticulously, he came to stand face-to-face with the white-clad figures.

The scene changed again. A new figure stepped into the center of the room. A bright orange whip hung from their hand—it wrapped around the neck of the mob king, who fell on the floor, writhing. Other figures with blood-orange whips formed a line before the leaders clad in white, but as they made to reach for the Sarris-Nakano brothers and their allies, their heads were thrown back in agony. The whip-wielders collapsed on their knees, then facedown on the carpet.

The only dancer left standing was the one wearing young Seto's face. He knelt by his brother's side as he drew his final breaths. The kurbantes-born's drumming beat became slow, mournful—

"Enough!"

Io turned. The real Seto was standing, leaning on a crutch. His face was lined with rage as he looked down at his younger self mourning his brother's corpse. With half a stride, he smacked his crutch against the side of the sofa. The sound or the jolt must have startled Urania; the indigo snapped out of her eyes. The illusion collapsed.

The room filled with the sound of panting as the kurbantes-born picked themselves off the floor. The dancer who had been playing young Seto was the oldest sibling, who had stood behind Seto. At his boss's infuriated gaze, the man dragged himself across the moquette to Seto's feet and slipped a knife out of his black robes.

"Forgive me," the kurbantes-born said, placing the knife at his own throat.

Seto moved fast—he grabbed the man's wrist just before he could slice himself.

"No," the mob king of the Shards said. There was anguish in his furrowed brow, defeat in his quiet voice. "No more rooster's wattle. No more Roosters' Silence."

CHAPTER XV

THE GREAT TIDE

A PLEADING TERROR spilled from Urania's lips—*"No, no, no."*

"It's all right," Nico whispered, instantly scooting closer to her. "He won't hurt you. It's all—"

"You don't understand," Urania whispered through her palm. "The g-group in white—that's the Agora. That's how th-they dress."

"The *Agora*?" Bianca said, voice shrill with incredulousness. "It can't be the Agora. They're . . ."

"Harmless?" Seto provided.

But the Agora *were* harmless. They were the sage mothers of the other-born community: benevolent, sheltering, advice-giving. They were composed of horae-born, descendants of the gods of time. Their powers imbued them with knowledge of the past, present, and future. In Io's experience, they held a kind of ceremonial role: they issued extreme-weather alerts and chimerini swarm warnings based on their readings of the future, they consulted on the placement of new settlements and the trajectory of businesses depending on their knowledge of the present, they advised on disputes and war by reminding people of the sins of their past. They made the trivial, everyday decisions associated with running the other-born population of the world—they didn't *arrange mass assassinations*.

"Sir." The oldest kurbantes-born rose from the floor and helped his boss back to his chair. "They have seen our illusion, but they know nothing yet. Give us the order and we'll make sure none of it ever leaves this room."

He meant none of *them* ever leaves this room. Io's heart rioted in her chest. There was no escape—if Seto gave the order, there was nothing she could do to save herself and her friends. She watched with her breath held as Seto settled back into his chair, deposited his crutch at his side, and gazed down at his guard's dagger. A detached sort of astonishment had settled on his features.

His eyes were glassed over when he spoke. "There will be no need for that, Emir. The Silence is broken. I will explain what I know, and in turn, they will explain what they know—isn't that right, Miss Rossi?"

Bianca nodded, almost comically fast.

"The first scene you saw in my team's illusion was the negotiations of the Kinship Treaty," Seto started. "After weeks of infighting among other-born, the Agora was formed. It comprised solely horae-born, a temporary solution because their kind were the only other-born the human delegation found nonthreatening and benevolent. Their knowledge of past, present, and future made them powerful orators. As you may know, they negotiated the recognition of other-born rights that is still in effect today."

Neon headlights had been turned on in the nightclub below, washing the room in muted colors. The kurbantes-born had stumbled back to their positions along the walls of the room. Seto's gaze lingered on Urania, whose face had collapsed into her palms.

"The second scene you saw was decades after the Kinship Treaty, fifteen years ago. By that point, the Agora had been ruling for nearly half a century. Their rule was just, prosperous even. But they were supposed to be a temporary solution. The horae-born were supposed to step down and reallocate their seats. My older brother Hinata began advocating for elections to ensure a governing body made up of representatives for every kind of other-born.

"Lots of other-born shared his opinion. Within months, our co-alition had two hundred members and a long list of demands. We began planning in earnest. If the horae-born were unwilling to step down, then we would form our own governing body, one chosen by the people and for the people. But strange things began happening, interrupting our meetings or setting our plans a few steps back. It was small things at first: floods, acid storms, icebergs reigniting the Wars, our allies suddenly changing their minds. Until Little Iy."

Little Iy, Io recalled, had been an island off the coast of the city-nation of Iyen on the southern continent. It had boasted a population as big as Iyen itself, but thirteen years ago, it had been swallowed by a tsunami wave in what was later called the Great Southern Tide.

There had been several Great Tides throughout the centuries, strange occurrences where mountainous waves appeared out of no-where, taking out entire cities with no warning and no explanation that scientists could provide. The Tides were why most of the popu-lation had migrated away from the coastline, settling farther inland in cities like Nanzy and Kurkz.

"That wind we saw," Bianca asked Seto. "That was the Great Tide?"

"Yes," said the mob king. "Little Iy was to be the setting of the first all-member meeting of our coalition, held in our family's estate. We were going to establish an assembly, allocate duties, coordinate on a common policy across all city-nations. Three days before my brothers and I were due to arrive, the Great Tide wiped out the entire island."

He paused, the silence heavy and forlorn. Io couldn't wrap her mind around it. The Tide hitting the island three days before the meeting couldn't be a coincidence. Yet the alternative was impos-sible: gods who could control the Great Tide? Who could send floods and acid storms, cause icebergs to reemerge, and alter people's minds? That kind of power was unfathomable.

"The third scene you saw was after we had returned to Nanzy with a new purpose. Hinata believed—and most of us agreed—that the Agora had intentionally not warned us about the arrival of the Great Tide. We began digging into their past, established surveillance on them, investigated their members. But there was nothing to find. The Agora have always worked autonomously and in absolute secrecy. Their members use aliases. They never discuss their past or display their powers in the presence of others. To this day, we don't know the color of their eyes while they're using their powers.

"But it didn't matter. We began meeting again and formed a new plan: to go public with our coalition at the Mayoral Assembly at Jhorr. We were hoping both the Mayors and the public would see the reason behind a governing body composed of a variety of other-born. We had proposals in place that would benefit the entire population, not just us other-born. We were holed up in cheap hotels all around the city, dozens of us, including me and my brothers." Seto's lids fluttered shut. "We heard screaming from Hinata's room upstairs. When I opened the door, I found a fury-born standing over Hinata. She snapped his neck and escaped through the balcony."

Io thought of the scene she had just watched in the illusion. Seto on his knees by his brother's side, the slow, despondent drum of the kurbantes-born beat.

"Within minutes, we got reports from our coalition: every hotel had been attacked by fury-born. Most of our leading members were dead. We sent out a warning to the rest of our coalition. To your sisters," Seto gently said to Urania. "The Moonset Riots began a week after that.

"Our coalition eventually dissolved. Our surviving members—myself, the Nine, the æsir-born of Jhorr—have been lying low all these years. The Agora have even granted a lot of our demands over the past decade. We had peace—or so we thought." Seto exhaled through his nose. "My brothers and I were attacked by seven wraiths on the same day the Nine were slaughtered. We were celebrating Hinata's grandson's birthday. My three brothers were killed almost instantly. My sister-in-law and most of my nieces and nephews managed to escape. The only reason I am alive is because I was in the piano room, singing with *them*."

His fingers splayed to encompass the kurbantes-born. They had been singing and dancing when they were attacked, at the prime of their powers. That was probably the only reason they managed to escape seven wraiths.

"Sir," Io asked. "The victims of the assassinations across the continent a few weeks ago—were they members of your coalition twelve years ago?"

Seto stressed each word. "Every single one of them."

Io's mind raced, all her scattered clues puzzling themselves into a cohesive picture. Seto and his coalition had tried to overthrow the Agora. In retaliation, the Agora had used the fury-born as an army to get rid of the usurpers once and for all. Then the Nine orchestrated the downfall of the fury-born, and ever since, they had lived in fear of being attacked again. They had hinted at the existence of gods, which Hanne and Urania had all but confirmed. Eerily similar coordinated assassinations were carried out all across the continent, by wraiths meant to bring back the line of the fury-born.

Were the Agora and the gods one and the same? Their goals and methods certainly aligned, as well as the shroud of mystery veiling their true identities.

But one part still didn't make sense: *Why now?* The gods could have tried to revive the fury-born by avenging their deaths at any time during the past twelve years. If Seto's claims that the coalition had been dissolved and their demands abandoned were true, then why were the gods targeting them anew? What had changed?

"Can you think of any reason why you would be attacked again now?" Io asked him. "Did something happen?"

"Not that I'm aware of," said the mob king. Then, in an authoritative tone: "Why, Miss Ora? What do you know that I don't?"

That was a hard question to answer. How did one even go about telling the most powerful mob king in the world that he was being pursued by *gods*? Io's mouth opened, then closed. She couldn't figure out where to start or how to phrase it; her mind was a bell ringing with realizations.

"For hell's sake, cutter," Bianca butted in. She turned to Seto. "It's the gods. The ones who sent the fury-born to kill your brother twelve years ago and the wraiths six weeks ago—*it's the gods*."

To his credit, the mob king didn't laugh. He did, however, smooth the creases of his trouser legs and drawl, "While I appreciate humor, Miss Rossi, now is not the right time for it."

"Do I look like I'm in the mood to crack jokes, sir?" Bianca replied in a dry tone.

Seto gave her a flat look. "You expect me to believe in the existence of gods. That in itself is a joke."

"What if I told you the Nine had suspected it for years?" Bianca said. "What if I told you they tried to find out the truth with their powers, but someone was blocking them? What if I told you that the person who made me into a lifeless weapon and launched me upon the Nine insinuated she was working for the gods? What if I told you that this one"—she nudged her head toward Io—"has held a god's thread in her hands and followed it all the way here?"

Seto's sharp gaze went to Io. "Elaborate," he commanded.

"The thread was golden," Io said. "Bianca and I have been

following it across the Wastelands, looking for the gods. We finally tracked it to a human, a norn-born, who warned me explicitly to stay away from *the gods*. I followed her anyway and found that she and the gods she serves are behind the Wastelands kidnappings. I believe the missing people are true fury-born. That's why we were in the northern tunnel. We were following a girl and my—"

Io paused. She wasn't certain how much to share, how much to protect Ava from the mob king's wrath. But the truth of the matter was that they needed an ally, and Seto Sarris-Nakano was the most powerful ally they could find.

"The girl escaped with the help of my sister Ava." From the corner of her eye, Io saw Bianca's head snap to her face, eyes wide. "I traced the glass vial they left behind to Salamander's, where my sister has been ordering sleeping tonics weekly. The oneiroi-born who ratted us out to you, Nautilus, seems to think that Ava is a tram driver in the City Proper."

Without taking his eyes off Io, Seto said, "Nehir, get a full statement from Nautilus."

In seconds, the hulking kurbantes-born woman behind the sofa disappeared from the room. Upbeat dance music spilled into the quiet room before the door closed behind her.

"You believe us, then?" Bianca said, voicing the question in everyone's mind.

"I have not decided yet," Seto answered.

"Sir," Io said, "you must know as well as I do what the kidnappings mean. The gods are collecting true fury-born from all over the world. They slice their love-threads to make them obedient. They're remaking the Order. They're building an army." Io glanced at Edei, remembering his words earlier. "I don't know what their ultimate goal is, but they are preparing for *war*."

The statement hovered in the room, a dangerous thing with sharp fangs and a snout dripping blood. Io looked at each of them in turn: Bianca's jaw was clenched, her eyes distant, as though she was lost in thought; Edei was a pillar of solemn calm; Nico could hardly keep still, his wide-eyed gaze locked on Seto; Urania was looking at her lap, rubbing her nails with a thumb; the kurbantes-born siblings were wearing various faces of surprise, suspicion, and rage; and Seto Sarris-Nakano was gazing at them over the bridge of his nose, his long forefinger tapping a slow, leisurely rhythm on his knee.

"I see," the mob king said. His voice was expressionless, as though he *did* see, he *did* believe the gods were creating an army—and that didn't sway his opinion one way or the other. "Before I can decide my next steps, I would like a moment alone with you, Miss Ora."

That was understandable; he wanted to squeeze more details out of her—

But Seto added, "And you, Mr. Rhuna."

Io's stomach clenched. She glanced at Edei, then back at Seto—the mob king was looking at her with eyes glimmering the rosy pink of an erotes-born.

Io's breath became stabbing inhales, trembling exhales. Her heart hammered a frenzied beat against her rib cage.

"Everyone else, please leave the room," ordered the mob king of the Shards.

CHAPTER XVI

TAMPER

DANGER HOVERED IN the room as Io's friends and the kurbantes-born filed out. Edei's mouth was a hard line, his gaze marble cold. Io herself was all bristling caution; it felt like one wrong move, one false word might turn the mob king against them.

Seto was watching them with his soft, rosy irises. "The Erotes," he started, "were five gods: Eros, god of desire; Anteros, god of requited love; Hedylogos, god of flattery; Himeros, god of unrequited love; and Pothos, god of yearning. I am the latest. I can see desire and longing in the form of concentric circles rippling out of each body, intersecting when the feeling is reciprocated. It is wholly serene and perfectly balanced—imagine a pebble tossed soundlessly onto the surface of a tranquil lake."

Seto paused and raised his pink eyes to them, nailing Io and Edei in turn.

"When I look at you two, however," he said, "I see waters in turmoil. Your feelings are like two torrents of opposing rivers clashing into each other. Their battle distorts the love-streams of those around you. Just now, my powers couldn't discern the ripples of anyone else in the room besides you two, nor affect them in any way."

Io turned red all the way to the tips of her ears. She could feel her skin burning, her cheeks, her neck, her clavicle—every inch of her sizzled with barely contained mortification. If Seto kept talking for another second, it was very likely she might short-circuit, explode, and take out the whole Moor District with her.

"If I am to commit to helping you," Seto said, "the task ahead requires my best focus, my absolute power. I will not embark on a fight against *gods* with my abilities hindered. You are a danger to me right now, Miss Ora, Mr. Rhuna. Please allow me to examine your rivers of love and resolve the issue, so that we may all succeed in our impossible mission."

Gods! *Examine* their *rivers* of love. Why did everything suddenly sound so suggestive? Io wanted to dash for the door. Any other day, she'd wager she could make it past all nine of the kurbantes-born, but now, with her hands clasped in these damned manacles, she only had her fast legs and quick wits to work with, and what use were those? Perhaps if she went along, this humiliation would be over more quickly—

"Our feelings," Edei said emphatically, "are none of your business, sir."

Io's eyes cut to his face. In her complete spiraling, she hadn't noticed him move, but he was now standing firmly between her and Seto. Even bound behind his back, his hands were clenched so tightly his knuckles were showing white.

"They are when they affect my control over my powers," Seto said with perfect confidence.

"I'm sure you'll find a way to work around that."

"Believe me, if there was a way, I would have found it by now—"

Io spoke up to interrupt their back-and-forth; she had a feeling it would quickly escalate into a proper fight. "We share a fate-thread, Edei and I. Could that be what is affecting your, um, rivers of love?"

Seto's eyes shimmered rapt and mesmerized, wholly pink, zapping back and forth over the air around Io and Edei with impossible speed. He reached for his crutches and rose on his feet, taking a step toward Edei. "Is that what I'm seeing? Destiny?"

Edei backed toward Io, matching Seto's every step. His hand pressed on Io's stomach, centering her behind his own body. "*Sir*," Edei warned.

The threat in Edei's voice seemed to startle Seto out of his trance. His eyes blinked back to their normal dark brown, his fingers hovered in midair. "Apologies," he said. "Please, may I take a look?"

Edei glanced at Io over his shoulder, searching her face.

"Just a look," Io told Edei, but she tried to imbue the words with another meaning, too: *We need his help. We need him as an ally.*

Edei's eyebrows grooved a severe line over his eyes, but a second later, he stepped aside.

The mob king's palm dipped in the air as though he was cupping water into his hand. There was no substance that Io could see on his skin, but she *felt* it. A great emotion of longing, dripping sweet and sugary like honey from a spoon. She shut her eyes and let the feeling pull her under. She was standing on the shore of the sea on a very hot day, the waves lapping around her ankles, higher and higher, until they closed above her head. The sea had the taste of Edei and the smell of him, and where the water touched her, it felt like his caress.

"I've only seen two fate-threads in my lifetime," Seto said softly. "The first was a traveler passing through our estate in Little Iy. The second I tracked down myself, after years of searching. I am the descendant of the god of longing, you see, and a fated love is the most transcendental longing in the world: across space and time itself. Which begs the question, Miss Ora, Mr. Rhuna, of why on earth you would ever attempt to tamper with it."

Io's eyes flew open. "What do you mean, tamper?"

"I can see some sort of lacerations on your love-streams. Think of them as rocks piled or dams raised on the riverbed. There is purpose behind these attempts, Miss Ora. To change the course of the river or stop it entirely. They could have been made by an external factor, like an other-born with powers such as yours and mine. But most likely, it has come from you or Mr. Rhuna. Such alterations are always stronger when they come from the self." The mob king paused and considered them through vibrant pink eyes. "Have you been aware of this fate-thread long?"

"Aware, yes," Io answered for both of them, avoiding Edei's gaze. "But we didn't, um, meet until two months ago."

"It could be," Seto said, "that your minds are rejecting this union and the fate-thread hasn't quite caught up yet."

Io was stunned to silence. *Rejecting* the fate-thread. It certainly aligned with what Edei had said earlier, in his gentle way: that these were hard times, it was understandable if their feelings had changed. But Seto had said minds, plural. Was this her doing, too? Were her own feelings changing? Io didn't think so, but change could be a quiet, insidious thing, slowly working in the dark of night, until you woke up one day, and the love you felt for someone was gone entirely.

"Sir," Edei said. "You have taken your look. You have made your hypotheses. What we do next is our decision. But what is yours? Will you help us?"

His crutches silent on the thick moquette, he retreated to his desk, where he opened the top drawer and pulled out two keys.

"It has been twelve years since Hinata died, but his loss cuts as deep today as it did then," the mob king said. "I did everything I could to protect my family. I silenced my fury, I buried my convictions, I crawled into my turf, ignoring the rest of the world. And it was still not enough. Six weeks ago, I had to watch the rest of my brothers die."

With his palm, he beckoned Edei to him and gestured at him to turn. Obediently, Edei presented his hands and let him unlock the cuffs.

"I don't believe in gods, Mr. Rhuna. But," Seto went on, "I do believe in avengers. I believe in justice. I think the assassinations were coordinated, the first step in a big plan. I intend to stop that plan by whatever means necessary. So, yes, I will help you. But I would advise you to resolve this situation between you soon, Mr. Rhuna, Miss Ora."

He deposited the other key in Edei's palm and regarded him and Io in turn.

"We are ruled by the shape of our longing," he said. "By threads that bind and hearts that cut, through tender flesh and deep into the bone. The choice is yours, as you said. But I implore you: choose peace, whatever form it might take for you."

And with a last nod, he walked out of the office, closing the door behind him.

Io and Edei stood alone in the mob king's office. Edei fit the key into Io's manacles and eased the heavy metal from her wrists, then flung it to the nearest armchair with far more force than necessary. The manacles click-clacked into a pile atop the smooth velvet. He took her hands in his and began rubbing the soft flesh where the spikes had carved death-white grooves into her knuckles.

"Is this what you meant earlier?" He spoke to the moquette on the floor. "About something changing in the fate-thread?"

In her chest, Io's heart hiccupped, as though it missed a beat or two. But lies or evasions were never an option with Edei; she had to tell him the truth no matter the cost. "The fate-thread is fraying," she said. "It started sometime after I left Alante. Its glow is weakened, its string unraveling."

She was watching him closely, eagerly. She craved for him to contradict her, she realized, for him to stomp his foot and tell her it wasn't happening, they weren't rejecting the fate-thread, it would all be as it was, complicated but easy, unspoken but felt, sweet and maddening in all the ways love was supposed to be.

But Edei said nothing. His fingers went on running circles over her tender skin. His brows cleaved over his half-closed eyes. He seemed at a loss.

Io felt desperation leak into her thoughts, coming up with things to say to fix this. In another time, she would have hurried to bridge the divergence, to fill the silence with her pleading voice, to appease Thais's dark moods in whatever way she could. But she didn't want to be that person any longer. She didn't want to bargain for love as though it was a transaction.

She wanted to be chosen, freely and completely. To be found worthy of love simply for who she was.

So, instead, Io said, "I could cut it."

And she would. She would choose a broken heart over this. Their fate-thread was fraying. Their love-stream was in battle. Their feelings weren't the same. Io knew that love didn't survive change—she had felt it happen with Thais, with Ava, even with her parents. Best to sever the ties entirely and start anew.

"It will ease this . . . turmoil," she added. "It will set us free."

His mouth scrunched up, teeth nibbling his bottom lip. When he spoke, his voice was so soft Io wasn't entirely certain he meant for her to hear it. "Is that what you want, Io?"

No, it wasn't, because she would lose this thing she had always cherished, this guiding light through every dark moment of her life.

And yes, it was, because these doubts, this un-love was hurting her. She had meant what she said: cutting the thread would set them both free. Edei, free to choose to love whomever his heart desired; Io, free of doubt and self-loathing, free to learn how to be loved afresh.

She took too long to answer.

"*What* do you want?" Edei said, a little forcefully, and finally looked at her.

Io's eyes dropped to his lips.

He saw. He noticed. He understood. The furrow was wiped from his brow in an instant. Calm washed over his features. He tugged at her hands, drawing her closer. His arm wrapped around her waist, his hand slipped into her hair and cupped her head back, baring her lips to him.

For a moment, he stood there, gazing down at her.

Then he leaned in, pressing his lips against hers. Io let her eyes flutter closed, let herself bathe in her senses: his soft, soft mouth caressing hers, his tongue twisting around her own, his breath rough and exhilarating. His thumb slipped beneath her jaw and tipped her head up. His lips dropped to the tender flesh of her neck, trailing kisses and then, suddenly, a nip. Io felt his teeth drag against her skin—a half-drunk gasp slipped out of her lips.

Her body seemed to move on its own, heady with craving. Her fingers ran over the hard muscles of his back and hooked into the loops of his belt. She pulled him closer, chest to chest—he exhaled in surprise. Her lips seized control. She rose on her tiptoes and kissed him, tracing his jawline all the way to his ear. A whimper left his mouth—Io acted on instinct, taking his earlobe into her mouth.

Edei unraveled. His hands hooked beneath her armpits, lifting her up. Io's legs wrapped around his waist as he backpedaled them to the wall. He pressed her against the cool glass, her body throbbing with the pulse of the music in the dance club below. Io thought she might erupt with joy, with desire, with pleasure. Edei was kissing her; Edei was pressing her up against a wall; Edei wanted her.

Their lips met again, hot and wet with kissing. Their mouths clashed, their tongues wrestled, their hands roamed beneath shirts and over smooth skin, a battle of yearning that Io thought might just be the end of her.

The door banged open. Music spilled into the room.

Io broke off first, twisting her head toward the newcomers. Edei lingered, his mouth skimming the skin of her cheekbone, his hands insistent on her body.

Emir, the kurbantes-born leader, marched into the room, going straight for the desk. Bianca stopped at the doorway, her hands uncuffed, and stared up and down at Io's and Edei's joined bodies against the window, then rolled her eyes dramatically. Nico and Urania appeared, and Seto pulled up the rear with his slow steps.

"Found them!" Emir exclaimed from the desk. "Emergency entry passes, I told you we had some."

Edei lowered Io to the floor and asked, "What's happening?"

"Nautilus and the Salamander's staff have confirmed Ava wears a City Tram driver's uniform when she comes into the Shards," Bianca supplied. "We were discussing how to best enter the City Proper when an announcement came in through the radio."

"The City Proper is in lockdown," Seto said. "Emir, there is no point in emergency entry passes. The gates have been sealed. You know as well as I do that they'll let no one in now."

"I'll get in touch with our friends in the police, boss, and see what they say."

Seto shook his head. "We'll have to wait until the gates are open again—"

"There's another way in," Bianca interrupted.

"This is my city, Miss Rossi. I'm pretty sure I know every way inside."

"Ah, but you don't." Bianca was smiling her trickster's smile, a fox in the body of a woman. "You and your brothers built your empire on swanky dance clubs and upscale restaurants, but I—I built mine on smuggling."

"Bianca, no." This one came from Edei, whose eyes were rimmed with panic.

"Bianca, yes," she said.

"You can't be serious. It's a miracle it worked back then—what makes you think it'll work now?"

"You got any other ideas?" she snapped.

No one answered, most because they had no clue what was going on, and Edei because he apparently *didn't* have any better ideas.

"Brace yourselves, fancy folk," Bianca Rossi said. "We're going swimming."

CHAPTER XVII

A BELLOWING SCREECH OF PANIC

HERE WAS EVERYTHING Io had learned about the Nanzese sewer system in the last twenty-four hours, all of it against her will: it was composed of thousands of sewer pipes that led to tanks beneath the residential levels. Sewage accumulated in these vast tanks all day, where it was—supposedly—filtered and sanitized, then piped out through exits located at the lowest point of the wall. All thirty or so gates opened simultaneously when the mud-tide was as its lowest, at which point, the wastewater was released right into the Shards surrounding the city. The gates remained open until the mud-tide began to rise again, so that none of that ooey-gooey filth could make its way back into the Golden City of Nanzy.

It was a disgusting, unfair practice, but it did present the perfect opportunity for anyone looking to sneak in or out of the City Proper. After the city dumped out the majority of its filth, there was a neat fifty-minute window where the pipes and tanks were empty. Any smart—albeit fool-headed—person could traverse the sewage system and climb out through a manhole on the other side of the wall.

It took Bianca all of five minutes to explain this, an hour to convince them it was safe, and almost an entire day to plan it. Now the sixteen members of their group—Io, Edei, Bianca, Nico, Urania, Seto, his nine kurbantes-born guards, and Pina, an asclepies-born healer and army doctor veteran—were dressed in waterproof wading dungarees with attached boots, face masks over their mouth and nose and headlamps on their foreheads. They were walking in pairs and trios in a cylindrical metal pipe that was barely as wide as they were tall; Edei had to bow his head to keep from hitting the grimy ceiling. The channel was one long stretch of metal, darkness lurking on both ends.

It had been almost half an hour since Bianca and the kurbantes-born had screwed the grate off one of the exit gates and their ragtag group had entered the sewers. Waste was still flowing in thick, oozy rivulets beneath their boots and would continue to do so for the next twenty minutes, when the gates closed and the tanks began to fill again. They had already crossed the most difficult part—the exit gate and two-hundred-step ladder up the tank—although not without casualties: their calves were burning and their nostrils felt like they might never recover from the stench.

Io's arms and knees were still trembling from the long climb and the fast pace Bianca set at the head of their silent procession. Her companions weren't faring any better, either. Seto's face was morphed into closed-off pain; often, he had to ask for his guards' help to guide his crutches through tricky parts of the piping. Pina, the medic, was panting so hard her mask was filled with condensation. Urania was an absolute heaving mess at the very end of the line, her normally sleek-smooth hair framing her sweaty face in wild curls.

For the first time since Io had been reunited with them yesterday, Nico wasn't keeping Urania company. He was a few steps ahead of Io, chatting animatedly with the tall kurbantes-born sister, Nehir. He was very pointedly not looking at Urania, although he had quietly positioned himself right behind her when they were climbing up the two-hundred-step ladder, monitoring her slow ascent and providing an arm to steady her when she faltered.

"They had a bit of a spat this morning," Edei whispered conspiratorially to Io, his eyes following hers to Nico.

"What about?" she whispered back, voice matching his playfulness.

Her head was a whirlwind of emotions, still very much unmoored, but in this at least, she had some clarity. That impassioned kiss against the wall was enough to put her in a—well, if not *good*, then at least slightly improved mood. They'd had no opportunity to speak or even be alone in a room together since then, but every time Io had looked at him across the meeting room, she had found his eyes already trained on her. And every time, Io hoped he'd cross the room and swoop her into his arms.

That kiss . . . Io would have liked to say that every sense and touch had been imprinted in her memory, but the moment had been too loaded with tension and exhilaration, and too interrupted. The whole make-out session had taken on the hazy quality of a dream. Io craved to reproduce it, to bathe in it, her lips against his, his hand in her hair, bodies pressed against each other, breathing the same air. She wanted it again and again.

How could their fate-thread be fraying, their love-stream battling, when all Io could think of was kissing Edei senseless?

Oblivious to her thoughts, Edei said, "As I understand it, they couldn't agree on the best food to pack for our journey. It devolved into a screaming match."

Ahead of them, Nico spun to glare at them. His steps dragged, allowing them to catch up to him. "It wasn't a screaming match," he said.

"He's right—I was being dramatic," Edei said with a half smile at Io. "But it did sound like you were being very . . . opinionated about whether raisins or almonds make for the best energy snack to bring on a sewer heist."

Nico rolled his eyes. "It's not about raisins and almonds, Edei. It's about the fundamental differences of our upbringing, which Urania fails to grasp. We can go to any local store and buy a pound of raisins for a note. But almonds are only sold in the Fen District and cost three notes. It is irrational to even suggest it."

All three of them glanced back at Urania bringing up the rear, looking about to keel over. Yet she kept putting one foot in front of the other, grim determination on her flushed, sweaty face. There was a smudge of brown on her forehead above her face mask, which Io hoped was something completely unrelated to the filth beneath their feet. A moment later, Urania caught them all looking at her, narrowed her eyes, and pointedly turned her attention to the kurbantes-born walking beside her.

An exaggerated pout of unhappiness lined Nico's face. "What am I supposed to do, Io?" he whispered. "Should I go talk to her?"

"I'm not the best person to ask," Io said. She had never been good at advice. She had always been the advice-receiver, never the advice-giver. Thais had handed out a dozen little instructions and corrections per day, and Ava's silence had made it seem like she agreed. If Io tried to contribute her thoughts on a serious matter, her sisters would look at her as if she was a toddler trying to counsel bankers on the day's interest rates. But here was Nico *asking* for her thoughts; perhaps he would find some value in them. "If she's willing to listen," she tried again, "then yes, talk to her about it."

Nodding at her suggestion, Edei added, "And if she's not, then it might not be worth your time."

It was a little harsh, but Io empathized. It was a conscious effort for her to mark a dividing line between wanting to make people understand her point of view and removing herself from the situation when she realized they never had any interest in listening to her.

Nico began to deflate, chin tucking into his neck, but a new voice joined the conversation.

"Don't listen to these two pushovers," Bianca said, her voice clear even through the mask. "Argue to your heart's desire. Argue till your throat's raw. Ava and I disagreed on pretty much everything. You don't know how many nights I've spent discussing the philosophical value of street music."

A smile drew at the corners of Io's lips, soft and sorrowful. That sounded like Ava, all right. But it surprised her that Bianca revealed this much; it was the first time the mob queen had volunteered information about her and Ava's relationship. Even when Io mentioned Ava's presence in the Guts again, Bianca had been silent and stoic.

"If you *had* let yourself debate the matter," Bianca told Nico, "you might have found out that almonds have five times the nutritional value of raisins, and you would indeed be getting quite a deal on your three notes."

Nico gazed at his former boss with rapt attention—then turned on his heel and made a beeline for Urania.

"It is ridiculous," Bianca said. She had eased her pace to fall in step with Io and Edei, as though she wanted to stay a part of this conversation for a little longer. "How invested you all are in your fleeting teenage infatuations when there are literal gods out to get us."

She raised a pointed eyebrow at them that made Edei go positively beetroot red.

Io harrumphed. After the utter humiliation that was last night's conversation with the erotes-born mob king, she would not be tolerating any teasing from the mob queen as well. "Oh, come off it," Io said. "Cheering on teenage romances is a balm to the tormented soul."

"I remember," Edei said, voice lilted with humor, "a certain very grand declaration of love that teenage Bianca commemorated with a poem—"

"You shut your mouth, Edei Rhuna," Bianca snapped.

"Please, don't, Edei Rhuna," Io countered. She leaned across Bianca to widen her eyes at him. "You were saying something about a poem?"

"Oh, yes. A love poem. It actually won a newspaper award, I believe . . ."

"There are *public copies* of it?" Io's voice was hued with exuberant thrill.

"Oh, yes," Edei repeated. "If someone very thorough looks into the Alantian news records of eighteen years ago, they might even find it."

"The moment we're back in Alante, I'm going hunting for it," Io said.

"I'll help," Edei offered. "The mob queen's first foray into romantic poetry is bound to be a riveting read."

A nearly hysterical giggle escaped Io's nose, the sound undistorted even by the mask.

"Yeah, yeah, you're both hilarious," Bianca said dryly. But she was, amazingly, smiling, and *staying* in place between them.

Ahead of them, the light of their headlamps began to fracture and climb up walls that were suddenly wider and thicker, made not of metal but cement. The sound of their footfalls was swallowed by the impossibly tall duct opening up above them. Ladders were built into the circular wall every ten feet or so, leading to about a dozen grated trapdoors on the ceiling.

"Gods." Urania's voice cut through the silence. "*More* stairs?"

"This is the home stretch, princess," Bianca said. "See those trapdoors up there? They lead to manholes at street level."

"How do we know which one to take?" Seto asked. He was resting against the wall of the tank, massaging his left thigh. The asclepies-born, Pina, was squatting by his side, eyes closed and fingers working circles over his kneecap, as though she was stirring an invisible cup of tea.

"That's why we brought the fire-moths." Bianca stuck her hand out for the jar that Edei obediently fished out of his backpack.

It was filled with a pretty chimerini hybrid of fireflies and moths. When Bianca eased the lid off, bright turquoise light burst from their furry little bodies. The fire-moths flew upward in a lazy, amorphous cloud. Neon blue green hued the walls and shimmered on the ladder steps as they made their way through the grate of the second-left trapdoor, slipping out of sight—

A muzzle snapped.

A great lump of the fire-moth cloud disappeared, its light snuffed between the gigantic jaws of a . . .

Io didn't know exactly what her eyes were seeing. The beast was huge, with a long crocodilian mouth, scaled skin, a deformed, ridged spine, and short legs that somehow allowed it to adhere itself to the ceiling like a gecko. It wasn't an obvious cross of two animals that would have marked it as a chimerini, but it wasn't a regular animal, either. It was too large, and no animal could survive in the sewers anyway. Its eyes were a glassy gray, from living in darkness, Io presumed.

"A leviathini . . . ?" It was Emir who spoke, his body planted in front of Seto, his golden-rimmed gun already in his hand. "They died out decades ago. How has this one survived so long?"

"What," Bianca spat out through gritted teeth, "is a leviathini?"

"Baby leviathans," Emir explained. "A rodent leviathan made its burrow in one of the hills around Kurkz, centuries ago. For decades ever since, our grandparents and parents were conscripted into army expeditions to hunt and kill its offspring. They looked like it, but much smaller."

"This one resembles what Le Cauchemar is believed to have looked like," Seto commented.

Le Cauchemar Junior, just great. Lurking right by the trapdoor they were supposed to go through. Would the world never give them a break?

"Is it part human?" asked Bianca.

The question was so odd that Io turned to glare at the mob queen for asking it, but she found Bianca studying the creature with eyes burning the orange flames of fury-born. Could she see something on the leviathini? Io called forth the Quilt—

Gods. She could see its threads. They were hazy, distorted, not quite the size and shape of human threads. But they were there. The bright one shooting upward was its life-thread; another strong one led to a crevice at the opposite side of the ceiling, probably its sleeping nest; and another led, astonishingly, to its own tail, which the leviathini was swinging lazily upside down against the ceiling.

"How is that possible?" Io mused. "Other-born powers only apply to humans."

"You can see it, too?" Bianca asked. "Seto? Pina? Everyone else?"

"Yes," Seto said, and a second later both Pina and Urania also mumbled a *yes.*

"We don't," Nehir said, "but our powers are not vision-oriented anyway."

A heavy silence followed, loaded with questions, until the scuttling sound of the leviathini moving across the ceiling startled them. It had inched down the wall, in their direction, as if they posed no threat at all. They probably didn't. Its size alone was inconceivable; Io doubted the creature had ever faced an opponent that didn't immediately turn tail and run away.

They needed to get out of here, fast. But the only way out was up, where *it* was.

An absurd plan was forming in Io's mind, which regrettably sounded like their only choice. "If I can see its threads," Io said quietly, "I can *cut* its threads."

She dropped the Quilt and turned to her team. Above them, the beast descended a few more feet. Io had no doubt it would attack the moment it got close enough to reach them with its gigantic jaws.

"Edei," she said, "get everyone back in the tunnel we came from. Bianca and I will lure it away from the ladder and keep it occupied. As soon as the way is open, you all start climbing."

"We can help," Emir offered. "We can fight it."

Io shook her head. "You're needed on the ladder. Bianca and I will have mere minutes before it realizes there's an easier, more exposed meal right behind it. Seto, Urania, and Pina need to be safe through that trapdoor when that happens. Then and only then can you come help."

It was a sensible plan; Emir seemed to think so, too, because he gave her a curt nod, grabbed her and Bianca's backpacks, and moved to the opening of the tunnel they had come in through. Edei was far less convinced, giving Io a lingering look, but did as he was instructed. Suddenly, it was only Io and Bianca on the floor of the large tank, like two toothpicks trying to pick a fight with a cat. They watched the leviathini advance on them with slow, methodical steps.

"What are you thinking?" Bianca said, hands on her hips.

"We draw it to the other side of the room. You distract it while I climb the nearest ladder. When I'm high enough, I grab its life-thread and slice it."

Bianca exhaled through flared nostrils, slow and furious, fogging her mask. Her hand clapped Io's back, as though they were teammates in a schoolyard game. "Let's get to it, then."

They launched in unison, crossing to the opposite side of the room in long, hurried strides. The floor was gigantic; it took them nearly three minutes to cross it entirely. The beast followed along on the wall, matching them step for step. When Io lifted herself up on the nearest ladder, the beast paused, then began moving again, much faster. Its spiked tail swished left and right in the slithery manner of a crocodile.

Io risked a glance at the other side of the room: Edei was silently motioning at everyone to hurry. Nico was leading the climb, Urania keeping close behind, while the kurbantes-born were taking turns helping Seto up. Pina brought up the rear. Io estimated it would take them four to five minutes to reach the trapdoor.

It would take the beast less than two to reach *her*.

"Hey!" Bianca called up from the base of the ladder Io was climbing. "Smell these? Delicious, aren't they?"

She had a slice of jerky in her hand, grinding it between her palms—to release its smell, Io presumed. It was working. The beast swung in Bianca's direction so fast, the movement barely registered in Io's eyes. It had been concealing its true speed; if it wanted, the leviathini could be on them in seconds, not minutes.

Io wasted no time: she traced its threads in the Quilt. If Bianca led it just a few feet to her left, then its life-thread would be perfectly aligned to where Io now stood. She would be able to grab and sever it.

The leviathini had slithered onto the floor. Compared to Bianca, its size was tremendous. It could swallow half her body in a single bite. Io waved her arm to grab Bianca's attention, then pointed left.

The mob queen instantly got the gist, taking small, unthreatening steps back to where Io had pointed.

The leviathini's life-thread was a neat vertical line of silver from its body straight up to the ceiling. But it was still a few inches away; no matter how far Io stretched, she couldn't reach it. Bianca glanced up at her, saw her struggling, and took a step closer to the wall, essentially trapping herself. If Io's plan didn't work, if she wasn't fast enough, the leviathini would snap Bianca's spine in seconds.

Across the room, someone slipped.

The sound of a boot hitting metal echoed in the circular space. The beast's head snapped in that direction. Edei and Emir were the only two still on the ground, looking up at the person who had slipped, Nehir. Their backs were exposed to the leviathini's jaws.

Io acted fast, all on instinct and adrenaline.

She hooked her knee around the ladder step and tilted her whole upper body toward the beast's life-thread. She could already tell she was going to hurt herself—her hip bone ground out a horrible sound—but she didn't care.

Her fingers closed around the leviathini's life-thread.

She clenched her abdomen and pulled herself back. Her legs bent awkwardly, pulled by her weight, and her knee zapped with pain, but she didn't fall. She hooked her elbow around the ladder and reached for one of her own threads with her free hand. All she had to do was touch the two threads together and the leviathini—

It gave out a bellowing screech of panic and *bolted*.

The beast sprinted away from her, toward the opening of the tunnel they had entered through, taking its life-thread with it. Its movement was so unexpected, so fast that the thread simply slipped out of Io's grip.

She was left to stare after it, wide-eyed and open-mouthed.

"Did it just realize you were going to cut its life-thread and"—Bianca hissed from below—"skedaddle?"

Io couldn't really wrap her mind around it, either, but they had no time to discuss. Emir called out, "Hurry up! The tank's filling again!"

Indeed, wastewater had started dripping from a large pipe opening on the bottom of the tank. All around them, there were the gurgles of machinery coming to life.

Io jumped to the floor, sprinted to the ladder, and scrambled up, through the grate, and into a narrow, dark, claustrophobic pipe, the only sounds her own panting and Bianca's frantic *go, go, go*s behind her. Peripherally, she could sense the walls of the duct were getting moister by the second and that something cold was plopping on her head—but she focused on putting one hand over the other, fast, fast, fast.

Then someone was grabbing her wrists and pulling her out of the manhole. Someone was slipping her mask off her face and clasping her shoulders and chuckling. *Everyone* was chuckling, squatting on the paved street or leaning against the walls, half-hysterical with laughter.

They had made it into the Golden City of Nanzy.

CHAPTER XVIII

A TORRENT

IO STOOD BEFORE the floor-to-ceiling windows of the Hôtel Du Jardin Blanc, eyes aglow with the gilded lights of the Golden City.

Nanzy was truly a glittering mirage; the radiant shimmer they had been able to see over the wall from the vantage point of the Shards didn't do justice to the extraordinary marvel Io was witnessing now standing *inside* the city. Every rooftop was dressed with golden signs: store names in swirly fonts, images of wares, extravagant strings of lamps. Every building was dressed in golden paint: the windows, the balustrades, the quaint little balconies. Glossy trolley cars zoomed past like beams of sunlight, streetlights zigzagged across paved streets and marble pavements, spotlights twirled their ivory glow into the overcast sky above.

Its skyline was all squares and spheres, prim and proper as the rest of it. Arches marked the intersection of avenues, domed cathedrals burst like the rising sun from the horizon. One in particular was a sensational sight. Situated atop a hill, the large, domineering structure seemed to be carved straight from the skull of Le Cauchemar. Even from this distance, Io could see the golden veins marking its ivory surface. Neat parks lush with greenery and ornate metallic structures speckled the ground, the fanciest trolley stations Io had ever seen.

There was not a drop of tidewater in sight. No piles of trash in back alleys, no homeless people camping in abandoned storefronts, no chimerini bugs scuttling across the streets. It was a city of extravagance, of luxurious cleanliness and wealth, "Proper" in every sense of the word. Its electricity bill alone must be the size of Alante's budget for an entire month.

Io wished she could feel anything but awe. She should be appalled by the comfort the city lived in when the rest of the population trudged along in the floating slums around it, furious with the hypocrisy of their opulence when so many had to survive in the filth they dumped out, disgusted by the unfairness of it all. But it was so beautiful. So clean. So golden. Her mind was already cataloguing ways she could stay here for the rest of her life, visit all its many wonders, be a part of its shimmering prosperity.

When she was in the Shards, she couldn't comprehend why everyone was sludging along in service of the lucky few inside the City Proper. She couldn't wrap her mind around the sacrifices they made, working in the factories all day, only to return to tiny, stifling apartments with questionable running water. They saved money all their lives like Torr's mothers had, in the hope of one day making it into the Golden City. Now, standing in the city itself, Io understood. Now she respected it.

In the wild, dangerous world that surrounded them, Nanzy was a haven. Who *wouldn't* want to live here?

She exhaled and turned back to the room. The penthouse suite of Hôtel Du Jardin Blanc consisted of a vast living room with a tiered dining area and an island kitchen, three bedrooms, and four bathrooms. Normally, it was occupied by Mayors or council members from other city-nations, merchants or entrepreneurs or wealthy landowners. At present, however, it was host to Io's ragtag group of sixteen.

They had climbed out of the manhole almost three hours ago,

into a side alley in the opulent Flowermarket District. They had scrubbed off the filth as best they could, draped themselves in cologne, and thrown fake chimerini furs over their shoulders, then spilled into the streets of Nanzy, dashing between passersby and automobiles to the Hôtel Du Jardin Blanc. They had waited at the back door of the twenty-story-high building while Emir slipped inside. A few minutes later, he had come out with a prim-looking maid, who had bowed her head at Seto with a quick "Boss" and ushered them through the service corridors and up to the penthouse.

The suite was currently undergoing renovations: two of the bathrooms and one of the bedrooms were in the middle of refurbishment, and the ceiling was almost entirely ripped out to install new lights. All furniture was covered by thick protective canvas, and the electricity had been shut down, but there was running water, steaming hot, and plush pillows and blankets that Seto's contact had brought up along with three large trays of leftovers from the five-star hotel restaurant.

Their group was now clean, fed and sated, slumped in various corners of the suite. Seto and most of the kurbantes-born had taken over the two bedrooms, while Edei, Nico, and Bianca were lounging on the canvas-covered sofas of the living room. Emir and two of his sisters had taken off the minute they had showered and eaten, to do some intel work on tram drivers in the city and get in touch with their contacts. Urania was drying her hair with a towel soft as a baby fawn; she had insisted on cleaning up last, so that she could really luxuriate in the experience of a proper bath.

"Cutter," Bianca said from where she lay on one of the sofas, her elbow draped over her eyes. "Stop lurking. Go to sleep. We're in for a long day tomorrow."

Tomorrow, when they would spill into the streets of Nanzy Proper in search of Ava's whereabouts. Io stepped away from the windows and settled on the sofa pillows she and Nico had arranged in the space between the two sofas. She removed her spectacles and set them on the floor by her pillow. On her right, Urania hummed a song as she scruffed her short hair with the towel. It was a popular tune, one of the cheesy love songs that Ava had hated to sing at the Fortuna Club. Nico seemed to know some of it; every few seconds he sang a word or two in tune with Urania's humming. Their argument seemed to have resolved, and they were back to longing looks and smiles hidden at the corners of their lips.

On Io's left, Edei was resting on the second sofa. His eyes were closed, his breathing slow. He and Emir had supported Seto all the way to the hotel. After climbing that final ladder, the mob king's legs had given out, despite Pina's attempts to heal him on the go.

Io gazed up at the ripped-open ceiling, the wires sticking out spite-fully. She wondered what kind of light fixture used to be there and what they would replace it with. It was a pitfall of luxury, she supposed, always wanting more. Better. Her mind turned to her sisters and the Ora legacy. *One day*, they had always hoped. One day, they would be successful. One day, they would be rich. One day, they would live in a city like this, in a penthouse like this, bathing in steaming water and sleeping on plush, lavender-scented pillows.

A smile etched itself on her lips. The memory was dressed in fondness. What a simpler time it had been, when all she could fault her sisters for was obsessing over success.

She closed her eyes and pictured their home. It was an exercise she did often, to help her busy mind fall asleep: She imagined she was walking through the streets of the Silts, turning into their building, then into her family's old apartment. In her mindscape, she went through every room, cozied up in her favorite armchair. She could almost imagine Thais at her back, shuffling around the kitchen, the smell of chicken soup and avgolemono in the air, the constant scratch of Ava's pencil as she went over instructions on her music lessons.

Io opened her eyes. Urania's humming had stopped, replaced by soft breathing. She rose to her elbows to check. Sure enough, the Muse's mouth was softly agape in slumber. Nico was facedown on his pillow, his nose flat against Urania's shoulder, snoring softly. Bianca's back rose and fell in a slow rhythm, her blond hair curtained over her pillow. A vial of sleeping tonic sat at the table next to her sofa; Seto had replenished her supply before they left the Shards.

As quietly as she could, Io stood and grabbed her boots.

A hand came around her wrist.

She glanced down and found Edei sitting up on the sofa. His eyes draped with sleep. "Where are you going?" he whispered.

Io didn't bother explaining much; she knew he'd understand. "I've got to find her first, Edei. On my own."

His fingers slackened. "How about," he said, "I give you a head start, then I come find you?"

"How will you find me?"

He tapped his chest over the fate-thread and said, with confidence, "I'll find you."

Io smiled, then nodded. Loyal and gentle, her Edei, and clever as a fox.

"Be careful," he whispered—and let her go.

The roofs of Nanzy were nothing like Alante's. No cat bridges, for starters, but also no hanging ladders, haphazardly placed planks, and tolled overpasses. The roofs were sturdy structures of smooth steel with solid rails and ornate streetlights, every bit as clean and polished as the rest of the city. Free of the night tide, Nanzy had no real use for them—they were a pretty remnant of harder times, like pre-Collapse artifacts in museums.

Io's first stop was one of the overground stations of the City Tram. She stood before the trolley line maps for a long time, mulling over her clues. Ava had escaped with Thais; she had been running supply trips to the Shards, often with Torr's help; she had a standing weekly order of sleeping tonics. The Guts tunnel she used was the same one where the wraiths who had attacked Seto's brothers were last seen.

Io's hypothesis was straightforward. Ava was working for the gods. She and perhaps Thais, too, were involved with the wraiths somehow, or the new fury-born, using the sleeping tonics to keep their bloodthirst at bay. But their operation needed to be covert, away from the public eye, especially in a city as opulent as this. Which meant they needed a place to hide.

That was where the City Tram came in. According to the map and the station manager Io had befriended, there were around seven discontinued stops on the trolley lines, making for perfect hiding spots. Of those seven, four were situated far too centrally to provide cover. Another two were in the middle of construction, the station manager said, but there was a final option, an old stop in the Trade District hosting the city's warehouses.

The roofs had grown gradually more deserted the farther into the Trade District she traveled, but police patrols walked every street in Nanzy, every rooftop and bridge. This morning, amidst planning the sewer heist, Io had asked Seto why he had all moira-born marked at border control. It wasn't his order, he explained. It came from the Nanzese Police. All he wanted was to find out for himself why moira-born were suddenly a public threat.

Io kept her eyes to the ground whenever she blinked the Quilt into existence. She had foolishly left her spectacles in the hotel; looking at long distances had already strained her eyes. Ava's thread still pointed north, to Jhorr.

A heavy breath huffed out of her. Of all the things Ava had done—siding with Thais, helping her escape, abandoning Io, tasking her with saving Bianca's life—this might just be the worst. Ava's power as a moira-born drawer allowed her to elongate or shorten someone's threads, making the accompanying feeling stronger or weaker. Drawing out her and Io's thread was a betrayal that outweighed actions, a betrayal of the mind, of the heart.

One soul in three bodies. That was how Thais had convinced Ava to side with her that day in the House of Nine. *When our sisters need us, we go. No questions asked.*

Mama used to say that. She would line them up by the door every time she and their father prepared to leave for a seasonal job at the Neraida Plains outside Alante, lay her palms on Thais's shoulders, and tell her to watch over her sisters. To make sure her sisters behaved. Mama was very particular about that last part of the phrase, *no questions asked.* One time, before this rule was introduced, Ava had asked to stay home from school that day but refused to tell Thais why. Thais had made her go. After school, police had escorted Ava back to their home. During the dissection lesson in anatomy class, she had elbowed her teacher in the belly and let all the frogs escape. Back then, Ava had been able to see the threads of animals.

Ava had been eleven, Thais thirteen, Io only five; she remembered that day sourly. Thais had been two hours late picking Io up from the daycare. For two hours, Io was convinced that her sister might never come.

Io wished she could free her mind of these memories. Of Thais having to shoulder too much too young, of Thais being the sole recipient of Mama's reprimands, of Thais learning early on that family meant obedience, *no questions asked*. She wished the entirety of Thais's self could be what she had done to Io, the manipulation and hurt and betrayal. No other sides to her, no fond memories of better times, no complexity to her character. But the present was never free of the past, an ebb and flow of memories that could grind it to dust.

She stopped at the edge of the roof.

This was a quiet part of the city, every block squared by tall, windowless warehouses, and between them stood a twenty-foot trolley station made of iron. An abandoned trolley car hung from the cables, long lines of rust running down its sides, likely from acid rain. Neon-colored images of animals had been painted on its body. No sign of life was visible to the naked eye, but in the Quilt, it was ablaze with threads—at least ten people that Io could discern.

She heaved a breath and started walking. A fire escape led her down the rooftop adjoining the abandoned trolley station. It was barbed with spiky wire, but there was an opening to scoot through, obviously carved out by trespassers. Io turned the Quilt on the abandoned trolley car hovering in the air before her. There was something odd about the threads in the right wing of the car—they looked too scattered, too few.

Slowly, she walked around the perimeter of the roof, seeking out a better angle. At the corner of the building, the view was unobstructed. Io could discern several severed life-threads lying on the floor of the wagon, nine or ten of them—wraiths, just as she had suspected. On the other side, there were three proper bundles of threads. One of them was Thais's.

Io knew not because of the thread they shared—that one still pointed north, along with Ava's—but because of the threads bursting from Thais's hands. Like sunrays on a cloudy day, they looked fuzzy, staticky, as if they were blinking in and out of existence. Newborn threads, spun threads.

Thais was weaving.

The Moirae had been three sisters. Clotho, the spinner of new threads of fate, Lachesis, the allotter of a thread's strength and length, and Atropos the Inflexible, who cut the threads and ended people's lives. Disuse had replaced their real names by the most straightforward terms used now for their descendants: weaver, drawer, cutter.

Of those, only cutters were feared, because a slice of their fingers could mean death. But Io had always thought weavers were the most dangerous. They could create a thread, falsify a connection of love and devotion between any two people. Io's was a skill of violence, yes, but Thais's was one of manipulation so nefarious that it could cause double the damage—Io had seen it with her own eyes. With Malena Silnova, a painter who had urged Thais to weave threads of admiration between her and gallery owners or art collectors. With Thomas Mutton, a scammer who had employed Thais to weave threads of love for various clients. With the wraiths, whose severed life-threads Thais had woven into a fury-whip. What new ploy was her sister entwining now?

Rage flared Io's nostrils, quickened her breaths. Before she knew it, her legs had taken her across the roof and onto the platform of the station. She was going to rip the door open, march right to Thais, and tear those sapling threads from her callous hands. She was going to fix this, all the damage her sister had done, and then she would make Thais pay for it.

She was halfway down the narrow bridge to the trolley car when its door burst open. Ava stood in the frame, illuminated from behind by the flickering rosiness of candlelight. Her eyes latched on to Io, brows pulled together in a face Io knew well: a sister's concern.

"Io," she said tenderly, and Io had to smother the urge to run right into her arms.

They both stilled. Ava drew the door closed behind her.

Io had known this moment needed to be just the two of them, alone, without the danger of Bianca and Urania and Seto Sarris-Nakano, without Thais and her tricks. Now that she was in it, though, she found herself at a loss for words.

Her sister looked tired. Gone were her luxurious, shiny curls, gone were her makeup and brass earrings. Her skin had broken out in blemishes, as it always did when she was stressed, and her clothes were lackluster, a simple, sleeveless black shirt and blue cotton trousers.

Her hands came up, palms facing Io placatingly, and she spoke in a slow, gentle tone. "Calm yourself, sister mine."

The Ora term of endearment brought a visceral reaction—it knifed through Io's rib cage, slicing through her heart. How dare Ava use it. How dare she remind Io of all they had lost.

"Why?" Io asked—*snapped* was more like it. "Thais is in there, weaving threads for gods know what. You were in the Guts yesterday, with a girl who's been reported missing. And that trolley car behind you is full of wraiths. Why should I calm myself? You're working for the gods!"

Ava's chin spasmed. "We're not working for the gods. It's not what you think—"

"Then tell me what to think," Io countered. "Tell me what this is. Tell me why I shouldn't just march in there and tear every hair from Thais's skull."

"Don't."

It was a sharp command, with a multitude of interpretations, but what made Io pause was the sound of it on Ava's lips; her sister *meant* it. Ava had spent her life as the mediator, the negotiator, the olive-branch extender of the Ora family. She was never exasperated. She never demanded.

The storm of fury and bitterness in Io's head quieted. "Why did you draw out our thread, Ava? Why did you want me to think you were in the north?"

Why did you not want me to find you? Io thought. She dared not ask this question out loud. It felt pathetic.

"If I tell you," Ava whispered, "do you promise to be calm?"

"I'm the danger now, then?" Io hissed. "I'm the one who needs to be calm, after our sister doomed women to death, tricked me into helping her slaughter the Nine, then abandoned us all to face the aftermath?"

"No, that's not what I meant."

"What did you mean, Ava?"

Io's sister tried again, gentler this time. "Just hear me out. Hear the whole story, then you can decide."

Decide what exactly, Ava didn't say. But the subtext was obvious. Io knew where Thais and the wraiths, known fugitives across every city-nation, were hiding. Where Torr, a missing girl barely twelve years old, had been taken. She could have the entire Nanzy police force here in less than fifteen minutes. Or worse, she could have Seto Sarris-Nakano here, and Bianca and Urania, all the people whose lives Thais and her ilk had wrecked.

Hear the whole story, then decide. Io could do that. Because this was Ava in front of her, her favorite person in the world, and *oh,* how Io wished the story would exonerate her. How she wished she could forgive Ava and have her back, on her side, as it should always have been.

Io made herself nod. She would let Ava tell her story. And by the time she was done, Io would have decided: if she had lost one sister, or two.

"When we left Alante," Ava began, "we did go north, to Jhorr, to find shelter until everything blew over. But when we arrived, the city was in uproar, the æsir-born and a council member murdered, wraiths on the loose. Thais tried to reach her contact there but was shut out entirely. She went into one of her depressions, staying in the hotel room for days on end."

Io knew those depressions well. Days of Thais locked away in her room, under the covers, not speaking to a single soul. Getting angry and snappy when Io or Ava tried to help. The last time Thais had fallen into one, it was after Io refused to cut Ava's thread to music.

"But I couldn't stay cooped up. I kept thinking of the carnage in the House of Nine. Of Bianca, her threads severed, her life twinkling out. I was in the Quilt for hours on end every night—that's how I found him. A wraith. He was a few years older than me, hiding in a half-demolished warehouse. His life-thread was severed, his body decomposing. But when I approached him, he let me bring him to our room and feed him. As soon as Thais saw him, he went ballistic— screaming, kicking, trying to harm her. He only settled when we gave him one of Thais's sleeping tonics. I dozed off sometime around dawn. When I woke up, the man was looking better. Livelier. Clear-headed. Because Thais had woven a thread between them."

The threads Io had seen Thais weaving—they were for the wraiths? But how? Wraiths couldn't sustain threads. Or at least, Bianca couldn't.

"Thais was rejuvenated," Ava continued.

Io knew that phase well, too. Give Thais a grand purpose, a way to *make the world better*, and she would take up the cause like a white knight on their stallion. Except Thais was the one who had created the wraiths in the first place. She was no noble knight, no savior—she was a liar, skilled and honed, even when it was herself she was lying to.

"She thought she could save them. Restore them to life. I found two more wraiths in Jhorr, and one in the tundra outside the city. I brought them to Thais, who wove threads connecting them to her, to me, to each other. The more threads, the more alive the wraiths looked. But unrest was growing in Jhorr, the æsir-born's followers fighting it out with the police right there on the streets. We decided it wasn't safe anymore. Thais was concerned we were being followed."

"By me, you mean," Io interrupted.

"By her colleagues, by the police, and yes, by you. You have to understand, Io, it wasn't just the two of us anymore. We had three dying people to care for and protect. I drew out the threads of the people who might be tracking us. You, Saint-Yves, Thais's friend Hanne. We were halfway across the northern Wastelands when we found two more wraiths. But our plan wasn't working as well as we had thought: the threads Thais wove kept unraveling. Thais believed her contacts in Nanzy would help us save the wraiths' lives, so we headed for the Golden City. All the while, Thais kept weaving and reweaving the same threads, trying to keep the wraiths alive. When we arrived in Nanzy and Thais tried to contact her colleagues, she was met with utter silence. They have cut all communication channels that Thais knows of."

That was suspiciously convenient, but Io didn't fault Ava. It wouldn't be the first time Thais had lied nor the first time Ava had gobbled the lie up.

"We rented a room in the Glade District and continued our work: I looked for wraiths, and Thais wove threads to keep them alive. I found four more and nursed them back to health. But it became very hard to keep what we were doing a secret. The Sarris-Nakano brothers were looking for wraiths. Thais knew of a place inside the City Proper where we could lie low"—Ava gestured at the abandoned trolley car behind her—"so we bribed our way in and have been holed up here ever since. I found a driver's uniform in one of the trolley's cabinets and have been using it for free passage back and forth from the Shards.

"I was always on the lookout for people with no threads. That's how I found Torr, the girl you saw me with. She had been hiding in the busiest neighborhood in the Fen District, which is always packed with people. She's a clever girl. She realized her love-threads had been cut when her feelings about her family began to change. She figured the man who had attacked her would be looking for someone with no threads and stayed close to people, so that their bundle of threads would hide her lack of them.

"When I approached her, her eyes flashed orange. She was terrified. She couldn't understand what was happening to her. She didn't know how to use her newfound powers and believed someone was watching her and her family. It took a lot of convincing to bring her back to our hideout with me. I had no way to smuggle her through border control, so I asked around for another way into the City Proper: the tunnel in the Guts where you saw us." Ava's jaw squared. "I didn't kidnap her. Torr chose to stay with us. She accompanies me on most supply runs because she likes to check up on her family. With the wraiths' help, we have been teaching her how to handle her fury-born powers. We have been trying to do good, Io."

But *do good* were just empty words. It didn't count as doing good, as making things better, when it was your own mistakes you were trying to fix. Should Io be applauding Thais for showing empathy, the most fundamental of human emotions? She was glad the wraiths were cared for, she was glad Torr was safe, but Thais was no selfless hero. Her sister was just afflicted by the unshakeable Ora legacy: shame, guilt, and the breaking of hearts. And yes, Io had purged shame from her own self, and yes, Thais might be able to do the same—but first, she had to *take responsibility*. She had to *apologize*.

Thais and Ava both had to apologize.

Io had promised to be calm, to hear Ava's story, and to decide: Was there a way to forgive her? Her sister had offered an explanation of her choices, a justification for her actions—but not for all of them. Not for what truly mattered to *Io*.

Her feelings were in turmoil, a torrent of desperation dragging the steady rocks of her logic downstream. She knew before she opened her mouth that it would all come out loud and aggressive, eyes wet and cheeks red and saliva threading between her teeth.

"You left me, Ava!"

CHAPTER XIX

SOOTHED AND VALIDATED AND CONTENT

AVA RUSHED TO her, her feet skimming over the grate of the station. She reached for Io's face and cupped her cheeks. "Io, I'm so sorry," she said in a hushed, hollow voice, "I know I hurt you, *I know*. I have thought about it every day since we left Alante. Please, forgive me, sister mine, please."

Then her arms were around Io, her curls tickling Io's face, the warm, soapy smell of her. For a moment, Io thought of pulling away, of pushing her back, but the embrace was a gift of solace. The apology she had been hoping for, finally delivered. This had always been the Ora sisters' praxis: comfort and hurt and comfort again, an endless ouroboros devouring its own tail.

"*Why?*" Io murmured. "You left me alone in the bloodbath, even after Thais revealed all that she had done. You drew out our thread, you avoided me, you made me think——" The words choked in Io's mouth.

Ava was still holding Io by the shoulders. "I had to make a difficult choice that day, in the House of Nine. Thais asked for my help——it's how we do things, us Ora sisters, no questions asked. She sounded terrified of whoever sent her to Alante. I was afraid her bosses would silence her in whatever way they could instead of let Saint-Yves arrest her. And I knew that the public would crucify her. Use her as an excuse to turn against all moira-born." She paused, then: "I made a split-second decision, Io, to save our sister's life."

But that wasn't true. There were twin streaks of tears on Ava's cheeks and an infallible sincerity on her forlorn brow. Slowly, Io took a step back, out of Ava's arms.

She looked her sister dead in the eye and said, "It wasn't a split-second decision, Ava."

Around them, a gust of wind tore past the district, whistling furiously through the iron structure of the station. Io shoved her hair out of her mouth.

"You had already decided," Io said. "Long before you saw Thais that night, before you heard her confession and feared its consequences. When Bianca found you, you told her to stick with me. That I would look after her, like I look after all wounded things. You *assigned* her to me because you had already decided to leave both of us."

Ava looked down at Io's feet, at her own boots that Io had borrowed what seemed like an eternity ago. She opened her mouth to speak, then closed it. She had never been good at confrontation, her sister; Io had always helped her avoid it, but not today. Not with this.

"Do you remember that day at Amos's, after Bianca's arrest? When you stood up to Thais to defend me?" It all came out in short, stubby bursts, as though Ava was trying not to cry. "There was a finality in your voice. You were done. Done with how Thais treated you. Done with Thais herself. I realized then . . . that you hated her."

Io sealed her breath in her lungs, pressure building against her rib cage. She didn't *hate* Thais. She was bitterly disappointed and darkly furious, but she hadn't hated her sister, certainly not that morning when she had still thought Thais was a shit person, but largely innocent of mass murder.

"Then a few hours later, Bianca came to find me, threadless and bloodthirsty for vengeance," Ava continued. "When she asked me to convince Saint-Yves to follow us to the House of Nine, I knew that whatever was to follow had to do with Thais. And I knew that if Thais was in danger, you weren't going to protect her. In fact, you might do the opposite—"

"She is a murderer, Ava!" Io cried out.

A trolley zoomed past nearby, silencing them. The quiet lingered.

"She has hurt a lot of people, I know that," Ava said at last. "But so have Bianca and Edei and Amos in the Iceberg Wars and pretty much everyone I know in this wicked world of ours. We do what we need to survive—"

Io opened her mouth to argue, but Ava raised a palm.

"No, let me finish," said Ava. "We do what we need to survive, and sometimes it's awful, shitty things, and we regret them, and the next time we have a choice, we *do better*. It doesn't undo the hurt, it doesn't absolve us, but we do better and try to help and that's something, isn't it?"

Io didn't know what to say. The principle was sound, full of kindness and hope, but could it apply to Thais? They had all hurt people, because that was the world they lived in, a kill-or-be-killed world. And they all deserved a second chance to do better—like Bianca was doing with this quest, and Edei with his new version of the Fortuna gang, and Amos with retiring from the Iceberg Corps and donating half their income to families of fallen soldiers. But Thais had stood there in her salmon-pink kitchen and admitted her mistakes, holding Io's hand and smiling. And the next day, she had manipulated Io's love of Ava into breaking Bianca out of jail and setting her loose on the Nine.

"Thais has had her second chances," Io said. "She doesn't get any more from me."

The statement dropped stone-heavy between the two sisters. It was the first time Io had thought it, but its truth was undeniable. Ava was right in a way: Io didn't hate Thais, not exactly, but she *was* done with her. Io had offered her all the compassion she could spare, all the second chances she deserved and then some—and Thais had squandered it all. Io had nothing more to give and nothing to expect in return. It was liberating.

"She gets more from me," Ava replied. A deep groove had etched into the skin between her eyebrows. "But, Io . . ."

Io sighed through her nose. Here they would come, all the excuses Ava, always the peacemaker, had invented over the years: *Thais has sacrificed so much for us. She's been working all day to take care of us; her temper is bound to be taut. Mama was hard on her in a way she never was with us. We have each other, but Thais had no one to fight for her.*

Io's mind jumped back to Amos's apartment, to the first real fight she and Ava had ever had. *Finally, we have comfort,* Ava had said then, trying to convince Io to drop the investigation on the wraiths. *Finally, we are safe.* Ava had always argued for safety. Shelter from the complicated feelings of being angry at Thais, from the betrayal of her sister turning out to be someone different from the person they thought she was.

Io didn't have the indulgence of forgiveness, the luxury of safety. Io knew, with absolute clarity, that tolerating violence was a violence in itself. If Ava tried to defend Thais and change Io's opinion now, it would be over. It would be unforgiveable.

Ava's eyes were fixed on Io, and her every word came out like a stab of gritty intention. "She gets more chances from me, but, Io, I won't let her hurt you *ever again.*"

Io closed her eyes.

She leaned into her sister's touch and relinquished herself. As though magnetized, her body found its way back into Ava's arms.

Her cheeks were warm with tears, sobs hiccupped from her lips, but there were some chuckles in between the sniffling, and Ava's arms were tight and infallible around her, and Io was soothed and validated and content.

She was happy.

They stayed like that for a good long while, sitting side by side on the steps of the station, holding each other's hands and talking: about the god's thread and the futile quest through the Wastelands, about the missing people and the true fury-born, about Seto Sarris-Nakano and the nefarious Agora, about Edei and the fraying fate-thread, Nico and Urania—about Bianca.

Ava buried her face in her palms when Io confirmed Bianca was alive and well. "I knew you'd keep each other safe."

Io rubbed her back, unsure how to comfort her. Words of encouragement felt empty. Bianca was not exactly an open-hearted, forgiving person, and besides, this was a matter only Ava and Bianca themselves could solve.

But as the conversation moved to their trek through the blasted city sewers and their narrow escape from the hundreds-of-years-old leviathini, Io knew exactly what to say. "We need to know about the gods, Ava. We need to figure out where to find them and how to fight them. They're gathering an army. Torr got lucky, but the other missing people didn't. I believe they're true fury-born and that the gods are abducting them because they're planning something big. We need to stop them."

Ava stood up without a second thought. "Thais never mentions the gods, and I haven't pushed her to. But I think it's time now."

She slipped her fingers through Io's and led her down the plank to the trolley car. Warm candlelight spilled beneath the door. Io's muscles tensed with dread and anticipation: beyond that door stood Thais. Before she could lose her courage, she reached around Ava and pulled the door open.

The trolley car had been completely transformed. The seats had been ripped out, the luggage bars packed with food and medical supplies. A tiny wood stove was burning by the left wall, a make-shift vent pumping wood smoke out the window. The floor was covered with cardboard, every window painted black or taped with dark cloth. A thick, old rug had been draped like a curtain in the middle of the room, separating the sleeping quarters from the small anteroom. In the Quilt, Io could see twelve people total in the room: ten wraiths, asleep in the far end of the wagon; the fury-born girl, Torr, curled up with a book against her chest; and Thais.

Io's sister sat on a stool before the fire, her brow scrunched in concentration, sweat beading her forehead and neck. Her eyes were alight with silver, and her fingers moved fast in interlooping maneuvers, like braiding someone's hair. Her mouth was a tight, white line; she was in pain, Io knew, because weaving a thread hurt. Much like Io had to sacrifice one of her own threads to cut someone else's, Thais—and all weavers—had to snip pieces of their existing threads to create a new one. It felt, Thais had described it once, like skinning strips of your own flesh off.

"I thought," Thais said without looking up, "that you were going to get rid of her."

Anger flashed in Io's mind like a red alarm, but she wasn't going to gift Thais with a reaction. "We need to talk," Io told her eldest sister, "about your former bosses."

"Oh, do we?" Thais challenged with a drawl.

"Thais, behave," Ava cautioned. "The information Io needs is necessary to stop—"

There was a knock at the door: two beats slow, pause, three beats fast, pause, two beats slow. The Fortuna's safe code.

"It's Edei," Io said to a startled Ava. Without asking for permission, she threw the door open.

It *was* Edei, wearing his white shirt with his sleeves rolled up above his biceps and scowling deeply, but it was someone else, too. Io barely caught a flurry of blond hair and a billowy black shirt, as the person barreled past her and Ava and tackled Thais to the floor. A tussle followed, limbs tangled and sounds muffled against the cardboard-covered floor. It ended quickly, with Thais pinned to the floor by the wrists and Bianca Rossi pressing a knee to her chest.

"Stop, stop—" Ava was frantically trying to pull Bianca's arms off their sister.

But the mob queen's grip was iron-hard. She positioned one of her boots on Thais's left wrist to free her own hand, then arced it above her head, her fist clenching something invisible. Within seconds, Thais began writhing, eyes bulged, mouth opening and closing like a fish out of water. Io couldn't see Bianca's face from where she stood, but she knew her eyes were burning fury orange and her whip was curled around Thais's neck.

"You promised to be calm, boss!" Edei cried out.

Stepping around Io, he went for the hand Bianca was holding her fury-whip with. Together, they all looked like one of those pre-Collapse statues in District-on-the-Hill: ancient gods tangled in combat, naked bodies rippling with deathful muscles. Io knew it would be futile. When caught in her fury-born's bloodthirst, no one could shake Bianca off.

But one could reason with her, as Io had been doing during their time together on the road. "Bianca," she said from where she still stood by the open door. "You need to let her go."

Through the shuffling and strained breathing came Bianca's snarled reply, "There are crimes that cannot go unpunished."

"Is death her punishment?" Io countered. "Who decides that? You?"

A moment of silence followed, then a low *"Yes."*

"And when she's dead, how do we find the gods?" said Io. "We need answers, Bianca, not an executioner's axe."

Io couldn't see Bianca's face, but Edei could. His eyes searched the mob queen's face with a concerned frown. He loosened his grip on her hand, then let it go completely. Ava wasn't as trusting, yet when Bianca shrugged her hold off, she eased away and sat gingerly on the floor next to them. The hand holding the fury-whip lowered. Thais coughed, gulping down air.

"Where are the gods, weaver?" Bianca asked.

"Get off me!"

Bianca shifted her weight to press down on Thais's chest. *"Where are they?"*

"I don't know! Do you think I chatted with them over tea and biscuits? They have an entire shadow network in place precisely so that no one will ever come close to them. I got my orders from my superiors, and they got theirs from someone further up the chain of command. I never laid eyes on the gods!"

Io stepped closer for a better view of her sister's strained face. "Do not lie, Thais. You shared a thread with one of them."

Thais's eyes narrowed with venom. "Are you enjoying this, sister mine? You'd have liked to be the one holding me on a leash, wouldn't you?"

It was a cruel, baiting question, but Io found it did not bother her in the slightest. She was at peace with her feelings for Thais now. No more forgiveness, no more second chances, because even here, trapped beneath the wraith *she* had created, Thais's instinct was to try to hurt Io. No, Io didn't enjoy watching Bianca hurt Thais, but she wouldn't stop it—not just yet. It appeared that moments of threat and violence were the only times Thais could be truthful.

She said simply, "Answer the question. Because if we have to ask again, it won't be me and Bianca. It will be Urania, Muse of astronomy, whose sisters you murdered. It will be Seto Sarris-Nakano, whose brothers were killed before his eyes by your faction's wraiths. It will be his kurbantes-born, who barely survived."

A breath hitched in Thais's throat—she exhaled and began speaking. "I never laid eyes on any of them. I only know they exist because of the gold in their threads. After we passed our initiation, we were brought blindfolded into a room, where we pledged our allegiance to them. When we were released back into the city, I had that silver-and-gold thread. My suspicion is that they have other moira-born in their ranks and that one of them wove that thread between us. Between them and all of their network. When I touched the thread, I didn't get glimpses of the person or thing it connected me to, as we usually do. I could only sense a purpose, our duty to restore the world to its former glory."

"Ah, yes," Io said, "your grand purpose. You are conduits of the divine. Justice is the virtue of great souls." She repeated Thais and Hanne's words that day almost verbatim, dripping enough sarcasm to fill a beehive. She was being a little cruel herself, but she didn't care.

"Who are your superiors?" Bianca asked. "I would like to pay them a visit."

"Good luck finding them." Thais's wiry neck muscles strained against Bianca's hold. "I've been trying every channel I know of for the past six weeks. It's been total silence. They have gone into hiding."

Bianca's head twisted to Io, those orange eyes filled with inquisitiveness.

Io contemplated all their clues so far: the wraiths set on a course of punishment, the Sarris-Nakano brothers' coalition advocating for elections, the white-clad Agora members in the kurbantes-born's illusion.

She reached into her pocket and unfolded the map they had found at Wilhem's room back in Tulip. "I found this map in someone from your shadow network's belongings. What do these markings mean?"

"They're weather predictions," Thais said. "We were all given one of these maps each time we were traveling outside Nanzy."

Weather predictions: that was what the Agora were known for. "Who made these predictions? The Agora? How are the gods connected to them?"

Thais took a moment before answering. Her sneer had settled into narrowed, calculating eyes, shining with something Io didn't quite like. When she spoke, her voice was calm, measured. "You've done a lot of digging, haven't you, little sister? I told you, I was only privy to what my superiors told me. But there has always been a sense of legitimacy to our cause. My comrades believed our missions had the Agora's stamp of approval. I got to see that firsthand when I was chosen to carry out the mission in Alante. A week later, the Agora endorsed Luc's Police Commissioner application and transferred a large sum to fund his mayoral campaign."

So, it *was* true. Rosa and Xenophon had been on the right track about Saint-Yves's shadowy funding. But why was Thais holding Io's gaze with such intensity? Why was she *willingly* offering information?

Her sister went on. "We were recruited by a network working for the gods. We were gifted with golden threads of duty. We served our orders loyally. We never doubted, we never questioned. But when the wraiths kept dying, when our mission was failing, I reached out to my superiors. Their reply was to keep trying. It wasn't just an order—it was a threat."

Io remembered Thais's frantic explanations the night of the Nine's murders. *You don't deny them, Io,* Thais had said. *I've seen what happens to those who do.*

"It isn't right, what they've done. Yes, the fury-born have been avenged. Their line has been revived. I don't know if that was their plan from the start, but they were successful. Now they're building back their army. But they abandoned all these helpless people." Thais shifted her head to point at the sleeping wraiths in the trolley car. "Used them and discarded them to slow, miserable deaths. They told me we were serving a great purpose, a mission of peace, but they abandoned me, too. After all I've done, all I've sacrificed, they cut me off."

Of course, Thais's change of heart was because *she* had been hurt, Io thought bitterly. Her wounded pride, her unseen potential, her severed aspirations—the world just had to revolve around Thais.

"I have spent every waking moment since I left Alante trying to think of ways to lure them out of hiding. To force them to face me and their failings." She paused, watching Io. "The gods have gone silent, and the Agora never leave their compound except to attend events of the biggest magnitude. Like the Mayoral Assembly gala tomorrow night."

Blood rushed through Io's ears, her trepidation heavy and disorienting. Thais was willingly sharing information because she was trying to get something out of this. Another manipulation, the cost of which would no doubt be high.

"But I know a way you can get their attention," Thais said. "I know how you can lure the gods out of hiding."

Io was quiet. No point in replying when the other shoe was yet to drop.

"You are going to use your connections to find a way for me to enter the Garden District to see Luc Saint-Yves," her sister bargained. "He and I can figure out how to get us into the gala."

Io didn't want to know the answer, yet still she asked. "How do you know the gods will be there?"

"Because I'm going to convince Luc," Thais said, "to put out an announcement that he has found the last surviving member of the Nine, the Muse the gods failed to kill—and that he will be bringing her to the gala."

CHAPTER XX

LET ME CHOOSE YOU

"YOU AREN'T SERIOUSLY considering agreeing to this, are you?" Bianca snapped.

They stood in the corridor of the top floor of the Hôtel Du Jardin Blanc, outside the penthouse room the rest of their group was sleeping in. Weak daylight filtered through the floor-to-ceiling windows at the other end of the corridor. Dawn had arrived incognito, the sky so overcast there was barely a difference between day and night. Edei had stepped inside to fill the others in on the events of last night, while Bianca had gestured Io aside with her chin, her crossed arms and venomous scowl promising a titillating conversation.

Io didn't feel like doing this right now. She leaned against the wall and shot back, "What's your plan, then?"

Bianca worked her jaw around, a lion flexing its muscles before its next meal. "Definitely not putting my trust in the person who manipulated me, betrayed me, and led dozens of people to their deaths."

"It won't be the same. Ava will keep her in line."

The mob queen's face darkened. After Thais had dropped her bombshell and started explaining where Saint-Yves was staying in the Garden District and how they could access it, Ava had tried to pull Bianca aside. Hissed murmurs had been exchanged, then the mob queen had jerked her arm away from Ava's touch and marched straight out of the trolley car.

"Forgiven her, have you?" the mob queen asked flatly. "You think

Ava can be trusted? All the wraiths sleeping in their safehouse—
they don't know who their caregivers really are. They don't know
Thais was part of the group that created them. Your wicked sister
didn't have the guts to tell them, and Ava thinks they need to focus
on their health. But they deserve to know, cutter."

"Wouldn't they be able to see the marks of crimes on her?" Io
asked. "Like you do?"

"We see guilt," Bianca snapped. "We don't see what this guilt
comes from."

Would any of the wraiths have stayed under Thais's care if they
knew she was one of the many hands that had condemned them to
an early death? Io doubted it, and Ava must have, too. Why then had
she mentioned it to Bianca to begin with?

Io considered. She craved to help, to alleviate Bianca's wrath. "Can
I tell you a story?"

"How will a story help with anything going on right now, cutter?"
hissed Bianca.

Io shrugged the comment off. "It's a short one. One autumn, our
father returned from the mines with a small, auburn canary. It trilled
every morning at dawn; we all loved it, Ava especially. Then, one day,
we woke up and the canary was gone. Ava had left its cage open, so it
could fly away if it wanted to. She was very pleased that the bird was
now free." Io paused, remembering. "I found its half-eaten carcass
on a corner of the roof a few days later. It hadn't flown away. A stray
cat had snatched it through the open door of its cage and eaten it."

Bianca blinked, infinitely bored. "Your point is?"

"Ava tries to help," Io said slowly, as though talking to a toddler.
"But she doesn't always know how—so she leaves the door open."
She made a *get it?* motion with her eyebrows, which Bianca did not,
apparently, get. "The reason Ava mentioned that the wraiths don't

know about their creators, about Thais, might be because she thinks you can help. That you are better suited to tell them the truth, in a way that neither she nor Thais ever could."

The mob queen's eyebrows shot up, as though the idea had never occurred to her. But in Io's mind, it was the most logical conclusion: out of all the wraiths, Bianca had been able to hang on to life the longest and had recovered her mind the fastest.

A small, uncertain whisper slipped through Bianca's lips. "What do I even say? How do you tell someone that the gods mutilated your threads to revive the line of the fury-born and that now you're half of a fury-born, too, except you're probably going to die, pretty soon?"

Io had no answer to that, but she could offer understanding. She reached out and laid her palm on the sharp jut of Bianca's thin shoulder. For once, the mob queen didn't shrug the touch off.

The door was thrown open, startling them both.

Emir beckoned them inside with a jerk of his head. The kurbantes-born had discarded his black robes and was wearing trousers and a shirt in dark gray. His siblings were dressed similarly, scattered in clusters around the room. Seto and Urania were the only ones sitting, the former in an armchair, the latter on the floor among the pillows. The Muse's eyes were trained on the floor-to-ceiling windows, glassy as though lost in thought. To her left, Nico was chewing on the inside of his cheek and casting glances at Urania every two seconds. Edei must have told them what Thais had proposed. Io wondered what the Muse had decided.

Edei was standing by the windows, his back to the room, his mouth a hard line. Io circled the sitting area to stop right next to him, while Bianca leaned against a wall by the door.

"Mr. Rhuna has explained your sister's plan," Seto said. "Entering the Garden District will not be easy. It's a gated community, one of the most affluent in Nanzy."

"But it can be done?" Io asked.

"My contacts can procure courier passes, but no more than two."

"That should be enough. I can accompany my sister."

"You cannot," Seto said calmly. "Not with so many police patrols going around. We will not risk you getting arrested. Mr. Rhuna has volunteered to accompany your sister. He believes the Mayor will agree to see him, as they recently did business together in Alante."

"Did they?" Bianca hissed, ripping off the wall. "What have I taught you about *no guns, no leeches, no paramours*, ey? You've taken my gang and ruined it, you big buffoon—"

"Hey!" Nico called out. "You're being unfair, boss. You don't know what it was like after the murder of the Nine. It was Edei who managed to put a stop to the riots. He struck a deal with Saint-Yves to recall all police presence in the Silts that allowed us to take back control from the other mob bosses. Edei's the only reason the whole city didn't die of thirst during the acid rainstorm. He and the rest of our gang agreed to brave the acid rain to fix the water purification system."

"Am I supposed to be impressed? That you sold out our gang's values to save your asses? I'm not." Bianca turned her gaze from Nico to Seto. "And you—I thought you were smarter than that. Are you really going to trust the success of this operation to one of the gods' former—let's hope—lackeys, the current Mayor of Alante, and a nineteen-year-old boy playing at king?"

Seto replied with a simple "It is an opportunity worth exploring. If it proves a dead end, we will proceed with another plan."

"If it proves a dead end," Bianca seethed, "we'll all be in cuffs."

"It will not come to that, Miss Rossi. My power reaches far beyond the Shards."

"How does your power square off against the entire Nanzese police force—"

"*Enough*," Edei cut in. He was scowling at them over his shoulder, his voice sharper than Io had ever heard it. "Thais and I will plead our case to Saint-Yves. He will either help or he won't, and we'll take it from there. Everyone here thinks this is the most viable option, even Urania, who will be risking the most if we manage to get into the Assembly gala—so for once in your life, *stop bickering, Bianca*."

The mob queen shifted her weight, hip jutting out. She raked Edei up and down with what Io thought was a half-irritated, half-impressed tilt of her eyebrows. But when she spoke, her voice dripped sarcasm. "Sitting on my throne helped you grow some fangs, ey, pup?"

Io expected him to fold, to drop his eyes and lower his head, as she had seen him do in the past before Bianca's wrath. But Edei didn't move in the slightest. He held Bianca's gaze and said, "That's right," as if the jab hadn't touched him at all. "You should get some sleep, Bianca. You too, Io."

Then he was moving across the sprawling living room. He picked up his bedding from the sofa and Io's from the floor and marched into one of the rooms at the back of the penthouse, leaving silence in his wake. Io cast a look around at Bianca's stunned face and Nico's proud one, then turned on her heel and followed him.

As her footfalls echoed on the marble, she realized: it was the first time she had heard him call Bianca by her name and not "boss."

The room Edei had chosen was under renovation. The floor was freshly laid milky gray marble, the walls fashioned with sleek, dark wooden wardrobes. It was dusty and colder than the rest of the penthouse, and it had no windows. Io could already feel the dark and quiet settling on her lids sleep-heavy.

She and Edei lay side by side, a few feet away from each other, atop the plush hotel comforters they'd laid on the floor. Io had kicked off her boots, unbuttoned her trousers, and rolled up her tight top. Edei had taken his shirt off completely. It was chillier than the other rooms here, but still uncomfortably humid.

Io spread her hair over her pillow, tracing the tips of her fingers on the cold marble. She was looking at the ceiling, the wisps of shadows that slipped into the room through the narrow gap between the closed door and the floor. The shadows shifted as the rest of the team moved about the penthouse, deep in planning mode, but no sounds reached them here. She could only hear Edei's breaths, long inhales and loud exhales of air—the sounds of barely suppressed infuriation.

"Are you all right?" Io whispered into the black.

"Not really."

"Bianca was just trying to rile you up. She probably felt threatened that you were finally—" She quickly swallowed her words, afraid of sounding obtuse.

"Standing up to her?" Edei supplied. "I did that plenty back in Alante, just not as . . . volatilely. I don't care what Bianca thinks of me, to be honest. It bothers me that she's right, though."

Io remained quiet, in waiting.

"I sat on her so-called throne for barely a month, after I recovered and before I left the city to find you. For years, I had thought about all the things I would do differently, all the progress I would bring. But when the time came and I had to deal with the aftermath of her arrest and the Nine's slaughter, the looting and riots, the increasing police presence, other gangs vying for our turf and our members abandoning us—nothing I had planned worked." Io could only see his outline in the darkness; his throat bobbed. "The only reason I managed to pull the gang back together and retake the Silts is because I abandoned my own hopes and did exactly what Bianca would do. What I had seen her do countless times before: rule with knuckles made of brass."

Violence. It had come to haunt Edei again.

"Edei . . ." Io began.

"I know what you'll say." He spoke fast, breathlessly, as though trying to get it all out. "At least I tried. At least I saved the gang and brought peace back to the Silts. I know that should be a comfort, but it isn't, Io. Silver linings have never been enough for me. For a long time, I could serve Bianca because she was the best option we had. But I tried to be another option, a better one, and I could change nothing. I just ended up repeating all the things I thought were her shortcomings, her mistakes—because they weren't mistakes. They are the only thing that works, and she was right. She was always right. You've got to have fangs to sit on the throne. There is no changing things, not in this world."

Io opened her mouth; he needed her help right now, kindness and hope. But what could she say? She, who denounced change? How hypocritical of her to champion change now, for Edei's sake, when she herself thought change was a bleak, insidious thing, an interloper.

Perhaps she could ask him. Perhaps they could help each other in this, as they had done in so many other things. "Why do things need to change? If it works, why change it?"

She heard him shift on his pillow, turning to look at her. "Just because it works doesn't mean it's right."

He was talking about morality again, but Io found the term far too nuanced. "But right is what we decide it is. What we think is right might not be what people like Bianca or Seto or the gods think is right."

"But see, even your examples, you're pitting *us* against *them*. The powerless against the powerful. Right has no uniform shape, that's true, but there's a—" He said a word in Sumazi that Io didn't quite catch, and paused briefly while his mind scrabbled for the Alantian translation. "A *communality* to it. If all of us with less power think something is not right, that it hurts us, then it probably does. And if it hurts us, it requires change. We need to have the choice, at least. Even if the world works as it is right now, even if it's nice and comfortable, it doesn't mean we can't choose something better, something just and kind and hopeful."

Just and kind and hopeful—it was a wonderful thought. Io turned it in her mouth like candy, achingly sweet. If it hurt, it required change; she could agree with that. She could implement that—was already implementing it in her relationship with Thais. Only a few hours ago, she had decided that she was done gifting her sister second chances. That was change, too, Io supposed, the good kind. "Growth" might be a better word for it.

Some impulse had her pulling up the Quilt. Her fingers reached over her chest, skimming through her many threads. She found the one that led to her sister by feel alone: Thais's intoxicating laugh, her silky hair in Io's hands as she braided it up, cinnamon and semolina clinging to her skin after she had made Winter Feast melomakarona cookies.

Io followed it away from her chest. Her fingers stilled.

"What's wrong?" Edei asked. "What are you looking at?"

"I think it's going to snap."

He was silent for a long, long moment. "The fate-thread?"

He sounded fearful. Io glanced at him, but his face was swathed in shadow.

"No," she said. "My thread to Thais."

"What would you feel? If it snapped?"

She didn't even need to think about it. The answer came easy and instinctual, in the way truth often revealed itself. "Relief. A sense of loss, too, but mostly relief."

"What does it feel like? When a thread snaps? When it's not there any longer?"

People had asked her that before, Rosa, Amos, her schoolmates, her clients. *Loss and longing*, she used to answer. But she didn't give Edei the answer she used for everyone else—she gave him the truth. "To me, it feels like cutting your hair very short. You imagine its phantom touch on your back. You reach out to put its invisible substance behind your ear. There is a sense of loss in it, yes, but you know you will get used to it, with time."

"Is that because you're a cutter?"

"I suppose. Knowing it will get better makes it easier to do what I do."

"Easier doesn't mean easy," Edei said. "I've always thought it's unfair that you moira-born have to lose one of your own threads to cut someone else's. Using your powers costs you something you love, which is not the case with most other-born."

"No, it's not," Io agreed.

This had been a point of discussion often in the Ora household, most often brought up by Thais. Her sister was always furious at the injustice of it. It hurt to weave a new thread, it was draining to draw a thread, it cost dearly to cut one. Io had listened to Thais's tirades as though it was the news on the radio, as though it concerned someone else. Sacrificing one of her threads to cut another person's was all she had ever known. It was how her powers worked, a law of nature as unbending as the pull of gravity. Losing a thread hardly mattered when Io loved in such multitudes. In a day, she could have a new thread.

But now she was no longer a beacon of silver, as Hanne had said. Now she was down to nineteen threads and hadn't been able to replace them. Now loving felt like labor. Io was so tired, so drained, so brokenhearted. Unmoored.

Edei was right: it wasn't fair. Sadness dropped on her chest like a weight, and a seedy sort of irritation. It had never been fair, so why was she only now realizing it? She should have questioned the nature of her powers before.

"Do they ever grow back?" Edei asked into the silence.

"Sometimes," Io replied. "If the feeling remains. If it's strong enough."

"But if the feeling remains, if it's strong enough, what does it matter if there is a thread to accompany it?"

Was he talking about . . . *them*?

Quietly, he added, "What does it matter if it has the stamp of approval from fate?"

He *was* talking about them. He was asking her, in his feather-soft and sunlight-gentle way, to cut the fate-thread.

Io turned on her side to face him, tucking a hand beneath her cheek. Only his outline was visible, his strong nose, his long eyelashes, the curls dotting his forehead.

"Can I tell you a story?" she whispered. "About the time when I first discovered our fate-thread?"

"Of course."

"My mother was very proud of it. All her friends were awed. One of them had a boyfriend from Poppy Town, a moira-born weaver.

She invited us over for dinner. Mama dressed me in Thais's old blue velvet dress and Ava's too-small slippers. When we got to her friend's apartment, it was full of people: not just her boyfriend, but his brothers, too, and their cousins, all of them moira-born. Their eyes shone silver the moment I stepped into the room. I was ten, a little shy, not much acquainted with people outside my family. They terrified me—they started asking me for permission to touch it, to tug it and draw it out. The boyfriend wanted to tear a strip of it away to try and weave his own fate-thread."

Io shuffled; the memory still made her squirmy.

"They didn't last more than ten minutes. One of them started complaining his head hurt. Another one's eyes became red and itchy. Those who were holding the fate-thread snatched their hands away—there were scorch marks on the tips of their fingers. For everyone but me, the fate-thread was too bright, too potent to behold for more than a few minutes. I stopped panicking. No one was looking at me anymore, no one was touching me. I ate my dinner in silence and asked for seconds.

"Mama said nothing, not a word to me, until we were back in our apartment. Thais had stayed up to find out how it went. Our mother looked at me over her nose and said, *Those were important people you just disappointed, Io. If you keep doing that, you'll end up all alone in the world, won't you?* Thais scoffed, loudly through her nose, which was odd—she never disagreed with our mother on anything—and told her, *Well, if you could see that fate-thread, Mama, you would know that Io is destined to be loved more fiercely, more resolutely than all of us combined.*"

Io had always loved that story. The justice of it. She loved it still, even if Thais was no longer her righteous defender.

"I've lived my whole life with that certainty," Io went on. "That there was someone out there destined to love me, unconditionally, even if I was a disappointment and ne'er-do-well, even if I made a living outing cheaters and cutting threads, even if I conspired to drive my own sister out of her home."

"Io," he said, "I didn't know—"

"I never told you," Io said, cutting him off.

She didn't want his sympathy right now. This wasn't about her terrible childhood and her mess of a family. It was about the two of them—and about destiny.

"It wouldn't be the end of the world to cut it," she told him in the darkness. "But don't tell me it doesn't matter. It would be different. The thread might disappear forever. Or it might grow back. But in either case, it wouldn't be destiny. It wouldn't shimmer and torch and burn."

"But it would be our own choosing," Edei insisted.

Io's throat tightened. Had she secretly wished he would relent and finally accept it? Yes. But she didn't fault him for disagreeing. In fact, she admired this in him, his infallible values, his honesty, his kindness. Always gentle with her, even when he was breaking her heart.

Because if he doubted the love with the fate-thread and she feared the love without it, then where did that leave them? Doubtful and fearful and *loveless*.

"I told you I would cut it if that's what you wanted, and I still mean it," Io said, trying to keep her voice steady. "I just wanted you to know what it was you were asking for."

Edei didn't miss a beat. His head turned to her, light dancing on his pupils.

"I know what I'm asking for," he whispered. "Io, let me choose you."

But what if he didn't? When the thread was cut, the destiny rejected, what if there was nothing left between them? Change was a clever pickpocket, a thief in the night—it bled you dry and convinced you it was your fault for carrying valuables in the first place.

"I'm too scared," she whispered back.

There was a short silence, then he gave a nod, his head susurrating against the pillow.

"Then," he said, his voice wide around a smile, "let me hold you."

He reached into the space between them and grabbed hold of the comforter she was lying on. He pulled; Io went with it, sliding across the floor until her body was lined up with his. His arm draped over her rib cage, his hand tangled in her hair. Her nose skimmed his bare chest, right in the nook where his clavicles met. His breath teased the wispy hairs at her forehead.

They fell into a soft, dreamful sleep.

CHAPTER XXI

NOTHING LIKE AN ENDING

MUCH AS SHE took pride in her patience, Io was not built to wait. She just hadn't known it before, because she was always the one following clues, making decisions, risking her life. But now, watching Thais and Edei get into the automobile in front of the Hôtel Du Jardin Blanc, Io couldn't keep her limbs from fidgeting, her mind from spiraling.

The plan was for Thais and Edei to pose as Hôtel employees, delivering six boxes of eclairs to Saint-Yves's mansion. It so happened that the Hôtel Du Jardin Blanc was renowned for its pastry chef, and its eclairs in particular. Io felt positively offended that she hadn't known earlier; eclairs were her absolute favorite pastry in the world. When Emir had brought six teal boxes of the famous Nanzese pastries to the penthouse, neatly gift-wrapped with a gauzy baby pink ribbon, Io glared at them with a vicious jealousy. Once past the guards and into the gated community, Thais and Edei would knock on Saint-Yves's door and plead their case. Seto, Pina, and most of the kurbantes-born siblings had taken off earlier in the day to hold strategic positions around the gated community—in case things went south.

The Hôtel vehicle took off down the avenue, taking Thais and Edei with it. Io's eyes trailed it as it wove through traffic. Her stomach was in knots, her shoulders clenched up with tension. Gods, this was going to be impossible.

A menacing presence sidled up to her, all furrowed brow and

crossed arms. "I was thinking," Bianca said, "that it could be a good time to visit the other wraiths."

Io just *mm-hm*ed.

"Would you care to come with me?" Bianca asked, a little pointedly.

The automobile disappeared around a corner. Io dragged her gaze to the mob queen. "What if something goes wrong?" she said. "What if we're needed?"

"Cutter. We've been explicitly instructed to stay out of this. You and I are far more likely to be recognized than anyone else involved."

"But," Io said in a small voice, "I want to be here when they return."

"I'm sure Edei will know where to find us." Bianca sighed loudly through her nostrils. "I'm begging you, cutter. I don't think I can bear listening to those two smooching any longer."

The living room of the penthouse was empty but for Nico and Urania on one of the sofas, in a tight embrace. The sounds of their whispering and giggling and, well, *smooching* had been the backdrop of this entire operation. Apparently, sometime after Io, Edei, and Bianca snuck out last night, Nico and Urania had shared their first kiss—and hadn't stopped ever since.

A kiss was a welcome relief, Io guessed, from the danger they were about to put themselves in. Edei had filled Io in on Urania's reaction to Thais's plan to use her as bait. Nico had instantly shot it down, but the Muse had taken his hands and said, *Yesterday, you told me I grew up in such privilege that I can't see when it makes me standoffish. I have an opportunity to use my privilege against the gods tomorrow. I'm going to do it, Nico, and you're going to help me.*

It might be good to give these two some privacy. It might be good, too, to see Ava and the wraiths without Thais present.

In the end, visiting the wraiths' safehouse did nothing to soothe Io's nerves. Io might go so far as to say it doubled them, because now, on top of worrying about Edei, she also had to navigate the very awkward interactions between Bianca and Ava *and* ten wraiths gawking at her with suspicious eyes.

Torr, at least, was easy to talk to. The girl had been elated to find out Io was a private investigator. She launched into a long recap of her favorite book series, The Mysteries of Thistle Manor, a twelve-volume-long escapade of a young detective moving into a haunted house with her family and solving the murders of all the different ghosts that lived there. Torr wanted to know about every case Io had ever worked on, which Io was happy to oblige, skipping over the raunchier cases of course. It didn't strike Io as strange at all that she felt instantly at ease with Torr—exchanging book plots and investigating cases was what her and Amos's friendship mostly comprised. Gods, she missed Amos.

"And then," Torr concluded, holding volume seven tight against her chest, "it turns out the ghosts weren't sabotaging Thistle Manor after all—it was the sketchy real estate agent who sold the house to them, because he had been making a profit by scaring the owners off and selling the house to someone else."

"That's a good twist," Io said.

"It's brilliant," Torr commented. The girl had a way of delivering the most enthusiastic of comments in the driest voice Io had ever heard come out of a twelve-year-old's mouth. Io found it very entertaining. "I wish Margaret Ellis would publish more of them, but unfortunately, she died a few years ago. My moms were going to take me to see the play in the Theater District when we moved to the City Proper."

The girl quieted, her fingers running over the dog-eared cover of the book.

"They still can," Io said. "When this is all over."

The look Torr gave her was cutting. "This will never be over. I am a fury-born now. I don't even know if they'll let us into the City Proper after all."

Io didn't deny it. Torr was too clever, too aware to be placated by white lies.

"I'll make sure you get in," one of the wraiths piped up.

He was an older man in his late sixties, with a patchy gray beard and a hooked nose. Ava had introduced him as Elias, a clerk in the Nanzese mayoral office. His deathly pale skin was flaking all over, as though he was a lizard changing skins. He was the last wraith Ava and Thais had found, holing up in a tunnel in the Guts. No one explicitly said so, but Io believed he was one of the wraiths who had attacked the Sarris-Nakano brothers. A long gash trailed from his temple to his ear, caked over with black pus.

The man had been warming up a soup on the gas stove and was now ladling portions into tin bowls for the other wraiths. Most of them were sitting on their cots or the cardboard-covered floor at the far end of the trolley car, but Elias and a couple of young women had braved Io's presence in the sitting area. In the Quilt, Io could see the sapling threads Thais had been weaving for them. They connected the wraiths to each other, but to Ava, too, and Thais and Torr. They weren't going to last long; their essence was faded, fraying at the edges.

But they were keeping the wraiths alive, and that was enough for now.

Elias extended a bowl to Io. "Should I serve them, or will they be staying out there long?" he asked, directing his gaze to Ava and Bianca.

The door had been left ajar to let in some of the much-needed cool summer breeze, and Ava's and Bianca's figures were visible through it. Ava was leaning against the metal framework of the station, eyes downcast, while Bianca paced up and down. Io could just barely hear their voices if she tried. She ignored them as best she could; it didn't look like the sort of conversation you would want someone eavesdropping on.

"Let's give them some more time," Io said. They had arrived here a little over an hour ago, and after introducing them to the wraiths, Ava had managed to pull Bianca aside for a private . . . argument, from the looks of it. "I'm sure they'll come back in when they're hungry."

"Is it true?" one of the younger wraiths, Costanza, asked, her drooping bloodshot eyes nailed on the mob queen. "That she's one of us? Threadless?"

Io cupped her hands around the sizzling hot tin bowl and gave a nod.

"She's different," Costanza said. "Seems much more . . . alert than the rest of us. I can barely last three hours without falling asleep. Does she drink the tonic?"

"Yes," said Io, "but not as often as you do."

Just within the hour she had been here, she had seen the wraiths take sips of the sleeping tonic twice. On the road, Bianca had only drunk the tonic when the fury-born bloodthirst gripped her in its claws, maybe once or twice a day. Io couldn't help but wonder: Did these wraiths truly need more of it to feel like themselves, or was it something Thais and Ava had suggested to keep them subdued? Io couldn't blame her sisters if the latter was true. She couldn't imagine what it must have been like, traveling with this many wraiths through the Wastelands. Some of them were far worse than Bianca ever was, wounds leaking, lips ashen, limbs moving with difficulty. Not to mention the fury-born bloodthirst; Io had caught at least four of the wraiths studying her with orange eyes.

Metal groaned, and Io glanced up to find Bianca marching toward them with a purpose. Elias, Costanza, and the other young woman watched the mob queen approach with an almost reverent kind of look. She came to a stop right where Io was sitting on the floor, hands propped on her hips.

"Cutter," she said. "Can I have a moment alone with my kin?"

Io was already standing, spilling a bit of her soup in the process. "Sure thing."

Torr unfolded from her cross-legged position as well, perhaps to join Io and Ava outside, but Bianca stuck out a palm. "Stay, girl. You're fury-born, too. You should hear what I have to say."

With a fleeting glance at Io, Torr settled back down, her face sobering with gravity. Whatever argument she had just had with Ava, Bianca had come out victorious. She was going to tell the wraiths about Thais. About the gods, too, and all that had happened since. Io had no place in that conversation; she slipped out of the trolley car and joined Ava where she had taken a seat on the steps of the trolley station.

Her sister was staring into the distance, her mouth a firm, unhappy line. Io began sipping on the soup—it was good, hearty stuff: potato stew with carrots, celery, and a strong hint of bay leaves. Dusk hadn't arrived yet, but the promise of it was thick in the air, a cool breeze chasing away the stifling heat of the day.

After a while, Io asked, "Is this Mama's yahni recipe?"

Ava nodded. "But I substituted bay leaves for oregano. Couldn't find it here."

"It's good." The potato stew was a staple of the Ora household, because all its ingredients were so cheap. Io softened her voice. "Ava—"

"It's all right, sister mine," Ava said. "You don't need to comfort me. Me and Bianca . . . I'm going to fix it. It might take time, but I'm going to fix it."

Io's lips curved up into a smile. Her sister, who did everything to avoid confrontation, who ran away the moment her relationships stopped being fun, was going to *fight*. Io felt proud and heartwarmed; she let her head drop to Ava's shoulder, and after a moment, Ava reached up to tousle her hair.

Minutes passed until Ava spoke again. "They're back."

Thais and Edei appeared on the roof adjoining the trolley station. Io's sister dashed ahead in hurried strides, while Edei followed, keeping his distance, hands in the pockets of his trousers. The whole metal structure vibrated when they reached Io and Ava.

"How did it go?" Io asked, heart in her throat.

Thais was wearing a pout of epic proportions. Her face dragged, as though someone was tugging down the corners of her mouth.

"He's going to help us," Edei replied.

Io's gaze went to him. He was still dressed in the red-and-white uniform of the Hôtel Du Jardin Blanc, which was a little tight on him; the shirt hugged his arms, the vest accentuated his chest and waist, the trousers showed off his long, straight legs. Some people were fond of arms or abs or strong backs in boys—but Io loved long, straight legs, a fact that Rosa enjoyed making fun of.

Only a few hours ago, she and Edei had woken up in each other's arms. She had had a palm resting against his rib cage, her face against his bare back; he had been holding her hand against his chest like a prayer. *Let me choose you*, he had said last night, and although Io was still terrified, she was also appeased. He had held her, he had wanted her. For today, at least, that was enough.

Io noticed his hands. He hadn't removed them from his pockets. Was he hiding them? She stood in one fluid movement, and Edei let her remove them from the pockets. On his right hand, he still wore the knuckles. Red welts had furrowed into his skin beneath the brass. He had used them, recently.

"It's nothing," he said, so low only Io could hear. "The phobos-born was there. He was surprised to see Thais. He thought we were a threat. But it's sorted now. They're going to help. Saint-Yves has been closely monitoring the disappearances—one of the missing people from Poppy Town is his former lieutenant. He had suspicions, too, that the missing people are other-born and that someone might be kidnapping them for a bigger purpose."

"And . . . ?" Io whispered with a nudge of her chin toward Thais.

Edei shook his head. If Thais had any notions of convincing Saint-Yves to take her back, they apparently hadn't been fruitful. Io could understand: Saint-Yves was an idealist. Thais's involvement in the murders of the Nine had put a stop to the Initiative, his career-long project for the integration of other-born in the police force, before it even had a chance to begin.

"What's *she* doing here?" Thais snapped.

They all twisted to look at the carriage. Through the open door, they could see Bianca speaking to the wraiths. The mob queen's head slowly swiveled toward them, her eyes burning foreboding flames of orange beneath her furrowed brow. Behind her, the wraiths were still, quiet, but their eyes, too, were orange, trained solely on Thais.

"What is she doing?" Panic shrilled Thais's voice. "Who the hell left her alone with them?"

She strode across the rooftop. Three steps, four, almost to the door—

Ava stepped in her path. She was shorter than Thais and less muscular, but her presence in that moment was domineering. She clapped her fingers around Thais's wrists and held her back.

"Thais," Ava said. *"No."*

Lithe and slow, Bianca sauntered to the door and shoved it closed.

Io stilled, her eyes traveling between her two sisters like a snared rabbit watching the hunter stalk out of the foliage. Never before had she heard Ava say *no* to Thais. Never before had she stood between Thais and what she wanted. This wasn't going to go down well.

Thais thrust a hand in the direction of the closed door. "She's going to— They will— *I did the best I could, Ava.*"

Io expected Ava to comfort her. To wrap an arm around Thais's shoulder, to tell her of course she did, everyone knew that, it would be all right soon. But Ava said nothing, *did* nothing, not even as Thais turned away from them all and covered her face with her palms.

"I'm not the villain," Thais hissed through silent sobs. "I'm not the enemy."

Ava's face was impassive. She abandoned her post before the closed door and moved back to the steps of the station, where she sat with her arms around her knees. "Edei," she said, "if you're willing to wait, I have some anti-inflammatory meds in the carriage. I can dress your knuckles."

"Sounds good. Is this yours, Io? Can I have some of it?" He had slumped down on the steps next to Ava and picked up Io's half-eaten bowl of yahni stew.

Io nodded, her thoughts dazed and confounded. It felt like the world had turned on its head. Thais was crying alone and muted.

Ava was stoic and determined, having stood her ground. Edei was reaching out with his free hand to pull Io down to sit next to him, then scooting her closer to him with an arm around her waist.

Would they have done the same, a month ago, a week ago, a day? Thais's sorrow would have been a firework, loud and bright for all to see. Ava's opinions would have been candied and suppressed so as not to grate the ear. Edei's affection would have been questioned and dissected, his intentions analyzed. And Io—her shame would have drowned out all other feelings. Her fear would have immobilized her.

There was still shame and there was still fear, but this—this was *change*, and yet somehow, in some wondrous way, it felt nothing like an ending.

CHAPTER XXII

A JOKE

THE GREAT ARCH was an ancient structure in the shape of, well, an archway, dated pre-Collapse if the chipped and grayed marble was anything to go by. The Golden City of Nanzy had a ton of these arches, Nehir had explained on the way here, erected to commemorate emperors' victories and long-gone gods. This one was by far the grandest, almost two hundred feet tall, each of its four legs fifty feet wide. The Nanzese were so fond of it that every year during neo-monsoon season, they dressed the whole Arch in metal casings, to keep the acid rain away. It was the number one tourist attraction in the city, and the perfect venue for the Mayoral Assembly gala.

Carvings of tearful survivors and nude fallen soldiers decorated its legs, while a colorful mosaic of gods on the battlefield adorned a principal vault sitting on transverse ribs in the shape of roses and thorned vines. Four wide, carpeted cage lifts carried passengers to the top of the Arch, the so-called Terrasse du Ciel—the sky terrace.

The Terrasse was a marvel: an elegant glass gazebo sat on one end, windows framed with gold, floor tiled with colorful slates. All around it there were green, sculpted shrubs and long climbing vines, ornate fountains spraying jets of water into ponds dotted with lilies and orange fish. Heavy, metal benches swathed with soft cushions were sprinkled between the shrubs, while lamps with wrought iron frames and textured opalescent glass pulsed subtle, rosy-kissed light into the space.

The guests numbered in the hundreds—Mayors and council

members, Nanzy's old money families and nouveau riche entrepreneurs, all dressed in their finest, carrying hair-thin champagne flutes and chatting in delicate voices. The world's elite in a great melting pot, brought together by gossip and free drinks.

What a facade, Io thought as she climbed the last step, cheeks flushed and lungs absolutely devoid of air. She had been forced to take the stairs; all personnel had to, and Io and her group were posing as exactly that: service staff.

There were ten of them in total: Io, Thais, Nehir, and her brother Hassan posing as servers. Pina, Emir, and Edei posing as the retinue of a distinguished guest, Seto, in a delicate gray linen suit. The mob king had insisted on joining them despite his swollen ankle with a stark *Miss Ora, I'm still the most powerful other-born among you. It looks like you're going to need me.* Urania had come as, well, herself, and Nico as her bodyguard.

The Muse's arm was looped around Saint-Yves's elbow. In a finely tailored burgundy suit, the new Mayor of Alante was all mirthful waves and polite smiles, shaking the hand of anyone who came to greet him, then gentlemanly introducing Urania to them. His friends' faces slackened in surprise, then furrowed in offered condolences. It was a performance. Everyone in this party knew the last surviving Muse would be arriving today, thanks to the rumor Saint-Yves had leaked to the political circuits.

Nico was a shadow behind the pair in a discreet black suit. On Saint-Yves's other side stood Aris Lefteriou, the Mayor's right hand, a powerful phobos-born that Io and Edei had faced back in Alante.

Io watched them all waltz around the greenery of the terrace, trying to catch her breath. She was wearing the same black suit and white button-up as the rest of the gala personnel, procured in secret by Seto's contacts. The uniform was stiflingly hot and ironed to unbending crispness; every movement felt like she was wearing armor. Wide-rimmed, dark sunglasses sat on her nose, as they did on all the other-born from her group, to conceal the color of their eyes. Seto had reassured them service staff, especially bodyguards, would be wearing the same glasses, and so far it looked as though he'd been right. The mob king had even managed to procure some with a long-distance refining lens for Io.

"Anything?" Thais whispered. The servers' uniform was a little large on her, the suit jacket jutting out like a hunting tiger's shoulder blades.

Io shook her head no.

Their plan was straightforward: scan the Quilt for the golden threads of a god. Once located, they would alert the others, then coordinate a quiet attack. Four pairs of other-born glove manacles had been smuggled inside the gala, inconspicuous among the medical replacement parts for Seto's leg braces in Pina's bag. The asclepies-born currently sat beside Seto on a bench facing the central fountain, where she had arrived half an hour before them in Seto's retinue. She was on alert, eyes roaming the crowd, ears perked. At their signal, she was to bring them the bag and the manacles inside it.

"Keep looking," Thais said. "I'll take the right side of the terrace, you take the left. Grab a tray and pretend to serve."

Io obeyed. As she crossed the terrace toward one of the four food stations positioned around it, her gaze caught Edei's. He looked stunning in his black tuxedo, all broad shoulders and long, straight legs. He leaned on one leg with an almost bored expression, his right hand in his pants pocket, no doubt fidgeting with his brass knuckles. The whole thing made him look like a spy out of a radio show, suave and elegant.

The afternoon had been a whirlwind of planning, preparing,

getting dressed, but when Io had come out of the bathroom in her server's uniform with her hair slicked back into a low bun, Edei had said, "I like your hair like this."

Io had run a hand over the wide expanse of her forehead, even more prominent now that her curls had been tamed to obedience. "You like foreheads longer than trolley tracks?"

He had bumped his shoulder with hers. "Your eyebrows look beautiful."

"Like two black boats barely holding on to this endless sea of skin?"

He had snorted, then: "They try their hardest, and for that, they should be applauded."

A chuckle had burst through Io's lips, drawing glares from every other tense member of this expedition. "You know what?" she had whispered to Edei. "That was a solid joke. Good repartee, steady back-and-forth, well-timed delivery. We've made strides, Edei Rhuna."

He had thrown his head back, a delightful, raspy chortle pouring out of him.

Io could still hear that laughter now, its cozy memory a balm to her nerves. She wanted to rush over there and smooch him right on his solemn, stressed lips. These smooching impulses made her feel like a giddy thirteen-year-old again, fantasizing about the handsome stranger on the other end of her fate-thread arriving with a bouquet of roses to save her from the misery of her life after her parents' death. Their death had long been forgotten, and there certainly were no roses in sight, but Edei was as beautiful as she had dreamed him.

She gave him a timid grin as she passed by, and Edei smiled back.

The moment she stopped before the food station, however, the manager began shouting frenzied orders at her, shoving a tray of soft cheese and olive canapes into her hands and steering her toward the crowd.

A pianist was playing soft chamber music somewhere on the other side of the terrace. Io followed the sound at a leisurely pace, keeping to the left side of the terrace and stopping every time a guest reached out for a canape. When she finally reached the glass gazebo, her cheeks hurt from all the polite smiling. The structure was small but impressive, entirely made out of glass and gold, plush with green sofas and thick cowhide carpets. An extravagant chandelier hung from the ceiling, constructed around a claw, one of Le Cauchemar's if Io had to guess, seeing how its talons were ivory inlaid with gold. A light fixture had been nailed on to the bone, like a threat jeweled in gems.

Beneath the gold and ivory sat the Agora.

They were all dressed in white, as in the kurbantes-born's vision. Silk dresses, finely tailored suits, and fashionable two-pieces in shades of white, cream, and light beige clad their bodies. Some were young, some older, of various races and genders. No physical trait revealed a shared heritage, not in the way the Nine had all had brown skin and long noses. There were eleven of them total: six seated on a plush emerald sofa and armchairs, five standing behind them. A wall of security people in black suits and dark glasses stood guard at the open doors of the gazebo, separating them from the crowd, which did nothing to stop the rest of the guests from craning their necks to take a look at them.

From this distance, the Agora's threads appeared silver, but Io wasn't entirely convinced. Only up close, between her fingers, had Io been able to make out the gold interlaced with the silver in the thread that had connected Thais to the gods. She needed to get closer—

Somebody reached out for a canape. Io pulled to a sudden stop,

243

patiently waiting as a group of Rossk helped themselves to a bite of soft cheese and olives. On the other side of the terrace, she glimpsed Thais, who had been detained at one of the two bars. She stood behind the counter, pouring champagne into an endless grid of glasses, her face an icy glower.

Ding, ding, ding!

The sound came from the center of the terrace, where a beautiful woman in a sequined green dress and black cat-eye spectacles tapped a spoon against her champagne glass, near a splendid fountain of a nymph sprouting out of water.

She must be someone important, because at once, the guests began flocking to her, forming a wide circle around the fountain. Even the Agora rose from their seats and approached, their security personnel staying in formation around them. In the innermost ring of the circle stood Saint-Yves, Urania at his side. As the guests pressed around them, Aris Lefteriou whispered an order in Nico's ear and peeled away from them.

Io let the crowd drag her along the periphery of the terrace. She couldn't pinpoint Seto from where she stood, but the last time she'd spotted him, he had been sitting at one of the benches right in front of that fountain. Movement caught her gaze—Edei was waving at her from a few feet ahead. He and Pina had retreated to the edge of the terrace, along with the rest of the personnel. Depositing her tray on a low table, Io scooted between them.

"Welcome, friends!" the woman crooned in a deep voice. "For those of you who may not know me, I am Charlotte Dubois, the Mayor of Nanzy." A round of applause rose from the audience. "It is my city's honor to host this year's Mayoral Assembly, and my personal honor to host this wonderful gala. Thank you all for giving back to the public—this year's proceeds will go to my good friends at the Toussaint Foundation, so they can continue their wonderful work on children's units in our city's hospitals."

More applause, this time directed at an older couple standing close to Saint-Yves and Urania.

"Our city—our world—is going through a grave time," Mayor Dubois continued, her face sobering. "Natural disasters threaten our houses and utilities. Neo-hybrids infest our cities and crops. Political unrest has broken out among our constituents. Crime is on the rise, as is evident in the recent brutal murders that have rocked the city-nations."

Murmurs from the crowd, grief striking the guests' finely painted faces and perfectly coiffed hair. Io doubted they actually cared about the other-born murders—it was the threat of unrest that worried them.

"But not all is hopeless." Dubois's arms opened magnanimously. "Yesterday, the Mayors and council members of all city-nations came together and unanimously agreed on the need to strengthen our policing bodies by beginning mandatory conscription of all citizens of age. It was a grim measure that would have certainly caused unrest—but I am very pleased to announce today that we have found an alternative. Just this afternoon, a couple of hours ago, our magnanimous friends, the Agora, have offered their new Order to our service."

Heads snapped to the white-clad members of the Agora, who stood statuesquely at the opposite edge of the circle, separated from the rest of the crowd by a wall of security guards.

"The new Order?" Edei whispered. "They can't mean—"

"It is my privilege to reveal to you today," Mayor Dubois announced gleefully, "that the fury-born line is active once again!"

As if on cue, the security personnel surrounding the Agora removed their glasses.

Their eyes simmered with orange rage.

The crowd murmured, uncertain how to react.

Io's stomach dropped. Her eyes cut to Thais behind the cocktail counter—her sister was looking right at her, hands trembling around the glass she was pouring champagne into. The fury-born would be able to see the crimes on Thais. On all of them. Their cover was blown; in a matter of minutes, a dozen fury-born might descend upon them. They had to get out of here, right now.

"This is a joke, right?" The voice rang out over the nervous crowd, nasal and girly—Urania.

The crowd shifted like concentric ripples on the surface of a lake. The man before Io stepped back, bumping into her. Edei's hand came around her waist to steady her. Urania moved into the circle with ferocity. Nico was clasping her wrist, trying to pull her back, his eyes on the fury-born, wide and rimmed with alarm.

Mayor Dubois smiled charmingly at the crowd before turning her attention to Urania. "You must be our Luc's guest," she said, "one of the famous Nine. We were all so aggrieved to hear about your sisters' deaths and so relieved to hear you survived—"

Urania snapped her hand out of Nico's grip. *"Stop."*

Someone in the crowd broke the silence with a loud noise of indignation. Feet shuffled, whispers rose in waves. On Io's right, a menacing form clad in a black suit elbowed his way through the crowd: Aris Lefteriou, wearing a desperate, almost panicked, expression.

Io's gaze returned to Urania as the Muse called out, "You didn't seriously cut a deal with them?" She wore indignation well: her face was smooth, her voice cadent. If not for the bulging veins in her neck, one would think she was merely conversing with an acquaintance. "After all that they've done?"

Io's heart hammered in her chest. She could see the trajectory of

Urania's ire; it would grow and swell out of size and then *explode* with the truth. The Muse's last hold of self-control had snapped loose— she would reveal everything to the crowd: the wraiths and the fury-born, the murder of her sisters and their old allies, the Agora and the gods.

The girl's mouth opened—

And froze. It remained hanging, tongue just peeking out.

Her hand jerked, as though drawn by an invisible string. It traveled slowly through the air, behind her body, where it met Nico's fingers again. For a moment, the two were touching, as they had been just a moment ago, then Urania snapped her wrist free once again.

An indignant snort echoed across the crowd. Edei's hand fell on Io's back—but hadn't it been there already, coming to steady her when the man bumped into her? Io scanned the terrace, going over every face in the crowd, every jerky movement and unnatural still-ness. Aris was still shouldering through the crowd toward them, even though he should have reached them by now.

Her gaze latched on the bar at the other side of the crowd. Thais was still pouring that glass of champagne. A single golden drop was falling from the mouth of the bottle—except it wasn't falling. It was *rising*, from the glass up to the bottle, moving in reverse.

What the hell was happening?

The moment distilled to that drop of champagne, traveling through the air. It joined the mouth of the bottle like a kissing lover, then—it was over. Champagne gurgled into the glass. Aris arrived at Pina's right. Edei's hand pressed on Io's back. The snort sounded loud and vexed. Urania slipped her hand out of Nico's grip. Her mouth closed.

"We apologize, child," a new voice called over the crowd.

A middle-aged man had stepped forward, his long hair combed

into a ponytail at his nape. He was dressed in white and flanked by four of the fury-born. Wearing a sympathetic smile, he extended an arm toward Urania across the fountain.

"It was inconsiderate of us to announce this in your presence," the man from the Agora said. "You must still be grieving. Please, let us treat you to a glass of champagne and discuss this in private."

Power, Io realized. This was power unlike anything she'd ever seen before. The kind of power that could bring about floods and acid storms, icebergs and Great Tides. The power of the gods.

"Edei," she said without looking at him, "get Urania out of here."

He asked for no further explanation; he threw himself into the throng, making a beeline for the fountain. Io was already squatting before Pina's medical bag. Out came bandages, vials of medicine, and syringes. At last, her fingers closed around the other-born manacles.

"Pina," Io said, straightening. "Find Seto. Tell him the gods are here."

Pina's eyes went round, her hands closing around the second pair of manacles Io was offering. She took off without another word.

Io turned to find Aris panting before her. "I felt a wave of fear," he said. "Someone was trying to influence Urania."

Not just influence—someone had been trying to *undo* what Urania was about to say. The Muse's lips had frozen mid-open, just before she outed the gods' secrets. And the world had malfunctioned, like a scratch on a record player. Io couldn't comprehend what had just happened, couldn't find a rational explanation, but she knew power when she saw it. She knew what had to be done.

"Are you in this?" she asked Aris. "Truly?"

The phobos-born was looking at her with those black eyes that had once so terrified her. "I am," he answered curtly.

Good. She needed backup, *powerful* backup, and she didn't have an array of choices right now. She dragged up the Quilt with such force it momentarily blinded her. Silver assaulted her senses from all sides, the guests and staff, the Agora. With her moira-born eyes, Io swept the crowd. Silver, silver, silver, silver—

And then.

On the other end of the terrace, by the staff entrance:

Gold.

CHAPTER XXIII

DRIVEN TO THE HILT

IO TORE THROUGH the crowd, never taking her eyes off the dot of gold across the terrace. She could hear Aris's raspy breath a step behind her, and beyond it, startled cries rising from the crowd at the fountain. However Edei and Pina were executing her orders, they were not being discreet about it. But she couldn't help, couldn't even spare a glance back—the god was all that mattered now.

Her surroundings were a blur in the Quilt, bodies and benches and flower beds. She navigated them by instinct alone, trusting the crowd to part before her. In seconds, she and Aris had pushed through the guests. The bundle of gold was right in front of them, moving at a breakneck pace, but Aris had pulled to a stop next to Io, which he wouldn't have done if there was an obvious path to follow.

She dropped the Quilt and took stock of the real world. They were standing before the service staff entrance, leading to the same stairs she'd had to climb up earlier. Io threw open the door and—

"*There*," she hissed.

A floor beneath them, a figure was dashing down the stairs, their heels click-clacking against the marble. She looked to be a woman, with dry, graying hair and a small, slim figure.

Io handed the manacles to Aris. "I will corner her," she whispered. "Hide in the shadows, wait for my signal, then *pounce*. We need to get these manacles on her, as fast as we can. We won't get another chance."

Aris Lefteriou nodded, his eyes childlike wide. "Cutter," he whispered when Io turned to leave. "Be careful."

Io merely lunged, down the steps, taking them three by three. Gods, if Aris, who had despised her from the first moment he saw her, was advising caution, what exactly was Io throwing herself into? She held the railing for balance, her stomps echoing down the staircase. Her heart thundered in her ears, her focus sharpened by dread.

She rounded another floor—and there she was.

Short-haired and sharp-faced, with prominently hooded eyes and long, bony fingers. Her skin was the white of fresh snow, her hair the black of charcoal, her eyes pure gold. The goddess must have heard Io coming; her feet were firmly planted on the landing between the floors, her body angled toward Io, her fingers splayed in front of her.

Io didn't stop or even ease her pace. She placed a foot on the balustrade and *jumped*.

She tackled the goddess to the floor with a bone-chilling *THWACK*.

Io's body seized with pain—she had landed on her left elbow and twisted her ankle—but adrenaline fed her mind with strength. The goddess was on her back, pinned beneath Io's weight. She grabbed blindly for the woman's flailing arms, first the left, then the right, and wrestled them both to the woman's chest, trapping them there.

Then she cried, "Aris!"

The phobos-born was just coming around the landing above Io's. He must have been watching, because the moment she called out, he tossed the manacles across the staircase to her. His aim was perfect. Io caught them in midair, their heavy metal frame smarting against her wrist.

The hand casings of the manacles were already open—clever, clever Aris!—and Io shoved the first around the goddess's right hand with minimum effort. It snapped shut with barely a sound. The goddess must have not realized what was happening, because suddenly, with the manacle around her hand, she began thrashing, rough and vicious. Her leg kneed Io in the ribs. Tears flooded Io's eyes, her side throbbed with pain, but she didn't budge. She threw her entire weight on the goddess, sliding her shin across the woman's chest and onto her throat, then used both her arms to pin the goddess's left hand against the marble floor. Nails and metal dug into Io's skin, her mind frantic with violence. Blindly, she gripped the woman's hand, slipping the manacle around her wrist—

Click!

It was on. The manacles were both on. The goddess was captured.

Dry sobs raked through Io's body. She pushed herself away from the goddess, backpedaling on hands and feet, ripples of pain coursing up her rib cage. At the foot of the landing, she came up to a half-standing position, blocking any escape routes the goddess might try.

She glanced up, to Aris, who looked as stunned as Io felt. He was huffing loud breaths, as though he had been the one doing all the fighting. His wide eyes were on the goddess, who was picking herself up from the floor, slowly and awkwardly thanks to the manacles on her hands.

"I need to get the others," Aris whispered. "Are you good, to keep an eye on her?"

No, Io was not good to keep an eye on a literal goddess, but what other choice did she have? Someone had to get the rest of the team, to tell them their plan *had worked*, to grab the goddess and get the hell out of here while they had the chance.

"She's cuffed, isn't she?" Io said, more to herself than Aris. "What can she do to me?"

Aris seemed as convinced by that as Io had sounded, but said, "I'll be quick," and dashed up the stairs.

In a matter of moments, the only sound in the staircase was their loud, labored breaths. The goddess had propped herself against the wall in the corner of the landing. Her dry, gray hair was sticking out in all directions. Her austere maroon dress was hiked up around her knees, revealing frail calves with stark blue veins. Her cheekbones were red, and scratches ran down her wrists and forearms.

"Who are you?" Io asked.

It was the first thing that came to mind; a silly question, all things considered. But Io's thoughts were blank, the aftershocks of pent-up adrenaline shivering down her spine. She couldn't believe that she was here at last, before a god, before the mastermind behind the wraith assassinations, the Wasteland kidnappings, all this hurt and death.

"What," the goddess said between hollow breaths, "does it matter?" She leaned her head back against the wall, bringing her manacled hands in her lap. Her eyes were slits, her golden irises locked on Io. "What matters is who *you* are. The cutter. The unseen blade. The reaper of fates."

Terror rippled down Io's spine. Bianca had been right to burn down the House of Nine and all evidence of the prophecy with it. On a goddess's lips, these words weren't merely a prophecy—they were a death sentence.

"It's not real," Io breathed out. "It won't happen."

The goddess regarded her with her hard, gilded gaze. "No, it won't. You won't be the death of us, my unseen blade, not on my watch."

A threat, as clear-cut as any Io had heard. But something bothered her even more, sending chills down her spine. *My unseen blade*, the goddess had called her. It was perverse in its intimacy, nauseating in its sweetness.

"Is that what you're trying to achieve here?" the goddess asked, raising her manacled hands. "Absolution?"

"I have nothing to seek absolution for," Io replied—too fast, she realized. She had revealed something about herself with this answer, with this refusal of guilt, something that had pleased the goddess.

Because her wrinkled face had now split into a satisfied smile. "What is it, then, that you hope to achieve by chaining me?"

Io knew she shouldn't reply, she knew she was being goaded, but *she* had the upper hand. Soon her friends would be here and this goddess would be their prisoner. So, she spoke with a clear, resolute voice, "We will hold you accountable for your crimes and deliver you to justice."

"Justice," the goddess said. "Now that's a word I haven't heard in a while. And what do you perceive are my crimes?"

The goddess was mocking her, but Io felt too terrified to be offended. "You," she said, "have orchestrated hundreds of murders. You brought about the destruction of Little Iy. You arranged the deaths of the other-born coalition. You slaughtered the Nine in their home. You used innocent people to do your bidding. And then you discarded them, threadless, to die in the streets."

"Is that right?" the goddess asked. "So convenient, your tale. Perhaps it will enlighten you to hear it from my side. My sisters and I have saved millions of lives. We have protected this land from catastrophe. We defeated the usurpers who would have jeopardized the balance of our world. We have revived the line of the fury-born, after *your* people wiped them out. We have made endless sacrifices, every minute of every day of our long lives, so that you and your kin can live."

"My kin?" Io asked quickly, to keep the goddess talking. "Moira-born?"

"*Humanity!*" the goddess spat.

Io whipped her head back as though struck. The goddess's entire face had morphed into a sneer, her eyes narrowed, her skin crinkled, her thin lips pulled back to reveal yellowing teeth.

"Condemn us all you want, chain us and deliver your justice," the goddess said in a low, spitting hiss, "but in the end, we are and have always been your only salvation."

From what? Io thought. This goddess and her sisters, what did they believe they were saving humanity from?

Above them, a door swung open. Boots pounded down the stairs. A voice called down, "Io?"

Seto. Thank the gods, Seto was here. He would take the goddess from Io's hands. He would stick her in hell-knows-where and squeeze some answers out of her. With the goddess captured, he could rally his allies again. They would find the goddess's sisters. They would handle this.

Io's part was done. She could rest now. She could leave this foul city and never, ever look back.

"We're down here!" she shouted.

The goddess's eyes snapped up, somewhere over Io's shoulder, to where Seto had just appeared, followed closely by Emir. "Oh," she said with a mirthless smile, "hello, old friend."

A shadow of doubt passed over Seto's face. "Do I know you?" he asked as he slowly descended the steps on his crutches.

"I suppose you don't. But I know you, Seto Sarris-Nakano," said the goddess. "Your family has been quite the thorn in our side this last decade. I would like for that to end, wouldn't you, old friend?"

Seto was as measured as ever, his only tell a tiny flare of his nostrils. "It depends on what this ending entails."

"Like all endings," the goddess said, "it entails death."

Io had always had one thing going for her: she was *fast*. She was leaping up before the last syllable had left the goddess's lips.

She was crossing the landing before the others even registered the words. She was reaching for the goddess, hands shooting out to interrupt whatever she was planning—

The goddess's eyes flashed with gold.

She rose smoothly from the floor, as though her collapsed state had been a ruse. She shook her hands, like wiggling them after washing, and the manacles simply fell off.

First the left one, with a loud *click*. Gravity didn't claim it; instead, it hovered in the air and traveled down the expanse of the goddess's arm. Its sharp edges dug into her skin, but they didn't break it. The metal traveled the grooves of her scratches, leaving smooth flesh behind. The right manacle soon followed.

The goddess tossed them aside, like a used napkin. The manacles scraped against the floor exactly where Io was standing. They jumped into the air and suddenly, impossibly, Io's hand was there to catch them. Her fingers closed around them, driven by an invisible force.

Her arm shot out of its own volition, in the direction of the stairs. The manacles flew through the air—Emir barely had time to step aside before they landed against the wall with a thundering crack. Exactly where Aris had been standing only minutes ago, when he had tossed the manacles to Io.

It was all happening again, in reverse.

A goddess of time, Io realized. *One of the Horae.*

Justice and deliberation were not a choice any longer. This had to end here, now, in the most resolute way possible—the goddess had to die.

The Quilt shimmered around Io, silver and gold. Her fingers closed around one of her threads. She propped a foot against the wall and jumped, swiping the goddess's life-thread from the air.

A guttural scream tore through the goddess's throat. She reached for Io, eyes wide and terrified.

Io brought her own thread down and *sliced*.

Her chest jerked with pain. Her breath hitched in her rib cage. Her legs gave out. She slumped against the wall, throwing one arm out to stop her body from tumbling down the stairs. One of her hands was empty, her own thread severed in sacrifice, but the other . . .

The goddess's life-thread was intact. How was that possible?

"Girl," the goddess hissed. Her eyes were still round, but there was a spark to them now, a menacing tilt to her jutted chin. Her chest rose and fell in stabbing breaths. "You forget your place."

No, *this* was Io's place: right in the goddess's face.

Io gritted her teeth and lunged again. She didn't go for the life-thread this time—she went for the woman's feet. She swept a leg out in a circle, hoping to topple her to the floor.

Gold pulsed bright in the goddess's eyes. Io's leg simply stopped in midair, then her whole body was sliding backward, her every move in reverse. Io had no control over her muscles—they obeyed the goddess alone, obeyed time. Her slipping leg spun her off balance. Down she went, tumbling over the steps of the staircase, her hip jolting with pain.

Io made herself stand.

Her body ached; her chest smarted with the loss of her thread. But her mind was clear with purpose, with *necessity*. She could fix this; she had to, because they would never get another chance like this. She needed to knock the woman out. Unconscious, they could carry her away and buy some time to figure out how to contain her powers. All you had to do to knock someone unconscious, Bianca had told her once, was push on their trachea for forty seconds straight.

Io lunged, going straight for the woman's throat. She only took three steps before that strange force claimed her body again. Back she went, down the steps, time reversing until she stood right where she had begun, heaving with pain.

A time loop.

The moment Io thought the words, it was obvious. Her eyes went beyond the goddess to the dome of golden dust lingering in the air around them in a six-foot-wide sphere. Beyond the dome of gold, Io could see Seto and Emir and Aris, all three of them frozen in place: Seto between steps with his hand on the railing, Emir with a gun aimed at the goddess, Aris behind them on the stairs, the manacles back in his hands.

Io had never seen such power before. She hadn't known such power even existed.

"Why," she breathed, a pleading fear coating her voice, "are you doing this?"

The goddess took a step, then another, coming to a stop right before Io. Her hand came to caress Io's cheek. "Oh, child," she whispered. "It is not personal. We are, all of us, victims of destiny."

Io tried to pull away but found that she couldn't move a muscle. Her body was caught in an infinitesimal loop: a pantomime of a step. The ball of her foot landed on the floor, her weight shifted forward, her weight shifted back again, the ball of her foot lifted off the floor.

"But my sisters and I have sacrificed our entire lives to save the world," the goddess said, almost softly. "I cannot let you end it. I cannot let you live."

She stepped closer. Her hand cupped Io's head, bringing her closer in a facsimile of a hug.

Then something was pressing against Io's stomach.

Something was slicing through her flesh. It was inside her, it was mangling her. It shouldn't be there, it was wrong, this was all wrong.

The goddess stepped away from Io, around her, and down the steps. Her feet made no sound. For a few seconds, the dome of golden dust held, then it crumbled, disappearing into thin air. Time resumed; Seto, Emir, and Aris stumbled onto the landing as though shoved forward.

Emir looked at Io and cried out, "No!"

Io's eyes traveled to her midriff.

A knife jutted out of her flesh, driven to the hilt. Already, she was bleeding, fast, the blood thick and dark. Her senses were dulling. Her vision was blurring.

Io fell to her knees.

PART III
THE REAPER OF FATES

CHAPTER XXIV

A MUTED SNOWFALL OF ASH

IO HELD HER stomach. Already, her fingers were slick with blood—too much blood.

Seto was above her, a blurry presence in gray. A cry tore through his lips. "Get over here, Pina!"

Pina had arrived. She was asclepies-born; she would heal Io. She would save her. But when her face replaced Seto's to peer at Io's wound, her brows were pinched together. Her eyes were aglow with olive green. Her hands reached for the knife.

Pain laced through Io's gut anew. Darkness surged for her.

When she came to, she was propped against the wall of the landing. Pina loomed before her, face scrunched in concentration as her hands hovered over Io's stomach. Io's insides were scalding with heat, with pain, with desperation.

Sounds came from the stairs above them, the pounding of feet.

Seto, one hand on the wall to support himself, didn't tear his gaze off Io and Pina. "Stall them," he said to Emir and Aris.

Emir sprang into action, taking the steps up two by two. Aris started after him but was cut short—he opened his arms to grab Emir as the kurbantes-born was flung back down the stairs.

Io's eyes went to the landing above them. Figures crowded it. Clad in black security uniforms, eyes enflamed with orange, stood the fury-born. Behind them, there were people swathed in white: the Agora. One of them had the amber eyes of a grace-born. Another had eyes the color of sapphire, a third looked down at them with eyes of molten iron—other-born, all of them. But none with eyes of gold. None of them the horae-born that the Agora was supposed to be comprised of. Io couldn't understand it.

Shouts burst behind them, complaints and barked orders. Io could make out other people coming down the stairs, in regular clothes: guests, jittery with panic.

Seto leaned heavily on his crutch and reached out, his fingers splayed as though stroking the back of an invisible pet.

"We know you," one of the fury-born hissed down at him. "We know what you've done. We can see your crimes on your skin."

"You've seen nothing yet," the mob king replied.

His fingers clenched into a fist.

The space around him distorted, as though flames were rippling the air. Io felt it in her chest—an assault of love, dutiful and boundless. She loved him, oh, how she loved him. She had to take care of him. She had to protect him. She made to move, to shield his body with her own, but Pina pushed her back down.

On the landing above them, the crowd—fury-born and Agora and guests alike—became utterly still. The lines of agitation smoothed from their faces. Their eyes glazed over. In their fancy suits and glittering jewelry, the guests began shouldering past the fury-born and the Agora. Their bodies filled the stairs, dozens of them, descending in a quiet, orderly pace. Two of them reached out for Emir, who was panting against the wall, and helped him stand. Mayor Dubois, in her green, sequined dress, her cat-eye spectacles lopsided on her nose, took Seto's arm to help support his weight.

Arms came around Io, around her waist and beneath her knees. Sharp stings of agony shot through her torso.

"Careful, careful," Pina was saying. "We shouldn't be moving her at all."

Io squeezed her eyes shut. Her mind languished in welcome relief as consciousness abandoned her.

Lights were rushing past overhead. Someone was gasping close to her ear, their breaths rushed and hot against her skin. She could see a sharp jaw, a goatee—Aris Lefteriou was carrying her.

On his left was Pina, keeping pace with his long strides, a hand placed firmly on Io's stomach. Warmth emanated from the asclepiesborn's fingers, but it wasn't comforting. Io's shirt stuck to her skin, from her clavicle all the way to her waist. Her blood had soaked Aris's suit; she could feel it in the sticky, wet sounds the fabrics made.

There was another person over Io's head. Two hands went in and out of focus as they moved in midair. Io glanced up to find thick eyebrows pulled over frantic eyes blazing with silver. *Thais.* Her sister's fingers flexed frantically. Io blinked on the Quilt.

Above her, spreading up to the sky, Io's life-thread was fraying, strands sticking out like split hair.

Io whimpered.

"Hush," Thais said. "Rest."

Thais was trying to weave her life-thread back into existence. Thais was here, her older sister, the only mother she had really known. All would be well.

"No," her sister called ahead, replying to something Io hadn't caught. "Forget the hotel. The Agora got Urania—it might be compromised. We need to get Io to the trolley safehouse. Ava's got medicine there that might speed up the heali—"

Io didn't hear the rest. The black came for her again.

She was on the ground, in Aris's lap. His breaths knifed the air, consuming all her senses. Pina's hand was still on her stomach; so was that horrible, painful warmth. Thais wasn't there.

Her sister was at the edge of the rooftop, her back to Io. Her shoulders were shaking with silent sobs.

Before her, the abandoned trolley car hung in midair, held aloft by a single cable line. Its tip, where the entrance had been, faced the ground. Pieces of cardboard, charred and burning, tumbled through the open door like a muted snowfall of ash. Its other end was engulfed in flames, painting the iron bars of the station, the rooftop, their faces in oranges and pinks.

There was no one in the trolley car. No Ava, no Bianca, no wraith.

"How did they find them?" Seto asked.

The answer was obvious to Io. She couldn't speak it; her lips wouldn't obey.

They had been betrayed.

CHAPTER XXV

CANARY YELLOW

IO WOKE TO a foreign room.

The ceiling was painted lilac. An ornate light fixture hung in the middle of it, unlit. A scarf rested on the bedpost, bright yellow velvet. Twin bookcases pillared the closed door, and the walls were decorated with portraits of long-haired dogs. The nightstand was packed with discarded medical tools and bloodied gauzes. In an armchair, Pina was asleep, her body curled in a tight ball. Thais stood before the window, arms crossed over her chest, weak cloud-filtered light grooving shadows on her sharp features.

Io glanced down at her body. Her midriff was wrapped in clean bandages, white and spotless. She could feel heat pulsing through her torso with every breath, but it didn't hurt, not even when she sat up on her elbows. The only evidence of her wound, of that insidious blade in her gut, was the tattered remnants of her uniform—the crisp white button-down had been pushed up just below her breasts, stiff and brown with dried blood.

"She performed surgery on you." Thais had turned to gaze at Pina. "She's depleted. Seto said it will take her weeks to regain her strength."

It had always bothered Thais, Io remembered, all the things other-born had to sacrifice to use their powers. For weavers like her, the cost was pain. For cutters like Io, the cost was one of their threads. And for asclepies-born like Pina, the cost was the strength and energy of their own body.

Thais's eyes returned to Io. "But you will be all right."

Images of the fight sprang into Io's mind: the staircase, the goddess, the uncuttable golden life-thread, the knife, the blood, the escape. Aris Lefteriou carrying her, Pina healing her, Thais desperately trying to weave her fraying life-thread back together. They had saved her.

Thank you, Io tried to say, only it came out in a ragged, formless gurgle, the croak of a parched throat. Thais went to the nightstand and poured her a glass of water, which Io drank in small sips. Slaked, she tried again. "Thank you. For saving me."

Thais was looking at her with eyes hooded with exhaustion. For a long moment, her sister said nothing, then: "One soul, even when we hate each other."

It was the mantra their mother had instilled in them since they were little: *Three bodies, one soul. When your sisters need you, you go, no questions asked.* In another life, the comment might have stung. It might have made Io miserable, desperate for forgiveness. But she had woken in a stranger's room among bloodied bandages after facing a goddess of time. Her ruined relationship with her sister, her mother's hard lessons and terrible truths, felt trivial now.

"Ava?" Io asked.

Thais's eyes flashed silver. Her hands went to her chest, to the thread she shared with their sister. "I've tried tugging on it," she said in a hard whisper. "The Ora sisters' call to arms. There has been no reply, no vibration, nothing."

But she's alive, Io thought. Otherwise, Ava's thread wouldn't be there in the first place. If she wasn't responding, she must be unable to, cuffed or unconscious. Io thought of the trolley car in flames, the ashes fluttering in the air like fresh snow. No sign of Ava or Bianca or Torr, or any of the wraiths.

"Someone betrayed us?" Io whispered.

"Perhaps," Thais said. "Or perhaps the gods knew about our side operation from the start and finally decided to put an end to it."

"Where is Edei?" Io asked. The last time she had seen him, she had ordered him to get Urania out of the Great Arch. But last night, Thais had said Urania had been captured, so where was he?

"We haven't heard from him. Or your other friend, Nico. Seto has sent three of his guards to look for them. Your fate-thread is still here. He's alive, somewhere in the city."

But what if he was captured, like Urania and Ava and Bianca? How would Io get them back? How could she ever face a foe who could alter time and undo the present?

"Can you stand?" said Thais. "We've been squatting in this empty apartment for most of the night. The mob king is eager to move. He and his people are conferring in the other room."

Io did *not* think she could stand, but there was something urgent and nervous in Thais's voice. She gave her sister a nod and gritted her teeth as Thais helped her sit up and swing her legs over the mattress. Hooking her hands under Io's armpits, Thais gently pulled her upright. Pain stabbed Io's abdomen, but it was surface-level. Stitches, if she had to guess.

She grabbed the bedpost for support—her fingers skimmed something velvet. The scarf, thin, long, and velvet, the vibrant color of canary yellow. It was familiar in some way, but Io's mind was foggy, pulsing with the memory of hurt and despair.

When she stood, the room swam. She had to stay there for a long time, waiting for her senses to settle. Then, one hand on her stomach, the other gripping Thais's elbow, she walked to the door, which Thais threw open.

Nine faces turned to them. Seto was sprawled on a kitchen chair, his eyes closed, his legs propped up on a stool. Towels dripping water had been laid on his shins. A couple of the kurbantes-born were still asleep in the sofas and armchairs on the other side of the room, while the rest sat around the long dining table. Hassan was bent over the kitchen counter, preparing a tray of food. Aris stood by his side, watching the kurbantes-born's hands move swiftly across the kitchen space. Last night, Io remembered, Aris had been the one carrying her to safety.

On Seto's left sat Emir, his face blemished with purple from his jaw to his temple. He smiled when he saw her. "Guzelim," he said in Kurkz, meaning *beautiful*. "I'm glad to see you up."

Seto's eyes flew open. He dropped his feet from the stool and pulled it back for her. Thais deposited Io on it, then claimed another for herself. It was a long, eight-seat table, cloaked with a daisy-patterned tablecloth. Stools and armchairs had been brought over so that all of them could fit around it. Hassan carried over a tray of biscuits and jams, a large kettle of herbal tea, and a jar of honey. The kurbantes-born siblings passed plates around with the amicable efficiency of people who had grown up together. Soon, there was a cup of sugared rose tea in front of Io, with three pieces of shortbread coated in jam around the saucer.

"Eat slowly," Thais cautioned when Io raised one of the shortbreads to her lips.

Io obeyed, chewing each bite until it was warm and gooey in her mouth. She washed it down with a sip of the tea, sweet and scalding hot all the way down to her stomach.

Then she placed her face in her palms and burst into tears.

It was sudden and unstoppable, like a torrent of thawing ice carving its way down a hill in springtime. Sobs racked her back, tears spilled between her fingers, snot dripped down her nose. It grew worse and worse, and Io couldn't stop it, couldn't regain control of her body—her breaths became so jagged, so gasping, that her rib cage hurt and her stitches pulled at the skin of her stomach.

She didn't know how long it lasted. She felt a hand rubbing circles into her back at some point, but she wasn't sure who it belonged to. All she could hear were her own blubbering sobs. When at last her breathing calmed, she wiped her tears on the back of her hand and looked at her team. She didn't know what to tell them, what hope to offer, what plan to conjure. Someone had deposited a napkin before her; she blew her nose into it, then scrunched it into a ball and cupped her hands around the warm teacup.

Seto's eyes had never left her.

When she looked up at them, he must have judged her ready—he spoke. "What we experienced last night was unlike anything I have ever seen before. Correct me if I'm wrong, but my interpretation is that the woman—the *goddess* snared you in a sort of temporal loop. The dome she cast around you made everything blurry, but it looked as if she kept throwing you back, reversing your actions. The fight only lasted seconds for us. Your movements were so fast that you looked like hummingbirds."

Io didn't correct him. He was perfectly right.

"My guess is that she's one of the Horae. A true goddess of time," Seto went on. "Those of us there also witnessed that the Agora themselves, the supposed descendants of these goddesses, are not horae-born at all. I spotted a grace-born, a nut-born, and an indra-born myself. Emir has informed me that there were also three matres-born and an oneiroi-born clad in Agora white."

Again, Io remained quiet.

"Our hypothesis," the mob king said, "is that the horae-born never existed. Hence our entire lack of information regarding their eye color and powers. We believe that the gods, the true Horae, have been controlling the Agora, which are in fact a variety of other-born dedicated to the gods' cause—would you say that you agree with that?"

Yes, she agreed, but what difference did it make? The Agora not being comprised of horae-born was the least of their worries. It was the gods themselves, the Hora who stabbed Io yesterday and her sisters, who were the true threat. The *invincible* threat.

"We are currently waiting for reinforcements from the Shards. Several of them are other-born with unique talents that will add to our already admirable force. When our people get here, we will embark at once, storming the gods' lair. We have set up a plan, with several alternatives and fail-safes should it go sideways. Thais," he said, gesturing with a palm at Io's sister across the table, "has located the whereabouts of your sister Ava and a young fury-born named Torr through the threads she shares with them. Both point in the same direction, toward the Cathedral of the Blessed Heart. Thais believes—and I agree—that it is a trap. The gods abducted Ava, Bianca, and the wraiths in order to lure us to them. Which means the gods will be there to ensure our destruction goes as planned. This is our chance, Miss Ora. If we play our cards right, we could use the gods' trap to our advantage."

Io couldn't keep it in any longer—"But what's the point?"

All heads at the table turned to her.

"Say the gods are indeed waiting for us in this Cathedral. Say we manage to get in, with all your reinforcements." Io took a long breath. "She could reverse my every move. She could undo all my attacks. Even if we find them, even if you have a clever plan and a hundred other-born, *what is the point?* We cannot win!"

"Rest assured, Miss Ora, we have tried to put that into the equation—"

"Mr. Sarris-Nakano." Io smoothed her voice, her face. She needed to show him she wasn't being obstinate or controversial; her warning was guided by neither fear nor panic. She needed him to understand the facts. "I had her golden life-thread in my hand. I sliced it with my own thread. It should have been severed. She should be dead. But her life-thread is uncuttable. She is *immortal*."

Seto's mouth shut into a tight line. His eyes roamed to the window and the gray sky beyond it. He said, "The Great Tide is here."

Io frowned. First, that was impossible. The Great Tide had been heading north across the Wastelands only a few days ago. Even if it changed direction recently, it couldn't have arrived here, this far inland, in such a short time. And secondly, what did it have to do with what they were discussing?

"The Great Tide is currently thirty miles outside Nanzy," Seto explained. "The mud-tide beneath the Shards has been affected. It's reached two-thirds of the way up the Spined Wall. Our people released the anchors and are now safe atop the floating districts, but stilt neighborhoods have been abandoned, entirely submerged in mud-water. The tide has found its way into the City Proper. Rumor is a giant leviathini has burst through the sewers and is now prowling around the Trade District. The same one, I'd wager, that we happened upon two days ago."

Io was already moving. Holding her belly, she made her way to the window above the kitchen sink. They were on the seventh floor of one of the fancy buildings in the Museum District. She had no idea where her spectacles might be, but evidence of the Great Tide was visible even in the distance she could see clearly. Across the street, the stout buildings that housed the city's museums were submerged in water, almost to their second floors. The streets were flooded, auto-mobiles dragged by murky brown water. Streetlights were leaning off their bases. The citizens of Nanzy were gathered on rooftops, holding their children and their belongings, while police boats bathed the gray morning in gyrating red and blue lights.

She turned back to Seto with wide eyes. "The gods are doing this."

He nodded. "I believe so."

"But how? It doesn't make sense. They are goddesses of time, not nature. Could there be other gods, also alive, working with them?"

"That I do not know. But it makes no difference. The Horae are our target, and our plan foresees their powers. We will storm their lair. The kurbantes-born will front the main attack, while a force of oneiroi-born will infiltrate the Cathedral and put the goddesses in a wakeless slumber. Then, while they're neutralized, we can figure out how to kill them in earnest."

Io trekked back to her chair, already light-headed from standing too long. "I don't think you're hearing me," she told Seto. "They could *reverse* time. They will throw you into a time loop and take control of your body the moment they see you coming."

"That's why they won't ever see us coming. My colleague, the chernobog-born mob boss of the outer Shards, is making their way to us through the City Proper as we speak. Their team will cast a veil of darkness over the gods' lair."

"But the gods know we're coming this time. Their trap will be meticulous. They'll have an entire army by their side, their disciples, the new Order of fury-born."

Seto leveled her with a hard gaze. "How much do you remember about last night, Miss Ora? About our escape specifically?"

A frown cast over Io's face. She remembered Pina's hands hovering above her stomach, Emir flying through the air, figures crowding the landing above them on the staircase of the Great Arch. She remembered Seto. His fingers had danced in the air, distorting the space around him. The guests had lifted Io into the air, carrying her to safety, while the fury-born and the Agora had remained perfectly still. Obedient, Io realized, to Seto's command of love.

The mob king of the Shards must have read the realization on Io's face. "Last night, I had almost a hundred people under my influence, the fury-born included. That is only a fraction of my true power. I can neutralize whatever army the gods have prepared."

Around the table, the kurbantes-born gave nods of affirmation; they must have seen their boss in action many times before.

Yet Io was still unconvinced. "If your plan fails, we will have handed them our entire force on a silver plate. They are expecting us—"

"So what?" Thais snapped from across the table. Her palms were flat against the wood, her whole body leaning in Io's direction. "Why are you fighting this, Io? Are you seriously considering leaving Ava in their hands? Get ahold of yourself!"

Io's mouth formed a soundless O. Her gaze dropped to her lap, where she was digging her nails into the soft flesh of her palms. The familiar guilt arrived, crushing her chest under its weight. Thais was right; Io hadn't been thinking about the actuality of the situation. About Ava and Bianca and Urania, about Torr and the wraiths. Of course she wasn't going to leave her friends in the hands of the gods, but—

She had been stabbed last night.

Her life-thread had been fraying, a mere eight hours ago. The desperate, all-consuming panic of her blood spilling dark and hot between her fingers hadn't left her system yet. Io doubted it ever would. Her resistance to Seto's plan wasn't cowardice, it was fear.

It was memory. Seto's plan of attack meant willingly marching into that knife again. He was asking too much of her, too soon.

"We could bargain with them," Io said. "We could strike a deal for the release of our friends."

"Miss Ora," Seto said. "I understand your reservations. I share them, we all do. But these gods killed my brothers. Assassinated my allies. Terrorized my people. They have abducted the mob queen who led me into the City Proper, the muse-born who risked her life for me. They have somehow brought the Great Tide to our doorstep. They have abducted dozens of true fury-born, building an army that they were going to gift to the Mayors to ensure our subdual and obedience. There can be no bargain, no deal. It is time to *fight*"—drops of spit shot from Seto's lips, his usually composed demeanor shattered with passion—"and I will do so, with every ounce of power I still have left."

"You cannot win," Io whispered.

"I will try nonetheless."

It was noble, and kind, and brave—Io admired him for it. This was the hero the world needed, the leader they craved, this was a man to march to your death with.

Io was not.

Io was scared. She was defeated. Gone was her patience, gone was her resilience, gone was her speed. The ghost of that blade was still embedded in her insides, the proximity of her own death imprinted in her memory. The next time they saw her, the gods would kill her, she was sure of it.

My sisters and I have sacrificed our entire lives to save the world, the goddess had said. *I cannot let you end it. I cannot let you live.* The gods knew about the Nine's prophecy, about Io's role in it.

Io was a cutter, an unseen blade, a reaper of fates—and none of the people in this room knew it. They were asking her to face the gods who were willing to kill her to stop the prophecy from coming true. They were asking her to march to the end, to her end. All because Io's destiny had been preordained, her future told in silver and flame and—

She stopped. Made herself pause. Made herself think.

You won't be the death of us, my unseen blade, not on my watch.

The death of *us*, the goddess had said. And when Io had tried to slice her life-thread, the goddess's eyes had gone wide, her fingers had trembled, a primal scream had slipped through her lips.

Suddenly, pieces began falling into place. *Why now?* Io had asked herself when Seto and the kurbantes-born revealed what had happened twelve years ago. For a decade, the gods had lain low, in relative peace with Seto and his allies. Why stir the waters now? What had changed?

The answer was *Io*.

All this time, Io had believed it was her decision that started this all. To follow Edei to Bianca's office and take on the investigation of the Silts murders. But that wasn't the true beginning, was it? It had never been Io's decision—she hadn't accidentally involved herself in the conspiracies of the gods. The gods had been conspiring against *her*.

They had sent Hanne to misdirect her and scare her into staying away. They had declared all moira-born fugitives for crimes against humanity. They had closed the borders to the City Proper. They had abducted the true fury-born, gathering an army around them. They were now flooding the streets of Nanzy, essentially prohibiting any travel within the city.

They wanted to keep Io away.

They wanted to keep her from fulfilling the prophecy.

Because the gods were scared of Io. Which meant that Io could indeed harm them. Kill them.

Io stood. She shuffled to the bedroom door. There, on the bed-post, was the thin, yellow, velvet scarf, the kind that was currently in fashion among the rich folk, draped on the forehead over carefully coiled waves. Io had known she had seen it somewhere before; that canary shade was unmistakable.

The prophecy had been painted in hundreds of portraits by the Nine's artists, big and small, on canvas and cloth and wood. Some had been charcoal, in black and white, but others were in color, thick swirls of vibrant oils.

In those, Io had been standing with a thread in her hands before a burning world, a canary yellow scarf billowing in the wind among her curls.

CHAPTER XXVI

ALBI, ALBI, ALBI

THE YELLOW SCARF was soft to the touch, its velvet smooth like running water. It was pretty, Io supposed, and definitely expensive, but hardly world changing. Yet a world-changing choice presented itself before her. Walk away, bargain with the gods for the return of her sister and friends and leave the rest of the fighting to Seto. Or wear the scarf, march into that Cathedral and show the gods exactly what kind of destiny she was made of.

The prophecy that the artists of the Nine had painted, of Io severing a thread that would end the world, was talking about the *gods'* thread. Last night in that staircase, Io hadn't managed to sever the goddess's life-thread with one of her regular threads, but—what if she tried the way Hanne had severed the boy's threads back in Tulip? The norn-born had twirled all his threads into a single line, then used one of hers to cut them all. Io could do the opposite: weave all her threads together in the hopes that their combined power was enough to sever the goddess's life-thread.

A world-changing, *wretched* choice: the love she felt for all the people and things she cared for weighed against the lives of so many, Ava and Bianca and Torr and the wraiths, perhaps Edei and Nico, too.

Wretched—but easy.

Io folded the yellow scarf and tucked it into the pocket of her trousers. In the living room, she found Seto and the kurbantes-born watching her return, while Thais fumed silently over her cup of tea.

"I'll join you," Io said, feeling a little silly at making a grand statement.

Seto replied with a direct "We're leaving in two hours, when our teams have assembled."

"I want to be with the sneak-attack team, with the oneiroi-born going after the gods."

"That can be arranged. But why, if I may ask?"

"I'm the only one who's fought the gods before," she lied smoothly. "I know what to expect."

"I see," Seto said, his gaze unwavering. He didn't believe her, not if he was as clever as he seemed, but he didn't contradict her, either. "Hassan?"

The stout kurbantes-born brother laid a notebook on the table among the teacups. A map of the Cathedral had been drawn on it, enumerating the various entrances and attack points. Hassan began going over each step of the plan, tracking the trajectory of the teams across the expanse of paper. He spoke in sign language, his siblings or Seto interpreting for the rest of them. Thais and Aris interrupted with questions, which were answered promptly by either Hassan or Seto.

Io remained quiet. The plan was to take control of all the entrances first in a coordinated attack. When they were in position, the chernobog-born mob boss and their team would veil the Cathedral in darkness. Under that cover, Seto's team would attack with the aim of immobilizing the fury-born, the Agora, and the other disciples of the gods. Seto was to mount the majority of the attack, assisted by the kurbantes-born, Aris, and a special team of grace-born who could enchant people into obedience.

At the same time, a covert task force of oneiroi-born, joined by Io, would stealthily surround the gods. The oneiroi-born would use their powers to put the gods in a deep sleep, which would then be taken over by asclepies- and horus-born, monitoring the gods' vitals so that they wouldn't wake up.

There were several fail-safes in the plan if things went south. Entrances would be held open at all times by other members of Seto's force. A group of regular, nonpowered members of the Sarris-Nakano gang would wreak havoc in the building with guns and bullets. And if all else failed, there would be an extraction team on standby to create a diversion for their allies to escape.

Hassan was going over the different exit points in the building for the third time when Io felt her chest tingle. She swiveled in her seat so fast her stitches burst with pain. Everyone at the table started, snapping their heads up in the direction of Io's gaze—

The door flew open.

Within seconds, several guns were trained on the intruders. Nehir appeared first, an arm slumped over her shoulder, then Nico, his head drooping and nose bloodied, and at last, Edei, carrying Nico's other arm.

Io's chair scraped back as she stood.

Edei's eyes traveled across the room, glazed and muted. There were tear marks on his cheeks. When he spotted her, the inner corners of his eyebrows rose, his eyes wrinkled, his lips pulled down. Without taking his eyes off her, he gently let go of Nico.

Io took a step toward him, clutching her bandaged stomach.

Edei dashed through the living room, his strides long and purposeful. He was in front of her in seconds—then he was holding her, his arms tight around her, his head buried in her neck.

Gasping breaths tore through his body. He whispered, "The fate-thread— I felt it fading— I thought I lost you—"

"It's all right," Io told him. "I'm all right."

His arms were around her, all of him around all of her, and Io knew he wasn't going to let go anytime soon.

"Albi, albi, albi," he kept murmuring into her hair.

And Io was certain now that it *would* be all right, because she'd heard enough Sumazi in her life to know his words meant *my heart, my heart, my heart.*

CHAPTER XXVII

A PAIR OF SHINY, BLACK MOCCASINS

IO STOOD BENEATH the Skull of Le Cauchemar, gazing up with furrowed brows.

The Cathedral stood atop a tiered hill. A large cupola was framed by four smaller ones, the once white marble now gray and eroded from acid storms. The building was dated pre-Collapse, and locals called it the Blessed Heart.

Above the Cathedral, as though resting its chin on it, sat the Skull of Le Cauchemar. The frontal bone was smooth ivory marred with golden lines. Twin hollows shadowed where its eyes had once been, and its jawbone hung ajar, revealing four rows of teeth, thin and sharp like a deep-sea creature's. The Skull had been scraped of debris and lacquered; even in late evening, under the dark light of the rainless storm, it stood out like a venomous guardian over the city.

Io rubbed her eyes—looking at long distances was straining without her spectacles—and followed silently up the metal escape staircase leading to one of the side doors of the Cathedral. Edei was a step behind her, Nico behind him. The ginger had insisted on coming, despite his busted lip and swollen-shut eye.

During the gala fiasco last night, they had followed the fury-born who had captured Urania, out of the building and through the streets of Nanzy. When the abductors stopped at a busy intersection, Nico and Edei had jumped them, even managing to get Urania away for a few minutes. The fury-born had caught up to them two blocks down the street, retrieved Urania, and left Nico and Edei bleeding on the pavement.

Nursing their injuries and hiding from the police patrols, Nico and Edei had crossed the city to find the hotel under surveillance and the abandoned trolley car in flames. Edei had started trying to find Io through the fate-thread, but in their weakened state and with the streets suddenly flooding with tidewater, their progress had been slow. Nehir and the other two kurbantes-born had found them on a rooftop not far from the commandeered apartment.

A hand shot up in front of Io and clenched into a fist in a sound-less order to stop.

The oneiroi-born task force was full of these tricks, complicated hand gestures and coordinated movements that hinted at army train-ing. Seto had explained the oneiroi-born were a sort of resistance group active in the factories around Nanzy. They worked as security for the factory unions and functioned like a well-oiled machine.

The person who had issued the latest command was Gray, the group's leader, a minuscule woman with hulking arm muscles and a baton strapped on her back like a knight's sword from a tale. She was eyeing the door at the top of the staircase, which was suspiciously left ajar.

"Jin?" she whispered to a younger man, her second-in-command.

Jin's eyes flashed lavender and turned to the wall, scanning the building beyond it. Io mimicked him, pulling up the Quilt. The Cathedral had two floors: the vast ground floor with the tall domed parapets, and a second floor of twin balconies facing each other. Io and the rest of Gray's team were on the staircase leading to the southern balcony. Another team, led by the chernobog-born mob boss, was at the northern balcony, and Seto's team would burst in through the main entrance on the ground floor. Their attack was to be carefully timed: first the chernobog-born, then Seto's team, then Gray's. But first, they all had to slip inside and secure all the exits, which meant getting an idea of what awaited them on the inside.

"Two directly behind the door," Jin reported to his leader, "ten more on the balcony. A bunch of them on the ground floor."

"Four behind the door," Io corrected in a whisper. "Another eleven on the balcony. They're huddling close together, precisely so we can't see them."

Or at least they were trying. But Io had an advantage over other kinds of other-born. She could see something that couldn't be altered or hidden: life-threads. They shot up to the sky, revealing fifteen people in total on the balcony.

And beyond that . . . there were almost a hundred people in the Cathedral if Io's estimates were correct. The vast majority were standing beneath the large dome, in a semicircle around Bianca and the wraiths, whom Io could detect by the loose threads hanging by their feet. The wraiths weren't her concern; the kurbantes-born and Thais were in charge of freeing the hostages. Io and Gray's team were going to face the gods—

Those three bright, golden life-threads in the very center of the dome.

Io dropped the Quilt and looked at Gray—just in time, too, because the woman was delivering soundless instructions to her team via a series of complicated hand gestures.

"Huh?" Io whispered under her breath.

Edei leaned close. "They're going to try to put the guards to sleep through the door."

"How do you know their secret codes?"

A smile tucked at the corners of his lips. "I don't. I'm just guessing."

He nudged a head in the direction of the oneiroi-born: three of them were silently ascending the stairs, their eyes aglow in lavender, their fingers moving as though plucking the strings of an invisible instrument. Gray herself was leading the smaller group, but she wasn't using her powers. Her eyes were clear and focused on the open door. She flattened her back against the wall, edging closer, then swept inside, gun first.

As one, the oneiroi-born rushed in after her. For every person using the dream-waves, there was another guarding their back in the real, corporeal world. It was done so fast, so quietly, so efficiently, that by the time Io, Edei, and Nico had climbed the stairs after them, the whole balcony had been cleared.

Fifteen bodies lay unconscious, the last one being lowered to the floor gently by Gray. Io leaned down to touch a finger to the neck of the closest one: still breathing. Good gods—Gray's team had lullabied fifteen people to sleep in less than a minute. It wouldn't take them long to wake up, though. Gray was already handing out handcuffs and gags. Io took the ones she was offered, turned the body at her feet to its stomach, and tied the guard's hands behind his back.

Something slipped out of the man's pocket. It was a rectangular piece of paper, haphazardly folded. When it slid to the floor, one of its corners propped open. The swirls and lines looked familiar. Io picked it up and twisted it toward the little light of the evening.

A map. Just like the one Io had found at Wilhem's apartment in Tulip, with the mystifying wiggly lines and arrows. Thais had claimed these weather warnings were handed out to the gods' disciples when they were carrying out a mission that required traveling. The strange shapes showed the trajectory of storms and floods, as predicted by the Agora—or the Horae themselves, Io supposed, considering the horae-born didn't exist.

But this man wasn't tasked with traveling today, so why was he carrying one of these maps?

Io smoothed the paper against the floor. Unlike Wilhem's map, this one didn't show the entire continent but rather a fifty-mile radius around Nanzy. Wavy squiggles surrounded the Spined Wall and wove through some of the outer districts of the City Proper. Small star-shaped marks dotted the streets. A large black spot was drawn over the Trade District.

What did it all mean? Io's finger trailed over the route she had taken to get here, on rooftops and across bridges hanging over the flooded, chimerini-infested streets below. The markings couldn't be weather conditions—the sky was overcast today, but there was no rain, no storm. And besides, how could the gods track something as unpredictable as a flash flood or a Great Tide? Their powers weren't connected to nature. They were the Horae, goddesses of time, future, present, and—*past.*

It all became clear to Io, suddenly and absolutely, like the snap of two fingers. *So convenient, your tale,* the goddess had told Io last night. *Perhaps it will enlighten you to hear it from my side. My sisters and I have saved millions of lives. We have protected this land from catastrophe. We have made endless sacrifices, every minute of every day of our long lives, so that you and your kin can live. Condemn us all you want, chain us and deliver your justice, but in the end, we are and have always been your only salvation.*

Io's mind reeled; the goddess had been honest. She and her sisters were humanity's salvation. Humanity's death. All evidence was here on this map.

"Io?" Edei whispered above her.

Her head snapped to him. She must have looked frantic, wide-eyed and shell-shocked.

"What's wrong?" he said.

Io opened her mouth—

"Comrades," Gray hissed, "in position."

There was no time to explain. They were on the move. Io folded the map into her pocket and fell into formation.

The oneiroi-born spilled across the balcony, moving swiftly on soft feet. Edei and Nico had taken their guns out, barrels trained on the floor. The whole group slipped like shadows down the balcony and onto the wide steps leading to the ground floor.

From the top of the double staircase, Io got her first glimpse at the interior of the Cathedral. No lights were on; the anemic light of dusk filtered in through the long, narrow stained-glass windows at the top of the dome. Thick stone columns curled up from the floor. Statues and gargoyles jutted through the darkness with their long noses and horned heads.

An altar sat beneath the dome, where diagonal swaths of light draped on three figures seated on heavy, tall-backed chairs. The one in the middle was the gaunt-faced woman who had carved a knife into Io's belly. The one on her right was a few years older, with white hair and deep lines on her neck. The youngest sat on the left, slumped back against her chair, her head tilted awkwardly as though she was napping. There was no doubt they were sisters; same brown eyes and dark hair, same downturned mouth and flat eyebrows, same long necks and narrow shoulders.

The Horae. Goddesses of time.

Flanking them on all sides were their disciples. Almost a hundred, standing ramrod straight in a semicircle around Ava, Bianca, Torr, and the wraiths. All gagged and bound by other-born manacles. Among them stood Urania, a gash across her brow.

Behind Io, Nico inhaled sharply. Edei reached out and clasped his wrist, holding him in place.

On the balcony across from theirs, the chernobog-born's team was already in position at the top of the stairs. The mob boss, a lanky young person dressed in all black, was speaking to Gray with those silent hand commands. Io glanced at the double doors at the main entrance of the Cathedral: in the Quilt, she could see people gathered on the other side, two dozen of them. Seto and his team, coming into position.

It felt like the entire room was holding its breath. Waiting for Seto's signal.

Io reached into the service staff trousers she was still wearing. Her fingers touched soft velvet; she pulled out the yellow scarf, pushed her curls back, and tied it atop her head.

At her side, Edei whispered, "What's that?" His gaze was hard, his brow an angry line. He knew; he recognized the scarf; he reached to snap it out of her hair. "Io, *what's that?*"

Io caught his hand and snaked her fingers between his. There was no stopping this now. Io had made her decision. She was going to cut and reap and end the world—whatever might be the cost.

She brought his knuckles to her lips and kissed the soft skin above his brass knuckles. She wanted to whisper *Don't be angry*, she wanted to tell him *I'm sorry*, but there were no words left in her mouth, no words to make this better for him.

"*Io, no—*"

It came fast, blessedly. A feeling of sweet longing flowed into Io's chest. Love, adoration, devotion. Seto was sending a wave of his power down the Cathedral—that was the signal.

"Him," a voice echoed through the vast space. It was the goddess in the middle who had spoken, addressing the room at large. "Him first."

Him? Io startled. *First?* Io panicked.

No, this wasn't right. It wasn't how it was supposed to go—

Someone barked an order. Doors burst open, footfalls filled the chamber.

Darkness dropped, heavy and absolute. The world collapsed around Io, all senses stolen from her—if not for Edei's fingers in hers, she wouldn't know whether she was awake or sleeping, alive or dead. Her first instinct was to call on the Quilt, but nothing arrived. The chernobog-born's power was immovable. No Quilt of silver could break their darkness.

Io could feel nothing but her own body: her heart galloping in her ears, the cold air whooshing past her parted lips, her eyes blinking furiously as though they could flicker the darkness away.

She decided to move, down the staircase, in the direction she thought the altar must be. Edei hadn't let go; he followed, gripping her hand. Io extended her arm and fumbled in the dark. Her fingers skimmed against stone—the railing. Using it as a guide, she hurried down the steps, reaching smooth floor in seconds. She started across it in the dark, toward the altar. She had to reach the gods. She had to finish this—only she could.

Her foot connected with something soft. She crouched down, taking Edei with her. Her fingertips grazed fabric, a shirt. The body beneath her was spasming. Io traced her hand across their shoulder blades to their neck, their head. Their hands were around their throat, as though they were choking—

The fury-born. The fury-born were attacking them.

But why wasn't Seto's plan working? The first step had been

carried out—the chernobog-born's darkness cloaking them all—but where was his power? Where were the kurbantes-born and the grace-born? Why weren't they taking on the fury-born?

Edei's hand lurched out of hers, there one moment, gone the next. She called out his name, the only proof of her voice the vibration in her throat. She waved her arms, stepping around on disoriented feet. A cry tore out of her lips, scratching her throat but making no sound.

Then something hot and stinging whipped around her neck. Air whooshed out of her. Her heart roared in her ears, behind her eyes. She knew there was nothing to grab hold of, but still her hands flew to her neck, fingers clawing at her own skin. The whip went taut—Io tumbled backward. Her head smacked against marble. Her stitches roared with pain.

The darkness winked off, as abruptly as it had descended.

Through eyes dusted with tears, Io turned to the side and saw the bodies lying around her. The kurbantes-born, the oneiroi-born, the chernobog-born's team—all of them on the floor, backs arched, hands on their necks. Edei and Nico on their knees, arms bent behind them. Dozens of other people sprawled on the floor, faces beaten up and hands in manacles. And Seto—a woman was holding up his limp upper body by his short hair, his eyes rolling into his skull.

A pair of shiny, black moccasins circled Io's body.

Io was instantly in the Quilt, shooting an arm up to grab one of the figure's threads—but there were none. There were no threads, no rivers of love, no dream cords to manipulate; that was why Seto's plan had failed. These weren't fury-born. They weren't any kind of other-born.

They were wraiths.

The figure stopped some feet away from Io's head. She folded on her haunches and rested her elbows on her knees, one hand gripping her invisible whip of fury. She cocked her head in that feline way of hers, face lined with sadness and pity.

"Oh, cutter," said Bianca Rossi.

CHAPTER XXVIII

AS YOU PROMISED

THE BETRAYAL DROPPED like a hammer on Io's chest. She lay there, on the floor, staring up at her partner in crime, her reluctant ally, her friend. A small, apologetic smile was plastered on Bianca Rossi's lips; Io wanted to reach up and slap it right off her face. They had set up an entire plan, called reinforcements and willingly marched into a trap to save *her*. Bianca and Ava and the wraiths. And this was the thanks they got? A knife in the back, plunged so deep it sliced through the heart?

"Don't," the mob queen warned.

She grabbed ahold of Io's elbow and dragged her forward. A great chandelier atop the gods' altar had been turned on. Io's allies were lined up beneath it: a barely conscious Seto, a tearful Thais, a grim Edei and a frantic Nico, the kurbantes-born, Gray and her oneiroi-born, the chernobog-born and their team, all cuffed and forced to their knees. Wraiths stood above the leading members of Io's team, Elias and Costanza and the rest of them, the very same wraiths Ava and Thais had spent weeks nursing back to life.

They hadn't been taken to lure them into this trap, Io realized. She recalled Bianca's narrowed gaze as she closed the door on Thais, on them all. The wraiths had walked away from the trolley car willingly, probably set it on fire themselves, then came here and offered their services to the gods. In return for what, though? What could possibly be worth the sacrifice of all their allies?

Bianca stopped before the gods' altar. The tip of her black moccasin jabbed the soft flesh behind Io's knees. Down Io went, the marble biting into her kneecaps. She glanced to her side; Edei was trying to reach for her, a stream of Sumazi curses running from his mouth. Bianca placed a foot on his shoulder and pushed—Edei toppled sideways.

The fury-whip around Io's neck went slack. Io gulped down eager, dizzying breaths.

"There, there." Bianca patted Io's head. Then she called out, "Goddesses!"

From this vantage point, the three goddesses looked like giants at the top of the altar. They wore long white dresses with high collars and cinched sleeves, made of a wispy fabric that fluttered with the tiniest movement. At the foot of the short steps that led to the altar stood Ava, Urania, and Torr. Ava's eyes were round and red over the cloth gagging her mouth. Urania's head was downcast, while Torr was looking back at Io with a level gaze, as defiant as the first time Io had seen her.

"The usurpers," Bianca called up. "Delivered alive and bound, as promised."

The goddess in the middle stood from her seat. She descended a couple of steps on soft, silent slippers and surveyed their group. Usurpers, Bianca had called them, but they were revolutionists, a resistance, the last line of defense between the gods and the rest of the world.

"Now it's your turn, Eumonia," Bianca pushed, voice heavy with demand. "Pay up."

Eumonia, Io thought. An old word that meant *good order*. The names of the other two Horae were dragged from the depths of her mind: Dike, meaning *justice*, for the eldest, and Eirini, meaning *peace*, for the youngest. In Io's old textbooks, Dike was the goddess of integrity and the past. Eumonia was the goddess of stability and the present. Eirini was the goddess of amity and the future. If looping a few minutes of the present was Eumonia's power, what were Dike's and Eirini's? What kind of temporal manipulation could they cause?

Was there a way Io could use them to her advantage? Seto's plan had failed; they no longer had the element of surprise. But Io's hands were still unbound. If she could reach the altar and take out Eumonia, then the threat of time loops at least would be eliminated. Her friends could still fight their way out of this—

"*Don't*," Bianca warned again, drawing out the vowel.

Io hadn't even moved. But Bianca knew her too well, as Io did Bianca, each other's little tricks and reflexes embedded in their memory after spending all these weeks fighting side by side in the Wastelands.

"Your payment," Eumonia said, dropping her icy eyes at Io, "will not arrive until the cutter is dead."

Io's stomach plummeted as though she had been punched. She knew the gods wanted her dead, but Bianca had agreed to be their method of killing? Io's mind flashed back to all the times the mob queen had *saved* her life: with Hanne, the lion-raptor, the police officers in the Shards. Just three nights ago, the two of them had volunteered to lure the leviathini away from everyone else, risking both their lives for the good of the many. Had Bianca been pretending all this time? Or had the gods offered something so valuable, so sweet that Bianca couldn't deny it?

"I promised to capture her for you," the mob queen said through gritted teeth. "I didn't promise to kill her."

"But it should be easy for you, no?" Eumonia said. "Kill her and we'll reward you instantly."

"Even a god should know not to hustle a hustler," Bianca hissed.

Then she lifted her hands from Io's shoulders. The wraiths around them mimicked her. Suddenly, the so-called usurpers were free to move again. Thais acted first—she scrambled up from the floor and dashed for where Ava was standing with Torr and Urania. Io's sister had barely made it to the steps before Eumonia called:

"Enough!"

At the command, one of the wraiths snatched her arm back. The invisible fury-whip connected to Thais's neck tugged taut. Io's sister went flying back, landing on the marble with a shattering smack. She cried out, cradling her right arm to her chest. Even from this distance, Io could see the dislodged bone pushing unnaturally at the skin on the corner of Thais's elbow.

"Our payment first," the mob queen said, hands landing on Io's shoulders again.

Eumonia flicked an irritated wrist at her sister. Dike's eyes glowed golden as the goddess of the past pulled her palms away from each other, slowly, as though dragging apart two magnets. A cold wind rippled through the room, spiked like icicles; the hairs on Io's skin rose. The goddess's fingers worked an intricate pattern, her long nails aglow with golden light. Then she brought her hands back together in a resounding clap.

The sound blasted through the room with more essence than any clap had the right to have. It knocked into Io and the other captives, making them stumble to the floor. The painted glass around the Cathedral vibrated as though with the crack of thunder. And the wraiths—

Their bodies shot upright, their spines arching, their eyes spinning up into their skulls.

"Wh-what are you doing to them?" Thais cried out.

"She is—saving them," Seto breathed. Io hadn't seen the mob

king come to, but he was now propped in Nehir's arms, his head cradled on her lap. His eyes were rose-pink.

Io blinked the Quilt on. Her surroundings became awash with silver. Above each wraith was a torrent of glistening metal, a thin string of liquid silver spinning around itself, stray particles weaving back together in midair. It took seconds, mere blinks of the eye, and then it was done. Their life-threads pulsed bright and silver, from their chest straight up to the sky.

This was what Bianca had bargained for: their lives. They were wraiths no longer. Despite her terror, despite all her failed plans, Io couldn't fault Bianca for that. A *pitiful imitation of life*, Bianca had once called her time as a wraith. Io was glad that these wraiths at least, these innocent people, would survive this.

Bianca's lids were closed, her face tilted skyward. Already the color had returned to her skin, her bones were less prominent, her hair had gone back to its former lustrous blond. It was as if no time had passed at all, as though Io was just walking into the mob queen's office to meet her for the first time. Bianca Rossi had been dressed in a pristine striped suit then, and she looked just as elegant now in an oversized button-down, form-fitting pants, and those shiny moccasins.

Her eyes opened slowly, like waking from the sweetest dream. When they dropped on Io, they weren't bloodshot or glassy. The mob queen was herself again, albeit changed by the touch of gods— when she blinked, orange filmed over her eyes. Bianca was still fury-born. Her fury-whip was still around Io's throat.

"Please remember, my queendomless queen. We can take this back as easily as we have given it," Eumonia called out, shattering the wistful silence of the Cathedral. "Now, do as you promised. Kill the cutter."

Without breaking eye contact with Io, Bianca shoved her forward. Io's palms smacked on the marble, but she was given no time to recover. The mob queen had clasped the collar of her shirt and was dragging her forward, toward the altar and her executioners.

Panic seized Io's thoughts. She began thrashing, screaming and kicking in no coherent direction. "No, stop! Stop!"

Io's wail rose unanswered, swallowed by the dark expanse of the cavernous room. Her feet scraped against marble, her fingers reached for something to hold on to. She was thrown at the foot of the steps, only a couple of feet away from Eumonia.

"There she is," Bianca said, still holding the collar of Io's shirt. "But I won't do your killing for you."

Io craned her neck: Eumonia loomed above her, a cutting figure in white. The goddess reached into the folds of her dress. Out came a knife, long and serrated. "Very well," Eumonia said, and began descending.

A plea gurgled out of Io's mouth, "No, no, no, no—"

Boots clomped against the marble.

Io's gaze cut to the sound. In the line of captives facing the altar, Edei was moving. He reached with bound hands over his shoulders, grabbing a chunk of his guard's shirt, then hauling them entirely over his body. The guard—a former wraith, a disciple, Io didn't know—skidded on the floor, landing almost at the base of the altar. Then, still kneeling, Edei's hand shot to his ankle, from where he produced a gun with a golden handle, just like the ones Seto's gang carried.

He aimed it with both hands, as they were still bound at the wrists. He fired—straight at Eumonia.

The shot tore through the Cathedral, magnified against the echoing marble and glass. Io's body jerked involuntarily; so did Bianca's. On the altar, Dike nearly jumped out of her seat, but Eirini . . . the youngest goddess didn't move in the slightest, her head tipped forward, her hair concealing her face.

Eumonia glanced down at her chest. Dark red spilled over her pristine white dress. She touched a finger on it, as though she had never seen her own blood before, then wiped the filth on her sleeve.

Her eyes flashed golden. Light dusted over her body, like sand dripping between fingers on a sun-soaked afternoon. The bullet rose from her wound, slowly at first, pushing through her skin like a worm from the mud, then faster—it zapped through the air, lodging itself firmly back into Edei's gun. The force of it smacked the weapon out of Edei's hand; he stared at his empty palm in astonishment.

But Io's allies didn't stop. Emir tried next, tearing a leg out of his forced kneeling position, stomping his foot on the floor, then thumping his bound hands against his chest. On the second beat, Nehir had joined him, and another kurbantes-born on Emir's other side. A rhythm was beginning to form: stomp, thump, stomp—

Eumonia flicked a hand. The kurbantes-born's legs snapped back into their kneeling positions.

But suddenly, Eumonia's head shot back, her mouth gasping for breath.

Io found her assailant in the line of captives: a former wraith, now turned into fury-born, had wrapped her fury-whip around Eumonia's throat. It wasn't the young girl's doing, though; at her feet sat Aris, kneeling and bound in manacles. His pitch-black eyes were locked on the young woman's and his mouth was moving fast with whispered commands. He had snared her in his terror, ordered her to attack the goddess.

Dike shifted in her seat, Eirini was motionless as ever, but Eumonia's eyes radiated gold. Gold dusted around her. In a moment, the goddess could breathe again. Aris's head jerked as though slapped by an invisible hand. His eyes tore free of the young woman, her fingers went back to his nape, forcing his head down to face the floor.

"*I can keep doing this forever!*" Eumonia screamed at the room.

"Then—I guess you'll have to," Edei snarled through his teeth, as he struggled to reach the altar against the hold of two more guards, "because Io—is not dying—tonight."

Eumonia opened her mouth, and Io knew what would come. She would order her army to kill them. All of them, the guilty and the innocent alike.

"Stop," Io cried out from the base of the altar. "Please. They don't have to die."

She took a shuddering breath, as though she could fill her lungs with courage. She had to say this just right. She had to find the proper words to convince the gods without the shadow of a doubt.

"They don't understand, they haven't seen what you and I have seen," Io said, forcing her voice into a whisper. An idea came to her fast, the words that would convince the gods: "They don't know what you're protecting us from."

She kept Eumonia's gaze, letting all her desperation gather in her eyes like unshed tears. This had to work.

"Show them," Io pleaded. "Show them what I'll do. Show them the end. You can convince them—please, they don't need to die."

Eumonia didn't respond; instead, she twisted her head at her older sister, Dike, goddess of the past. Not a glance in Eirini's direction, Io noticed, as though her youngest sister wasn't there at all.

"Can we?" Eumonia asked her sister.

Dike's gaze was all calculation, nailing Io with the violence promised in a tiger's snarled snout. "We can," she replied. "The cutter is right. They won't stop fighting, and I'm growing so tired of their little whims."

Dike's eyes blazed golden. The light grew brighter and brighter. A flash of gold boomed across the room. The world around Io unraveled, like a tapestry hacked into bits.

From the tatters came an image of Nanzy. The city was burning.

CHAPTER XXIX

WALL OF BLUE

IO STOOD AT the hundred steps leading to the Cathedral of the Blessed Heart. In her hands was a silver thread. She felt her mouth snarl, she heard a roar tear through her teeth. She sliced through the thread, its silver essence whisked away. Red assaulted Io's senses—it flamed past the wall, taking over the Shards, the factories, the valleys beyond. The world burned, as far as the eye could see.

Pure golden light pulsed as the scene changed. Hillside rolled across the horizon, the earth glistening with wetness. The vision showed a small town, festooned with chimerini bugs scuttling across every roof and wall. Around the town, its crops rotted with disease, neon-colored bugs nibbling at every fruit and leaf. Farther down the valley was another, bigger town. Storms churned in the dark sky above it; sizzling hot rain dropped from the clouds, eroding wood and metal and flesh.

Then tidewater was filling a vast expanse of green. The ridged spines of large chimerini slipped in and out of the water. In the depths of the flooded valley was another city, its buildings almost completely engulfed with dark waters. Birds of prey soared above it, plunging down for their meal.

Several seasons came and went in the blink of an eye, rain, drought, rain again. Rocks jutted white and jarring like a fanged mouth above the sea. Far out into the crashing waves, a shape was moving through the water. A scaled back with a ridged spine, a long tail with spiked ends, a crocodilian snout. Sea foam sprayed up as the leviathan broke through the water. Its claws dug into the earth, its legs pushed against the rocks of the shore, its belly slithered onto land. It tore in the direction of a city, barely visible on the slope of a forested mountain.

Time sped past; now a small, squat village sat atop a cliffside. The earth roiled, rocks snapping free. Screams tore through the night. The ground gave way. The village collapsed in on itself, the cliffside and surrounding hills soon following. The entire island was gone in a matter of seconds.

Another burst of gold. A city stretched for miles in every direction. The sky was an unnatural gray, the air heavy with smoke. Black objects rained from the clouds above, leaving trails of flames behind them—asteroids. The city was smoldering, ashy water trickling through the streets, towering glass buildings caving in on themselves. There were no sounds but crashing, no screams or pleas of help; the citizens were already dead.

At the edge of the horizon stood a giant wall of blue, abnormal in its height and breadth. The tsunami waves of a Great Tide—they towered above everything in their path, so tall she couldn't even fathom their size. The water would crush everything in its path.

There was no doubt in Io's mind, not a single sliver of hope:

This would be the end.

CHAPTER XXX

THE NAME IO

THE VISION CRUMBLED, leaving Io in the middle of the Cathedral once more, chest panting with heavy breaths. The chamber was silent and still, the shock thick enough to cut with a butter knife.

Io could sense the eyes on her back, the room's attention on her. But she was looking at the goddesses. Eumonia at the top of the steps, smugly satisfied. Dike, perched on her chair, her eyes still aglow with gold. And Eirini, the youngest, the goddess of the future: her hair laid over her face, her head slightly askew. She hadn't moved, not *once*, this whole time.

"Miss Ora."

Io knew it was Seto speaking to her. She didn't turn.

"Was that you?" the mob king asked from where he lay on the floor in Nehir's arms. "In this vision of death?"

She didn't answer—she knew Eumonia would be more than willing to.

The goddess shot an arm in the direction of Urania, the one holding the serrated knife. "The Nine prophesized the end of the world at the cutter's hand two months ago. Their artists began creating poems and drawings of this girl here, destined to bring about the end of the world. Tell them the poem, Muse."

A guard behind Urania roughly tore the gag from her mouth and held her down by the nape. Io recognized him as one of the other-born who had posed as Agora members at the gala. To Urania, he snapped, "Do as you're told."

Words spilled through Urania's lips, fast and jumbled. *"The cutter—the unseen blade—the reaper of fates. She watches silver like a sign. She weeps silver like a mourning song. She holds silver like a blade. Sh-she cuts the thread and the world ends."*

There was a long silence. Bianca's fingers were digging into Io's flesh, but Io didn't care. The mob queen's panic didn't matter. Her own fear didn't matter. Fate had taken the reins now. They were merely passengers.

"Do you see now?" Eumonia called across the Cathedral. "The Nine tried to keep this prophecy a secret, but our agents were able to obtain a copy of it. Ever since, we have been trying to prepare. To gather our forces. Reclaim our most powerful allies. Support the city-nations."

Whispers shattered the silence, shuffling feet.

"All we have ever done is protect you," the goddess said. "We've been keeping you safe from all the natural disasters of this world, from every beast that has crawled out of the darkness. We've spent our lives in service to you. And now we must put an end to this newest threat. This girl who will bring about the end of the world we have all fought to preserve. The cutter *must* die."

Io tossed her curls off her face and called up to the goddess, "You're lying."

Eumonia's fingers whitened around the hilt of her knife.

"I'm not the one who will end the world," Io said, addressing the room at large. "Because the world is already ending, isn't it?"

At the altar, Dike leaned forward on her chair.

It was all the confirmation Io needed. She started speaking fast, loud, getting as much of it out as she could, because at any moment, the goddess might reverse her actions. "Those tsunamis you showed us: they were the first Great Tides. The asteroids raining from the skies were the debris of the moons. The island swallowed by the earthquake was Little Iy. The floods, the acid storms, the chimerini infestations—those have already happened in the Wastelands. They are happening now in towns all over the Wastelands, in the neo-blizzard in Jhorr, even here in Nanzy."

Io raised her hands up, unthreateningly, to show Bianca she didn't mean any harm. When the mob queen didn't stop her, Io reached into the pocket of her pants and took out the map. She raised it above her head, unfolded, for anyone to see.

"You've handed out these maps to your disciples every time they travel. But these are not weather predictions, are they? Look at today's map. These waves are drawn over every district and neighborhood currently flooded by the Great Tide. These small spots are the streets infested with chimerini. And this black dot over the Trade District— that's where the leviathini is prowling, isn't it?"

Io raised her voice. "I found another map like this a week ago. Every natural disaster that has struck the world over the past few weeks was marked on it. The Great Tide, the acid storms, the neo-blizzard in Jhorr. For a long time, I couldn't understand how the goddesses of time could be influencing nature. But now I know. Now I've seen it with my own eyes.

"It was Dike, goddess of the past, who shared this vision with us. Not Eirini, the goddess of the future. Your younger sister didn't even move. She hasn't moved once since I was brought before her. In fact, I'd invite every other-born in the room to take a look and tell me what is wrong with her."

Not two seconds passed, then someone behind her shouted— "She is alive, but she's not there. Her mind is a husk."

Io hadn't taken her eyes off Eumonia. She saw plain as day when the goddess's lips thinned. Io was right.

She was *right*, and so she kept talking. "I'd wager that the goddess of the future has been like this for a long time. Since the asteroids began raining from the sky. Since the tsunamis began destroying the old world. I'd wager," Io said, stressing every word, "that her life was forfeit the moment she tried to *reverse the Collapse.*"

A shudder went through the room.

Io didn't stop. She wanted to get it all out while she could, because Eumonia would try to undo this, of course she would. Io would get only one chance, here, now.

"The Collapse never ended, did it?" Io shouted into the room. "That's why the tides never settled. That's why the storms always strike around the same time of year. That's why chimerini infestations shoot up, and why new icebergs are discovered to reignite the Wars, why the raw materials of the Guts are replenished as if by magic. Because you've placed us in a never-ending time loop. The end of the world, again and again and again, each disaster wielded as a weapon in your hands—"

"You ungrateful child—*WE SAVED YOU!*" Eumonia shrieked.

The cry echoed over the domed ceiling. The goddess's chest rose and fell in angry stabs of breaths.

"Do you think it was easy, watching the world Collapse?" Eumonia screamed. "Do you think it was easy, throwing up this giant loop? Keeping it under control? It has taken every ounce of power I have. It has taken my sister's life!" She spread one arm in Eirini's direction. "She foresaw the end moments before it happened! She transferred all her power into me—it cost her her mind, her life! All so that we could stop the Collapse, so that we could stall the apocalypse, for *you!*"

"For us." Io repeated the words with no emotion, but her mind was churning with fury, her chest braced with unshed tension. "Did you send the Great Tide to Little Iy, where the other-born coalition was supposed to meet, *for us?* Did you let that neo-monsoon destroy the fury-born compound and lead the fury-born right into your waiting arms, *for us?* The acid storms, the chimerini infestations, the gods-damned leviathans, did you place those strategically in the towns where other-born were congregating, *for us?* And these women you made into wraiths, then sent out to assassinate your enemies— was that *for us,* too?"

Now Io was panting. Her breath came in bursts. Her stitches pulled at her skin, her muscles thrummed with rage.

"Your desperate attempts to cling to power have killed millions!" Io screamed.

"We have been forced to make hard choices. Sacrifice some areas so that our strongest assets may survive. If we weren't leading you, child, you would have all died already!" Eumonia threw the arm with the knife in a circle. "All of you! Humanity would be dead!"

"But we're not," Io said. Her voice settled back to normal. Her mind was filled with sudden clarity. It was time now. Time for the world to end. "Humanity didn't die. I think that says something about us."

"Who the hell cares what you think, child?" shrieked Eumonia.

"No one. But you—you should definitely care what *they* think."

Still holding the map, Io cast her arm in the direction of the Cathedral, encompassing the entire room. Her allies, yes, but also the former wraiths, whose lives the gods had cut short, and the fury-born, whose predecessors the gods had manipulated, and their various disciples, who must have had family—like every person in the world had family—that died in one natural disaster or another. Disasters that the gods knew exactly where and how they were going to strike. Disasters that could have been *prevented*.

"In the past two months, there have been countless storms, neo-monsoons, chimerini infestations, and floods across the world," Io said. "We thought that nature had gone berserk. But the disasters were no accident, were they? You placed each and every one of them strategically across the Wastelands to block my path. You were willing to sacrifice the lives of thousands just so I wouldn't find you. But these lives, goddess—they were *our people*. Our families, our friends, our neighbors."

Eumonia's eyes went round as they darted across the crowd behind Io. Did the goddess see wrath on their faces? Did she see the betrayal and doubt?

A man spoke up, one of the disciples who surrounded Ava and Urania. Io recognized him as the Agora member who had spoken at the gala last night. "Is that true, mistress? Could you have stopped all those tragedies?"

The goddess's mouth had plopped open, at a loss for words.

"Sister," Dike called from her seat in a lazy, almost bored tone. "Why are we still living this moment? Reverse it, please, and I'll just never show them the past."

Io's breath hitched.

No, no, no—

"Yes," Eumonia said. A veil of serene control had fallen back over her face. "I'll do just that."

Io panicked. She elbowed Bianca's rib cage and threw her head back, smacking Bianca right on the nose. She rose on her legs and took a step toward the altar—

Bianca's arm came around Io's throat, blocking her movements.

"Good girl," Eumonia said to Bianca. "Now bring her to me, will you?"

Bianca shoved Io forward, slowly up the steps. Io thrashed, kicking her legs out, trying to topple the mob queen. There was no way to fight the gods, not really, but oh, Io would try. Io would try until her last, dying breath.

That serrated knife awaited her at the top of the altar. She was getting closer to it with every inch Bianca pushed her forward.

"What," the mob queen hissed between panting breaths, "have I told you about standing still, Io?"

It made her pause: the name *Io*. The mob queen had never called her Io before.

It made her pause—and think. What *had* Bianca told her about standing still?

Staying still is rot and death, the mob queen had said after they had killed the lion-raptor. *The more you stand still, the more the world finds obstacles to place in your way. Grit your teeth and just go for it.*

Bianca was still holding her back. Still keeping her in a headlock. Their breaths knifed the air between them. Io couldn't see Bianca's face, but she didn't need to. She knew what the mob queen meant:

Violence, decided on the spot.

CHAPTER XXXI

A DELUSION

BIANCA RELEASED IO. Her arm shot out, flicking her invisible fury-whip. A choke tore through Eumonia's lips—with a pull of her arm, Bianca brought the goddess to her knees.

Io dashed up the last two steps and kicked the knife from Eumonia's hand. She twisted, her fist already pulled at the level of her head, and punched the goddess in the gut. Eumonia went down, a heap of white robes on the marble.

"Free the others!" Io screamed to Bianca over her shoulder.

Eumonia was trying to rise, but Io pressed a knee on her back, keeping her down. The goddess slumped back to the marble, with a shuddering breath.

In the periphery of her vision, Io saw Dike's white-clad figure take a few steps toward them—then her back arched, her head shot back. She writhed in pain, tufts of wispy white hair sticking on her lips and tongue. But the arm holding the fury-whip, the arm choking her, was not Bianca's; the mob queen had barely taken two steps toward the dais.

Torr was the one sowing her vengeance on the goddess of the past. Her tiny figure was huddled close to Ava, but her slender arm was extended toward Dike's throat.

"Good girl," Bianca smirked, then she aimed her fury-whip at Dike, too.

The elder goddess gasped anew and stumbled back into the dark wooden frame of her dais. Her trembling limbs attempted to keep her upright and failed—she collapsed in a heap on the foot of her dais.

Shots rang out, six of them in fast succession, then more pulls of the trigger, the quiet clicks of an empty chamber. Io's shoulders had scrunched to her ears in surprise; she lowered them now and looked around.

Nico stood at the base of the altar. In his extended hand, the barrel of a revolver wisped a tendril of smoke. It was aimed in the direction of the youngest Hora, Eirini. He was a lousy shot, Io remembered. There were several bullets rammed around the goddess of the future: on the back of the chair above her head, on the wall behind it, on the chipped floor by her feet.

One was lodged in her throat. Red spilled over her pale skin, dripping across her clavicles to her white dress. Her chest spasmed with soft gurgling sounds, but her body was unmoving, empty of thought.

"NO!" Eumonia screeched.

Io reached for her moving arms, but the goddess was surprisingly strong. Her nails scratched at Io's legs, her forearms, whatever flesh the goddess could get ahold of. Io instinctively leaned away, which was just what the goddess had wanted. She arched her back, dislodging some of Io's weight, and rose to her elbows.

Her eyes flashed golden.

Io did the first thing that came to mind—she slapped her.

The goddess's head snapped to the side, her eyes pressing shut. Io fumbled for the goddess's arms, trying to pin them down. She had no time. She had to end this now, before the goddess threw them into another time loop and undid everything.

In an instant, she had the Quilt blazing around her, reaching over the goddess's head for her life-thread.

Golden dust began falling on Io's skin. No, no, it was too soon—

A dome of light burst outward from Eumonia. It zapped over Io's skin, surrounding the two of them in a hemisphere of suspended time.

Io's body pumped panic with every heartbeat. She scrambled away from the goddess on hands and feet, her back hitting the golden warmth of the time-loop dome.

Eumonia stood up. The skin across her cheekbone was pink. She touched her fingertips to it and massaged her jaw. Her feet dragged across the marble; she had lost a shoe in the fight with Io. She leaned down at the edge of the dome and picked up the serrated knife.

A small sound of terror escaped Io's lips. Her empty hand went to her stomach, to the stitches burning hot against her muscles, no doubt bleeding anew after her fight with the goddess. She remembered the knife burrowing into her. The pain. The immobilizing knowledge that she was dying.

"Please," she whispered. "It doesn't have to be this way."

"Child. It's far too late for that." The goddess's voice had a lack-luster quality, laden with pain and exhaustion. "We gave you the choice to walk away."

Choice.

Choice was a delusion. Io's life had been formed by the choices of the gods. She had grown up in a world of constant peril because the goddesses had kept the Collapse in a time loop. She was feared and persecuted for being moira-born because the gods were terrified of the power of other-born. Her parents had died young in an accident the gods could have no doubt stopped. Her sisters, her friends, her allies—they had all been used as pawns, with no thought to how much it would cost them.

There was no choice that Io had made that was hers and hers

alone. Except this one, right here. To wear the yellow scarf. To face the gods. To fight—and kill them.

"I cannot let my sisters die," the goddess said. "I cannot let the world Collapse. I cannot let the whims of a brazen child define our future."

But that was a delusion, too. There had never been a future. There was only the past, laid over the present like a mourning shroud. Io had lamented the past: all the love she had had for Thais, all the care she had taken to build a life without her. She had cursed the coming of change, blamed it for her myriad of hurts. But she had been wrong. Change was uncomfortable, sometimes filled with growing pains, but without it, there was no way forward. No way to keep going, to shed the scabs of your past and heal yourself in the present. Without change, there was no future.

Io lowered her gaze to the floor and let her curls fall over her face, hoping the goddess would not see the silver in her eyes as she pulled forth the Quilt.

A tapestry of threads bloomed around her, iridescent with light. Io didn't move her hands, but her gaze whisked over her remaining threads. Her love of her friends, of the places she cared about, the many little things she loved about this life . . . Could she sacrifice it all to sever the goddess's life-thread? But what other choice did she have? Her only hope was to weave her threads together and attempt the cut that Hanne had employed on the boy in Tulip. And it might still not work. The goddess was immortal, a being outside of time—

A memory scratched at her mind.

It's an extraordinary thing, a fate-thread, Sonya, Thais's moira-born tutor, had once said. *All threads exist outside the concept of place. No one can see or touch them but our kind. But a fate-thread also exists outside of time. It is a thread of the future, bound to you in the present.*

And just a few days ago, Seto had said about the fate-thread, *A fated love is the most transcendental longing in the world: across space and time itself.*

Io thought back to that night in Hagia when she had found Hanne. The norn-born had taken a particular interest in Io's fate-thread. She had been pleased at its fading light, its fraying essence. And then, when the dioscuri-born had tracked Hanne's paths, they had revealed she had often visited Lilac Row. Where the Fortuna Club was seated. Where Edei had been lying in a bed, recovering from his bullet wound.

Io had believed the fate-thread began fraying because Edei's feelings, or her own, had changed. But what if that wasn't true? *Let me choose you*, he had said. *Albi, albi, albi*, he had called her this morning, enfolding her in his arms as if she was air and he a drowning man.

No, she was certain now: it wasn't his feelings that had changed the fate-thread. It was Hanne. The norn-born cutter had snipped at the fate-thread before she left Alante, bit by bit, hoping that Io's doubts would do the rest. Because the gods didn't just fear Io or the prophecy—they feared the fate-thread.

Fate was powerful. Fate was deadly. Fate could topple gods.

Io rose on one knee, then the other, and stood. She could feel Eumonia's power washing over her, pushing against every inch of skin, every move of her muscles. Her knee folded back down, obeying the god's power.

But her fingers didn't open. The goddess's life-thread was still in Io's hand.

Io gritted her teeth, fighting against the goddess's power. One knee, then the other; she stood, yet again.

With her index and thumb, she reached into the Quilt and plucked her fate-thread.

A cutter could only sever a thread by sacrificing one of their own.

It was unfair, just like Edei had said a few days ago, like Thais had been saying for years. It cost the thing that mattered the most: love. Io had thought there was nothing that mattered more to her than the fate-thread, the promise of being loved one day in the future.

But things had changed. It was still unfair and still painful, but now Io could comprehend the depth of her sacrifice. She would surrender her fate-thread not because she had been forced to accept the nature of things and the injustice of her powers, but because it was her choice.

She no longer needed the hope of one day. She was loved in the here and now.

"What is that in your fingers?" Eumonia hissed.

Io didn't answer. She gripped the fate-thread in one hand, the goddess's life-thread in the other.

"Stop this," Eumonia snarled. "You don't know what you're doing."

Io knew precisely what she was doing.

She was the cutter, the unseen blade, the reaper of fates. She watched silver like a sign. She wept silver like a mourning song. She held silver like a blade.

"Stand down," the goddess screeched. "Accept your fate or the world will end!"

"Then let it end," Io said.

And sliced.

CHAPTER XXXII

NO ONE LEFT BEHIND

IT WAS INSTANTANEOUS. The goddess's eyes rolled back into her skull, her neck became limp, she toppled onto the floor. The dome of the time loop popped like a soap bubble, raining golden dust around them.

Io took a step toward the goddess's body. She pulled up the Quilt, just to make sure: no threads of any kind, golden or otherwise. When her gaze returned to the corporeal world, Io found Eumonia's body—Dike's and Eirini's bodies, too—had started to deteriorate. Their flesh flaked over in patches of gray. Their bones crumbled into white dust. In seconds, all that remained of the goddesses were human-shaped piles of ash beneath stained white dresses.

A cry of anguish tore across the vast space.

Something sharp and hot struck Io's shoulder. She stumbled to her floor, clutching her upper arm. Hot blood coated her fingers.

A second shot rocked past the altar, striking the marble inches from Io's leg.

"Io, Io—"

Hands slipped beneath Io's armpits, hauling her across the altar. Edei deposited her against the back of one of the seats and checked her bleeding shoulder, cursing under his breath and placing both hands on the gunshot.

"It looks like a flesh wound," he said. "How much pain are you in?"

It doesn't matter, Io thought. "She's dead, Edei. I killed her. Using our fate-thread."

His gaze found hers beneath furrowed brows. "It's all right," he said deep and reverent, full of meaning. "Do you hear me, Io? We will be all right."

Io's hand reached up to graze his jawline. Words popped into her head: *I had to* and *I'm sorry* and *forgive me.* But they were the instincts of her old self. Spoken now, they would hold no truth. She could feel it in her heart—she felt no guilt or shame, no remorse. She had made a choice, the first real choice in her life it seemed like, and she did not regret it.

She was filled to the brim with clarity, determination, justice, and something else, too, elusive and unfamiliar—"hope," she guessed, was the better word for it.

"Stand down!"

A booming voice rang through the Cathedral, vibrating off windows and columns. Io and Edei leaned out of the dais they had taken cover behind. The floor of the Cathedral was filled to the brim with bodies locked in combat. In the middle of it stood Bianca, her invisible fury-whip clenched in her fist, her back against Ava's, who was holding a silver thread in one hand and a gun in the other. The two of them paused midstrike.

All of them paused, every single person in the room, some caught in arms, others lying on the floor, others still halfway to the exits.

Every pair of eyes in the room glazed a rosy shade.

Io scoured the cavernous space before the altar, her eyes latching at last on Seto. He was splayed on the floor, propped up on a shaky elbow, but his other arm was extended, fingers wide open. Io recalled Eumonia's order: *him first.* The gods must have known the power the mob king could wield—an entire room, hundreds of people, now under his command.

He did not bother to stand or even raise his voice. He said only, with finality, "It is done. The gods are dead. The Collapse will come to an end. There will be no more fighting, no more death. You can leave, or you can stay and discuss our next steps. We need each other now more than ever."

A female voice screeched on the other side of the chamber. "Do you know what she has done?" Io tracked the sound and found silver eyes peeking through the shadows, obscured by tendrils of bright red hair—Hanne. "She has brought down the Collapse on us all! We are doomed, king of the Shards, and it belittles you to pretend otherwise!"

Io's heart hammered in her chest. Her legs felt weak and jittery with tension, but she stepped out of her cover. None of them noticed her at first, not until she opened her mouth and called out, "We will survive."

"Oh, will we?" Hanne snapped back, walking out of the darkness at the edge of the chamber. "You think yourself so clever, so brave. You took on the gods and won—a big round of applause to you, Io Ora, reaper of fates!" Hanne turned around theatrically, arms spread wide. "But did you think about what comes next? All those things in their vision, all the catastrophes they have stalled—they will come for us, and there will be no one to stop them this time! Tell me, since you're so very clever, how will we survive the apocalypse, girl?"

Her voice had risen to a shrill. It echoed through the chamber, grating against Io's ears.

Slowly, Io looked at the faces around her. Hanne's was lined with ire, but behind her, the gods' disciples wore a mix of desperation and grief. Io hadn't thought of them in those final moments. She had not thought of the hurt she would cause, the unrest she would sow, all these devotees now adrift and purposeless, bent on revenge.

A professional breaker of hearts, once more.

But perhaps, these hearts were supposed to be broken. Perhaps this faith was undeserved. Perhaps what came after heartbreak was just as important: when you rose on one knee, then the other, and stood. When you realized that you could piece yourself back together, little by little, slowly and painfully. You might not be whole ever again, but you would survive, and that was—that was salvation, in its true form. Not what the goddesses had been trying to do. Not what Hanne was relying on.

"We will survive," Io said again, raising her voice to carry across the Cathedral. "Look at this city, with its wall and its floating slums. Look at the dams and coastal barriers. Look at all the little towns and villages in the Wastelands. Look at us here, other-born of every shape and kind—"

"And if we work together, we can save each other?" Hanne mocked. "How idealistic! Just like your sister. Well, I have news for you: we can't survive the apocalypse on the power of unity alone."

"But we can," Io stressed, taking a few steps forward. "Don't you see? We *have been* surviving the Collapse for centuries."

Edei hurried past Io, slipping down the steps. He picked something up from the base of the altar and raised it in the air. "We have this now," he said to the room. "You must have more of them, for every month and year the gods sent you to carry out their orders. Don't you?"

A few of the gods' disciples nodded.

"With this information in hand, we have the chance to do it right this time," Edei went on, scanning the Cathedral with his steady gaze. His face was lit with zeal. At long last, he had a way to cast his brass knuckles aside. "No more villages sacrificed to the storms and the chimerini infestations. No more islands lost to the Great Tides. No more Iceberg Wars."

A heavy silence filled the room.

Io's mind went to that Kurkz man, helping her up the radio tower outside Tulip. He had so little, yet he had offered it all to her. Such was the way of the road, of the Wastelands; such needed to be the way of the entire world.

"This time," Io said, walking to stand by Edei, "there will be no one left behind."

Hanne opened her mouth to speak, but one of her friends grabbed her arm.

They were a younger person, with a burst of red curls and stubble on their jaw, a pleated skirt flowing around their narrow hips. Their eyes were the vivid green of a morrigan-born. "I had family in the Southern Peninsula when the Great Tide hit," they said, their voice carrying in the silent room. "Liesl"—they pointed to a middle-aged woman that Io recognized as one of those ten people who had posed as the Agora at the gala—"her husband and son died in the Iceberg Wars. Mani and Erica, their siblings were in Little Iy when it sank. All of us have lost someone because the gods chose to protect their 'strongest assets,' Hanne. All of us here"—they gestured at their side of the room—"and all of them there." They gestured at Io's allies.

It was true: Io and her sisters had lost their parents when the dam collapsed in the valleys outside Alante. Bianca had lost her sisters in a mining accident. Urania had lost seven of her sisters. Torr had lost her threads of love.

"You cannot bring them back, Aoife," Hanne said.

"But we can make sure it never happens to anyone else. The cutter is right, Hanne. Look at all the other-born in this room. Think of all our powers combined. Think of all those maps we have, dating back decades. If we put our heads together, we will know each and every disaster the Collapse will be throwing our way." Their gaze focused on Io and Edei. "No one left behind."

Hanne searched their face for a long moment. Then she pursed her lips together, snapped her arm out of their hand, and walked away. Her boots clipped against the marble of the Cathedral, a ticking clock of fury all the way to the double doors. When she disappeared through it, there was more movement in the gods' ranks, first a couple of people, then dozens.

They joined Hanne, leaving this fight—for now at least. Io held no delusions; they would be hearing from them again in the future. She knew firsthand how deeply rooted the weeds of revenge could snarl into someone's mind.

But the grand majority of the gods' disciples had stayed. They came out of the shadows or rose from the floor to join the redheaded morrigan-born. They would stay and they would help, and Io knew Aoife was right. There were almost two hundred other-born in this room, each with their own power, and thousands still in the rest of the world. They had the gods' maps detailing precisely how the Collapse would unfold this one last time. They would arm themselves with all the mistakes the goddesses of time had made, all the selfish, terrible choices, and they would make better ones.

At last, Thais's axiom was being shaped with truth and forged with compassion: *Be better, make the world better.*

Io was made to sit on the steps while a horus-born, a healer from Suma who had been one of the gods' disciples, worked on her bullet wound. The flesh stitched itself back together, leaving a trail of burning hot skin in its wake.

Pew chairs made of dark mahogany had been brought for Seto, Aoife, Bianca, and a middle-aged man who was a leader among the kidnapped fury-born. Io's assessment had been right; the gods had severed the true fury-born's love-threads to make them more pliable. Thais and two more weavers from the gods' faction had already volunteered to weave the threads back for them, an arduous endeavor that would take months.

The leaders sat in a circle on the side of the grand chamber, where a fireplace had been lit. Everyone else was either leaning on the walls or sitting on the floor. Ava had propped an elbow over the back of Bianca's chair; Urania lounged between Nico's legs in front of the licking flames; Thais had scrounged up notebooks from somewhere and was taking notes against her lap, her dislocated elbow sitting in a makeshift sling across her chest; Torr sat cross-legged before Seto's chair, with the kurbantes-born spread all around him.

They were talking fast, several conversations overlapping, until Seto raised a palm and called for a vote or for volunteers. Within minutes, decisions had been made—every once in a while, one of Seto's or Aoife's people would shoot up from their seat and run to the side room where the Cathedral's radio was situated, to alert the appropriate channels of the newest orders.

Io didn't attempt to listen. She ought to and she would, later on, but her mind had become hazy with loosened tension, heavy with grieving apprehension. It was done. It was over. And now the aftermath had come, and Io didn't quite know what to do with it.

Her eyes sought Edei again, barely visible through the open doors of the Cathedral. He stood before the hundred steps leading to the building, pacing back and forth. He had volunteered to lead the security team with Aris, against potential retaliation from Hanne and her group, from the Nanzese police, or other allies of the gods that they didn't even know about.

The moment the gods died, Aris said, he had felt a mass surge of fear in the world, sudden and powerful. His guess was that it was a subconscious reaction to the power of the goddesses of time disappearing from the world, a metaphorical rising of the hairs on your arms. Fear brewed violence—best to be careful. Within minutes, he and Edei had assembled a team to guard the entrances, until this new coalition decided on the most pressing issues.

Io rose on tired feet, thanked the horus-born, and made her way through the chamber. Bianca looked up as Io passed by, acknowledging her with a simple nod of the head. Ava gave her a brilliant smile. Thais didn't look up from her notetaking at all; just as well. Io didn't quite know how to deal with her eldest sister just yet. She had not forgiven her—she didn't think she ever could—but perhaps there would be a time when Thais could earn Io's trust back, a time when things would change.

Change. It was strange, how the word comforted Io now.

The world beyond the doors of the Cathedral was burning. It was all violent red and sparking orange—but they were not real flames. The gods had tricked them, even in this. The sun had finally made an appearance, peeking beneath the gathering storm just as it dawned anew. Lifted by the Great Tide, the slums floated nearly at the level of the City Proper. The horizon was all glass, the gilded roofs of the Shards and the inner city creating an endless sea of glittering mirrors.

The blazing colors of the rising sun reflected on the looking glass, the sky dragged down to the earth in all its red glory.

Io tore her eyes off the mirrored sunrise and found Edei. His back was to her. She approached slowly, every step more hesitant than the last. She was suddenly feeling nervous all over again, like that day she had seen him from afar standing at the balcony of the Fortuna. She had thought him so handsome then, a painting of dripping sunrays and cheekbones sculpted by a master's hand. He was handsome still, and she was just as wonderstruck.

"Hey," she said, touching his elbow.

He must have sensed it was her or had been expecting her, because without turning his head, he raised his arm over her head and pulled her in to his side.

A grin tugged at Io's lips. He was here, he was holding her. But gods, why did she feel so embarrassed? She wanted to burrow into the crook of his arm until this whole day, this whole week, this whole *year* was over. Instead, she forced herself to glance up at his face.

She found him already looking at her. A crooked smile was on his lips, one that she had never seen on his face before: not quite gentle, not quite teasing—but almost surrendering. His hand skimmed over her bandaged shoulder.

"All good now?" he asked, his breath soft and warm against her cheeks.

"All good," she echoed.

His gaze traveled up from her eyes to her hair—and narrowed. "Gods," he whispered, "when you put on this damned scarf . . ."

Io remembered the moment: his gaze had been hard, his brow furrowed. He had recognized it. He had reached out to grab it. *What's that?* he had whispered, then with anguish, *Io, what's that?*

"I'm sorry," she whispered.

His face sobered. His eyes did that thing again, moving between hers very fast. He didn't let go of her, but his forehead was lined with worry and his voice dropped to a whisper. "What do you feel?" he asked.

He meant about them, Io knew. About the fate-thread being gone.

"I don't—" she started. She was having the sudden urge to burst into sobs, emotion building in her chest like a dam fighting a torrential storm.

No—she wouldn't cry. She wouldn't mourn. The fate-thread had been her guiding light since she was a child. The one thing that had been hers and hers alone. The promise of better days to come. But in its essence, the fate-thread was love, and Io couldn't mourn that, because she hadn't lost it.

"I don't feel any different," she said at last.

A bubble of a laugh burst out of him, vibrating between their joint chests. "Good," he said, then again, deeper, "*Good.* I don't feel any different, either." After a moment's hesitation, he added, "What does the Quilt look like now, without it?"

Io had been too afraid to check. But she was in his arms now, laughing like schoolchildren at recess, and she felt brave and certain and whole. She leaned away from him and pulled forth the Quilt.

In the space between their bodies, there was silver.

You could barely call it a thread, thin and flimsy like the vein of a maple leaf, but it was silver and it was spinning around itself, getting thicker and shinier with every second. Weaving itself into existence.

Edei must have seen the shock on her face; he asked an agitated "What?"

Io couldn't reply with words—she started laughing, childlike giggles of joy and relief, and in a moment, he joined her, because he understood, he realized, what her bliss meant. His arm came back around her, his lips dusted pecks on her forehead, their chests vibrated with joint laughter. Behind them, the world burned scarlet and pink, in the blaze of a new day.

ACKNOWLEDGMENTS

I wrote the acknowledgments of my first book, *Threads That Bind*, half a year before the book even came out. I knew little of what was to follow; my gratitude was a wishful, dreamful thing of the future. As I write these acknowledgments now, for my sophomore book and finale of the series, *Hearts That Cut*, I know so much more. Of what it took to get here and what it will take moving forward. My gratitude is a deep, deep thing, built on foundations of experience and fortified by wonder.

First and foremost, my deepest thanks to my publishing team. It is a privilege to work with my editor, Gretchen Durning. The pride I feel for this series and growth I've made as a writer is almost entirely owed to Gretchen's extraordinary insight. A huge thank-you to Felicity Vallence, Shannon Spann, and James Akinaka, Lizzie Goodell, Christina Colangelo, and Bri Lockhart for their amazing enthusiasm in getting this series into readers' hands. To Jen Klonsky, Krista Ahlberg, Sarah Liu, Brian Luster, Jayne Ziemba, Alex Campbell, and Rebecca Aidlin: thank you for making every step of the publishing process a dream. To Kim Ryan, Abby Fritz, Trevor Bundy, Debra Polansky, Brooke Sufrin, and Chrissi Konopka, as well as Sam Devota and the team at Penguin Canada: thank you for all your hard work in the amazing special editions of this series. To the remarkable Mia Hutchinson-Shaw, Molly Lo Re, and Lauren Klein: my deepest thanks for a fantastic audiobook. To Corey Brickley, my cover artist, and to Kristie Radwilowicz, my cover designer: How? This cover just arrived in my inbox one day, fully formed, and I was instantly blown away. It has been an honor to work with both of you on this series.

To my team at PRH UK: the lovely Amina Youssef, Carmen McCullough, Millie Street and Libby Thornton, Arabella Jones,

Saskia Nicholls, Tom Rubira, Alicia Ingram, and Adam Webling for the stunning trade and FairyLoot editions of the series. A special thank-you to Chloe Parkinson and Michael Bedo for their love and enthusiasm for this series and its readers.

My deepest gratitude to the authors who read and blurbed this series: Alexandra Bracken, Leslie Vedder, Amanda Joy, Nicki Pau Preto, Lyndall Clipstone, Claire M. Andrews, and Sarah Underwood. To Amanda Joy, Laura Silverman, Anna Meriano, Kat Dunn, Emma Finnerty, and Bea Fitzgerald: your support and enthusiasm mean the world.

To my amazing agent, Michaela Whatnall: I cannot thank you enough for supporting every wild idea I have and helping me battle each one into shape. I could go on and on about what a joy and privilege it is to work with you. Many thanks to my team at DG&B: Lauren Abramo and the co-agents for getting this series to readers across a dozen different countries; Gracie Freeman Lifschutz; Andrew Dugan; Nataly Grueder; and Michael Bourret. To my publishers across the world: thank you for loving and trusting this story.

To my family, always: I'm profoundly grateful for the myriad of ways you've loved and supported me through the years. To my friends: thank you for your love, your humor, and your unwavering support.

To George: I won't get soppy this time. I'll only say: here's to many, many more dreams.

And lastly, a huge thank-you to everyone who has read, reviewed, posted, and shared this series. To independent booksellers, librarians, educators, and critics. To the wonderful teams at Barnes & Noble, Waterstones, FairyLoot, and OwlCrate. To the readers: Io's story is one of hurt and longing, of fate and choice—but most important, it is a story of hope and change.

You have changed my life and for that, there can never be enough words.